JOSEPH O'CONNOR

Cowboys and Indians

WITHDRAWN

Flamingo
An Imprint of HarperCollins*Publishers*

I would like to thank my family, particularly my father Sean and my stepmother Viola. I would also like to thank Marie O'Riordan, my agent Lisa Eveleigh, and – for suggesting the original image for the cover – David Ryan.

Flamingo
An Imprint of HarperCollins*Publishers*
77–85 Fulham Palace Road,
Hammersmith, London W6 8JB

Published by Flamingo 1992
9 8 7 6 5 4 3 2 1

First published in Great Britain by
Sinclair-Stevenson Limited 1991

ISBN 0 00 654458 4

Author photograph by Jerry Bauer

Set in Imprint

Printed in Great Britain by
HarperCollinsManufacturing Glasgow

We had fed the heart on fantasies,
The heart's grown brutal from the fare;
More substance in our enmities
Than in our love; O honey-bees,
Come build in the empty house of the stare.

YEATS

E_{DDIE} V_{IRAGO} had a serious case of the shakes.

He leaned back hard in the pullman chair and swigged at his plastic cup of Sealink gin, noticing that when he swallowed he raised his shivering little finger in the air, like some kind of crazy duchess or something. Like Lady Bracknell, or some other deranged old bat. Good breeding. His father was right. No amount of education could stamp it out.

That finger made him feel self-conscious. It betrayed him, sticking up like that, giving him away. And if somebody had been with him, he might even have made some smartass quip about it. But nobody was with him. Eddie Virago was alone, just him and his guitar and his ego. And at twenty-four, you don't worry too much about that. It's exciting to be alone. You don't know what being alone is, not yet, but it's a big deal to you and that's something.

The air in the pullman lounge was stale and smoky, redolent of disinfectant and greasy food. His lips tasted of salt. And the light from the shell-shaped glass wall lamps was so sleazy that he had to squint, especially if he wanted to make out something over the far side, where the huge window looked out over the oncoming waves and the night.

Underneath him Eddie felt the churn of the sea, far below the car deck. He imagined the vast cold hulk of the mailboat plough-ing through the water in the darkness, an explosion of white metal and froth. He could almost see it, rearing into the air, smashing down into the waves, hammering the water like a weapon. And for some reason that brought a hot tingle to Eddie's face.

It was a good-looking face, there was no doubt about that. Eddie's face looked like something out of a Pre-Raphaelite paint-ing, or so Jennifer had told him once, the fucking pseud. First-year History of Art in UCD and Jennifer thought she was Melvyn sodding Bragg or something. Still, no matter what she said, Eddie knew he was a looker. He said looks weren't important. He said it every morning when he preened himself in the mirror and every night too, when he brushed his gleaming teeth. He said it at every available opportunity, to anybody who'd listen. But extremely good-looking people always say that, and they usually look particularly good when they're saying it. Eddie was a head turner. He always had been, he was now, and with just a fraction of the good fortune that always goes with good looks, he reckoned he probably would be till he dropped. And even then, like his hero Sid Vicious, Eddie'd be a good-looking corpse.

His lashes were long and girlish. His ears were just the right size. His nose looked like it'd been chiselled out of a block of granite. His eyes were big and bright, with just the correct hint of practised doe-like innocence. His skin was tanned and smooth as glass. And his mouth relaxed into a well-cultivated and arrogant pout that seemed to say, to whoever was interested, 'You can kiss me if you want to, but hey, if you don't, that's fine too.'

But the eyes weren't in great shape just now. Even Eddie would have had to admit it. Usually leafy brown and sparkling, but now suffering from last night's alcoholic goodbye, they stung and itched in their sockets, almost as scarlet as the lurid mohican haircut that crowned his head.

Eddie's hair was something else. He'd got the first mohican in Dublin. This was back in early 1978 when hardly anyone in the city had even heard of The Sex Pistols or The Clash, specially not the old barber in Glasthule, who was still saying that Mick Jagger looked like a bloody girl and that nobody could write a good melody any more. Eddie used to tune into John Peel late at night, while his parents fought downstairs, imagining what it would be like to be over in London, the eye of the storm, the rotten apple, the monstrous and fetid birthplace of punk. And the rampant phony roar of 'Anarchy in the UK' and 'Pretty Vacant' would drown out the sound of the real anarchy that raged through the kitchen below. When he swanned into Monday morning religion class with the haircut, he'd nearly been expelled on the spot. The next year they'd moved him from Blackrock College to one of those trendy experimental schools on the Northside, where the teachers wore polonecks, and all they seemed to teach was sex education and woodwork. By then everybody in the city knew Eddie. He'd catch people pointing at him, trying to take his photo on Grafton Street when he was hanging out beside Freebird Records on a Saturday afternoon, chewing gum, looking mean, arms folded in a gesture of threatening tolerance, heel of his right-foot two-tone Doc Marten clamped against the wall behind him.

But nobody wanted to take his photo now. Eddie was in a state. For someone about to unleash himself on the world, Eddie was looking rough.

Eddie was shaking like a puppy shitting razorblades. He was hungover so bad that his brain and stomach felt like they were turning into spaghetti. Nothing had any reality any more and everything felt seriously weird, like it was all underwater. His fingers trembled as he dragged on his cigarette. Eddie felt like downtown Beirut on legs.

He asked a fat nun in a long grey habit to keep an eye on his guitar. She looked up from her paperback book, 'Home Before Dark' by Hugh Leonard, and she smiled back, sweetly, a real nun's smile.

When he staggered into the bathroom – up on A-Deck – Eddie splashed water over his face and his skin felt tight, stretched over his bones like cellophane. His haircut was beginning to look limp, like some kind of rapidly expiring rooster. He pulled a tube of gel from his hip pocket and fingered the stuff in to his mohican slowly, pulling at strands and tapering them away until they stood up, vertical and spiky, to their full and majestic eight inches. He leaned in close to the mirror, wetting his fingers and running them along his eyelashes. His stomach was really churning now. Percussive sounds seemed to throb from it. It felt to Eddie like he'd swallowed a pogo stick.

A young guy in a sharp suit emerged from one of the stalls, took one terrified look at Eddie and began straightening his tie with unnecessary nonchalance. Every liquid substance the human body is capable of producing seemed to be represented on the stinking floor. And when Eddie closed his eyes, the grind of the engines seemed closer.

Back in the lounge the fat nun was asleep and the engine whine sounded somehow far away again, in the back of what was left of Eddie's mind. It reminded him of the chatter of conversation he used to hear on the middle floor of the university canteen, a great full noise which, if you listened to it for long enough, would trip you out better than any drug. Dean Bean used to say the middle floor felt calm like a ship when they sat there at night, watching the sun melt behind the glass walls, in the lengthening evenings before their finals. But Belfield, with its squat grey buildings full of stark modernist sculpture and its brutal perspex tunnels, had always seemed to Eddie much more like some weird spacerocket than a ship. The corridors were dark and draughty and the toilet paper was always hard and everybody, absolutely everybody, seemed to have something to prove. When he thought about it, it seemed a pity that in four years of university, these were his main memories. Well, he knew that wasn't true, but if anybody ever asked him, Eddie'd long since decided that this is what he would say.

One day Eddie knew people would ask him stuff like this. People would be interested – journos and groupies and television producers and liggers and hangers-on and lithe inebriated girls with faraway looks and designer drug habits. Eddie was going to be a star. Simple as that. Dean Bean, Jennifer, even the old man, they'd all said it. With Eddie it wasn't if, it was when. 'When I'm rich and famous,' he used to say, and almost everybody believed he would be. Or if they didn't, they said they did, which was almost as important to Eddie.

Dean Bean probably would have said it anyway. That's what best friends were for, in Beano's book, and in Eddie's too. Dean had come over from Arkansas on some ridiculous endowment scholarship to study the influence of Yeats and Lady Gregory on American culture. He'd ended up with a pretty short thesis, but Beano had fallen in love with Dublin. He'd become a vegetarian, changed his name from Dean Butcher to Dean Bean, persuaded his extravagant folks to buy him an apartment in Donnybrook and settled into a life of Guinness, sarcasm and late late nights, the kind of life that American academics think real Dubliners lead.

Eddie watched the girl totter in backwards through the lounge door, mouthing a silent curse, swaying in the middle of the floor, with a rucksack on her back. Suddenly the ship bucked. Somewhere a glass shattered, and the girl extended her long hands sharply on both sides of her body, like a surfer. Her face was dark, exotic, and she moved as though she knew somebody was watching her.

Her jeans were loose and unfashionable. She wore a khaki anorak with a red and blue target on the back. Eddie saw the target when she – wincing – unhooked the rucksack and dropped it painfully to the floor. She was dressed like a mod, a mess of mohair, black brothelcreeper shoes. Eddie remembered a joke of

Dean Bean's. Why are there no mods in Northern Ireland? Would *you* walk around Belfast with a target on your back? He was going to miss Beano, the stupid Yankee imperialist bastard.

The girl snapped her head to toss back her long black hair. She looked scatterbrained to Eddie. She looked like the type who might forget how to spell her name when filling in a form. She ran one hand through her thick hair and gaped around, as though she was looking for an old friend among the dozing couples and chattering stewards. She looked like she was waiting for something to happen. The ship went up and the ship went down. Deep in his gut, Eddie's enzymes were doing the lambada.

Yeah. She looked like a real space cadet. And if anyone could spot them at a fifty-mile distance, it was Eddie Virago. Girls like that, he had their number alright. He knew the score. It was all down to experience. Or so he liked to believe.

In the corner by the port-holes sat a huddle of rugby supporters, beetroot-faced middle-aged men whose movements and laughter reminded him of his father. They looked odd and a little sad, these runaway men, bellies rounded under their V-neck emerald-green jumpers, striped woollen green and white scarves around their necks. There was something naughty and childish about them, about the way they giggled at the passing waitresses, and whispered to each other, and about the way they tried to sing raucous songs which didn't quite come off because nobody knew all the words.

One sickly man talked rapidly to the man beside him, counting off points on the fingers of his left hand. He looked agitated, like he was fending off an accusation.

Eddie tried to figure why these men were slumming it on the boat instead of travelling, executive class, by plane. They looked tanned, wealthy, like they weren't short of the folding stuff. At first he couldn't reckon it. Then it hit him. Like himself, they'd left it too late. Ireland were playing England at Twickenham. You couldn't get a flight out of Ireland that weekend, not for love or money. It felt like a movie Eddie had seen once, about some South American country where everyone had to leave real fast for some reason when the solids hit the fan and the CIA came tumbling in. That's what it felt like on the boat that night. Exciting. Illicit. Like some serious shit was about to come down.

Except for one man, a very thin guy with silver hair and bright anxious eyes, they all looked as though secretly they were having a terrible time. They squirmed on the couches, too narrow and hard to accommodate their prosperous bodies. When the ship heaved they laughed out loud and groaned fake vomiting noises. A haze of blue cigarette smoke hung over the two long trestles they had taken over. Miniatures of Cork Dry Gin and Johnny Walker toppled and rolled against the high table rims.

Eddie tried to feel the way an emigrant is supposed to feel. Sentimental songs and snatches of poetry drifted like remembered smells into his consciousness and then eluded him. And although he was vaguely aware of the thousands of petulant Paddies who had crossed the same stretch of sea over the decades, and over the centuries too, he couldn't actually feel anything. Eddie was a cerebral kind of a guy. He prided himself on it. He could listen to Vivaldi's 'Four Seasons' without thinking once of Franki Valli. His awareness was all intellectual. Pain, loneliness, isolation, they were just words, and you could have used any other words to describe the same things but it wouldn't have made any difference to Eddie.

He was beginning to feel really sick now, and he closed his eyes again to blot out the rising wash of nausea. His spit tasted sour. His shirt clung to his wet skin. His nipples throbbed. He tried to think about something, anything, to take his mind off his stomach.

He found himself trying to calculate a figure, adding first the average amount of emigrants for one month, then a year, then a decade, and so on until the warm seductiveness of the gin melted his calculation away and he let it go, like somebody in a movie letting go of a hand coming up through a hole in the ice. He felt too lousy, sipping at the lukewarm tacky gin, with his stomach swaying like the waves and the remains of a greasy cheeseburger disturbingly solid in his gut. Eddie had never been a great sailor. And the girl had usurped all his attention anyway, wandering around the Charles Stuart Parnell Pullman Lounge, like a lost child in a shopping mall, with a self-consciously cross frown in her eyes, searching for somewhere to park herself. She just looked like she didn't belong.

Apart from his mother and a couple of college friends, Eddie hardly knew anybody in London, and when he thought about that he felt a little freaked out. There was his Uncle Ray in Greenwich of course, who was also his godfather, and there was his neurotic boozy aunt in Tufnell Park about whom his parents seldom spoke. But he didn't really feel like barging in on either of them, listening to sibling gossip, answering endless questions about what his relations euphemistically referred to as his career. If he wanted family hassle, he figured, he could have stayed at home.

In any case, Eddie's father had been having an argument with Uncle Ray for as long as Eddie could remember. And it had all got worse since the separation of Eddie's parents the year before. Side-taking had made it worse. It was one of those stupid disagreements that friends get over and laugh about, but which turn serious in families over time. Something about politics, Northern Ireland, extradition – something. Some bullshit that made no difference to either of them if truth be known, which of course it never is, not in families, not in Eddie's family at any rate.

His father had insisted on scrawling 'Mam's' address in London on the back of an envelope for Eddie, and made a great show of it in front of Eddie's sister Patricia, as if to prove that in times of need family disagreements could be forgotten. As if that's all it was, a silly family disagreement. But Eddie knew it would hurt his father if he rang that number, and he didn't want to do that, whatever else happened. Things were bad enough. He just couldn't have handled that. He had taken the address tactfully and said, 'We'll see', and his father had nodded, 'Well, of course I'm not forcing you, but you never know', in that reticent way of his that pretended everything was alright, and communicated so much in spite of itself.

Eddie saw the girl again, right across the lounge now, way over the other side, in the semicircle of seats that looked out through the glass over the thrashing white sea. She was remonstrating with one of the stewards and her features contorted in exaggerated and angry grimaces. Her back was now facing Eddie but he saw her jerking her thumb repeatedly over her shoulder, standing up straight with her hands on her hips, tossing her head in anger. The steward stood very still, arms folded, head slightly bowed, speaking stubbornly into the ground. He looked like one of those calm bastards, you know, one of those unbearable pricks who's done a course in customer relations and won a little gold star.

An old man in a pork-pie hat cocked his head above the back of his pullman and said something to the steward, pointing an accusing finger. But the steward ignored him and continued arguing with the carpet. And after a minute or two the girl dragged the rucksack up onto her back and stalked away, leaving him jabbering away to himself, in mid-sentence. She was gnawing her lip and looking mean. Like she was on some kind of a warpath.

Eddie felt the cramp spreading through his intestines. He farted. Something inside him made a gurgling noise. His lips felt dry.

She weaved through the bulging cases and overfilled seats towards where Eddie was, looking around with defiance, then yanking the yellow bag of duty-free that adorned the seat in front of him, the seat beside the fat nun, onto the floor. She sat down determinedly, like she was expecting somebody to tell her not to sit there. Nobody did.

The fat nun woke up with a start, squirmed uncomfortably and went back to sleep again, snoring like a motorbike. Her book fell from her lap and softly hit the floor. The breeze flicked through the pages and made them flutter.

'You'd think,' the girl said, 'for the money you'd be guaranteed a seat.'

It was the kind of thing Eddie's mother would have said. And the way she said it too, straight out to the air like that and not to anyone in particular, was in the manner of something an older person would have said, not someone like her who was twenty, maybe twenty-one, twenty-two at an absolute push.

Eddie pursed his lips and said, 'Yeah, you're right there.' But then he bowed his head, cracked open the spine of the paperback that lay on his knees and began to pretend to read. He didn't feel like talking just now, even though close up the girl looked prettier than he had imagined she would. His fingers ran up and down the columns of words, caressing the yellowed paper. But he couldn't concentrate, no matter how he tried. The black words just seemed to mock him. Eddie had too much on his mind.

He thought about Jennifer, about their farewell on O'Connell Street with the wind howling like Siouxsie and the Banshees over the roof of the GPO, about the way she'd blinked back her tears at the bus stop, and the way the Coca Cola sign's reflection had blurred scarlet in the black and squalid surface of the Liffey.

Jennifer had upstaged them all. After all the endless world-saving talk on the middle floor, all the glib undergraduate extremism, Jennifer had announced one day that after the graduation she was going off to Nicaragua to teach English for a year. And the way she'd dropped it too – even Eddie had to admit it had style. She just came out with it like she was going for a walk around the block. Just like that. Matter of fact, and it was all set up. Jimmy and Ruth and everybody else had said that was great, but Eddie remembered the way they'd all looked at him when she said it, and not at her, expecting him to say something. Dean Bean'd been gobsmacked. And Eddie had been as surprised as anybody else. Shit, he'd been more surprised, to tell the truth, not that he could admit that, not even to Beano.

'Fair enough,' he'd said. 'That's cool. I mean, everyone's going to Nicaragua. I'd prefer Guatemala myself, but fair enough, if that's what you want.'

The girl was still seething. She lit a cigarette and tapped the match with her thumb to extinguish it. Her hair was thick and not black, as he had thought, but dark brown and dirty. In between sucking on the cigarette she gnawed the thumbnail of her right hand until drifting smoke watered her eyes and she began to squint and blink. Her cheeks were pink, but that could have been from anger. Her eyes darted around like a bird's. Coughing, she slapped her chest with her free hand.

'What's that you're reading?' she said.

She spoke briskly, with a soft rural Northern Irish accent. Eddie looked up and stared her down. Something pounded in his head. He felt like telling her to fuck off and bother somebody else, but he didn't. She looked like the kind of girl who'd slap you if you said that. Maybe it was the accent too. You didn't fuck at somebody with a Northern Irish accent, not if you wanted to continue a meaningful relationship with your kneecaps. Her eyes were green and defiant like a witch's eyes, that was one thing he noticed. He folded a corner at the top of the page and closed the book.

'Lyons,' he said, '*Ireland Since the Famine*.'

'Mmm,' she said, in mid-drag, 'thought that's what it was.' She balanced the cigarette lengthways on a Coke can and wriggled out of her anorak. She was thin. Her pink knees shone through a frayed hole in her Levis. 'Thought that was it,' she said again, like she was trying to make something of it. She unbuttoned her mohair cardigan and peeled it off.

A silver crucifix glittered on the soft part of her neck. She wore a T-shirt with the words 'Hothouse Flowers' transferred on, and a silhouette of the lead singer, a guy with an Irish name whose hair had a perverse logic that rivalled even Eddie's.

'You a student?' he asked.

· 9 ·

'No,' she said, 'I mean, I was.' She paused. 'But not right now.'

Eddie couldn't think of anything else to say at first. He didn't want to ask where she'd studied, firstly because he was afraid he might know someone who'd been at the same college, and that would have led to a conversation. Secondly, because it was the obvious thing to say, and Eddie prided himself on never saying the obvious thing. He was beginning to feel really bad anyway, totally strung out and shaky and hot.

'What do you think of it?' she asked, nodding at the book.

'Oh, it's OK,' Eddie said, surprised by the question, 'you know. If that's what you're into.'

Suddenly he was aware of his middle-class Dublin accent, its flat nasal tones, its unexpressiveness, its utter poverty of cadence. Her own voice was musical and textured, all vowels and moist intonations, undulating softly like the wilds of Donegal from where she obviously came. That's what Eddie reckoned anyway. Things like that occurred to Eddie. Eddie fancied himself as a bit of a poet.

'What do *you* think of it?' he said, to take the attention away from himself. With her fingers she combed her hair behind her ears.

'I think it's crap,' she half-laughed, in a matter-of-fact voice, without looking, dropping her cigarette butt into an empty polystyrene cup and shaking it from side to side. Then she said it again, and she glared at him as if to say, 'So what do you make of that, pal?' She looked like a tough one.

Eddie began to swallow hard. Hot moisture filled his eyes. Pain chewed its way up his windpipe.

'Oh fuck,' he moaned, grabbing onto the armrests.

'What?' she said, 'what's the matter?'

Eddie bent over and cursed, hands to his mouth.

'Oh Jesus fucking Christ,' he said. The fat nun woke up and stared. 'Fuck me,' said Eddie.

The girl started to laugh.

Eddie leaned over till his head was right between his knees, and he puked up like a fruit machine. He gawked up steaming vomit all over his Chinos and his new Doc Martens, and when he clamped his mouth shut, puke oozed from his nostrils. Sweat soaked through his forehead. Puke gulped through his tightened lips. His spit was thick and ropey as he spat. Puke dribbled down his chin and dripped into the pocket of his shirt. He slithered down on all fours and puked even harder, and his puke splashed all over the girl's feet and his own fingers. And the sound of his puke, splashing on the floor, made him want to puke again.

The ship gave a sudden lurch.

'Jesus,' the girl said. A look of unadulterated horror invaded the fat nun's saintly face.

The rugby supporters, one by one, stopped chattering. They looked at Eddie and to his great surprise they didn't laugh. They all looked aghast, all except for the little man with the anxious eyes who picked up a sandwich and bit into it absent-mindedly. The fat nun called for a glass of water but Eddie couldn't drink. He retched again, even though there was barely anything left in his stomach. The fat nun said he needed a cup of hot sweet tea. She kept saying it. And every time she said those words – hot sweet tea – Eddie swallowed up another steaming mouthful.

'Come on,' the girl said, tugging frantically at his puke-sodden sleeve.

Out of the reach of the ship's lights the sea was dark and oily, flecked here and there with the kind of glossy light you only ever see in postcards. Closer in, it was banknote-green and mucky. Eddie's head whined. He looked out over the deck and tried to focus on the point where the light stopped and the darkness began. Gulls flapped around the stern, screaming and colliding as they followed the ship, hoping for food. Once in a while, one of them would try to land on the paint-chipped railing, hover, fail, and crash downwards with a surprised croak towards the spray, swooping back upwards only at the last minute.

They stood watching, unsure for some time of what to say. Eddie gripped the cold steel railing and tried not to cry. The girl tried not to laugh.

'Seagulls are so fucking thick,' she said eventually, with real contempt, 'you'd think they'd try it once and realise it can't be done. You'd think they'd know that much.'

A big brutish bastard landed on the rail, staring at Eddie with almost a sneer on its menacing beak.

'Oh well,' moaned Eddie, 'they're Irish seagulls, I suppose.'

They were so far out to sea now that no land could be seen, on either side. The sky was white, full of milky clouds, and the breeze wrapped the little green white and orange flag hard around the mast where it struggled unsuccessfully to unfurl. The wind sounded even sadder than the sea. And the more the flag struggled, the more tight around the pole it was wrapped.

'Yeah,' she said, 'I suppose,' and she flicked the glowing tip of her cigarette out over the side, where the hoard of gulls circled around it in a screeching cloud of destruction.

'They're Irish alright,' she said, 'no doubt about that,' and Eddie sank to his knees, clutching his abdomen, wishing aloud that he was dead.

It worked.

A few minutes later, they found themselves kissing.

On the train they got off with each other and Eddie was glad he'd dropped into the men's room at Holyhead station to brush his teeth and get his act together with one of those pathetic traveller kits you buy for two quid fifty and then immediately regret. She kissed him hard and their teeth scraped. Her lips were cold and she smelt of aniseed and soap. The way she kissed him, she sort of ground her lips against his, as though she was dunking for apples in a basin full of water at Halloween. When he put his hand up inside her shirt and touched her back she jumped, and then softened.

Her fingers stroked the back of his head and she wriggled closer to his chest, chewing at his lips. It felt to Eddie like she had learnt to kiss from a series of photographs in a teenage magazine. She pulled her anorak across their wriggling bodies and opened her jeans.

When she pushed her hand down the front of his trousers he didn't object. She jerked him off before she even knew his name.

Afterwards they didn't say much. She smoked a few cigarettes, then a lot of cigarettes; and she read a magazine for a while before leaning over on Eddie's shoulder and falling into a murmuring sleep.

At four-thirty a fat black woman came waddling down the aisle with a trolley of sandwiches and she shot Eddie and the girl a look of sympathy that faintly disturbed him.

Lights on the distant hills prickled and blurred in the train windows. The hills retreated back in greater gloom until they disappeared into the sky. Eddie watched his face in the window.

He kept looking away, and trying to catch himself, surprised, in the glass.

Inside the train was dark and smooth and the chatter of steel on the tracks was broken only by the laughter of the young boys down the other end, playing poker for roll-up cigarettes. Their voices were Irish and the music on their ghettoblaster was Irish too, sentimental maudlin lovesongs and country and western standards. All broken promises, wayward rovers, lonesome cowboys.

The distant orange haze of Birmingham sped past with the smoke rising into the night and being coaxed away from the sleeping city by a timid breeze. Colours bled together in the rainy window. The city looked like some kind of weird animal, slumbering in the murk with a million brooding orange eyes. It just didn't belong. Somehow it had insinuated itself into the landscape, like the wrong piece of a jigsaw forced into place.

Eddie thought about the Birmingham Six, the Guildford Four, the Winchester Three. Like Dean Bean said, Anglo-Irish relations were becoming a set of fucking soccer results.

And Eddie thought of Yeats, the 'rough beast' he prophesied in his poem, 'The Second Coming'. He looked at Birmingham, menacing in the orange haze, and that's what he thought of. The rough beast, come to life in the flat and lifeless heartland of England. He thought of lit crit lectures in Theatre L on frosty February mornings when his heart had pounded with the thought of having to speak to the person beside him, the student-union guide way to make friends. And the first day he saw Jennifer, on the stage of Theatre L when she was running for election as class rep for English, her gorgeous movie-star face in the arc lights of the stage, her skin, white like new paper in a pad. He remembered her speech, how that awful American girl who walked like she had a corncob up her ass had spoken before her, saying she thought everyone should vote for her because she was so 'nahce' and so damn good at English literature.

'Well,' retorted Jennifer, in her best seductive tones, 'I'm not so good, but that probably means I represent more of you.' Then Eddie remembered the roar of male cheers, loud, like an aeroplane taking off, and the screech of wolf whistles too.

Yeah, Jennifer Swift was an operator. Swift by name, swift by fucking nature. She was then and she was still, and Eddie knew it. And somehow it wasn't that fact that got to him. It was the fact that now he knew it was a fact. He could see it now. That's what bugged the shit out of him. It really did. Eddie reckoned he could handle anything once he didn't have to think about it too much. Facts were just confusing, in the end.

The girl twitched in her sleep, pulling the anorak tight around her small wiry body. Eddie pulled open the magazine and read an article about some guy who had built a motorcycle Wall of Death in the middle of a Kildare bog. Obviously a major-league fruitcake, and now they were making a movie about him. What could you do? The world was full of fruitcakes, primadonnas and assholes, and nowhere more than in Ireland. You couldn't be anything in Ireland unless you were a few kopeks short of the full rouble. Really and truly. You just couldn't. Now he could see that too.

Euston station at six in the morning was no great shakes. The breeze galloped in under the electronic doors and slapped them full in the face as they trudged through the barrier. Manky pigeons flapped up in the girders and everything felt cold and secondhand. Eddie saw the fat nun again, clutching a small tartan suitcase and a carry-all bag with 'Italy 1990' on one side and 'Give it a Lash, Jack' on the other. Another nun was waiting for her by the Sock Shop, stomping her thick shoes to keep warm. The two nuns embraced and kissed the air on the side of each other's faces. They seemed to know where they were going. They seemed confident, and capable, like they really were glad to see each other, like they were old friends and they weren't just hamming it up.

Dozing winos lay huddled in corners and evil-smelling alcoves. On the low grey wall that sectioned off the elevator to the Underground was a marble plaque announcing that the station extension had been opened by H M the Queen in 1977. Around the edge of the hall the shops were closed and shuttered up, metal hoardings tagged with hip-hop graffitti, plastic neon signs extinguished, all except for the one outside the Thresher Off-Licence, which flickered and hummed as they passed it by, like there was some kind of weird electricity in their bodies. Which, in a way, there was.

A black man in a blue uniform and a tartan hunting cap walked up and down, pushing a throbbing industrial cleaner that left swathes of shiny surface slashed through the grime of the floor. When he got close up they could see he was wearing a Walkman, and every so often he threw back his head and sang softly along with some rhythm that only he could hear.

The girl said she wanted a cup of coffee so they wandered into the station McDonald's and she sat down at a table. Eddie knew that wasn't too right-on, but at six in the morning, in a strange city, the Amazon rain forest just goes right out the window. The light inside was white and glaring and it bathed the joint in a freaky and torpid oppressiveness. Tinny music trickled from the speakers. Ronald McDonald leered down from the wall, looking like some kind of crazed child molester from the 1960s. Eddie returned from the counter with two polystyrene cups on a plastic tray and one skinny bag of fries. The girl's feet rested clumsily on his guitar case, but he said nothing. She didn't touch the chips.

'Do you pluck your eyebrows?' she said, sipping painfully at the coffee.

'No,' Eddie said, 'do you?'

'I don't have to,' she murmured, and her face melted into a weary dark-eyed smile.

'No,' said Eddie, 'I guess you don't.'

'My name's Marion,' she said. 'Mangan.'

'And mine's Eddie Virago,' he said.

'Fair enough,' she said.

'Crazy name, crazy guy,' he said.

'Whatever,' she shrugged, wrapping her pink fingers tight around her cup. 'People's names aren't important to me.'

Eddie said he hated to mention it, but he was a bit short of the old dosheroonie. Money, he said, for the coffee and stuff. She fiddled in her purse and shoved a one pound coin across the plastic table. He said thanks. She didn't want to be under a compliment.

Eddie was about to speak when behind him he heard a splash and a sudden scuffle.

The two men wore ragged grey clothes and their faces were dark. Even from ten yards Eddie could smell their warm and rotten stench. Their faces were the colour of their clothes and their eyes were sunken into their skulls, glowing like angry coals in a fire. They stepped out from the table squaring up to each other, pushing each other's shoulders, slapping. The tall man had a hole in his right shoe and Eddie could see his black toes.

A mangy dog tethered to the table leg howled. Behind the counter all the bleary-eyed workers stopped moving. They looked like they knew something was about to happen. Something familiar.

'What did you ever do for me?' the smaller man spat. 'Nothing.'

'You bastard,' growled the other, slapping his face, challenging, 'you'd be nothing without me, d'you hear me? Nothing.'

It wasn't the kind of fight you see on television. When the first punch connected there was no punch sound, just a dull groan from the sudden exhalation as the little man bent over, one hand extended in a gesture of pleading. The tall man grabbed his straggly hair and pulled hard. Then the little man looked wild with pain, crazy and kicking all around him. The two men held each other, almost like dancers, and the big man wept as the little one butted his face. He lunged forward and kneed the little man in the crotch, smashing his elbow downwards into the back of his neck. The little man groaned, and he staggered forwards with his arms outstretched, making claws of his hands. And then each man looked as though the only thing keeping him on his feet was the weight of his opponent. Blood streaks stained both faces, but Eddie couldn't tell whether they were both hurt, or whether the blood of one had somehow got onto the face of the other. At the time, it didn't matter. The two men punched each other hard, in the chest and shoulders, and they scratched each other's faces with black grimy fingernails.

Eddie and Marion stared at this scene, as though it was a performance, unable to move or to intervene.

Then suddenly, the dog broke loose from the table, a black moody-looking mongrel with a limp and a lollipop stick stuck in the shaggy fur under its hind leg, and one horrible white and red eye. That's what Eddie noticed. It bent its head low to the ground and began to growl. Marion screamed. Eddie laughed like a superhero. The dog sniffed at the air, seeming uncertain of where the noise had come from. It turned and stared at Marion, saliva dripping from its jaws.

The dog padded over towards Marion and she stood up quickly, upsetting the coffee, which dribbled over the side of the table. She began to pant now, holding her hands in front of her breasts and her groin as though she was naked in a crummy seaside postcard. Her shoulders shook and she bit her lip.

'Shit,' said Eddie. He stood up. The dog looked curious at first. It jangled its raggy collar, scratching itself, looking bemused.

'Get away,' she screamed, crumpling a paper cup.

'Shit,' said Eddie again. The dog seemed almost reluctant. But just as it looked like it was sloping away towards the two struggling men, it turned, yelping now, snarling, pawing the tiled floor, drooling, licking its nostrils. Marion stood on her seat. The dog stared, shaking its collar and its mad head. 'Fucking fucking *shit*, man,' said Eddie. The dog took one more bewildered look and then, almost as if it was easier to do so than to turn away, it seemed to lift its two front paws and come flying through the air, a howling streak of black matted fur, almost in slow motion.

Eddie stepped into its path. He found himself offering the dog his arm, because he knew the dog was going to bite something, and he didn't want it to bite his face.

So he held out his forearm and he felt the yellow teeth clamp shut around his sleeve. He heard himself make a noise, 'Ugh', like that, a noise that came from the pit of his lungs, a dull and empty noise of disgust and then it took a second or two for the pain to come.

The dog gurgled with savagery, way down in the back of its throat. It shook and tugged at Eddie's arm like the arm was a rat or some other cornered struggling prey.

Eddie felt tears prickle in his eyes. When he lifted his arm the mongrel clung on, and Eddie lifted it clean into the air several times, kicking hard at its underbelly every time. He yanked his arm forwards and back, and the dog slid its hunkers across the floor, whining through its teeth, still hanging on. And Eddie felt like a spectator, watching all of this, watching the dog snarling and slobbering over his arm, watching Marion lunge at it while he tried to keep her off, hearing her screams and the grunts of the dog far away, and the howl of a train about to move off from a platform somewhere.

He only saw the policemen from the corner of his eye, their navy uniforms flashing somewhere in his mind. Somebody shouted a man's name. Somebody else shouted 'Cunt'. Eddie heard a clatter as a helmet fell to the floor, rolling around on the circumference of its rim. 'Cunt', he heard again, an ugly and hard word, the ugliest word in the English language, as his mother had said once. Cunt!

The rubber torch came down with a crack, right in the middle of the dog's skull. It screeched like a monkey and bit even harder. Then the torch swung again and two gloved hands pulled at the dog's ears. It staggered to one side, toppling and confused, and one of the policemen dragged it away by the soft skin on the back of its neck, walking rapidly, holding the dog at arm's length like he was going to drop it into a dustbin.

Marion was shaking like she had the DTs. 'Oh my God', she kept saying, 'oh my God'. When she unclenched her fists her fingernails had left tiny crescents of white on her pink palms. She wasn't crying but she looked appalled and disbelieving. She looked like something terrible had happened, not just a dog biting some guy she hardly even knew. She held her hands to her temples but she said nothing at all except 'Oh my God', which she kept saying, 'Oh my Jesus', as if it was some litany she had learnt off by heart.

'Off the boat, are we?' said the policeman.

Eddie sensed Marion stiffen.

'Yeah,' he said, 'off the boat.'

'Irish?' said the policeman.

'No,' said Marion, 'Swahili.'

Eddie clutched his arm. He stared up at the roof in desperation and then he glanced back at the policeman, who pursed his lips and looked strict, tapping his rubber torch into the leather glove of his left hand.

'Yes, well,' said the policeman, 'we'll let that one go.' He looked like he was thinking about something important. His nose wrinkled.

Eddie's tear-stained face shone with relief, but Marion just picked up her rucksack and looked unconcerned. She dragged the sack behind her across the floor, and a plastic Safeway bag got caught in the strap. She stared in the newsagent's window and lit a cigarette. Eddie could see the flame's reflection in the glass.

He looked at the young policeman, wishing that he would say something to crack the apprehension inside his head.

'You want to get that seen to, sir,' said the policeman, nodding vaguely at Eddie's ripped sleeve.

'Yeah,' said Eddie, kneading his flesh, 'you're right.'

'You never know,' said the policeman knowingly, 'these days.' It was as though he was letting Eddie into some secret.

'Right again,' agreed Eddie, 'you never can tell.'

The policeman spoke politely, but it was an artificial courtesy, the politeness of a teacher scolding a pupil in front of a parent. The Geordie accent sounded a little like an Irish accent, with its squashed consonants, its vowels swallowed up from the back of the throat.

'Good luck, sir,' he said.

'Yeah,' said Eddie, 'that's one thing I need.'

'That's one thing we all need, sir,' said the policeman, 'specially these days,' and he smiled, and shook Eddie by the hand. It occurred to Eddie that this policeman who was calling him 'sir' was two, maybe three years older than him. Eddie saw Marion glare over her shoulder, then back at the newsagent's window.

He walked over to where she was standing, feeling hot, tense, shocked. His heart still hammered inside his shirt and his body smelt sour. Stickers ran up and down the little window, advertising teenage whores and cheap hotels. And in the middle of them all, a tiny blue postcard announced, a little unconvincingly in the circumstances, 'Jesus Saves'.

'Well,' said Eddie, 'I hope you're fucking happy.'

'Oh don't start, for Christ's sake,' sighed Marion, with an exhausted resignation that he found chilling. Last person Eddie had heard speaking like that was his mother to his father. It was as though they had been married for ten years. Eddie felt trapped.

She ripped into him, blinking at the floor all the time, gesturing around her while she cursed, never looking straight at Eddie.

'Typical,' she said, 'they know you're Irish, they look at you like that, it's just always the same. Fucking Brit bastards.'

'Look,' he said, 'just chill out, will you?'

'Innocent until proven Irish,' she interrupted, 'nothing ever changes, does it?'

'For Christ's sake,' he snapped, 'will you fucking cool it?'

Now she did look at him. She held a finger close to his face.

'Don't you tell me to cool it,' she roared, and her face distended into rage. 'Don't talk to me like a child, Eddie fucking Virago.' Way across the floor the man with the industrial cleaner stopped and looked around. He took off his cap.

'Listen,' said Eddie, with false calm, 'I don't need this, y'know?'

'Go on then,' she said, 'just fuck off, I know what I am to you, go on.'

'What you are to me?' He heard his voice croak. 'What are you talking about?'

'Fuck off,' she said.

'Look, I don't even know you.'

'Get away from me then,' she roared, 'leave me alone. Fuck you.'

Her voice began to crack with tears, which made her screw up her face into ugliness. Eddie just didn't want to see. Tears always had this effect on him. They made him feel sick and guilty and despairing. They made him feel transcendentally pointless.

'Right then,' Eddie said, and he grabbed his guitar case and stalked through the glass doors.

'Go on,' she yelled, across the concourse, 'go on.'

'Oh, fuck you too,' said Eddie, but under his breath.

Outside the station doors, Eddie sat on the concrete edge of the pond and tried to suss things out. Burger wrappers and cardboard boxes and newspaper pages floated in the scummy water. London was waking itself up. Traffic droned. The sky looked like porridge and the air felt smoky, exhausted, old. Eddie's arm ached, but it wasn't a serious cut. Brown-blue bruises were spreading out already from the graze. He felt sorry for the girl, Marion. She was just a bit shaken up. He knew that. She hadn't meant to be rude. You had to be understanding with girls like that. You had to give them a break.

Eddie looked out at the sprawling grey mess of the Euston Road. And underneath his great understanding, Eddie felt something which, he tried to persuade himself, was not loneliness.

When he went back inside she was sitting at the table in McDonald's, eating, calm, as though nothing had happened. She hardly seemed to notice him. After a minute she told him to eat his chips before they went cold. He did. She bought him a fresh coffee.

The hotel on President Street was called the Brightside Hotel. Marion said some friend from the UCG Student Union had used it a few times, knew the manager there and had made a reservation for her. Eddie said he couldn't argue with that.

When they pressed the buzzer, an Indian guy in his mid-thirties came out of the back room with a baby in his arms. The place smelt of apple-scented air freshener, not like apples, but like a committee's idea of what apples smell like. The Indian smiled and he rocked the gurgling baby. He had a well-trimmed moustache and bright eyes. He had hair on the back of his hands. He was handsome.

'We'd like a room,' Marion said.

'Yes,' said the Indian, scanning the register enthusiastically, 'it's possible.' He put the baby on the counter, placed his hand lightly on its chest, and ran his finger up and down the columns of his book. 'It can be done,' he said.

The baby was ugly. It screwed up its little face and squinted at Eddie.

'I have a reservation,' said Marion. 'My name is Mangan.'

'Ah, OK, you should say so.'

He had a friendly mischievous smile. The sweet smell of incense drifted out from the back room.

'Mangan,' he said, 'I think is not a British appellation.'

'That's right,' said Eddie. 'It's Irish.'

The Indian smiled again.

'The Emerald Isle,' he said, and he nodded, eyes wide, like he was waiting for a conversation to start. It didn't. 'For how long?' he said.

Marion looked at Eddie, but he shrugged.

'We're not sure,' she said.

The Indian shrugged too.

'No matter,' he said, scribbling in his book, 'you tell me or the old lady in the morning.'

He showed them to a small room right up on the top floor and he hung around waiting for a tip. Eddie tapped his pockets, frantically tutting. Marion said he sounded like Skippy the bush kangaroo. She gave the Indian a few coins, and he said 'most kind'.

'What's your name?' said Eddie.

'Patel,' he said. And he picked the baby up from the bed, and held it high so they could see its little gurgling face. 'Patel and son,' he laughed.

Marion wanted to do it in positions that Eddie had only ever read about. She fucked him hard like there was just no point to what they were doing, no reason at all, except the essential longing for some sort of escape. And the weirdest thing of all was that when he touched her body she said 'Oh baby' and 'Baby, that's good' in an attempt at a languid growl that just sounded so utterly out of character it made Eddie wonder what the fuck was going on. She sounded like a character in some cheap 1970s airport novel.

When she came she wrenched something out of herself, from deep down, and winced silently as though she was in agony. And when Eddie came he clutched at the bedspread and felt lonelier than he'd ever thought possible.

They lay in the bed all day. Even when they woke up they lay there, all afternoon, saying nothing at all to each other, while the light greyed down outside the window and the smell of sweat filled the room, strong and sweet now, like cut grass in summer. And after a while as the clouds came down the only light left in the room was a rectangle of warm gold spread over the pile of discoloured underwear that lay in a heap on the carpet.

The room was pretty small but it had a tiny blue bathroom attached and a balcony that looked over the grey and green roofscape of King's Cross and the slender skyscrapers of the city, in the distance. St Pancras station, the great pile of arrogant sandstone Victorian tat, blocked the view. That building had power written all over it. 'Fuck You, Bud,' it seemed to say to the passing traffic and to the legions of red and yellow cranes that seemed to threaten the streets.

Eddie looked out the window for a while, but he felt no thrill. He knew this scene so well from television and movies that it was like he had always lived here. There was nothing surprising about it. Nothing new at all, except perhaps the freshness of the air when the thunder cracked the sky and the rain finally came, producing a forest of umbrellas in the street below. For a second Eddie thought the white flash was lightning. But when he turned around she was standing by the bed with his camera in her hands, winding on the film, smiling boldly.

She was wrapped in a towel and her straggly wet hair touched her shoulders. Her toenails were long. He noticed that. And her fingers quivered when she wound on the film.

Ignoring him again, she sat down at the dressing table, leafing through a magazine she had found in one of the drawers, singing softly to herself. Eddie wondered what would happen next. He sat on the windowsill, smoking a cigarette, watching the way she moved. He wanted to go to her and touch her frail goosepimpled shoulders again, and hold her very close. But for some reason, he did not.

Then suddenly she clapped her hands, laughed out loud, a childish and happy laugh that chilled his heart.

'Brilliant,' she said. She pulled nail scissors from her purse, and carefully, slowly, began to clip the letters 'ABC' out of the headline on an article about the TV channel. The tip of her tongue protruded as she cut. 'What do you think?' she said, holding the cutting up to his gaze.

'Very nice,' he said, confused.

Unrolling sellotape, she bit a length off, and delicately fixed the big black letters to the wall above the bed, smoothing the paper out with her fingers. Then she stood back, admiring the sight, grabbed Eddie's camera again, and took a photo of the wall. This time the flash made him rub his dazed eyes.

'I just like alphabets,' she shrugged. 'I don't really know why.' Eddie said fair enough.

'*Chacun à son goût.*' He had to translate. 'It means whatever bag you're into,' he told her. 'You know, do your own thing.'

'So why didn't you just say that?' she said, and Eddie couldn't think of an answer.

Down in the street there was noise and wild music, and as the night came on it got worse. The sounds of London were what made it different. The kind of cacophony you never heard in Dublin, full of foreign accents and roars and insults and seductions. And the walls were so thin that they could hear the shouts and moans and the hiss of showers from the adjoining rooms.

'Why did you come here?' Eddie said, while she put on her warpaint.

'Why did you?' she answered, hanging a blue dress in the wardrobe.

'For a job,' he said. 'You know how it is.'

'Me too,' she said, 'to see my sister, and maybe look for a job.' Then she laughed. 'Jesus,' she sighed, 'why else would anyone come here?'

'I don't know,' said Eddie, 'different reasons.'

'Oh well,' she said, pouting lipstick in the mirror, 'I don't know about that, there's nothing different about me at all.'

'I wouldn't say that,' said Eddie.

'Well,' she said, '*you* probably wouldn't, but you can take it from me.' She pronounced that 'you' as though she knew Eddie inside out, and that kind of irritated him. 'No,' she said, 'there's absolutely nothing different about me.'

'Tell me about yourself,' he said, in a self-mocking Californian accent that made him feel awkward as soon as he said it.

'What do you want to know?' she said, cupping her breasts in the mirror.

'I don't know,' he said, 'about your family. Your father. What does your father do for a living?'

The crassness of the question evaded him. He picked up his guitar.

'He stuffs sausages,' she said, glaring at him, 'why?'

'No!' he said, strumming a melancholy chord. 'You're kidding me.'

Her frown softened to a smile.

'I'm not,' she said, pinking. 'He's a foreman in a sausage factory.'

'Oh well,' said Eddie, 'I suppose somebody has to do it.'

'Yes,' she said, 'that's what he says too.'

'Yeah, that's OK,' Eddie shrugged, 'somebody has to do everything.'

They went out to eat that night in a Mexican restaurant called Remember The Alamo. They hung their coats on a giant plastic cactus right in the middle of the floor. It was the kind of place where the menu's made of plastic and too big and they play Richard Clayderman playing Barry Manilow and the waitress tells you her name even if you don't want to know it. Eddie noticed the way Marion said 'Please' and 'Thank you' and 'Excuse me' to the waitress, and he felt guilty then, because he hadn't done this. And he felt she'd only done it to show him up. She had tostados and chilli con carne and drank a whole pitcher of beer. He had enchiladas and iced water because his stomach was still bad. He kept wanting to fart, and he squirmed on the seat.

Marion was from Ballybracken, a seaside town in Donegal that Eddie had never even heard of. She said it was a quiet place, where nothing much ever happened. The kind of place where you plug in an electric toothbrush and the streetlights dim. She'd been to college in UCG for a term, doing politics, but she'd had to leave when her father'd caught himself in a machine at work and her mother needed extra help to look after things at home.

'Jesus,' said Eddie, 'what bit of himself did he catch?'

'His nose,' she said, brazenly. 'My father hasn't got one.'

'So how does he smell?' asked Eddie.

'That's an old joke,' she said. And then she said she wanted to change the subject.

She had eight brothers and three sisters. A real typical Irish family, she said, real typical, boys who couldn't wash a dish, girls who had been bred for ironing.

'Why was Christ an Irishman?' she said. 'Because he hung around with the boys all the time and he lived with his mother till he was thirty.'

They had all moved away from home now. All except for her little brother, Pascal. Two of her sisters were married, one to a nice guy who'd been in the police for a while, the other to a complete bastard who had a cowboy boots shop in Mullingar. One brother was in the army, serving in Lebanon. Two were in Dublin on the building sites, living in one room in Rathmines. One was in New York, a washroom attendant in a big hotel. Another was in Leeds on a psychiatric nursing course and everyone in the town thought he was mad himself. That left two more brothers she just didn't want to talk about.

The guy in New York had a girlfriend who was a transatlantic air hostess for Aer Lingus. Every weekend she brought a parcel of washing home to Ballybracken for his mother to do, which she would then bring back to New York on the Monday morning flight.

When she said that Eddie nearly choked on his guacamole, but she swore it was true.

'Pathetic,' she said, 'but it's true as God.'

'Fuck,' said Eddie, 'beam me up, Scotty.'

'Yes,' she said, 'it'd be funny except for the way they treat her. She's like a black.'

Eddie told her his Dad was a deputy assistant bank manager, and he had been for ten years. He had one sister, Patricia, and she was in Trinity now doing psychology and sociology. And he told her about everything that had gone down last summer when he'd been working on his thesis, his mother, his father, how surprised everyone had been when she'd phoned from London to say it was all over and she wouldn't be coming back. Telling the story made him feel apprehensive, the way it always did. It was hard to tell it without appearing to solicit a sympathetic response. It wasn't that he *wasn't* looking for a sympathetic response. It was just that he didn't want that to show.

'One good thing,' he said, 'we all do our own washing now.'

She smiled. Then she asked Eddie what kind of music he was

into and he said he couldn't put it into words. Music that said something, that was all, not wallpaper for the ears. She said she liked George Michael and people like that. Eddie said that was too commercial for him, and he reeled off some names of bands she had never heard of, The Stone Roses, Screaming Blue Messiahs, New Model Army. They had an argument about U2. She said she didn't like them and Eddie couldn't understand why. She said they kept saying stupid things about the North, a situation that they just didn't understand. Her eyes sharpened when she argued, and that made Eddie uneasy. She said she supposed Eddie was one of the five million people who had claimed to have seen their first gig at the Dandelion Market.

'Seen it?' laughed Eddie. 'I played at it, support you know, with my first band, The Honey Bees, really decent blokes actually, U2, they always send me tickets when they're playing the Point Depot.'

Marion said big swinging deal. Eddie said they had done a lot about apartheid and that you couldn't buy their records in South Africa. Marion said lucky old South Africa, and Eddie told her that was a cheap shot. Marion thought it was all very well ranting on about oppression far away, but didn't Ireland have apartheid in the North? What about internment, shoot to kill, torture of prisoners?

'No,' scoffed Eddie, 'that's crap. Things may be bad up there, but they're not that bad.' He thought Ireland was full of people knocking other Irish people and that U2 were a right-on bunch of guys who had done wonders for the country's reputation abroad. She said it all depended what Eddie meant by 'the country', and as far as she was concerned Ulster was part of the country too.

'Listen,' Eddie sighed, 'spare me the green flag bit.'

'Well, don't you give me the line.'

'What line?' scoffed Eddie. 'I don't have any line, I couldn't care less, to tell you the truth.'

'The Thatcher line,' she interrupted, 'the establishment line, I've heard it all before from the likes of you.'

'The likes of me?' said Eddie.

'Yeah,' she said, 'the likes of you. Middle-class, chip-on-the-shoulder lefties from Dublin 4.' She looked like a bold child when she said it, but Eddie just didn't feel like starting a fight. 'Yeah,' she sighed, 'you're surprised, but I've met them before.'

Eddie laughed.

'Look honey,' he said, 'if you want to believe the hype that's fine you know. Just don't guilt trip me, OK?'

A bald man in the corner looked at Eddie, took a cigarette from a pack and waved it, raising his eyebrows. Eddie tossed him a pack of matches, which he tossed back when he had lit his smoke.

'Look, Eddie Virago,' she said, 'first of all, I don't think it's very right-on' – she sneered when she said the words – 'for you to call me honey.'

'True,' he smiled. *'Touché.'*

'And second of all, I think I should tell you, my father's a Sinn Féin councillor.'

'Big deal,' he shrugged, plucking at a bread roll, 'I'm impressed.'

He was too.

Back at the Brightside, Marion went up to the room while Eddie rang his father from the phonebox in the foyer. Everything was OK, he told him, the trip had been a bit rough but he'd just run into a friend from college on the boat and he was going to stay with him for a couple of days.

They talked for a few minutes and the phonebox swallowed Eddie's coins with a disturbing alacrity. Patricia was fine, out somewhere with her guy, some dinner dance or another in aid of child abuse in Ireland, a funny way of putting it, if you thought about it. Eddie agreed.

'Ireland won anyway,' said his father.

Eddie flicked through his copy of *NME* while he talked into the receiver.

'Great, Dad,' he said, 'did you watch it?'

'Yeah,' his father said, 'I got in a couple of beers.' Watery echoes and crackles distorted his voice. 'It was good, you know,' his father said, 'but it wasn't great.'

'I thought we won,' Eddie said.

'Yeah, but it's only a game, isn't it?'

Eddie saw Mr Patel walking through the hall with a cup of coffee in his hand, lifting the hatch at the side of the counter and slipping into the back room. He moved gracefully. He looked like he really belonged, and he knew the layout so well he didn't even look where he was going. Eddie envied him. Blue lights and shadows flickered on the walls of the lobby. The TV must have been on.

'Yeah,' said Eddie, 'it's only a game.'

'Still,' said his father, 'you're right, we won.'

'I better go, Dad.'

'Yeah,' said his father, 'don't be running up bills.'

'Sleep well, Dad,' Eddie said.

'Thirty-eight pence a minute now, that's what it costs to phone the mainland. Bloody disgraceful.'

'Yeah, it's crazy, Dad. Listen, I gotta run.'

'OK son, listen, what I wanted to say to you . . .'

The line clicked and went dead before Eddie could slip in the last word. Eddie stood in the dark little telephone booth for a few moments, just thinking about his father and wondering whether to ring him back just to say goodnight again, properly. But he knew that'd be dumb and embarrassing. He felt like he wanted to ring somebody else, but he couldn't think who. He opened the telephone book and looked up under his own name. There were quite a few Viragos, seventeen to be precise, when he counted. In Dublin they'd been the only ones. That had made life very easy. All he had to say to people was that his name was Virago and they could look him up in the book and that he was the only one. Simple. London was obviously going to be tricky.

On the open page of the *NME* he noticed something. An article on DEF JAM records, the hip-hop company in New York. Eddie laughed out loud to himself, and he leaned his fingers across the page, ripping out the letters that said DEF.

Then turning, he peeled a little sticker off the inside of the phone-booth door.

'United Islamic Party,' it said. 'Ban *Satanic Verses*!!'

Out in the lobby, he peered over the counter. Mr Patel was perched on the side of the little sofa, watching some halfwit situation comedy and chuckling to himself. The set was up way too loud so that when the canned laughter came on it howled and rattled the tiny window at the back. On the wall was a poster of some Indian movie star with a tiny red dot in the middle of her forehead. There was an answering machine wired into the phone on the floor and the little red bulb flashed on the side. On top of the TV sat a roll of toilet paper, all corrugated like it had fallen into the toilet and been pulled out.

When he saw Eddie he nodded and smiled and asked him if everything was OK. In the icy blue light he looked so handsome.

Eddie said yeah, everything was fine, and Mr Patel smiled again. His cheeks rounded into little globes when he smiled. He sipped his coffee, and his lower lip curled up over his moustache.

'You beat us,' he said, wagging a finger. Eddie asked him what he meant. 'In the rugby,' he said, 'injury time.' The laughter roared from the speakers, filling the whole room. 'Ireland four, England nothing,' sighed Mr Patel, holding up four fingers. Eddie told him he knew that already, but there was always a next time. 'Yes,' said Mr Patel, 'you have to be philosophical.'

Eddie asked for an early alarm call. Then he went outside for a quick joint. He walked up the whole length of President Street, and back down the other side, allowing smoke from the reefer to drift up his nose. The smell of hamburgers and pubs filled the air. He felt edgy and tired, full of apprehension. He found himself wondering what Jennifer was doing right that moment, and if she'd ever think of him again. Sitting on the steps of the Brightside, he closed his eyes and tried to see her face, but it wouldn't come. As he mashed out the joint he thought of Dean Bean. Hip-hop music drifted in over the street, and down on the corner four laughing black guys swigged from bottles. Eddie stared desperately up at the stars and the King's Cross moon, smug and cherry red in the clouds.

Back in the room, she laughed as he stuck the DEF to the flimsy wall.

And when he pulled back the bedclothes, she was already naked.

Next morning, Mr Patel was not happy.

He hefted great stacks of white cups and plates into the grotty grease-smelling breakfast room and he made a big vaudeville fuss of spreading out napkins and emptying the ashtrays. Dressed in a black suit with a thin black tie, he looked sharp and smooth, like a comic-book detective. But although he did his best to be polite, nodding fervently when somebody said 'Good morning' or 'Nice day', anybody could see he was miffed, and not quite the sweetie he'd been the day before. His lips were clamped closed tighter than a camel's ass in a sandstorm. He scuttled around the breakfast room swatting angrily at the air with his tea towel, straightening the pictures on the walls, most of which were straight already, muttering profanities to himself. Even though the room was cold he looked hot, and he kept running his fingers through his black hair and reaching a hand up to open his collar, which he had already opened and closed several times by the time Eddie and Marion reached their table.

His wife was getting a rough time. Every so often he'd butt open the swing door to the kitchen with his ass, look despairingly up at the ceiling, fold his arms, close his eyes and holler something Eddie and Marion couldn't understand, but which sounded like it might very well be rude. She'd creep in then, eyes down at the floor, carrying a bucket or a mop, barely daring to look at her husband, or at the few people scattered around the battered tables, or at anything else except the threadbare carpet. Plaintive eastern music wailed from the kitchen, and the screech of the newspaper man on the pavement outside was so loud that it seemed to rattle the windows.

Mrs Patel was a small, very lean woman. She wore a yellow and purple sari that draped her body from neck to toe, and a white veil across her nose and mouth, which made it impossible to guess her age. She had beautiful almond-shaped eyes, purple as wine, which Eddie saw when she glanced guiltily in his direction and took off her horn-rim glasses. Her skin was a little lighter than her husband's, and just as smooth. And she moved like a bird, with rapid, quirky darts, as she scrubbed down the skirting boards and polished up the cutlery with a yellow cloth.

Marion was in a better mood today, which was just as well. The reality of Eddie's situation was beginning to dawn on him. The drone of the traffic had woken him at five-thirty. He'd lain in the dark listening to the muffled echo of a distant radio, lying flat out in the single bed, with a sore throat, his legs intertwined with hers, his buttocks squirming in the still damp sheets and tiny crumbs of stale toast pebble-dashing his back. Eddie didn't really know what to do. He had to admit it. Deep down he knew this was a one-night stand that would end up turning into something else. Like every single other one-night stand he'd ever had. Typical. Only off the boat and he was in deep shit already. The very thing he'd promised himself he wouldn't do – get tied up with somebody too quickly – and now he'd done it. This had all the potential of a real Torvill and Dean situation. Thin ice all round, and Eddie could already feel it beginning to crack.

The bed was a real hotel bed too, way too soft, with nylon sheets that gave out static shocks and springs that must have been heard a mile away. The air was crisp and Eddie watched his breath turn to steam as he lay there very still beside her, wondering why this had happened, and how he was going to get out of it. He felt a hollow feeling deep inside the very core of his existence. But it wasn't emotion. It was hunger.

Just for a second he contemplated getting up and sneaking away without saying anything, just stealing down the back stairs like Errol Flynn or something, and never coming back. In the months to come, he was often to wonder why he hadn't done it, just slithered away in one of those sleek black London taxis, no questions asked, over to his mother's place. He could have been there before she even got up. Or anywhere else but the Brightside Hotel. He could have done it too. It was early, nobody was around, and he could have got away with it. But even Eddie wasn't that much of a bastard. And anyway, looking at it practically, he never could have got the guitar down the stairs without making a noise.

When he looked at Marion now in the breakfast room, her tiny hand shaking under the coffee pot's weight, deep in the tough little muscle that passed for Eddie's uneasy heart, he was almost happy that he hadn't taken the risk. Almost, but not quite. She just looked so vulnerable.

She held his fingers across the breakfast dishes and smiled in his face, a strangely mournful smile. Then she reached out her thumb and wiped something off the edge of his lips. He blushed. She looked better this morning, there was no doubt. She'd slept anyway, no mistake about that, grinding her teeth and snoring softly like a kitten. Now her green eyes were clear and she had put on some makeup and her skin was still pink from the ridiculous force of the shower. She'd put her hair up in a thick yellow band that made her look like Simone de Beauvoir, or one of those other Left Bank nettle eaters. Eddie could see his own reflection in those green eyes. They really were green as the sea off Sandymount, though, knowing what got pumped into it, he wasn't sure she'd necessarily take that as a compliment. Still, he could understand now why people talked about green eyes like that. Looking at Marion, it was obvious.

Strictly speaking Eddie wasn't in favour of makeup. It was one of those things it wasn't hip to be into, sexist, all of that. But Marion looked very pretty with makeup on and he stared at her, trying to believe that this time yesterday they'd barely even known each other, and now they'd done stuff to each other that most people don't do in a lifetime of marriage. And under the guilt, the strongest sensation he felt was that he couldn't wait to tell somebody about it, preferably Dean Bean, who collected other people's erotic experiences the way carbuncular youths collect the numbers of trains. Yeah, this would get Beano going. Eddie could almost see his big, thick, generous Yankee face going, 'Jesus Christ, you did not, you mother, you did not do that, gag me with a freaking *spoon*, man. Jesus.'

'You look very nice,' he said. Well, it was a start. They hadn't exchanged one word since they'd woken up, after all, and that just couldn't go on for long. Eddie had felt embarrassed watching her walk around the bedroom naked and pale, selecting clothes from her rucksack and wriggling into tights. He'd pulled on his boxer shorts under the eiderdown when her back was turned. He knew it was ridiculous, but that's the way he was. She hadn't even bothered to laugh at him.

While she was in the shower he'd made up the bed, quickly, reversing the sheets, tucking the blankets tight in under the mattress. He hadn't been motivated by any vague domesticity. It was just that he didn't want her to see the stains. And he didn't want to see them himself. He wanted to hide them away.

'You look nice too,' she said, 'but then you know that already, don't you?'

Eddie tried to switch into smartass gear, but it was too early, and his head was still clouded with the joint they'd shared before falling finally asleep at two-thirty in the morning, having rewritten the *Kama Sutra*. Words tumbled through his ravaged mind, but nothing came.

'I can't win with you,' said Eddie.

Mrs Patel scurried past the table, bent under the weight of a huge metal bucket full of slopping soapy water.

'No,' Marion said, 'you can't.'

He raised her hand to his lips and kissed it, a smoothsville trick that usually worked for Eddie. She shot him a look that made him feel faintly ridiculous and went back to prising open a plastic pot of marmalade with a fork. As she did so, her halter neck slipped and Eddie could see purple lovebites on the soft part of her throat, beside the silver crucifix. She caught his guilt-moistened eye. 'Look what you did to me, you savage,' she said, touching his hand again.

Eddie blushed and he chomped into his cold, soggy toast.

'Heat of the moment,' he said. But he felt like a bastard. Hell, she'd been no angel herself. Eddie's foreskin felt like it was currently residing somewhere around his ankles. But she seemed so gentle and vulnerable now, certainly not how she'd been in bed, and the sight of his teethmarks on her neck did make him feel like a neanderthal pervert. He felt too as if those marks exercised a control over him which he didn't like at all. They didn't of course, they were only crummy purple-black lovebites, but that's still the way Eddie felt. Sensitive. Eddie saw the symbolism in things. He was just that type.

She pulled off her hairband, tossed back her hair and looked deep into his eyes until he wished that she'd stop.

'Cut it out,' he laughed, when he could feel his own eyes crossing under her gaze.

She didn't. She squeezed his hand between hers, stared even deeper, as though she was searching for something familiar in his face. Her eyes were curious and mocking.

'We must look like jerks,' he chuckled, nervously looking around the room for something – anything – to talk about.

'You're so beautiful, Eddie Virago,' she said, suddenly, 'it's a pity that you're such a bullshit artist.'

'Hey, thanks,' he said, 'I love you too, honey.'

She laughed then, softly, and went back to her breakfast.

At ten-thirty Mrs Patel came to the table and mimed looking at a watch. Then she pointed at the door.

As they walked out, Marion slipped her arm around Eddie's waist, one hand in his back pocket, and Eddie distinctly heard Mrs Patel and her husband laugh quietly behind him. His face burnt, but he didn't turn.

Back up in the room they stood by the window with their arms around each other, saying nothing and not sure of what to feel. Eddie stared at their hugging reflection in the wardrobe mirror. He really would have to get something done about his mohican. It was in serious need of a trim.

Marion wanted to know what happened next and Eddie said he didn't know, but how about a bonk? She tutted and said she hated that Brit word and that wasn't what she'd meant anyway. Eddie pulled away from her and opened his guitar case. He lifted his guitar out and sat on the bed, frantically trying to concentrate on appearing to tune up the machine heads, turning against the strain until the strings got so tight he was sure his treble E would snap. Marion lit a cigarette and stared at him, running her hands through her hair. A nervous knock broke the silence. When she went to the door it was Mr Patel, looking sheepish.

'Room alright?' he asked, in a friendly voice. Marion said yeah, and Mr P said that was good. 'Our room,' he pointed, 'is just down the way, so if you want anything in the night, do knock us up.'

Marion said she was sure she wouldn't want anything, but if she did, she would.

'Thank you,' she said. 'Thank you, Mr Patel.' He smiled again.

'May I?' he smiled, stepping into the room. 'For a moment?'

'Sure,' said Marion, 'it's your room, after all.' Mr Patel laughed.

'I suppose so,' he said, 'I didn't think of it that way.' He paused, then; 'Why are you here? Do you mind telling me?' Marion pretended to laugh. Then she said she was here for a job. 'Well, look,' he said, suddenly enthused, 'I can help you out.'

Eddie found himself becoming rapidly aware of the sweet taint of cannabis that scented the room. He hauled the stiff window open wider. Then he sat on the sill gazing at Mr Patel, who wrung his hands together with great anxiety as he spoke.

Mr Patel said that Angela had left this morning, giving no notice and that he hated to say it, but it was typical of the blacks, they just didn't want to work. It turned out Angela was the maid and she was going back to Barbados to live with her maiden aunt. Mr Patel was real pissed off, because he said he was just about to start up a little carpentry and plumbing business with his brother-in-law and he just couldn't devote as much time as he wanted to running the hotel any more.

'I,' he sighed, 'have been dropped in the shit by Angela. Pardon my French.'

All the time he spoke his eyes kept drifting to Eddie's guitar, stretched out across the eiderdown. It was beautiful, admittedly, a real '56 Fender strat with sunburst finish and Gretch pickups. But the way he couldn't stop looking at it, well, it was like Mr P'd never seen a guitar before, which maybe he hadn't, not close up at any rate.

'What's all this got to do with us?' Eddie said.

'I have a proposition,' he smiled. 'I make you an offer you can't refuse,' and he walked to the bedside, leaned over the guitar and touched the strings, with an attitude that was almost reverent, gently, like he almost expected the strings to bite him. Eddie told him you had to plug it in before you got any really cooking sounds out of it. Mr P looked puzzled.

The deal was that Marion would take over from Angela, do some cleaning, make some beds, help out with breakfast, generally 'row in', and in return she'd get free live-in accommodation.

'You can stay in this room,' he said. And if her fiancé wanted to help out once in a while he'd fix him up too. If he behaved himself.

'Who?' said Eddie. 'Me?'

'Nobody will be empty handed,' he said. 'Stay with us here. What do you say?'

'He's not my fiancé,' she said. Mr Patel held up his hands.

'I ask no questions,' he smiled, 'you tell me no lies.'

'Why me?' she said. 'You don't even know me.'

Mr Patel said he just liked her and she seemed like a nice girl, and anyway, he knew the Irish were great workers. He'd run into lots of Irish people in the building trade, and he knew they were made of tough stuff. He chuckled from time to time while he spoke, and he stared, shyly, at the floor. He said he could see they were young, and he knew very well that when people were young they were hungry for opportunity. He could remember that himself. He stepped towards Marion and touched her hand as he spoke. There was opportunity here, he said. It was a great city. She should look on it as a start. Little acorns, all of that. And anyway, to be frank, he was desperate, and these YTS kids were lazy little shits from the council flats more interested in sniffing glue than putting in a decent day's work. He laughed when he said that, a guilty little laugh. He could see she and Eddie weren't like that. He had an instinct about people, he said, and it was never wrong. Eddie and Marion gave him a feeling. Eddie chuckled, frantically.

Marion looked at Eddie and asked him what he thought. He swallowed hard and said he didn't know.

'I know you don't *know*,' she sighed, 'but what do you think?'

Eddie started to panic. Silently. This was just getting out of hand now, way out of line, just the way he'd known it would. He began to wish fervently that he'd never met her. All he wanted was to hang around maybe for a day or two, then spin her a just-good-friends line and run for the hills. OK, so it wasn't exactly right-on, but it was the way things were between consenting adults and anybody who didn't know that was kidding themselves. He didn't want to be asked for an opinion on how she should live her life. That was just too much. He'd have to be courageous now, come clean, before anyone got hurt. He turned to face her. The look in Marion's face defied disappointment.

'Well?' she said. 'Would you like to stay?' Eddie sniggered and stared at the floor.

'Faint heart,' said Mr Patel, waving his finger.

'It's make-your-mind-up time,' Marion said.

Eddie thought about it. He hardly even knew this girl. They had nothing at all in common. Hell, he didn't even like her that much to be absolutely honest. All he wanted was a one-night stand, nothing more serious than that. Jesus. Why was it always so difficult? You go to bed with somebody, next minute they're asking you for a fucking opinion. She made him so nervous. Everything he said she had an answer for, usually before he even said it. She wasn't like any girl he'd ever met before, certainly not at all like Jennifer or the other girls he'd done a lap of the track with, and that was the truth, straight up. Deep in his heart he knew it would be a complete disaster. It couldn't possibly work out. They had two chances, slim and none, and that was being optimistic. It was utterly and absolutely doomed. There was just no question about it. He had to be tough.

She looked at him, chewing gum, eyebrows raised in anticipation.

'Well?' she said again. 'Are you staying or going?'

'Sure,' he stammered, 'I'd like to stay, OK? If that's what you want.'

She blew a gum bubble, and it burst against her lips.

'OK,' she smiled, 'you can stay so.'

'Whatever you like,' he said, palms raised. 'It's up to you.'

Mr Patel said she could think it over, but she said no, no point in thinking, she'd stay. He clapped his hands in delight.

'True love,' he beamed.

'Yeah, well,' said Eddie, as she covered his face with kisses, 'let's not get carried away here.'

He felt like his father. He felt himself stiffen like that, all prickly with bullshit resolve and maturity. Still, he enjoyed the way Mr Patel looked at him, laughing away, while Marion kissed his neck and threw her arms tight around him.

She'd have to hang around for a few days, she said, because she had a few people to see and important stuff to do. Then she'd have to go home to Donegal, collect her stuff, explain to her folks and come back again. The whole thing might take about a week. There was a problem with cash but Mr Patel said he'd lend her the money for the boat home and she could work it off week by week. She said not at all. She'd borrow it from her sister.

'So everybody is happy?' said Mr Patel, brightly.

'Yes,' said Eddie, loosening his collar, 'everybody is delirious.'

'It's a great day for the Irish,' beamed Mr Patel, 'as the old song goes.'

Mr Patel stopped in the doorway and he turned around, one finger raised as if he had forgotten something. Grinning like a schoolboy he pulled a little card from his waistcoat pocket and handed it to Eddie.

'My new business card,' he said, 'I would value your opinion. The Irish have a talent with pretty words, isn't that so? It's the thing your country is famous for, yes?'

'Yes,' said Eddie, 'pretty words,' and he took the card.

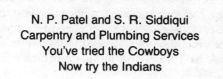

N. P. Patel and S. R. Siddiqui
Carpentry and Plumbing Services
You've tried the Cowboys
Now try the Indians

Marion sat down on the bed curling her knees up to her chin. She looked at the ABC on the wall, and the DEF, and she smiled like a child, a stupid, heartbreakingly innocent, lingering smile.

'It's great,' said Eddie, and he slipped the card into his pocket. 'I'd hire you anyway.'

Mr Patel looked pleased. He said they'd talk about arrangements later, and he left the room, closing the door gently behind him. They could hear him whistle an Elvis Presley tune as he walked briskly down the corridor. Heartbreak Hotel.

'And if I needed a bullshit artist,' said Marion, hugging him hard, 'I'd hire you, Eddie Virago.'

'Thanks,' he said.

'You're welcome,' she replied, with a defiant face.

Eddie felt suddenly very nervous. When he moved around the room he felt her eyes. He felt too that he wanted to be alone, somewhere far away from this strange girl and her silences.

'What's up with you?' she said. Eddie laughed.

'Nothing at all,' he said, 'just thinking about something.'

'Who?' she smiled. 'Is she good looking?'

'Nothing like that,' he said. Then he spoke again, to change the subject. He clapped his hands and said, brightly, 'So, I guess opportunity knocks, huh?'

'Well, I know it's only cleaning,' she said, 'but I'm happy now that you're here.' She was blushing deeply when he looked at her. 'Maybe I'll clean you up, too, Eddie Virago,' she said, 'what do you think?'

Eddie shrugged and turned away. The room felt cold now. He asked her for the loan of a few pounds so he could go get some cigarettes. She had to break a tenner, but she said she didn't mind.

They spent the morning sightseeing.

Buckingham Palace looked a vast doll's house that some bully-ing skinhead big brother had kicked down the Mall, tatty, frayed at the edges, in need of a good paint. Leicester Square was nothing to write home about either, full of Union Jack burger joints and overbright pizza parlours and those little circular public toilets that look like something straight out of a cheap episode of 'Doctor Who'. Garish stalls glittered importantly, selling trashy postcards of punk rockers and soap stars, black plastic bobbies' helmets and little red London buses that scurried along the ground when you wound them up.

When they walked across Trafalgar Square the sky darkened with pigeons, starlings, crows, a great squawking cloud of them, all screaming and fighting and shitting over the statues. Outside the South African Embassy, three weary-looking guys in black jeans strolled up and down shouldering placards and collecting money in buckets. Eddie threw in an Irish ten pence piece.

'Keep up the good work, comrades,' he said.

The National Gallery was full of chattering Americans, franti-cally photographing each other in front of the Leonardo da Vinci cartoon, thundering through the plush rooms and the souvenir shop like a herd of wildebeest, or a plague of Nikon-garlanded locusts.

Marion didn't like it anyway. She said Picasso was crap, and Eddie, although he disagreed with her, couldn't find the words to explain his opinion. Jennifer had told him all about it once, one drink-sodden night in the Belfield Bar when they'd been going out for such a short time that they were still interested in each other's opinions. But now he couldn't remember what exactly was supposed to be so hot-shot about Cubism. So he said yeah, Picasso was a bit overrated, that was a fair point alright.

Marion said she didn't care what anyone said, nobody ever looked like that. Eddie told her she should see some of the girls he'd gone out with. She didn't laugh. He did.

She liked Caravaggio's 'Supper at Emmaus', and she *loved* the huge Monet called 'Water Lilies', because she said it looked exactly like water lilies do. Eddie was surprised to hear they had water lilies in Donegal, but she said yeah, they had everything up there, it was like Disneyland and Paradise all rolled into one. She bought a postcard of Van Gogh's 'Sunflowers' in the shop, and a set of tablemats of 'The World's Great Artists'. For her mother. Eddie said they were great, although secretly he thought they were tacky and crap.

In the piazza at Covent Garden they watched a blue-haired clown with big yellow lips emptying buckets of water over a little guy with a miserable expression and a striped suit. All the kids roared, 'Yeah, yeah, yeah,' when the tall guy asked, 'Will I do it?' – the little creeps. After the fourth or fifth soaking, the little guy jumped up, grabbed a bucket and emptied it down the front of the big guy's tartan trousers. Then he went running through the crowds of screaming scattering kids, yelling, blowing a whistle, waving another bucket, which turned out to be full of confetti when he dumped it over a hapless looking kid with a fat face.

Over lunch Eddie was jittery. The music in the Hard Rock Café was way too loud, and the place was chock full of people in polonecks, all shouting and waving filofaxes and trying like crazy to impress each other while simultaneously appearing bored. There was something he wanted to ask her, but he was hoping it would just come up in the conversation. Needless to say, it didn't.

They talked about all kinds of bull, movies they liked, The Fine Young Cannibals, the incredible filth of London streets, Ireland's chances in the World Cup.

Eventually, over the coffee, Eddie came out with it. It was precautions, he said, in a hushed and conspiratorial voice. He was a bit concerned. Had they, as it were, been safe?

She told him she hadn't got AIDS, if that's what he was concerned about. He said it wasn't that. It was safe sex, in the old-fashioned sense.

'Well, it's a bit late to ask that now,' she said, 'isn't it?' Eddie concentrated like hell on his cappuccino. He felt his face flush. She let him stammer for a few minutes. 'You needn't worry,' she sighed, eventually relenting, 'it's all taken care of.'

Eddie did one of his wry smiles.

'Well, I don't mean to pry,' he said, 'I mean hey, it's a woman's right to control her own fertility.'

'Yeah,' she said. 'You mean it's not the man's problem.'

'OK, OK,' he nodded, blushing, 'point taken.'

She said maybe next time he might ask in advance. There was no good crying over spilt milk. Eddie smiled. He thought it was some type of crude joke, the kind of cringe-making thing Dean Bean would have come out with just when it was least expected. But she wasn't smiling. She was serious. 'Yeah,' he agreed, 'OK, you're right.' She said she knew she was right, thanks very much. Then he asked what did she mean anyway, next time, and she said, 'Next innocent young peasant you pick up and molest.' Eddie did one of his hurt faces and said there was no need for that. She told him to relax, she was only messing around.

'You can't take a joke, Eddie Virago,' she laughed, 'you really can't.'

They walked through Hyde Park, eating ice-cream cones and pretending to have a good time. But it was cold, and they had little to talk about now and October had deadened the trees and blasted the flowerbeds.

Grey misty light lay folded across the pavilions and everything looked mysterious and vague, as though it held the same shape as its appearance, but was actually something different and threatening. Steam rose into the air over the lake, like some lousy heavy-metal video, with someone cranking up the smoke machine. Great circles of deckchairs stood spread out in a spiral around the bandstand, but most of them were empty, their pastel-striped cloths flapping hard in the breeze. Here and there a few lone pensioners dozed, hats on their crotches, handkerchiefs knotted optimistically over their bald heads. But apart from them, and the dazed-looking businessmen crunching along the gravel paths, and the couples snogging against the trees, nobody.

At Speakers' Corner, when they stopped to look behind them, their feet had left two sets of black prints in the crisp frosty grass, way across the park, as far as they could see, all the way over to where the colour of the grass changed to grey and then to white and then disappeared into the lake. Once or twice the lines of footprints intersected, where she had danced from side to side in front of him as they walked, gaily chattering about nothing at all. The traffic roared down the Edgware Road.

Marion said she'd stay in London for a few days, go see her sister, then go home to Donegal to get her stuff. She talked quickly, excitedly, and she laughed out loud. But her enthusiasm oppressed him. Eddie fought hard against second thoughts. Sure, sure, he'd gone along with her. When the time had come he hadn't said anything. But here in the cold light of Hyde Park, all Eddie could see was a whole trainload of hassle coming straight down the line at him. He was such a coward. He knew it. He watched her joyfully spinning out plans, most of which seemed to include him, and he just couldn't get into it.

'Sure you don't want to think about it?' he said brightly. 'Emigration's a big step, you know. I mean, it's not something you take lightly. It's serious big-time shit.'

She looked at him like she was about to laugh.

'Oh yeah,' she said, 'why should I think about it? If I think about it I'll only fuck myself up. What have I got over there? Another three years making hairnets and washing underpants?'

She spoke with a weird kind of pleadingly hysterical undertone that seemed to imply that he'd better not try to warn her off. Her mind was made up.

'Don't get me wrong,' he said. 'I mean. I'm not trying to put you off.'

Hey, he thought it was a great idea. It was just *her* he was thinking about. But hell, if she was sure, no problem, and after all, it was her decision, nothing to do with him. He'd even lend her the cash, he said. She could fly to Belfast, get the bus and be home in Donegal in no time. Otherwise it would take days, on the boat, train up from Dublin, bus over from Derry. *That's* how good an idea he thought it was.

'Here,' he said, pulling out his wallet. 'Let me give it to you.'

'I thought you were broke,' she said.

'Well, no,' stammered Eddie. 'I'm alright now. Just being careful, you know.'

'Oh OK,' she said, to his great surprise. 'Thanks very much.'

They went into USIT and got the flight then and there. Eddie paid with one of his last fifty pound notes.

'Is that the last of your money?' she said. Eddie laughed, a little too loudly. He said no way, forget it, he was loaded. She told him she'd pay him back anyway. Eddie said that'd be great, but whenever she could spare it, like next week would be fine.

She told him not to worry, she wasn't going to run off with the rich kid's cash. 'And even if I do,' she said, 'you can think of it as payment.' Eddie said there was really no need for that kind of talk.

It was the last seat left on the Ryanair flight and it would have to be non-smoking. Eddie knew the guy behind the counter, some bright spark hot shot who used to be auditor of the UCD History Society. He pretended not to know Eddie, but it was him alright. They'd had a row in the Belfield Bar one night about Marxist literary criticism. He was wearing one of those cheap suits that get smelly after a couple of days' wear, one of those suits that look great on shop-window dummies and under disco lights, crap the rest of the time. He looked embarrassed. He looked like he didn't want anybody to know he was working there. When he handed over the tickets he didn't smile. He bent his head low and started scribbling rubbish on the back of a form.

Back outside, she pocketed the ticket and asked Eddie what he was going to do. That, he said, was the question. He'd maybe take in a movie, or just chill out somewhere, and he'd see her back at the hotel later. She shook her head and said tomorrow. It was ages since she'd seen her sister, so she might have to stay the night. She held up her bag.

'You know how it is,' she said. 'Girl talk.'

'Yeah,' he said, 'I know how it is.'

'I wonder will you be there when I get back,' she sighed, as if it didn't matter to her, 'or are you going to do a runner?'

A police car came screaming around the corner, wailing its siren. The fat man in the passenger seat held his arm out the window, clamping the blue light onto the roof.

Eddie said he'd be there. She smiled, as if she didn't believe him, and she told him he didn't have to be there, but just not to lie. He insisted he wasn't lying.

'I never lie,' he said, 'especially not to people I've slept with.' She smiled again.

'I don't think we're married or anything,' she whispered, 'if that's what you're worried about.'

'Hey,' he laughed, 'who's worried? Me?'

'Maybe you should go see your mother,' she said.

'Yeah,' said Eddie, 'maybe I will.'

They kissed under the marble arch. A dirty-bearded, sad-eyed man in an outrageous floral dress and Wellington boots shambled over wielding a camera, muttering something about a photo-graph. Marion laughed at him and Eddie said no. Then they kissed again, hard, and she pulled on a pair of black fingerless mittens that made her knuckles look pink and raw and cold.

'That's what I'll do,' he said, 'I'll go see the old dear.'

In the corner of his eye, Eddie could see the dirty old guy squatting down a bit, legs apart, aiming the camera at them. Eddie found himself turning, ever so slightly, so the lens could catch his good side.

'Wish me luck, then,' she smiled.

The dirty-looking man walked up and down, cradling the camera in his arms like a baby, rocking it, stroking it.

'Good luck,' said Eddie, and she went, swinging her little overnight bag back and forth like a child on a school trip. He watched the target on the back of her anorak disappear into the crowd. He kept hoping she'd turn and wave, but she didn't.

The man in the dress shambled over with a polaroid, stinking of stale semen and Guinness. His voice was hoarse and Eddie had to lean close to his evil-smelling mouth to hear it. The man said he'd taken the picture anyway, and Eddie could have it for the price of a pair of stockings. Eddie sighed and gave him fifty pence. The guy stared at the coin, looked unhappy. He whispered a few words that Eddie couldn't make out, and then he suddenly turned and marched determinedly down the steps to the Under-ground, brandishing his camera in the air like a weapon.

Eddie looked at the photo, at the two faces emerging out of the tacky paper. He held it between his thumb and his forefinger, blowing, waving it from side to side. It wasn't a great picture. His eyes were red, and Marion looked like she was about to throw up all over him. It looked like the kind of crummy picture they show on the TV news when someone goes missing from home. Still, he stuck it in his pocket, and he didn't really know why.

It did strike Eddie, on his way down the escalator, that what she'd said just before she left, well, it was a funny thing to say. Wish me luck then. She was only going to Lewisham to see her sister. Wish me luck. Hell, he'd heard it was a rough neighbour-hood, but it wasn't exactly a safari. Still, women were weird. If there was one thing Eddie knew, it was that. Women were just not all there. And this one was weirder than most. Wish me luck. Weirdsville Arizona.

Eddie sat on the dusty platform and let three trains go by. Exhausted women and men in suits staggered out towards the exits, and other men and women clawed each other out of the way to get on before the doors made that farting sound and slammed shut. Eddie was in one of those moods where you don't want to rush. He didn't have to. He watched the scramble for the exit, umbrellas and briefcases held high over heads, and he wondered where all these people were coming from and where they were going to, and if any of it all really mattered.

He sniffed in the warm dead stale air of the Underground and he felt freer than he had in a year. He pulled out his diary and looked up his mother's address. And then a few more grafitti-splashed trains slithered out of the tunnels, but he let those go by too, thinking that if he hung around long enough he might see something interesting.

He didn't.

At half-past four, after forty-five minutes of pacing up and down in the cold, Marion went up the steps and in through the big black glass doors. She took the lift to the top floor, just like she'd been told.

The dying sunlight slanted in through the blinds and everything in the lobby was hard, black and golden. The reception room was nicer, full of lush plants in huge earthenware jars, with two black coffee tables, across from the counter, in front of the sofa. Marion introduced herself and was told to sit down for a moment. An anxious-looking woman flitted around flicking at the leaves with a duster, and squirting water from a white plastic bottle. One of the low black tables was spread with leaflets about condoms and diaphragms – the word 'secretion' caught her eye and made her shudder. The other had neat piles of glossy magazines, on their covers the faces of Kylie Minogue, Gorbachev, the Princess of Wales, Madonna, Robert de Niro, and a thin white-faced Irish girl who was making it big on TV, Salome Wilde.

Marion wondered wistfully what it must have been like to be her.

A coffee machine bubbled on a shelf in the corner. A handwritten sign that said 'HELP YOURSELF' was taped to the wall above it, but there were no cups. Somewhere a radio played 'Dance in the Old-Fashioned Way' in a slow version, all slinky with saxophones. The floor was black rubber, tiled. Everything was calm, efficient, clean. The telephone, when it rang behind the counter, made a gentle, modern bleep and the beautiful blonde woman who answered it said, 'Hi, can I help you?' in a sing-song voice, like she really wanted to help whoever it was, and wasn't just saying it for the money. Her fingernails were long and dark red, almond shaped, like a model's.

Marion looked around, and she took off her dark glasses. It was dumb to be so paranoid, she knew that. And anyway, she was the only one in the reception room, just her and the beautiful receptionist, who was laughing quietly as she whispered into the phone. Marion pinched the bridge of her nose hard and her eyes blurred. When she put her fingertips to her temples she felt her blood pulse, but it was just a tension headache. She knew that too. From experience.

She picked up a magazine and flicked through the pages. 'Is Your Man Cheating On You?' mused one headline. 'My Heaven With Rock Hudson,' sang another. 'Everything You Should Know About The Big O,' tempted a third. She took out a biro and started doing an 'Are You Assertive?' test. But when she looked up the back to get the answers somebody had ripped out the page. She wondered why someone who would tear a page out of somebody else's magazine needed to do an assertiveness test in the first place.

She flicked through an article in one of the Sunday supplements. '100 Things Every Woman Should Know About Men.' Marion found she knew most of them already. Then she read an advert for something called a fat transplant and nearly retched. She thought of the sweaty surgeon, mask over his mouth, elbow deep in a vat of molten fat, scooping it into somebody's wide open abdomen with a trowel, or a spatula.

She thought about Eddie Virago too. Eddie wasn't fat. He had one little roll of flesh across his abdomen, but you couldn't have called it fat. His navel was an outtie. That's what her Daddy used to call them. Navels were belly buttons. It was where God had kissed you, on the production line up in heaven, to show you were finished off. Some were innies, and some were outties. If you unscrewed your belly button, your bum would fall off. That's what Daddy used to say. She shuddered. It was cold.

And when she thought about Eddie she felt warm again, odd inside, reluctant and evasive, but vaguely happy too. She closed her eyes and thought about his tongue, his fingers, his soft and girlish lips. He was so unlike anybody she had met before, certainly not like the blokes from Ballybracken. Jumped-up bog-galloping farmers who talked about tumescent slurry tanks and rapidly dying parents whose farms they'd inherit to try and seduce you. Alcoholic county councillors who would promise the stars to get into your pants, then run home to their wrinkled wives in their Spanish hacienda bungalows. Slick showband managers with premature ejaculations and secondhand Hiace vans, the leatherette of which felt sticky on your bare behind in the church car park after closing time. Maybe, she figured, this one would be different. Christ almighty, she thought, please let this one be different.

'Next please?' chirped the woman, an old woman with silver elegant hair and a navy blue twinset, who was now standing with a graceful hand on the shoulder of the blonde-haired receptionist. Both women seemed to gaze at her, kindly, softly. The way they were posed, it reminded Marion of one of the paintings she'd seen in the National Gallery, but she couldn't remember which one. That was an odd thing to think about, at a time like this.

The woman looked a little like the Queen Mother with her hair all candyfloss grey. She spoke like her too. She looked at the clipboard in her hand. 'Next?' she asked, raising her eyebrows, 'Ms?' She pronounced the word 'Ms' deliberately, over the top, like the noise made by a dentist's drill.

Marion smiled as she stood up.

'Miss,' she said. 'Wilde.'

'We like to keep it on first name terms here,' said the lady.

Marion swallowed hard.

'Salome,' she said, 'Salome Wilde.'

'Charmed to meet you, Salome,' said the lady, beckoning towards her. 'What a beautiful name.' When Marion came to the counter the woman raised the hatch, stood back, beamed, and gestured for her to squeeze past. The telephone bleeped again. 'Ms Callaghan next, Audrey,' the older woman said to the receptionist, who nodded, holding the telephone between her chin and her shoulder. She smelt nice, expensive, but not exotic. A pair of pince-nez spectacles dangled on a chain around her neck. She had a gold ring on her wedding finger. She put her arm lightly around Marion's shoulder as they walked.

'It's funny,' she said, looking into her eyes, 'I always thought that name was pronounced Salom-ay.'

'Oh, well, no,' said Marion, blushing deep, 'well, yes it is sometimes, but that's the way I pronounce it. Without the ay.'

'Well, that's lovely, dear,' said the lady, quietly, pushing open a door. 'Whichever way you want it.'

They sat at a table shielded by an open-plan wall partition. It was like visiting a bank manager. Her name was Margaret, she said. There would be a few questions. Marion said, yes, that's what she would have expected.

Margaret took Marion's full name – Salome Bernadette Wilde – and a couple of other details in a friendly way, as though what they were doing was an everyday thing, which, of course, it was. But when Marion went to light a cigarette she tutted in exaggeration, frowned and said, 'We'd prefer not, dear, if you please.'

Marion crushed out the cigarette, awkwardly, on a Wedgwood saucer.

Margaret picked the saucer up between her index finger and her thumb, nose wrinkling in exaggerated disgust, and she moved it at arm's length to the windowsill. Marion blushed. Margaret grinned. She had a tiny trace of lipstick on her lower front teeth.

'Nationality?' she said. 'Just for our research.'

'Irish,' said Marion.

'Yes,' she beamed, 'thought I recognised the accent.' She leaned her left sleeve across the form as she wrote, carefully, in block capital letters. 'Lovely country,' she muttered, 'delightful.'

'It is,' said Marion.

'We have a friend,' she said, 'lives in Galway somewhere, little place.'

'Do you?' said Marion.

Margaret looked a little scatterbrained. She looked like she was trying to think of something, then she shrugged her shoulders, beamed, and looked Marion in the face.

'Near Connemara,' she said. Marion nodded.

'Beautiful country,' said Margaret, 'I mean, just so *untamed*, you know.' Marion agreed. 'Well, when I say he lives there, it's more of a *pied à terre*, you see. I mean, a rural *pied à terre*, if there is such a thing.' Marion didn't know what a *pied à terre* was, but she wasn't in the mood to ask. She just nodded again and said that was nice. 'We get a lot of Irish girls here, you know,' she said, raising her eyes as she scribbled. 'Understandably, I suppose. Since that amendment business.' Margaret pursed her lips and shook her head regretfully. 'Very unfortunate,' she sighed. Marion said nothing. She reached into her bag, pulled out a tissue, and four fifty pound notes which she placed on the desk. 'Or women, of course,' Margaret laughed. 'We're supposed to call them women now dear, aren't we? Not girls.'

Then she laughed again, suddenly, as though she had said something hysterical. And Marion laughed too. Margaret pursed her lips and asked whether a receipt would be required. Marion shook her head. Margaret nodded. Would there be any visitors? Marion said no, there wouldn't.

'Fine,' said Margaret, ticking a little box on the form, 'fine. No visitors. Do you know, dear, sometimes I think that's actually preferable.'

'There's girls, there's women and there's ladies,' Marion said. 'Do you know that song?'

Margaret looked over Marion's shoulder, and into the middle distance. She knocked the end of her biro against her teeth and her bright eyes sparkled with delight behind her glasses. She repeated the words.

'There's girls, there's women and there's ladies,' she said, a few times. 'Delightful, delightful really.' But eventually she shook her head. 'No, dear,' she sighed, 'I don't believe I do. Who sings that one?'

Marion didn't know. She said it was just some stupid country song.

Margaret shrugged and her smile melted away. She was required to ask whether Marion had thought everything through, and Marion said yes, she had, with a sureness of tone that surprised both of them, yes, completely, she had absolutely no doubts at all.

On the way down to the operating theatre, Margaret put her arm very gently across Marion's shoulder and told her to buck up like a good thing.

'Have *you* ever been to Connemara, dear?' Margaret asked. And for some reason she could not really understand, Marion said no, through her tears, no she hadn't. 'Well, I'm sure you will go, Salome dear,' she whispered, reassuringly. 'One day you'll get your chance. I'm sure of that.'

When Eddie got home that evening he was seriously pissed off and sorry that he hadn't got it together to get on a sodding Tube out to Richmond and see his mother. A waste of time? Sure. But even that wouldn't have been as much of a waste as what he had done, i.e. nothing.

Things hadn't gone to plan down at the dole office. He'd queued up for two hours, surrounded by skins with tattoos and braces, only to be told by a guy with a face only a very kind mother could have loved that he was in the wrong queue and that it wasn't 'Signing On' he wanted but 'New Enquiries' and that 'New Enquiries' was about to close now because they were short-staffed in 'Signing On'. They were short-staffed in 'Signing On', apparently, because not enough people were signing off. After some minutes of this, the guy changed tack and began hassling him about his address. Eddie said he didn't know exactly were he'd be staying, and the guy said he couldn't claim anything at all unless he had a permanent address. So Eddie told him about the Brightside, picked up a couple of forms and booklets and went for a cup of coffee in the local greasy spoon.

But there's only so much cappuccino you can drink, and by the time he had figured out one leaflet it seemed to contradict the next. Income Support. Supplementary Benefit. Social Fund. Unemployment Allowance. What the fuck was the difference? And how could he get a social security number when he'd never worked here? And why hadn't he sussed all this out before he'd left home? The Students' Union never stopped ranting on about it, *Your Rights in London*, all of that – the brochure was almost handed out to you with a copy of your degree when you graduated. He knew Jennifer had been right when she told him to suss out as much as he could before he left. Jennifer was just always so fucking right. That's what was really bugging him now. If this was Jennifer, she would have arranged her first dole payment to be flown over specially and delivered to the fucking front door by Norman Tebbit himself, she really would. Not that Jennifer would ever be on the dole, of course. Some chance of that. People who talked a lot about unemployment usually managed to scrape along somehow. That was the sickening thing.

Eddie's mood was worsened by the fact that Marion wasn't there. And analysing this made him feel even worse than before, so he stopped. He sat in the café feeling moody, imagining the effect of a direct nuclear strike on the dole office, watching the three red-faced Irish labourers at the table across from him, laughing and smoking cigarettes, until the sky became dark red and white outside the glass, like a great big streaky rasher, with a greasy fried-egg sun.

Back at the Brightside, Mr Patel wasn't at the desk. There was nobody at all around in fact, and the lobby seemed quiet and spooky, drenched with the fragrance of incense and Jeyes fluid.

Up in the room, he could still smell Marion's sweet smell, whatever stuff it was she put on herself. He picked up his guitar and put it down again fast. He ripped a page from his pad and started scribbling a letter to Dean Bean, but by the time he got to the end of the first paragraph he was already bored. What could he say? Dear Beano, Well, here I am, holed up in a King's Cross dosshouse with some spaced-out woman I hardly even know, and I've only been in the frigging country two days. You're right, Dean, I'm an Oscar-winning asshole. Love Eddie.

So he lay on the bed with his hands behind his head, staring at the ceiling and listening to the whimpers of the couple in the next room. Was that how they had sounded, he wondered, him and Marion? Like little animals, pleasuring each other in a cheap hotel room? Well, it wasn't a bad sound. He had to admit it. It wasn't the worst sound Eddie had ever heard. It was just the sound of two people who probably didn't love each other, making love. And it was nothing more than that.

He cut a beautiful glossy red 'g' out of the 'Welfare Rights For EEC Nationals' leaflet and he added it to the chain of letters on the wall.

They certainly seemed to be enjoying it next door. Spanish, they were. Or Italian. Foreigners anyway. Every so often there was a slapping sound, *slap*, like that, followed by two tumultuous giggles, a great creaking of bedsprings and a convulsion of ecstatic moaning. Jesus, Eddie thought. People are pathetic when their hormones take them over.

He got up and went to the bathroom, where he shaved the sides of his head with the electric razor. He shaved until the sides of his head were smooth as an egg, then he looked at himself for five minutes in the mirror, suddenly turning towards it, arranging the cabinet doors for maximum multi-angled effect, trying to catch himself unexpectedly. He knew he'd have to cut this out. It was becoming a bad habit.

Back down in the lobby he phoned up Jimmy Shaw at his office. Some bimbo answered the phone and couldn't pronounce Eddie's name. Eventually Jimmy came on the line, sounding hassled. Eddie was lucky, he said. He was working late. There was a big push on, a majorly serious account, otherwise he would have been at home with Ruth.

Eddie wanted to talk, but Jimmy kept going, 'Look, I won't hold you up. I know you must be busy, man.' Eddie said yeah, he was real busy alright, run off his feet as a matter of fact, but he could probably fit Jimmy in if he wanted to meet later in the Bunch of Grapes. Jimmy laughed.

'That's real big of you, Eddie,' he said, 'I'll see you at eight.'

Out in the street it was cold and Eddie raised the collar of his jacket up around his ears. He came down President Street and right out in front of St Pancras, thinking of his father and his mother too. He watched a group of striking ambulance men collecting signatures outside the station, the yellow light from the brazier wet on their faces. They stomped their feet on the ground. They blew their knuckles and sipped from flasks. And they turned and waved vaguely at the street, whenever a car horn sounded in support, rattling their buckets, calling out to the haggard commuters who pushed wearily past them and into the station. When Eddie signed the petition, the young guy in the uniform said, 'Fair play to you, pal.' He was Irish. From Dublin. There was just no escape.

On Gray's Inn Road Eddie bought a kebab which smelt like a dog's breath, took one bite and chucked it in the gutter. Then he went to a newsagent where he bought two Mars bars and a girlie magazine, which he stuffed inside his shirt and down the front of his trousers.

Back home at the Brightside he flicked through the magazine, lying face down on the bed, chomping the Mars bars. Naked women cavorted in four-poster beds, on all fours, buttocks facing the camera, legs apart, staring backwards over their shoulders like speculative cows surprised in a field. The centrefold featured a nude woman who could put her ankles behind her head. 'Shy Wendy', said the caption. There were letters from readers about seducing secretaries at office parties and spying on lesbian neighbours. There were lists of phone numbers you could call and some housewife would ring you back and talk dirty to you while you jacked off. He knew about them. Dean Bean had called one up, but you had to have a credit card. The pictures didn't arouse him. Not at first. They made him feel vaguely nauseous. He told himself it was good that you couldn't buy stuff like this in Ireland. Sure, he was against censorship, but still, this stuff was pornographic degrading junk. He tossed it self-consciously into the dustbin, as though somebody was watching him. He strummed a few minor fifths on his guitar, but his fingers were too cold, too stiff, to manage anything more complex than the four-chord riff for 'Smoke on the Water'.

Half an hour later he retrieved the magazine, walked into the bathroom, opened his fly and jerked off into the sink, looking at himself in the mirror while he did it.

In the Bunch of Grapes pub Jimmy and Ruth were already waiting when he got there, sitting on a long bench, both of them glowing and pink with sweat. It was maybe a year now since he'd seen them. Not that he'd ever liked them that much, but Eddie'd just got to know them somehow in the first week of college, the way you do when you're so desperate you think you'll have no friends at all unless you drop your standards and talk to any old airhead who shapes along your way. When they'd left for London back in '87, Eddie had said he'd definitely ease on over to see them from time to time. They'd be sick of the sight of him, he promised, he'd be over so much. Sick of it. But somehow or another, as they had loudly predicted at the time, Eddie'd never got around to going.

Jimmy's face had got chubby and his hair was so short that his ears, one of which was studded, appeared to protrude a little too much. Ruth was still the same, a good eighteen inches shorter than Jimmy, very dolly, but with a mouth like a fishwife and a mass of undisciplined brown curls. She wore a maroon blazer with a phoney crest on the lapel. Her face was whitened with powder and her lips were red as a pack of Marlboros.

Ruth and Eddie had got off with each other once, on the night the exam results came out in first year. But she probably didn't remember, and Jimmy certainly didn't, and a hell of a lot of things had happened since then anyway, so big deal.

Jimmy waved when he saw Eddie's mohican advancing over the throng of suited glaring yuppies and tight-skirted secretaries.

'Eddie Virago,' he roared, at the top of his voice. Eddie stalked over and sat down on a stool, unwrapping his scarf from around his throat.

'How's the crack?' he said. Jimmy and Ruth gave him that secretive up-and-down look that only friends do, when they haven't seen each other for a while.

'Just in from the court,' Jimmy said.

'Oh yeah?' Eddie said. 'What have you done now?'

'No, you prat,' said Jimmy, 'squash.' He mimed a forehand stroke with his left hand.

Eddie threw his eyes to heaven.

'I know that, you dickhead,' he said. 'I see you haven't had a sense of humour transplant since you came over here.'

Jimmy laughed, sardonically.

'A sense of humour,' he said. 'I love it, Eddie, that's just beautiful coming from you.'

'Anyway,' said Eddie, 'good to see you guys, how long is it now?'

'Oh,' sighed Jimmy, scrutinising Eddie's face, 'about six inches, I guess,' and he reached over and slapped Eddie hard on the thigh. Only two years in the country and Jimmy had lost whatever Dublin accent he'd ever had buried in his Foxrock drawl. Now he was talking like a Home Counties wideboy. 'So,' he cackled, 'how's the old sod, and I'm not talking about Charlie Haughey?'

'Same as ever,' said Eddie, 'shit, you know.'

'Good old cynical Eddie,' said Ruth. Eddie did one of his tolerant smiles.

'Fuck off, Ruth,' he grinned.

'Swivel on it, Eddie,' she beamed.

'Right,' said Jimmy, rubbing his hands, 'now we've got the pleasantries out of the way, what are you drinking?' Eddie said he'd have a pint of Guinness. 'Are you sure?' said Jimmy, his face twisted in disgust. 'It's like pisswater over here.'

'I'm sure,' said Eddie.

'Peasant,' sighed Ruth, sipping her Perrier.

'I'm sure,' Eddie said, again.

Jimmy ordered a round and came back to the seat with a tray of pints.

They sat in silence for a minute or two. Nobody seemed to want to start things off.

''Scuse me,' said Ruth, 'have to go freshen up.'

Ruth stood up, shaking the table, and eased past Jimmy, who made clenching gestures in the vague direction of her buttocks. Eddie stared at the plastic oak rafter ceiling and counted, silently, to ten.

'Anyway,' said Jimmy, 'so you still have the hair.'

'No,' said Eddie, 'it's an astral projection.'

'Yes,' said Jimmy, 'that's what it looks like.'

Eddie didn't feel up to the usual cut-and-thrust routine, so he sipped deeply at his pint, nicked a cigarette from Ruth's pack, lit it, and asked, 'So how's advertising been treating you two yuppy bastards?'

'Oh, pretty good, Ed, you know, can't complain. 'Course, to someone of your principles it's all totally materialistic,' and Jimmy held up two fingers in the hippy V-sign, '*maaan*.'

'I told you before,' said Eddie, 'I hate hippies.'

'Well, for someone who hates them, you sure talk like one sometimes.'

'Oh, sit on my face,' sighed Eddie.

'Why?' said Jimmy. 'Your nose bigger than your prick?'

'There's an answer to that,' said Eddie.

'Mmmm,' said Jimmy, in mid-gulp, 'just you can't think of it.'

When Ruth came back from what she called the Little Girls' Room, Jimmy told her that as Eddie couldn't take a slagging any more, they'd better get down to the serious 'deep' conversation pretty pronto. Ruth ignored him. Eddie let it go too. He said he was tired and he just wasn't into an argument.

'Give me a break,' he said, 'OK, guys?'

'Pax,' said Ruth.

'Tampax,' said Jimmy. 'OK, OK, I'll shut up, I swear.'

They talked for a while, about mutual friends, college *faux pas*, what Dean Bean was up to, who was screwing who (or 'whom' as Ruth said), where everybody was working now, how well all the old gang were doing, except Eddie, of course, but that was only a matter of time, they had great faith in him.

'You should ring up Salome Wilde,' said Ruth, 'and get her to plug you.'

Jimmy said he was sick to the back teeth of Salome Wilde actually.

'Yeah,' said Eddie, 'I keep seeing her name. Who the fuck is she?'

'You remember her,' said Ruth, 'she was in Belfield, year ahead of us, History and Ancient Civilisation. Jimmy made a tit of himself trying to chat her up at the Trinity Ball one year.'

'She's making a name,' Jimmy sighed, rolling his eyes. 'She presents that "Art Attack" load of camel droppings on Channel Four.'

'Oh yeah,' said Eddie, 'that Arts thing, midnight, nobody watches it?'

'The very one,' said Ruth, 'it's quite tacky really. Culture for the proles, you know, the Laughing Cavalier and Jeffrey Archer. But they sometimes have bands too. And Salome's really very good on it. I must admit that.' Jimmy said every time he opened a sodding magazine he saw another sodding frank profile of her.

Ruth said some folks had all the luck. 'But I'm not jealous, honest,' she sighed, 'skinny bitch.'

Eddie was surprised. From what he could remember, Salome Wilde had always been so quiet in college, one of those standoffish types, sensible shoes, in the library all hours, first bus home after lectures. Good looking, yeah, but a bit on the silent side.

'Plotting, Eddie,' whispered Jimmy, 'plotting away all the time. It's those quiet ones you have to watch. And she *is* a Proddy too, of course, definite advantage for television, oh yeah.'

Eddie told them about his parents and they said that was an utter pain, and a total downer and a drag.

'Divorce?' asked Jimmy. Eddie said that in case Jimmy had forgotten, there wasn't any divorce in Ireland. Ruth looked at Jimmy and shook her head in mock disbelief. Jimmy went even more pink and said of course he hadn't forgotten, he'd meant annulment or whatever the hell the Church called it. Eddie said no, he doubted it, they didn't seem to want to make it official. Then he told them he'd rather talk about something else actually.

So they talked about the strange phenomenon whereby all their college friends seemed to be getting fat, specially the guys. Jimmy said it was all those student years of living on chips and lager.

'Thirty fucking something,' he said despondently. 'Why watch it when you can live it?' Ruth said yeah, and they were only twenty-four.

Ruth was big into callanetics, a form of keep-fit famous for being used by the Duchess of York. It was particularly good, apparently, for people with a problem in the bot department. Jimmy, who was fatter than most, kept trying to bring the conversation away from flab and cellulite and liposuction and around to house prices. He and Ruth had bought a flat in Golders Green, not as a serious heavy cohabitation vibe – Ruth made inverted commas gestures – but mainly as an investment. But since the crash, house prices were falling faster than you could say 'I bet he drinks Carling Black Label'. Now they were paying twice as much for the mortgage and the flat was worth less than they'd paid for it. Pitsville Arizona. Eddie didn't care. He had heard it all before, when Dean Bean had come back from visiting them last year. He told them that's what they deserved for being Thatcherite scumbags.

'Oh, you're not still into all that,' groaned Ruth.

'All what?' pouted Eddie, in a tone that made it clear he knew exactly what she was talking about.

'All that,' she giggled, and looked at Jimmy, 'all that up-against-the-wall bullshit bolshie stuff.'

'I am,' he said.

'But I mean,' she said, 'even Russia's given up on communism now, Eddie, and look at East Germany.'

'What about it?' Eddie said.

'Well, Honecker's gone, for a start.'

'Oh well,' Eddie said, 'I'll have a Carlsberg then.'

'Hoot hoot,' she said crossly. 'I'm just hooting with laughter, Eddie.'

When he'd finished chuckling, Eddie said you didn't want to leave all your principles behind when you graduated.

'Oh well,' sighed Jimmy, 'we don't care, do we, Bubble? You can have the scruples and we'll have the jacuzzi.' He slapped Eddie's thigh again. 'We're your flexible friends, Eddie, so why don't you just trot on up and order us all a double vodka' – he smiled broadly – 'comrade?'

Eddie told him he was a complete idiot.

'Scruples,' he scoffed, 'you have the nerve to talk to me about scruples. You probably think scruples is the name of a night-club in fucking Carnaby Street.' Jimmy said that was a good one.

'If it isn't,' he said, 'it should be.'

As the night dragged on they had a little too much to drink. Jimmy went on to whiskies and soda – 'On the rocks?' Eddie asked. 'No,' he said, 'I'd rather drink it' – and Ruth started an argument about her brother, who had just come back from Australia with no money, literally, in the stinking Hawaiian shorts he was wearing on the plane, bullied her father into paying off his student loan, and then gone out the next day and bought three new suits with another loan, and a Jean-Paul Gaultier designer umbrella, whatever that is, the only one to be had in the whole of Dublin anyway, had to be specially imported. Jimmy got more and more adamant that she was being an utter pain, and that her brother needed suits to do interviews and that you couldn't turn up in an insurance office looking like Bob fucking Geldof and she got more and more aggressive, saying she loved her brother to absolute death but sometimes he was a selfish little prick, and Jimmy should have known that, and all Eddie could do was sit there in silence thinking about Marion and counting the number of women in the Bunch of Grapes who were wearing white stiletto heels.

At half-past ten a suntanned girl in glittery earrings and a tight red dress breezed over and announced, 'Hello, strangers,' to Jimmy and Ruth, in a smug breathy voice. She was introduced to Eddie as Audrey Beckett, a friend of Ruth's from way back in the convent-school days. She was over here working for Daddy's meat-packing firm, holding the fort in the old PR department. But she was keeping up a bit of modelling on the side too, just bits and pieces. Eddie offered to buy her a drink but she was in a bit of a dash. She had to get over to Hampstead and put in an appearance at a party. She thought she'd met Eddie before though, somewhere; did he know anyone in Dublin rugby? He didn't? Was he a friend of Dean Bean by any chance?

'Yeah, yeah,' sighed Eddie. 'Jesus. London seems to be that guy's fan club or something.'

'Oh well,' she laughed, 'I'm not surprised. I could tell you a few stories about our Beano.' Eddie asked if she was sure about the drink, but she was absolutely pozzo, the Bambino was on a double yellow outside Harrods, down the road. 'Next time,' she smiled, 'get my number from Ruthie Pops and we'll do something.'

As soon as Audrey Beckett's bangled waving hand had disappeared through the glass doors of the Bunch of Grapes, Ruth's smile faded, and she called her a cow.

'Maybe,' panted Jimmy, absent-mindedly, 'but my god, she's easy on the eye, I'll say that for her.' Ruth pinched his face, hard. Jimmy winced and told her to fuck off.

'Fuck off yourself,' she said, 'you fat idiot.' Eddie didn't bother asking for the number.

'Look, guys,' he said, 'I've gotta split.'

Jimmy said yeah, they'd be hitting the old frog and toad any minute themselves. Ruth nudged him in the ribs and he looked at her questioningly.

'Go on,' she said, 'ask him.'

'Oh, yeah, yeah. We're having a few people over for a nosh-up on Saturday,' sighed Jimmy. 'Why don't you come?'

'You can bring someone if you like,' said Ruth.

'No,' said Eddie, 'I'll come on my own.'

'Well,' said Jimmy, 'you usually do.'

'Boom boom,' giggled Ruth, clapping her hands in glee.

Jimmy laughed until the tears ran down his fat cheeks. He

kept trying to stop laughing, then suddenly he'd snort into his drink and start howling again, looking up at Eddie, holding his nose to choke back his giggles.

'Hey relax, Ed,' he kept saying, 'I'm only fucking around with you.'

Eddie looked at his two friends, in their matching 'I FED THE WORLD' white sweatshirts, holding hands and shaking with laughter, and he was happy for them, with the particular kind of happiness you reserve for people you think are pathetically inferior to yourself.

'See you fucking reactionaries on Saturday then,' he said. And Ruth blew him a kiss, which he stepped backwards suddenly to avoid, upsetting a tequila sunrise all over what he was told, adamantly, was a Bruce Oldfield suit.

'Who the fuck is Bruce Oldfield?' he said. 'Mike's big brother?'

When he got back to the hotel, Mr Patel was sitting behind the counter, reading a copy of *Today*. When he saw Eddie he stood up quickly, looking worried, and relieved in equal measure, as though he had presumed Eddie was never coming back. He stood up very straight and ran his fingers through his hair.

'Thank God,' said Mr Patel.

Eddie asked what was wrong. Mr Patel told him that nothing was wrong exactly. But Marion was back, and she was asleep upstairs.

'How do you know?' said Eddie.

'She is not well,' said Mr Patel. 'We brought her hot milk. She is really poorly and ill. Shaking.'

The hot room smelt of dirty socks and talcum powder. As the triangle of light from the corridor spread across the bed, Eddie and Mr Patel could see that Marion was asleep now, on her back, breathing hard, with her arms folded across her chest like a corpse. Her face looked tense and worn, as though she was in pain. Her long hair looked matted and sweaty. Beads of sweat studded her forehead and her cheeks shone in the light. She wore a long black Chris de Burgh T-shirt, and her left leg was folded underneath itself which made her white thigh look fat.

'She came back just after you left, Eddie,' whispered Mr Patel. 'Very pale, very trembling. She sat in the lobby for a while, with her head in her hands like this, and then she asked the trouble and strife for some painkiller.' Eddie looked at him quizzically. 'The wife,' he explained, 'Mrs Patel.' Eddie reached out a finger and prodded Marion in the ribs, but she didn't wake. She snorted softly and rolled over on her side, curling her legs up towards her chest. 'She is knackered,' whispered Mr Patel, 'I think.'

Eddie flicked on the bedside light. In the far corner of the room, he saw the porno magazine, lying on the dresser, torn, lengthways, in two.

'Shit,' he said, 'fucking shit, man.'

He turned around to look at Mr Patel's confused face again. But Mr Patel just made the sign of the cross, tutted, and left the room, closing the door gently behind him.

Eddie peeled off his clothes in the cold and slipped in beside her.

She woke up in the middle of the night and told him everything was alright now, and that she was so happy to be here with him she didn't think she'd ever be able to leave.

Eddie said he hadn't been expecting her back until tomorrow. He touched her breast through her T-shirt, but she took his hand away, murmured something about true and endless love, and almost immediately fell asleep.

It was a week later when Marion finally left for Ireland and Eddie, to tell the truth, was pretty relieved. He told himself it wasn't because he didn't like her. Not that at all. It was just that they'd had to change the ticket and pay a surplus charge and make innumerable phonecalls and it had all just got on Eddie's nerves the way she'd been hanging round the musty bedroom all day, moody and weird, looking gaunt and sulking, making out to be sick. Well, she said she was sick, but every time Eddie suggested calling a doctor she'd go all crazy and beg him not to. She really did get uptight about it. And as for the day he offered to phone her parents. Jesus. A display of fucking fireworks that Led Zeppelin would have been proud of.

From the day she went to see her sister she just hadn't been right, there was no doubt about that. No matter how he tried, Eddie couldn't figure it. He wondered if they'd had a row or something, some sisterly thing maybe, but he didn't like to ask. Eddie knew better than to pry into family feuds, and no hint was offered, so he said nothing at all.

When she began throwing up in the mornings, it even occurred to him in a panic-stricken moment that she might be pregnant. But when he plucked up the courage to ask her about it she said that no, she wasn't, and then went all quiet again, and didn't speak to him for the rest of the night. So he couldn't think of anything else except some vague women's problem that he'd really rather not know about.

Mr Patel was getting iffy. He said he realised she wasn't healthy, but then neither was his bank balance. He'd have to get staff soon and if she didn't want the job there were plenty of other willing hands who did. She'd have to show a little enterprise. He pointed out that he wasn't a registered charity, as if that needed proving, and he went on and on until Eddie told him to chill out and Marion said not to worry, she did still want the job, and she'd go home and be back with her stuff by the weekend. That was a promise.

She went out to Luton on the Thameslink, straight from King's Cross, still looking peaky and pale. She told Eddie she'd be thinking of him, and he said that was nice. On the draughty platform she began to cry and she held him so tight that he could barely breathe. He told her to be sure and bring back some duty-free.

'I can't, you fool,' she sobbed.

'Why not?' asked Eddie.

'Because it's Belfast,' she said, 'I mean, it's not another country.'

The day after she left, Eddie finally managed to sign on, but he was told he'd have to wait two weeks for his first cheque. Money was running low. The £250 his father had given him was very nearly blown away on meals out with Marion, her plane ticket, phonecalls, the occasional cab, Tubes, booze, a ten spot they'd scored from a hapless hippy outside the Sir George Robey one night, when he'd dragged Marion along to a Napalm Death gig to cheer her up. Bad choice.

When he added it all up he could only actually account for spending £150. He had fifty in cash, so that only left a shortfall of another fifty, pretty good for Eddie, a guy who Beano used to say had the financial-planning ability of El Salvador.

In addition to the fifty of his father's he had fifty of his own, the last cheque he'd cashed on his student loan-cum-overdraft before he'd left the country. Eddie thought of Kieran Casey, that obnoxious moustache-wielding twat in the bank who was so keen to give you cash when you needed it, and then took it as a personal insult that you didn't mortgage your first child to pay it back. With women, Kieran was a flirty bastard. Jennifer never used to have any problem with him. She'd just wind the guy round her little finger and come out wrapped in banknotes. But guys, well, that was different. Guys got a hard time. Guys had to queue up outside his office like they were going to confession every time they wanted to see him. Which, in a way, they were. He'd ask you anything. He'd look through your cheque stubs going, 'Nice meal out, was it?' and 'Good holiday?' and 'Jayzus, but the women are fierce expensive, aren't they, Eddie?' Yeah. Kieran Casey was the kind of student banker who makes people invent rhyming slang.

Eddie thought of Kieran Casey, sitting in his subterranean office on College Row, surrounded by his framed photographs of the debating society and the rugby team, reading Eddie's cheque, the one that said 'Dublin Airport' in big black letters on the front and 'Fuck You, Kieran' in small ones on the back. Boy, would he go spare. He really would go crazy. Eddie laughed out loud when he thought about it. He could just see the smarmy bastard, hopping up and down and pulling out what was left of his hair transplant.

But that's the way Eddie was with money; live now, pay later, his father had often said it, and his mother too, not that she was anyone to talk.

'You don't seem to understand,' his father'd sigh, 'you don't make the connection, son. When you put that card in the wall, that's the bank's money that's coming out, not yours. You're going to have to pay it all back one day, you know? Why can't you just make the connection, Eddie? You're an intelligent guy. That's their money, you sap. Jesus.'

But now he exulted that once again he had given Kieran Casey something to worry about. That would show the greasy louse to flirt with his girlfriend. What was that Jennifer had told him, something Kieran had said to her once, during one of his endless monologues about his wife? 'It's not that I don't love her any more. It's just the passion I miss.' Jennifer thought that was quite sad actually. The fucking chancer. Eddie knew very well that Kieran had said this to every fresh-faced female undergraduate probably since James sodding Joyce had been to UCD.

'And if James Joyce was alive today,' he told her, 'he'd still be paying off his student loan. That bastard would make sure of it.'

But secretly he knew his father was right. His father was nearly always right.

'How do you think a bank works, for Christ's sake?' he'd say. 'I should know, Eddie. I've been in banking since I was eighteen. It's in their interest for you not to pay it back. You're playing into their hands. Can't you see that? Think about it. Jesus, Eddie. You confuse me.' 'Course, Eddie wasn't the only one his father used to say this stuff to.

On Charing Cross Road he remembered long nights sitting on the stairs with Patricia, listening to all that stuff down in the kitchen. The crash of broken crockery, the sound of his parents' bodies struggling with each other, grunting, pushing each other against the radiator, the sound of crying too. Now that was a sound you didn't want to hear. Then it had all seemed to get better for a while, after the counselling business, until that time suddenly last year, when it had all exploded again and she'd called from London, from the house of someone called Raymond, who nobody had ever heard about, to say she wouldn't ever be coming home again. Suddenly last summer. Just like the lousy play.

He dropped into the offices of the *NME* and left a classified ad.

> **SINGER AND LEAD GUITARIST**, (Dublin),
> seeks fellow travellers for seriously
> glittering future. Infls: Clash, Pistols,
> Doors, Smiths, Stooges, Velvets. No
> headbangers or hippies need apply.

The cute woman behind the desk was from Dublin too. She had big blue eyes and a ring through her slightly upturned nose. She looked Eddie up and down as though she recognised him.

'I know you,' she said, 'don't tell me.'

'Yes,' said Eddie, 'I *am* a friend of Dean Bean's.'

'Yeah,' she laughed, 'that's it. That's it. How is he?'

'Fine. Jesus,' Eddie sighed, 'this is crazy. I haven't met an English person in London yet. Everyone's from Dublin. It's like the Mafia over here.' She nodded.

'Yeah,' she said, 'the Murphia.'

They talked about Dean Bean for a few minutes. Then he asked if she wanted to go for a drink some time, but she said well no, not really, she only ever went out with hippies and headbangers. Then she licked her finger, and made a little invisible stroke in the air, and laughed. Eddie did his most casual shrug, and hauled his ego out of the office.

An hour later, looking in the window of Collet's bookshop, a pimply faced American youth walked over to him with a camera.

'Wow, man,' he said, 'neat mohican, can I take a picture?'

He was a short little fat kid with a T-shirt that said 'Sudden Death' and a real bad case of BO. He wore blue shorts and sneakers, just like his little girlfriend, or maybe his sister, a hip-hop peaked cap, and a leather jacket that must have made him sweat in that hot October weather. He looked fat as a beachball on legs. He said they'd been looking all over London for a genuine punk rocker and they hadn't been able to find one anywhere.

'They're all gone,' he said. 'Punk's just dead, this town's full of wimped-out Kylie freaks.'

Eddie wanted to say fuck off, which he thought would actually have impressed the kid much more than consenting to a photograph, but he didn't. He stood beside the fat kid, arm around his shoulder, looking mean and making a thumbs-up sign. Then the kid took a snap of his girlfriend, or his sister, with her arm around Eddie, and she looked at Eddie and she made a thumbs-up sign too, giggling, as though it were some secret and terrible signal.

'Jeez, Louise,' breathed the fat kid, 'this is just so neat.'

His name was Herb, and the girl's name was Tess.

'How do you get it to stand up?' Tess asked, nodding at his hair.

'What you do,' said Eddie, 'you get a tube of toothpaste and you rub it in.'

'Oh yuk,' said the girl, 'gross.'

'Far out,' gasped the kid, 'really, is that what you do?'

'Yeah,' said Eddie, 'toothpaste or glue, y'know. Or anything sticky.'

'What, like marmalade or something?'

'Yeah,' said Eddie, 'that would do it, but I think you better ask your mother.'

'Ask my mother,' said the kid, his face a study of incredulity. 'Can you, like, *believe* this guy? My mother can kiss my ass, pal.'

'Do you ask your mother?' said the girl.

'No,' Eddie said, 'I haven't seen my mother for a while. They threw me out, you know, for being such a rebel.'

The girl said that was a shame. She said, 'You should go see her.'

'Are you a real punk?' the kid said. 'Did you know Sid Vicious?'

'Know him?' said Eddie. 'Are you kidding? See these arms? Sid Vicious died in these arms. I was the one who found him, over in New York, in the Chelsea Hotel, when he was dying. I was the road manager for the Pistols.'

'No way,' said the kid, 'get outta here. You mean when he killed Nancy?'

'Straight up,' said Eddie, 'his last words were spoken to me. He said' – Eddie looked up at the sky – 'he said, "Eddie, tell 'em I didn't do it. Tell 'em I was framed," like that, that's the way he said it.'

'Jesus H Christ,' said the kid, 'that's unfuckingbelievable.'

His girlfriend, or his sister, clattered him across the back of the head and he called her a total fascist. Then Eddie said he'd have to be going. He had to get to the record company offices. He was in his own band now. He had a meeting with some pretty important people. The two kids wished him luck, and said they'd look out for his first record. They got him to sign his name on the back of a dollar bill. He signed it with a flourish, 'Eddie Honey Bees Virago'.

Marion called from Donegal a few times. But whenever she did, Eddie was always out, traipsing round the city, doing the James Joyce act, trying to get his bearings together and somehow sort the place out. They left vague, euphemistic messages for each other with Mr Patel, but they never actually spoke.

'She's very besotted with you, Eddie,' Mr Patel would say. 'You're a lucky, lucky man.'

London was a weird place to get to know. It was way too big to walk around and the public transport system didn't really help much. It never seemed to work properly. The ingenuity and diversity of the Tube platform announcements almost impressed Eddie. Burst pipes, fire alarms, staff shortages, suicidal yuppies chucking themselves under trains, the excuses seemed to be different every day. But even when the whole shoddy mess did somehow manage to work, travelling by Underground gave Eddie absolutely no idea where anything in the city was, relative to anything else. Days were a bewildered succession of flashing lights and savage ticket machines and mangled escalators and angry steel worms roaring out of hot tunnels. And Eddie would come home at nights feeling even more confused than when he'd set out, consoling himself with the thought that in *Ulysses* Stephen Dedalus had done pretty much the same thing, but with a much less impressive haircut. If you had to sum up the plot, that was about it.

One day Eddie set out to see his mother, but got so lost on the Northern Line that he gave up and found himself stranded in the tunnel at Stockwell for half an hour, just him and five large thick-necked black guys who kept laughing at his hair and playing 'Funky Cold Medina' on a painfully loud ghettoblaster. Not a great place to end up when you're headed for Richmond. Not a great place full stop, as far as Eddie was concerned.

But Marion and Mr Patel had everything sorted. They'd talked over most of the arrangements on the phone and now he knew for sure that she was definitely coming back to the Brightside, Mr Patel seemed to be seeing things a bit more calmly. He kept telling Eddie she was a lovely lady and a real star, and Eddie kept agreeing as enthusiastically as possible, feeling vaguely edgy, as if Mr Patel was trying to tell him something, which maybe he was.

Mr Patel had spoken to her parents too. They'd wanted to have a little chat, make sure everything was shipshape and above board. No offence, but they said they didn't want their daughter working for just anybody. They had nothing against people of the coloured persuasion, but still. Quite right too. Mr P said you couldn't be too careful in this day and age. He admired their integrity.

'Lovely decent people,' he said, 'but of course you know that, Eddie.' Eddie said he'd never met them and Mr P was surprised. He looked like he was about to ask something, but then he changed his mind at the last moment. He had the kind of discretion that only cheap hotel owners have. Eddie told him to get Marion to leave a number where he could call her back, but Mr Patel said it was a callbox. Marion's family didn't have a phone in the house. 'They're good working people. Things you and me take for granted' – he gestured ruefully at Eddie and himself – 'they don't have.'

Sometimes at night Mr Patel would knock on the door and invite Eddie to join him for a cup of tea down in the Engine Room – one of his expressions for the lobby. Mr Patel didn't drink. It was against his religion. But sometimes he got lonely, late at night, sitting down at Mission Control – the lobby again, – and he liked a good conversation to help him pass the time. Eddie didn't like these tea sessions much, mainly because Mr Patel wanted to talk about himself all the time. But he went along and sat in the freezing little room, with the television going full blast in the corner, drinking tea that tasted like weedkiller, because there was nothing much else to do, and because Mr Patel was a decent enough bloke if you made the effort. Hell, it wasn't even that much effort. All Eddie had to do was clamp an interested look on his face and go 'Yeah' every few minutes, something for which four years of third-level education had equipped him very well indeed.

Mr Patel talked rigorously about his past, like he had one day written down the facts of his life and learnt them off by heart. He had come over from Pakistan in 1974 with his brother-in-law and their two wives. Eddie asked him was that two wives between them or two wives each and Mr Patel looked a little shocked.

'Cool it, Mr P,' he laughed, 'I'm only pulling your wire.' Mr Patel looked even more shocked then, so Eddie shut up.

At first they'd all slept in one room, on the floor. This was up in Kirkstall, a terrible place, according to Mr Patel, that God had dropped at the last minute half-way between Leeds and Bradford, a cold and foul grey sprawl full of steep hills and rottweilers and knifemen and curry houses and concrete bunker pubs and fervent social workers scurrying around the place in secondhand Volkswagens, taking people's children away. Mr Patel shuddered when he said the word 'Kirkstall'. He said that Kirkstall had escaped bombing during the war, and that the only reason for this was that the Germans had looked down from their planes and presumed it'd been bombed already. He laughed then, his high-pitched girlish laugh, 'Heh, heh, heh,' and Eddie laughed too.

They'd had absolutely nothing, he said, when they'd come to England first. All his wife's dowry money had gone to pay for the flights. But then they'd got a loan from a cousin, moved down to London and bought out a newsagent's in Catford. It hadn't lasted. The money was good, but Mrs Patel was having her first child and Mr Patel didn't want to have to work so hard and be away from her. His cousin hadn't liked that very much, but it had been a difficult pregnancy, and the child – a son – had only lived two weeks. They'd decided to change their lives and try again straightaway, somewhere else. So they had sold the shop at a profit, paid off the loan, invested the surplus in British Steel shares, cashed in after a while, got another loan and a Tax Incentive Area grant and finally made the downpayment on this hotel. 'The Brightside,' he breathed, 'the Brightside Hotel,' and when he said it, he made the words sound like poetry. Their son, Ali, had been born the week they moved in.

The building had been a real tip when they'd seen it first, but Mr Patel and his brother-in-law had ripped it apart, put in new floorboards, new plumbing, new wiring, new roof, new walls, new furniture, new secondhand carpets, everything. Mr Patel said his brother-in-law was a whizz with all that kind of thing.

'But you should see the bills, Eddie,' he said, rolling his eyes. 'Wow.'

Mr Patel said that it was hard to believe, but in the old days the Brightside had been a famous society hotel, frequented by the talented and the beautiful.

'Just like now,' Eddie said, and Mr Patel laughed.

'It may interest you to know, Eddie,' he said, 'that the great Irish writer Oscar Wilde stayed here in his heyday and during his downfall too. Oh yes. We have done our homework here. It seems that the then owner was a kind and civilised woman, compassionate, educated you know, and she took pity on the poor hounded chap when all the world was against him. She hid him upstairs when the police came to take him.' Eddie was fascinated. He said he had a friend in Dublin who was writing a thesis on Wilde, and who'd be very jealous when he heard this. Patel laughed. 'Tell your chum to come and see us any time,' he said, 'We can show him the room that we think poor Wilde used to stay in, poor bugger.' Mr Patel laughed quietly and then he shook his head. 'Such intolerance, and for such a great man, Eddie, really, it's tragic, is it not, the things that people get distressed about?'

Then Eddie asked Mr Patel about racism, but Mister P didn't like to talk about that. He said he hadn't seen much of it, not personally. He knew it was there. He wasn't denying that. You read about some terrible things in the papers, attacks on Asian schoolchildren, things the police did, all of that. But he'd been lucky ever since he'd first set foot in GB, no doubt about it. And he didn't worry too much about it, anyway. Him and Mrs P, they didn't worry at all, in fact. They just kept to themselves and worked very hard. He said it was better not to get too obsessed with all that racism stuff. Better to put your energies into work. Nobody could work like an Asian could work. Nobody at all, and he'd met people from all over the world.

'You see, that's why the English don't like us, Eddie,' he said. 'We can out-shopkeeper the nation of shopkeepers.'

Eddie said they didn't like the Irish either but Mr Patel scoffed and insisted that was rubbish. What about Terry Wogan? Everybody loved him. Eddie said that was different, but he couldn't exactly explain why.

Mr Patel liked Eddie. He talked to him openly, even allowing himself to swear every once in a while, as a sign of taking Eddie into confidence. He talked about personal things. He talked about his little dead son Josuf, how upsetting it had been for them. And sometimes Eddie talked to Mr Patel too. He told him about his parents and Mr Patel was sympathetic, but in a way that wasn't embarrassing. He sat with the tips of his fingers touching, nodding wisely in the corner, pursing his lips as he nodded. Families were so important, he'd say, and Eddie would agree.

But there was one thing that Mr Patel just couldn't understand. Why didn't Eddie go see his mother? He didn't want to be personal, he said, but he just couldn't figure it out. Eddie laughed out loud, but he couldn't think of an excuse. He told Mr Patel he probably *would* go, soon as he'd settled in a bit. He just hadn't got around to it yet, but it was only a matter of time. Mr P said he really should.

'The world is full of women, Eddie,' he sighed, 'but you only ever have one mother.' Eddie asked him whether that was an ancient Muslim proverb. And Mr P said no, it was a country and western song.

A couple of replies came in to Eddie's *NME* ad, and on the Friday night, he met up with some people in De Hems Dutch Bar on Macclesfield Street.

There was a short-haired American girl called Ginger O'Reilly, who was a bassist, and two English guys, Brian Smith, a drummer, and a guitarist who insisted his name was Clint Saigon. Eddie asked if that was his real name and he said yeah, of course it was. He said it wasn't his *christened* name, but it was what everybody called him, therefore it was his real name. Brian said Brian Smith wasn't *his* real name either.

'My real name is Tokyo Cosmonaut,' he said, 'but it wasn't exciting enough, so I changed it.' Clint didn't like that much, but everybody else did.

Eddie said he'd been in and out of bands since he was sixteen but now he'd had enough of messing around. He was into giving it a serious go, an all-out, no-holds-barred assault on the big time. Of course he'd got a good bit of experience, supporting The Police when they played at Slane, stuff like that.

'Jesus,' whooped Brian, 'that's the biggest venue in Ireland, isn't it?'

'In Europe,' said Eddie, 'please.' Of course, Eddie's band had only been bottom of the bill, but still, they'd got fabulous press and word had been sent out specially from the backstage village-cum-mobile rain forest that Sting himself had really 'dug' them.

Everyone was impressed. And they all seemed to like the same bands, so Eddie handed out copies of his demo tape and they agreed to meet up the next week for a jam and for what Brian called a 'See What Happens'. Ginger said she wanted all band decisions to be taken democratically, and even though Clint said he didn't think democracy and art went together, Eddie agreed with Ginger, Brian was persuaded by Eddie, and Clint was outvoted in the end. He was going to have to be democratic, whether he wanted to be or not. Then they talked about band names.

'The Honey Bees,' Eddie said, 'that's what my old band was called. It's a really happening name, actually. People just seem to remember it, you know. I'm pretty set on that, I must admit.' The others didn't seem too keen, but the only other suggestions were Imelda Marcos and Her Shoes, from Ginger, or Oliver North and His Performing Paper Shredders from Brian, so The Honey Bees faction won out in the end. As a working title anyway. And that was the trickiest part of forming the band over with.

They chatted for a while about acid house parties and Michelle Shocked, and everybody bought a round. The beer in De Hems was strong, and the night was hot. Eddie watched them all argue and laugh and tease and insist on the validity of opinions that contradicted utterly what they'd said five minutes earlier. This was OK. They all seemed to click with each other, although Brian was maybe a little too quiet, specially when Ginger was talking. Still, Eddie reckoned they'd be fine, after a little time.

He was sure of it. These were the right personnel and he was the leader of the gang. Things were looking up now, at last. he could see that wheels were starting to turn. He drained his glass and begged one of Brian's cigarettes.

Just before his second round came up, Eddie slapped his forehead, cursed loudly, and suddenly remembered that he had to be somewhere. He left The Honey Bees in De Hems, arguing about The Waterboys' second album and what you *actually* heard if you played 'Sergeant Pepper' backwards, and he felt so light-headedly happy that he treated himself to a taxi home.

That night a Dutch aeroplane was hijacked in Vienna by a gang of crazy Libyans. It was very inconvenient for everybody. Everybody except Eddie. Sighing with satisfaction he clipped 'HIJ' and 'KLM' out of the *Evening Standard* headline, and, very delicately, he added them to the letters already on the bedroom wall.

Then he lay on the bed, thinking. Things were definitely looking up. Only a couple of weeks in London, and here he was, set up with a woman, and on the verge of joining his very first band. Yes. Things were looking up alright.

Now that was what Eddie called progress.

Jimmy and Ruth's flat turned out to be quite something. It was in the vast refurbished attic of a sour-faced Victorian house that looked out over the old Jewish cemetery in Golders Green. The floors were polished and smooth, and stained-glass skylights ran along the roof. All the furniture was black and Jimmy said they'd got it from Shabitat, a joke he had to explain to Eddie, who was new to such things.

Crisps and peanuts and little salty things were laid out in black bowls on the black coffee table. Charlie Parker honked out of the black stereo speakers. Ruth kissed the air on both sides of Eddie's face and hung his leather jacket on the black coat hanger.

'Help yourself to nibbles,' she said, wiggling her ass as she backed through the swing doors and into the kitchen. Her tight black dress looked like it probably had to be put on with the aid of a pulley and winch.

Jimmy breezed into the room wrapped in a black towel, his beer belly flopping over the edge.

'Streuth, Ruth,' he yelped, 'everyone's here already.' He picked up a beer can and said hi to Eddie. 'You know everyone?' he said. 'This is Eddie Virago, folks, late of Dublin town, now one of the great unwashed migrants of the Ryanair generation. He's unemployed by the way, so don't flaunt your fabulous wealth in front of him.' Eddie told him to butt out and put some clothes on.

In addition to Jimmy and Ruth, there were a couple of other old college friends. Well, not exactly friends. People whose faces Eddie knew.

A guy called Creep – nobody knew his real name – whose eyebrows met in the middle, and his girlfriend Fiona who was an assistant subeditor in what she called the trade press – actually, on a magazine called *Meat Trade Monthly*. Eddie remembered them vaguely from Commerce. They'd been one of those couples who hold hands during lectures and snog in the bar. Creep was working as a refuse-sack salesman on what he called 'the northern run'. His girlfriend kept telling him to tell a particular story about a really funny thing that had happened to him up in Carlisle once, but he didn't seem to want to.

'You had to be there,' he explained.

There was another girl, also called Fiona, who wore a yellow cheesecloth blouse and was into the Greens. She was a vegetarian, so the subject of *Meat Trade Monthly* was discreetly avoided. She was working as a fundraiser for the Committee to End Animal Experiments, she said. When Eddie asked what that was like she smiled and said, 'Oh, mustn't grumble.' She had a guy with her who seemed shy and awkward and didn't say much and kept cleaning his fingernails with a toothpick. He was a poet, apparently. Eddie didn't catch his name. He wore black-rimmed glasses like Buddy Holly's, and a black poloneck jumper. He looked like someone who'd come to an Islington fancy dress party, *dressed* as a poet. But in fact, a poet was what he really was.

'In real life,' as he put it.

Things were a little tense while they sat around the room waiting for Jimmy and Ruth to come back. One of the Fionas kept looking at Eddie's face, as though she was trying to remember him from somewhere. Eddie kept hoping she'd stop, but after fifteen minutes he decided to put her out of her misery.

'Yes,' said Eddie, resigned, 'Dean Bean.' Then she snapped her fingers and laughed.

'Oh yeah, that's it.' Eddie sighed. 'He's a real sweetie,' she said, with a demolishing smile, 'so what's he doing now anyway?'

Creep got to talking about wheel clamps for some reason and the poet got down on his knees to leaf through the record collection, occasionally scrutinising the small print on the back of an album cover. Any time somebody said 'Fiona' the two girls would turn around simultaneously, and everybody would crack up laughing, as though it was really funny. But there were whole minutes of agonising silence while everyone waited for everybody else to start a conversation, and when Jimmy finally came into the room Eddie was so relieved he could have kissed him.

'Fuck me,' said Jimmy, staring around, 'let's join hands and try to contact the living.' Jammed into a tight pair of stonewash denims, Jimmy looked even fatter than he had the other night.

Jimmy apologised for not having any methylated spirits, a supposedly ironic reference to Eddie's haircut. Then he slapped Eddie hard on the back and laughed.

'Good one, Jim,' said Eddie.

'Only jerking you off, Ed,' he said. 'What'll you have really?'

Eddie said he'd have a gin and tonic.

'Ices and slices?' said Jimmy.

'No,' said Eddie, 'straight up.' Jimmy looked him in the eye. 'Don't even think about it,' said Eddie.

When Ruth came out of the kitchen she asked Eddie not to stand on the rug, if he didn't mind. They'd got it on their holidays in Tunisia, and it was *très* special to them. So Eddie sat on the fat window ledge, listening to the small talk and everybody else stood around the rim of the rug, as though it was a swimming pool full of piranhas. The poet put on Nina Simone.

'Corso didn't get the Beeb job,' said Fiona the vegetarian, and Fiona the carnivore shook her head in dismay, saying if she'd been let down as many times as Corso she'd probably just give up breathing or something. 'Yes,' said the veggy Fiona, 'he's very peed off, waiting for a bit of feedback.' Now he was applying for the Royal Film School at Elmers End. Jimmy said he hadn't a chance, he knew that place well, if you weren't shafting someone on the inside you wouldn't get within spitting distance. Creep laughed, and Eddie asked how Jimmy knew this. He winked boldly, and tapped the side of his nose.

'*Vorsprung durch Technik*,' he said. 'Contacts, Ed.' The poet said that was absolute rubbish. 'No, serio,' said Jimmy, 'we do all their advertising.'

'Shall we?' said Ruth, beckoning towards the door.

'Shall we what?' said Eddie.

'Eat,' she said. 'It's all ready.'

Eddie had never tasted vichyssoise before. He said it was wonderful what Marks and Spencer could get into a can these days, and Ruth told him to fuck off. He told her she was looking very well. She told him to fuck off again. Ruth was in one of her nervous moods.

Jimmy sniffed the wine.

'Rough little vintage,' he said, 'wouldn't like to meet it down a dark alley one night.' Nobody laughed. Jimmy had obviously forgotten, but he'd been making this joke ever since first year, when they used to sometimes chip together for a bottle of Moroccan Hock or Asti Spumante and bring it back to Dean Bean's flat.

Beano's flatmate Johnny Speed had been working for the Simon Community at the time. He'd spend the whole night driving around the streets of Dublin, force-feeding sandwiches and soup to bedraggled winos, only to come home at two in the morning and find everybody in his flat almost as pissed and twice as incoherent as anyone he'd met all evening. Then, when they ran out of cigarettes, he'd break open the ration of Players that each Simon worker got issued for the gasping dossers, and they'd pass them round in frantic gratitude before getting into a fight about who was more middle class than whom. It was, as Dean Bean often said, a beautiful time.

When Ruth brought in the huge dish of steaming nut roast she beamed with anxious pride as everyone said how nice it looked. She looked incredibly nervous now. When she chewed her nails, Eddie noticed her hands trembling. That wasn't like Ruth at all. He wondered if she was alright. She kept smoothing down her hair and looking up and down the table, as though she'd forgotten something. Jimmy put his arms around her and squeezed her shoulders. He told her to chill out.

But it hadn't gone well. Even before the avocado salad was shared out, there was a big argument about the SDP. Ruth said she was going to vote for them because she fancied the ass off David Owen, which was about the most intelligent thing anybody said all night. Both Fionas agreed that the Greens would be getting their vote. They kept saying, 'We've destroyed the planet, we've ruined the world,' in a guilt-tinged voice, as though they, personally, had destroyed the planet and ruined the world. Creep said it didn't make any difference, the whole country was run by the banks anyway. Jimmy said he was staying with Maggie and he didn't give a wank about the Poll Tax. Labour were all very well, but you couldn't trust them on the Unions. He said Scargill had Kinnock by the goolies and he made a squeezing gesture with his right hand, forking a knot of pasta into his mouth.

'I know Maggie's a cunt,' he said, 'but she can do the fucking job, you have to give her that.'

Eddie tucked into his nut roast, and said it was very nice. He just didn't feel like a big political discussion. He kept thinking about Marion, for some reason, hoping she was alright, wondering what she would make of a night like tonight, wondering what these friends would say if they ever met her, not that, of course, they ever would. Ruth asked if he'd had any luck on the job front, and he told her there were a few definite possibilities, nothing confirmed, but fingers crossed. The poet said, 'Isn't "definite possibility" an oxymoron?' Jimmy told him not to be such a pedantic fucker.

After dinner the carnivorous Fiona pulled out a big bag of dope and rolled a joint. Jimmy called it 'whacky backy' and that made everybody laugh. It was good stuff. Eddie sucked hard at the damp joint end and felt the blast tingle slowly up from his feet. He felt better.

Jimmy brought a bowl of sliced-up kiwi fruit and banana from the kitchen, and Ruth carried in a huge jug of whipped cream. The vegetarian Fiona said she went absolutely crazy for kiwi fruit, just flipped out totally for it, and for some reason the poet laughed, slightly too loud.

Eddie started talking to the poet, who seemed to have been ignoring him all night. He said he'd written some poetry himself. The poet didn't seem to be too interested. Eddie asked who his influences were and he said Oh, people like Ginsberg.

'People *like* Ginsberg,' said Eddie, 'what does that mean?' The poet said it was hard to explain exactly what he meant and in fact he didn't like explaining his work at all. He preferred it to stand or fall by its own abilities.

'A bit like Eddie's hair,' said Jimmy.

Eddie asked if he'd got anything published and the poet said, 'Here and there, little magazines mainly, you probably wouldn't know them.' Eddie said he should enter a poetry competition, but the poet said he didn't agree with competitions for art, as they merely replicated the hierarchical fetishism of bourgeois society at large. That seemed to be the end of that.

Creep started talking about the release of the Guildford Four, and a documentary he'd seen about them during the week. He said it was terrible what had been done to them, and he looked genuinely upset about it. Jimmy held up a glass and said, 'Here's to them,' and everybody nodded devoutly as they chinked their glasses. Ruth said it was an absolute disgrace. The poet said he wouldn't mind spending fifteen years in jail if he was going to get all that money at the end, and both Fionas said that was absolutely crass. He said he'd only been joking, and anyway, all this hypocrisy made him sick. Eddie said he agreed actually.

'What about Nicky Kelly?' he said. 'He was framed, in the land of so-called Saints and Scholars.' There were dodgy things happening in Ireland too, but nobody, Eddie said, nobody seemed to give two tosses about that. There was silence for a moment. Then Creep said that was true, but still. 'Typical,' said Eddie. 'Just typical.'

Northern Ireland came up over the camembert. Some guys had been shot dead in a bar during the week, builders' labourers who'd been working for the British Army. The usual row started then, about whether the old IRA were terrorists or not, compared to the Provos. Creep said they were, that they did all the things the Provos did, kidnapped, killed, tortured. Fiona said this wasn't the case, that she didn't know exactly how to put it, but they'd just been somehow different. The vegetarian Fiona said she was opposed to all violence except in South Africa and the poet said, 'Why, do moral rules stop at the South African border or what?' The whole thing limped back and forth across the table, everyone churning out opinions Eddie had heard a million times before. Eddie couldn't concentrate anyway. He felt embarrassed that he'd gone over the top earlier. He said nothing. And all this talk about Northern Ireland kept bringing him back to Marion. It was weird. He was stoned. But it was true.

He thought about the shape of her face, the way she laughed, the way she held a cigarette, the way she turned the page of a magazine, the way she stirred her coffee, the way he sometimes caught her looking at him, the way she smiled, without showing her teeth and laughed when she was saying something sad. He discovered himself comparing the three girls around the table to her, asking himself, if Marion was here, what would she say about that? He sucked on the joint again and tried to forget her. He couldn't.

Half-way though dessert, the phone rang with a shattering

glass sound, interrupting the lethargic discussion that was just breaking out on censorship. And in his irrational state, Eddie was convinced it was going to be her. He was sure. He prepared himself to go out to the phone and take her call.

But then they could hear Jimmy from the hall going 'Serious shit' and 'Heavy duty' and 'Drag city Arizona'. And when he came back in he looked worried. Hugo Rogers was in trouble. He'd gone out to celebrate his new job in Foreign Affairs, pranged the old dear's Volvo on the way home from the Leeson Street strip and run over the foot of a policeman who'd tried to stop him on Baggot Street Bridge. He was in deep shit, and he wanted to get the number of Jimmy's brother, Paul ('Pablo', Jimmy called him), a lawyer.

The room filled with gasps. Somebody asked whether the policeman was hurt.

'Well, he's not over the moon, y'know?' – and Jimmy did his Groucho Marx routine with an invisible cigar.

Eddie said it had only been a matter of time, and that Hugo had always been an irresponsible wanker.

'Eddie,' cautioned Ruth.

'Well,' Eddie said, 'the guy thinks with his dick.'

''Course, you've always been a heartless fucker, Eddie,' said Jimmy, pleasantly, 'you don't care about anything except principle, do you?'

'Principle?' said Eddie. 'The guy ran over a cop, for Jesus' sake.'

'A pig, Eddie, isn't that what you used to call them? A fascist pig?' Ruth started clearing away the dishes. Eddie said that wasn't the point. He said they could all drag up stuff from the past if they wanted to. 'Well, you've changed, haven't you, Ed? The conscience of the middle class, is that what you're passing yourself off as now?'

The vegetarian Fiona followed Ruth into the kitchen, holding the joint in front of her like a crucifix to a vampire.

'You'd know about middle class,' said Eddie.

'Yeah, and you wouldn't. Dragged up in the slums of Ranelagh.'

'My father,' said Eddie, stabbing the air with his finger, 'is working class.'

Jimmy began to clap his hands, slowly, and to speak in the insistent Sean O'Casey accent he reserved for these occasions.

'Oh, it's that time of the evening, is it? Let's drag out Virago

Senior, the aulfella made good. Here he is, meladies and gents, not an arse in his proletarian trousers. Take a bow sir, bejayzus, take a bow.' Creep and his girlfriend started playing with the cutlery. The poet took off his glasses, wiped them on a napkin, and put them back on again. 'Ah, yeah,' said Jimmy, 'you've changed, Eddie, old son.'

'You haven't changed,' said Eddie, sourly, 'you never will.' He could feel himself getting drunk now, on top of the stoned feeling that was weighing down his jaw.

'Why don't you write a song about it, Eddie, eh? That'll have them manning the barricades, that'll have the bourgeoisie shaking in their shoes.'

Eddie blushed. Jimmy whinnied with laughter, and everybody else was quiet. Fiona started asking Eddie about his music, but he wasn't in the mood.

'Look,' said Eddie, to Jimmy, 'when I first met you you used to draw penises on newspaper photographs. When did you stop that?' Jimmy hissed a mouthful of smoke across the table.

'I stopped drawing them, Ed, maybe you should stop acting like one.'

Creep sighed loudly, and he said the conversation was becoming a little too heavy.

'Maybe,' said Eddie, 'but he's becoming a fucking caricature of himself.'

'Oooooo,' whined Jimmy, 'you're so sexy when you're butch, Eddie.'

In the kitchen the Fiona with the long hair was slumped over the table, weeping. Eddie stood in the doorway, watching her, but she didn't seem to notice. She was busily telling Ruth how life sometimes made her feel like 'a prawn in aspic', beautiful, delicate, but just slowly rotting away. Ruth kept hugging her and telling her everything would be alright.

Just as Eddie sat down at the kitchen table Fiona's head slipped from Ruth's shoulder. Her body slithered to the floor, and she lay flat out on her side, with one arm pointed out straight, still holding the joint. She looked like the Statue of Liberty, keeled over in a strong breeze.

Eddie helped Ruth do the dishes. It wasn't that he wanted to. It was just that he wanted to get away from Jimmy, who was busily insisting on showing the poet how the gas central heating worked. They stepped back and forth over Fiona's snoring body as they put the dishes away.

She asked him whether he'd heard from Jennifer. Eddie scoffed.

'What do you think?' he asked. 'You know what she's like.' Ruth said yes, that was true. She asked whether anybody new was flipping his pancake just now and he told her no. Then he said, well, yeah, kind of. She said that was nice, but she didn't ask for any details, which surprised Eddie a little, and even disappointed him too. When he said Jimmy was being a bastard again she looked surprised that he'd even mentioned it.

'You know what he's like,' she shrugged.

The kitchen walls were plastered with photos of Ruth and Jimmy, with the Eiffel Tower sprouting out of their heads, clinking pina coladas on sunset-washed balconies, poking their faces through cardboard cut-outs of the Mona Lisa, making eyes across sun-spattered café tables.

When they had put the dishes away, Ruth and Eddie sat in the kitchen for a while, polishing off a bottle of gin. They talked about the old days and Eddie got more and more drunk. At one point he reached across the kitchen table and touched Ruth's hand.

'You know,' he slurred, 'I've always found you very attractive, Ruth, physically.' Ruth peeled his fingers off her sleeve.

'Fuck off, Eddie,' she said.

They went back to the gin, as though nothing had happened. They talked, for some reason, about Ireland's chances in the Eurovision Song Contest, something neither of them knew the first thing about. And after another joint Ruth got a serious case of the munchies. Eddie got some bread and took a pack of butter from the fridge. They sat in silence, eating, for ten minutes, saying nothing, catching each other in the eye and then looking away, as though they had something to feel guilty about.

'Fair play to Ireland,' she said, eventually, 'they invented the first really spread-from-the-fridge butter.'

'Yeah,' said Eddie, 'it's a great country.'

When it was time to go Eddie retrieved his leather jacket from the bedroom. Creep and Fiona were asleep under the coats. Creep woke up and looked at Eddie with a bleary confused gape.

'Oh,' he yawned, 'it's you.' He said he could probably get Eddie a job in National Bags'n'Sacks, if he was stuck. Eddie told him thanks but no thanks, he didn't really think that was his thing. Creep made him take his card anyway, even though Eddie said there was honestly no point. Creep told him if he heard of anything else he'd give him a bell. 'We Paddies have to stick together,' he hiccupped. 'Have to keep the fucking flag flying, Eddie, what?'

Downstairs in the front garden Jimmy was rueful and apologetic. He told Eddie he could crash upstairs if he wanted to. They had a sofabed. Eddie said he'd take a raincheck.

'Come on, Eddie,' he said, 'no hard feelings, man.'

Eddie stuck his hands deep in his pockets and stamped his feet in the cold. Wafer ice had formed over the puddles in the drive and the grass felt crisp underfoot. Jimmy said at least he should let them call a cab, but Eddie said no, he just couldn't afford it.

'We're not all set up like you two,' he pouted. Jimmy said he'd bung him a few quid, but Eddie just shot him one of his best offended looks.

The moon was a hard red eye over Golders Green. Deep blue light seemed to dribble through a hollow sky.

'You know me, Ed,' pleaded Jimmy, 'too much fire water. I'm a fucking Barclays Banker when I'm pissed.'

'Yeah,' said Eddie, 'that's true.'

Jimmy threw his arms around Eddie.

'I love you man, you know that, come on Ed, give me a break.' Eddie told him to relax. He said it was just the dope, he'd been overdoing it lately, too much of it made you aggressive. Jimmy said, yeah, he didn't do it that much any more. 'In fact, I'm really a boring bastard now,' he sighed. 'I mean, it's not as if I don't know that, honestly. I do know that. I'm boring as the fucking Channel Tunnel, Ed, I really am.' They stood in the garden, looking up at the yellow-lit windows of the flat, and at the shadows moving across the curtains. Jimmy looked restless and despondent. He said it was good to see Eddie again, and Eddie said, yeah, yeah, sure it was. Jimmy asked if Eddie was really sure he wanted to go home, and Eddie said, yeah, he was positive, he had things to do next day, people to see. Jimmy looked like he was going to cry. 'Come on back up, man,' he said, 'just for old times' sake. Let's have a nightcap or two and bitch about somebody, eh?'

'No,' said Eddie, 'look, I'm really not in the mood, OK?'

'That sofabed,' Jimmy sighed, 'you know, it cost us three hundred and fifty quid and we've never used it once.'

Eddie said they should trade it in. Then he told him no hard feelings, but he really had to split. Jimmy stood in the gateway, waving sadly, as though Eddie was going off to war. And ten yards down the road, Jimmy called out his name again. Eddie rolled his eyes, and he turned. Jimmy seemed to be suddenly drunk again. He was swaying a little on his feet, one hand on the gate post to steady himself.

'You see all those stars up there, Eddie,' Jimmy hissed, 'you know what they do up there?' Eddie shrugged. 'All those planets out there, man, far away, all silver, you know what we are? We're the shit that all the people on those planets produce. They fire it all out into space, Ed, and it comes down here and that's what we are. Inter-planetary shit, you and me, all of us. That's the truth, man, I mean, like, that's what it all comes down to, in the end, as far as I can see. Intergalactic turd, you know what I'm saying?'

Windows began to light up white along the tree-lined street.

'Great, Jimmy,' sighed Eddie, 'that's just great.'

He walked down the road to a phonebox and he called a minicab from there.

When Marion came back things started to get weird.

Eddie'd been out at an interview for a job selling encyclopaedias door to door around the council estates in South London. The guy had taken one look at his hair and immediately started going on about what bastards they were up in accounts, setting him up like this, and how had they known it was his birthday? He fell around the office laughing, then he buzzed his colleague up on the fourth floor to come down and have a look. He couldn't believe it wasn't a practical joke or a punk-o-gram. When Eddie finally convinced him it wasn't, and that he really did want the job, the guy got all flustered and said he hadn't meant anything personal; he looked convinced Eddie was going to mug him. He pointed out that although he understood young people had to express their individuality, there was no way they could do it on his time.

When Eddie opened the bedroom door she was sitting on the bed, hugging her knees, staring into the mirror on the wall above the table. Eddie jumped when he saw her.

'Hiya,' she said, 'I'm back.' She looked happy to see him. Eddie stepped into the room, and she saw his suit for the first time. 'Christ almighty,' she said, 'a terrible beauty is born.'

The first thing that occurred to Eddie was that she looked

taller than he remembered, even though she was all scrunched up like that, hunkered on the eiderdown. She wore a thick white cotton shirt and a black skirt, with black woollen tights and a pair of scuffed ankle boots. She still had the crucifix round her neck. The room smelt of the rain. She looked well, but her eyes were a little moist and it occurred to Eddie that she'd been toking already. The window was wide open too, that was another clue. And when she moved he saw a packet of rizlas on the pillow. Her coat hung from a hanger in the windowframe. A battered yellow rose sagged from the lapel buttonhole. It looked out of place.

'So did you get the job?' she said.

'Nah,' he said, 'wasn't really what I was after.'

Eddie reefed open his red paisley tie and threw it into the wardrobe. Her shoes were arranged neatly along the wardrobe floor. Her clothes swished on the hangers. He took off his shirt and stuffed it into his rucksack. She got up from the bed, pulled it out, and draped it over his shoulder again.

'Please,' she said, 'there's a basket over there for dirty washing.'

She'd tidied up the room, stacking up the books properly, gathering the pile of Eddie's dirty clothes into the bath. The bathroom was tangy with the taint of ammonia and bleach. Her washbag lay beside the sink, toothbrush and paste sticking out the top. Powder puffs and emery boards and a pack of strawberry-scented shampoo lay on the shelf. A box of tampax and a bottle of vitamin pills sat in the cabinet and when Eddie closed the door he looked pale in the mirror. He pulled down his eyelids with his index fingers and he stared at himself for ten whole minutes.

He shaved his head and washed his armpits and the buzz from his razor rattled through his skull, making his teeth feel hollow.

The place was so damn tidy. Somehow when Eddie tidied, it didn't look the same. It was never more than the sum of its tidied parts. But when she did it, the place looked pristine and new and fresh, and it was almost a shame to crumple the sheets or pee in the toilet. She dusted under the bed, for God's sake! She was just that kind of girl. Real domesticated.

When he came out of the bathroom she was smoking another joint and reading some article in a colour magazine.

'You don't have to clean the place,' he said.

'Somebody's got to do it,' she said, and she offered him a drag, without looking up from her magazine. He took it. She beckoned to him to finish it off. 'Did you see this?' she said, holding up the front page of a paper. The headline announced gloomily that the Labour Party's position in the NOP polls was improving by the week. Eddie said that was great. 'Isn't it?' Marion said, brightly. 'We need NOP, they're the next three letters.' She sat up straight, back to the wallpaper, groped for her scissors and cut them out, in four quick movements of her wrist.

'So,' he said, after he'd taped them to the wall, 'how was Donegal?'

She lit a cigarette and flicked the match out through the window.

'Same as ever,' she shrugged, 'y'know.'

Leaning on one arm, she rested her head sideways on her hand and peered intently as Eddie moved around the room, arranging things, picking them up, moving them, pretending to look for something. He felt guilty under her gaze somehow. He felt she might have found something incriminating, something that might give him away, even though rationally he knew there was nothing. She asked if he'd missed her, and the way she looked at him made Eddie think somehow she knew more than she was saying. He told her he hadn't, that they weren't married yet, and she laughed, shrilly, as though what he'd said was preposterous.

'Did you go and see your ma?' she said.

'Yeah,' he said, peering out the window, 'she was out.'

Marion smelt of soap and sweat, and when they kissed her ears were cold. Her fingernails were chipped. She'd been chewing them. Something wasn't the same between them. Eddie could feel it. It seemed so long since she'd been there, even though it had only been a week. He realised that in his heart of hearts, he'd secretly expected never to see her again. Maybe he'd even been hoping for that. Maybe not. She confused the hell out of him anyway. That was the one thing he could say for sure.

She wanted to know what he'd got up to since she'd been away, and why he'd never been in when she rang.

'Have you another woman, Eddie Virago?' she said, pinching his arm till he flinched in real pain and slapped her fingers off.

So he told her about the new band and the terrible party and all of that, laughing as he told the story of the party even though she didn't seem to understand. He felt implicated as he told it, and he said cutting things about his friends to try and put some distance between him and them. But nothing he said could wipe the bemused smirk from her face. She said his friends sounded like jerks, and to his surprise that hurt him. It wasn't that he didn't know they were jerks, but still, they were his friends, that was his decision.

When she went to the bathroom Eddie sat on the bed, flicking through her magazine. There on the inside page was a grainy black and white photograph of someone he recognised. Jesus. So Jimmy was right that time.

'The Importance of Being Salome Wilde,' roared the caption. Eddie stared at the photo for a minute. She really was very good looking, he could see that now, smooth skin, gorgeous mouth. 'Rightly or wrongly,' said the strapline, 'I like being me.' Eddie threw it in the bin.

'Pseudy cow,' he grunted.

Mr Patel, as he put it himself, was totally over the moon. He was so thrilled she was back that he brought a big bunch of flowers up to the room, great big floppy green carnations, and he told her she was very welcome, and that he had enjoyed talking to her parents very much indeed. Then they sat on the bed, sheafing through word-processed schedules of what had to be done, where the cleaning stuff was kept, hours of work, all of that. Mr Patel talked anxiously, as though he half-expected her to change her mind and go away again. He ran his hands through his sleek black hair as he spoke. And he kept saying, 'Are you sure that's satisfactory?' and 'Are you sure you understand?' touching her wrist when he spoke.

Eddie took his guitar and went to leave the room. He was feeling creative all of a sudden. Getting turned down for job interviews always made him feel creative. Marion asked if he was going to change out of his suit trousers. He said no.

'You'll ruin your good suit,' she scolded. But he said he'd change later. Mr Patel said when he was wealthy he could buy a new suit for every day of the week, God willing. Marion did one of her sardonic laughs. She was becoming very good at them. Better than Eddie in fact, and that was something.

'I'll be up on the roof,' he said, 'if anyone wants me.'

Eddie had never mastered the art of finger playing. All he knew were the chords, and he didn't even know all of them. And for solos, he only knew three or four that he'd nicked from obscure Clash B-sides, and even with those he had to cheat, resting his little finger on the bridge to keep his hand steady. Joe

Strummer was his guitar hero. If he couldn't hit six strings he just wasn't interested. Eddie was no virtuoso, but then he didn't even want to be, that wasn't necessary.

He sat on the roof, trying to figure out a couple of tricky progressions, until the pads of his fingertips ached and his wrist got tired. When he stopped playing he chewed the hard parts of his fingertips, gnawing at the tough flesh that guitar players get there. He could taste the sour mix of sweat and steel from the strings.

Eddie hadn't written a song in ages. In fact, despite everything he told people, Eddie had hardly ever written a song. Eddie was an ideas man. He got loads of ideas, for nifty little chord patterns and hammer-on riffs, snatches of word play that would have done as lyrics. But he found it hard to work them up into anything. And any time he played a couple of bars to somebody they always seemed to think it sounded like somebody else, The Slits or The Damned or The Subway Sect. All of them, except Dean Bean, who thought everything was wild and far out, even when it was crap, which it was mostly. But Dean Bean was a friend. He'd say anything you wanted. That was certainly one thing Beano had going for him.

When Eddie ran the cloth up and down the strings, a soft whistle sawed out of the box. It was a satisfying noise. He did it again.

The trapdoor lifted and Marion came up on the roof. She swept her hair behind her ears. The wind blew it back in her eyes, and she tossed her head angrily. She said nothing.

And the moment Eddie looked at her, he knew he was in love. Just like that. Just the way she moved or something, and the way she looked across at him, with one hand shielding her green eyes. No violins, no soft focus. Just a feeling that big trouble was coming and that it was too late to turn anything back.

It was a pain in the ass but he knew that he couldn't stop gazing at her. Those green eyes looked too beautiful to be true, certainly more beautiful than they were. Eddie recognised all the signs. The same primal terror, the same sense of things falling around him and doors opening in his head, the same sense of torpid inevitability, they were all there and it was always the damn same. Eddie swallowed hard. His fingers formed a chord. The dying sun glowed, magnificent on her face.

He felt a bond between them and she moved towards him as though attached to some thin filament that would draw her so close they would end up touching. She moved like some kind of tiny animal. She walked like she had no right to be in the place, like she was a burglar, or a bewildered creature in a zoo. She came out of the shadow of the cooling stack with her head towards the ground and her hands extended towards him.

They kissed awkwardly, like bad actors in a crummy daytime soap. Then she stood with her back to Eddie, clamping his arms together around her abdomen. He rested his chin on top of her head. He almost put his foot through his guitar.

They stood on top of the building and they stared out over the grey and hazy sprawl of King's Cross, way down over the shabby shops of Gray's Inn Road. The sky was clear and darkening, and the plasticine-coloured skyline looked like it had been painted in with an airbrush. The smell of chips and diesel drifted up from somewhere in the street.

'What is it about London?' she said, after a moment. 'It's all launderettes.' She laughed. 'Have you noticed that, Eddie Virago? It's all launderettes and minicab offices.' Eddie said he hadn't noticed, but yeah, she was right.

'That's what keeps the dump going,' he said, 'clean clothes and places to go.'

They sat on the wall, kissing again, with a new tenderness. Eddie touched the side of her face and she caressed his bald scalp. She kissed the corner of his mouth. He held her fingers. Magpies squawked in the air.

They sat for a long silent time, holding hands, staring into each other's eyes like two cartoon characters on the front of a Valentine's card. Then Eddie stood up real quickly, packed away his guitar with a lot of fuss and said he wanted to talk.

'I thought you would,' she sighed.

He wasn't into a big heavy love thing and he told her that. She said that was fine. He didn't even know the meaning of the word love, he said, and 'in love' was just something ridiculous, just words. She agreed. It was all chemical, she said, like magnetism or something. She'd seen a documentary on BBC2.

He'd just come through a really heavy relationship and he didn't want to get hurt again, not now anyway, maybe not ever. He just didn't want to take that risk again. He didn't want to expose himself.

She said she felt the same. That surprised Eddie. He hadn't thought of Marion ever being in love with anyone else. Of course, she must have been, but Eddie just hadn't counted on it. That's what occurred to him, like a crazy revelation. It was just that she'd never mentioned anybody.

She said she wanted to know where she stood. Whether they were an item. Whether they were going together or not.

It was a long time since Eddie had heard that expression. Going together. In college you were 'having a relationship', or 'seeing somebody, no pressure'. If you were Jennifer, you were 'hanging out together'. Or if you were Dean Bean, 'making the beast of two backs'.

Going together. It sounded like something a child would say. He remembered his father saying it once. 'When your mother and I were going together, men had respect for women.' And the inexpressible look on his face when he'd said it too, a childish and happy look that nobody saw much any more.

'Let's just see what happens,' Eddie said, 'I don't want to get too committed, you know?'

Marion said she wasn't talking about Kylie and Jason, she just wanted to know where she stood. Eddie rolled up his sleeve.

'What do you want?' he said. 'Blood?'

She stared at his arm, as though she had never seen it before. She took hold of it, shaking it limply, like it was a dead thing. She stared at the teethmarks of the crazy dog, still indented in his flesh from the first morning they'd met. Her face liquefied to a smile.

'It can be arranged,' she said.

Then they went downstairs, took off all their clothes and lay beside each other on the bed. It was cold now. The mark of her elastic waistband had cut pink into her skin. They lay in each other's arms without saying a word. And Eddie wished he'd changed the sheets.

One night shortly afterwards The Honey Bees had their first rehearsal, in Clint's bedsit up in Highgate. It was a disaster. Brian hadn't been able to fit all his kit into the taxi for a start. Then it was almost impossible to assemble what he *had* brought. He ended up banging away at a solitary snare on top of Clint's coffee table, while Clint looked sulky in the corner. There were no guitar amps, so Eddie and Clint plugged into the music centre and the speakers blew. Added to that, Ginger was simply the worst bass player Eddie had ever heard. She didn't even know what to tune the strings to, and her bass looked like she'd bought it that afternoon, which, eventually, she confessed she had.

After five solid hours they managed to get through one complete version of Elmore James's 'Madison Blues', the only song they all knew, a straight twelve bar that Clint said nobody but nobody could screw up, not even Stockmarket and Waterman. Eddie could see this was going to take quite a while. When he got home he told Marion that everything had gone brilliantly.

'A few problems,' he admitted, 'naturally enough, but you'll always get that at the beginning. It's just like anything else.'

Marion smiled, thinking he was being ironic.

The next few weeks were the most fun they had. Talking for hours, finding out all about each other, staying up way too late, drinking too much, making love even more, all the things you do when you're in a strange city and you've nobody to answer to and you're falling reluctantly in love. And they couldn't have known that as time drifted on they would each remember this time, as though it had never happened, in that misty sardonic way that lovers do after things have got so bad there's no redemption.

Sometimes Marion went to meet some friends at the local Irish pub, the Pride of Erin. But Eddie only went with her once. Marion's friends got on his nerves. They were all gossiping culchies, from Donegal like her, and the Pride felt more Irish than any pub he'd ever been to in Ireland. It was Irish in the same way that Disneyland is American. Something about it just bugged him, and after the first night he said he didn't want to go again. She honestly didn't mind. In fact, she preferred it that way, or so she said.

On Guy Fawkes Night they walked all the way over to the South Bank to watch the fireworks. They strolled arm in arm across Charing Cross Bridge, as though they were a real couple in a lovesong. The air over the river was full of acrid smoke, weird colours that formed blurry faces, and the dull sound of distant explosions. Eddie didn't like fireworks much. They never quite filled the sky the way they filled a TV screen.

They got wrecked on Bacardi in the tatty bar of the National Film Theatre and Marion said Guy Fawkes was the one person in history with the right attitude to the British Parliament.

November came down over the city, and everything was sleek and glamorous in the rain. A Tube strike was announced. Eddie was drafted in to help Marion and Mrs P deal with the frantic suburban businessmen who invaded the Brightside, sleeping on fold-up beds and stinking mattresses, and eventually, when all the rooms were taken, on cushions in the corridors. It was an absolute bonanza. Mr P was coining it in. The place looked like a hospital in downtown Saigon.

Eddie enjoyed strolling up and down the corridors like a sergeant major ordering everybody around the place. 'Prerogative' became his favourite word. 'If you don't like it you can leave,' he'd say, 'that's your prerogative.' It gave him a big thrill that these overweight chartered accountants and self-important Tebbit-Heads had to take orders from someone who looked like their worst collective nightmare, a walking argument for compulsory military service. And Marion would laugh at him as he strutted up and down the hallways, in a way that made her look like she was proud of him, and embarrassed by him at the same time. Which she was.

One Sunday afternoon they went for a walk by the river and got their portrait done in charcoal by a spaced-out guy on a folding stool outside the Tate.

'She loves you a lot,' said the artist, a Russian exile, or so he said. 'Yes,' he kept murmuring, 'I can see it in her eyes. She loves you, very much, my friend. You are the lucky sonofabitch.' It wasn't a great likeness.

At nights Eddie knew he was in too deep. He found himself drifting away into soppy thoughts, and staring at Marion as she walked around the breakfast room arranging the stuff. He even tried to write a song about her, but let's face it, what rhymes with Marion? 'Carrion' was all he could think of, not an entirely appropriate word for a lovesong, not even a post-punk lovesong. But there was something special about this, and the delicious pain that flowed from the fact it couldn't last – well, Eddie almost got to enjoy it.

Marion kept cutting out her letters, and pretty soon the first alphabet was finished – 'Trade Union Vote To Go' yielded the elusive TUV – and she'd started on the second line. In a strange way, the little alphabets made the room look homely and warm, and finding the next set of letters became a real challenge between them. One of those games that lovers play. Mr Patel got them a secondhand black and white portable TV from his brother-in-law. One day Eddie found a battered electric fire in the back of a skip on President Street, and when he brought it home it worked. Marion was overjoyed. They made love in the red light. The room was comfortable and warm and snug, and though it was small Eddie felt good going up there with Marion, closing the door and shutting the whole crazy world outside.

In late November they began to have arguments. That was when they really knew there was no going back. Marion started asking for help. She wanted help writing letters, job applications, enquiries about courses. Eddie told her she already had a job, here at the Brightside, but she said she had too much spare time and one of them had to do a little work. Eddie thought that was below the belt. If she thought he liked scabbing all her money, then she had another thing coming.

She got this big thing about night courses, and at first Eddie thought it was great. She said she wanted to educate herself and learn a little about the world. She said London seemed like a good place to do that.

But it was the way she did it, it just bugged Eddie till he wanted to scream. She'd ask him what she should say, and how she should put things into words and he'd tell her, 'Say whatever you think you should say, don't ask me, what do *you* think?' The first few times he said this, he meant it well. He knew that she needed to be made feel independent.

But after a while it got to be a drag. They fought one night, after Eddie had dropped a tab of acid, and Eddie said she was stupid, which made her cry a little at first, and then a lot. Afterwards he told her he was sorry, and she said she was sorry too, but she realised he was better with words than she was, and she just wanted a little help. It wasn't too much to ask, she wept, a little help. She would have helped him, if there was any way she could have.

Eddie felt about two feet high. He said that she did help him, every day, and that there was no way he could go on in London without her, absolutely no way in the world. Then he started to cry too, which made her cry even more. They sat on the bed, arms around each other, weeping like babies. He was just so frustrated he said, so down. No matter what he did he couldn't seem to get a start in this fucking kip of a city. He was afraid. All he could see was failure. All his friends were making a start, but not him, and he knew they were laughing at him behind his back. She held him tight and told him not to worry about anything. It was just an argument. He wasn't a failure and everybody had arguments, and everything between them would work out in the end, she knew it. And she said that you had to expect all of these things. This was the price you had to pay when you fell so deeply in love. Eddie asked her not to use those words, and she said OK, but he knew what she meant.

'Look on the bright side,' she cried. 'That's all.' And Eddie laughed.

But from that night on Marion never asked for Eddie's help again. He pretended not to notice, but he knew. She wrote her letters and filled in the forms herself. She'd sit quietly in the room, gazing out the window over King's Cross and sucking the end of her pen, wrapped up in her thoughts, like a blanket around her. Like a womb. And no matter how much Eddie offered his advice, she never took it.

From the night the second XYZ went into place, the writing, as Eddie grew fond of saying, was on the wall.

In the first week of December, Eddie got a job with the same rubbish bag firm that Jimmy's friend Creep Malone worked for. That was all he could get. He'd bought *The Guardian* every Monday and applied for maybe fifteen media jobs a week. (Marion had helped with the typing on Mr Patel's word processor.) He'd planned at first to get something that would help his musical career along. Working for a record company, pop videos, something like that. Gradually, the definition of what would help his career got broader and broader, until eventually, it simply disappeared. Eddie started just churning out applications for whatever he could, with the fury of a government minister putting out leaks to the papers.

But most people didn't bother answering, and the ones who did were so patronising that they made him feel worse. They meant well, obviously. But why did people feel that to be told the standard was unbelievably high would be consoling? That only made things worse. It got so Eddie could tell from the outside of the envelope whether it was going to be a refusal or not. He just knew. Refusals felt light. Interviews felt a little heavier and the address was usually written in pen.

When Creep phoned up about the job with National

Bags'n'Sacks Marion told him to take it. And Eddie knew he didn't have much of a choice.

The job would keep him going until he got his act together with the music, or so he told his father. His father wasn't so sure. He said this wasn't what Eddie had spent all that time in college for. But Eddie told him he couldn't afford to be fussy and that he'd have to take whatever he could, for the moment anyway.

'What's the money like?' his father asked.

'Oh, I dunno,' said Eddie, 'ten a year plus commission, something like that.' His father said it didn't sound like very much. 'Hey, thanks Dad,' said Eddie, 'thanks for the input, OK?' His father said he was only trying to help.

His boss was called Miles Davis, 'no relation'. He looked like one of those young far-right Tory MPs, all blond hair, thin lips and mail-order suits from the Next catalogue. Miles was from Romford, Essex, the same town as Steve Davis, his hero and namesake. He had an ugly little souvenir plaque on his desk saying MAKE THAT SALE!! for which, he admitted, he'd paid £145 plus VAT, at a weekend course on 'How To Sell People Things They Don't Really Need'.

National's office occupied two units of a windswept box of breezeblocks, called 'The Blue Moon Business Park' located somewhere between Slough and the M25. National Bags'n'Sacks was the only office there. This was because the rest of the building was beginning slowly to subside into the mud, and the architect had disappeared off to South America with great speed, a shitload of debts and his former partner's squaw. Or so Miles said.

Miles talked about the secretary as 'it' and his BMW as 'she'. Half-way through Eddie's interview, unconscious of any irony, he said, 'I let it drive her round the block last week.' And he talked about bags and sacks as 'B'n'S'. He said that B'n'S had been good to him, and that B'n'S was a wide open field and that if you had respect for B'n'S, then B'n'S would have respect for you. 'Course, it had its old timers, just like anything else, but not here, not at National. National was a go-ahead, kick-ass, big-time, thrusting outfit. Miles was going to make some changes, and shake up the world of B'n'S until it didn't know what had hit it. For a start, he was already negotiating with the board of directors to change the company letterhead from the rather outdated 'National Bags'n'Sacks', to slick and punchy 'Natty Sax'n'Bagz'. And he was very keen on advertising his product.

'Anyone ever tells you advertising don't work, Ed, you know what to say?' Eddie said no, he didn't. Miles winked. 'You tell 'em,' he beamed, 'we all know what beanz meanz, Ed, you just tell 'em that.'

Miles leaned over his desk when he talked, rapping the blotter with his pen. He said he'd heard a lot about Eddie, and that Creep had spoken very highly of him. But for a start, he wanted to run a few concepts up the flagpole to see if anyone would salute. He wanted to know what were Eddie's career horizons, and where was Eddie coming from. Eddie said Rathmines, via King's Cross, and Miles said no, backgroundwise. What were Eddie's parameters?'

Eddie groaned, to himself. He could see that, in its own way, this was going to be a very demanding interview.

Miles's hair was so full of gel he looked like if you lit a match in the same room he'd spontaneously combust. He had a notice on the wall behind the desk. 'You don't have to be crazy to work here,' it chuckled, 'but it helps.' Beside that he had a framed photograph of Samantha Fox, autographed, 'To Miles, with love from Sammi XXX'. And beside *that* hung a poster of a shapely young woman on a tennis court, with her back to the camera and a short white skirt riding up over her buttocks. 'Crazy', Miles called it.

Along with 'buzzword' and 'parameter', 'crazy' turned out to be one of Miles's favourite words. He talked about his sales team, whom he called the Lads, as being a little crazy, but *basically* decent enough. 'Basically' was another favourite buzzword. Profit margins, projections, spreadsheets, everything was basically crazy.

Eddie asked about his wages. Miles said he'd be started on four K plus commission and seven quid's worth of luncheon vouchers a month. Eddie said that'd be fine.

'Hunky dory,' said Miles, 'you're in. I'll show you round the old reservation.'

Eddie was to work in a room with four glass walls and fifteen red telephones, called the Goldfish Bowl. There were no seats at the desks. On this famous weekend course, Miles had been told that people made more efficient sales while standing.

'Keep 'em on their toes, Eddie,' he said, 'and they'll keep *you* on yours. That's my motto.'

Eddie's job was to call up people on a list the company got from some mortgage outfit. He got £1.71 commission for every lead. Before tax. A lead was when he got someone to agree to a salesman coming to give them a free estimate 'for all their bagging and sacking needs'. Miles said it was surprisingly difficult. A lot of people just put the phone down straightaway. Other people thought they'd won a Cornflakes packet competition or something, and it took you maybe ten minutes to explain. Almost everybody would ask where you'd got the number. One or two would tell you to fuck off.

Miles didn't like Eddie's hair. He said you had to have respect for yourself, then punters would have respect for you. Eddie pointed out that if there was anyone he did have respect for it was himself, and anyway nobody could see him over the phone. Still, Miles was reluctant. He said they ran a pretty tight ship, suit and tie-wise. It was all a question of attitude. When Eddie refused outright to get it cut, Miles looked blank for a second, something for which his naturally vague face appeared to have been specially designed. Then he said, 'I must be crazy, but I'll make an exception with you, Ed. I've got a good feeling about you. I mean, take me away to the funny farm, Ed, but I'll bend the rules for you.'

Keith, Russell and Johnny K were the Lads, the three 'team leaders'. They dressed the same as Miles, except for the fact that they wore white socks. Johnny K was quieter than the other two, but, in his own way, just as much a tosser. Each of the Lads ran a gang of ten local agents, of which Creep was one, dotted up and down the country.

The Lads pronounced the word fuck to rhyme with park. 'Farking hell,' they'd say, and they said it at every available opportunity. Other times, they lost the 'fuck' part completely and just used the suffix ''king,' or the exclamation, ''kinnel'. They slagged Eddie off about his hair. They said all that hairspray would play havoc with the 'king ozone whatsit. Eddie told them he only used ozone-friendly hairspray, and they broke into a chorus of whoops, calling him a 'king poofta. Then they told Keith there was no chance of him damaging the ozone thingummy, as he hadn't used a 'king deodorant in years. Occasionally, when boredom set in, one of them would stand up quickly and grab another between the legs, which would induce hysterical laughter from the third. Maria the secretary told them they were bloody children. The Lads fell about the place.

'Farking lesbian,' said Keith, blushing, 'can't take a 'king joke.'

Still, Eddie made enough cash to keep the wolf from the

Brightside door – or, as Mr Patel said, out of the lobby, at any rate – and to pay to get copies of his demo tape made. The demo tape had two songs on it, written by an old friend of Eddie's called Jonesy, who was now in Saudi Arabia working as an engineer. It also had two instrumentals, written more or less by Eddie, with the emphasis on the less. At night he and Marion would pack the cassettes up into jiffy bags, compose pithy letters which were a subtle mix of arrogance and pleading, and get everything ready for the post. Sometimes the tapes were back home by the time Eddie got in from work, biked straight back over to the Brightside from the record companies with a perfunctory note saying this was not exactly what they were looking for. The stream of returned demo tapes got so remorseless that Eddie dreaded coming home. Mr Patel said people in the creative arts always had these problems.

'Look at Jeffrey Archer,' he advised, 'the poor guy was nearly bankrupt before he made it as a writer. Look at him now.'

The Lads were slobs, but once Eddie realised they were *complete* slobs, he managed to deal with them.

They recited endless stories about their trips up and down the country, invented tales about frustrated housewives and nymphomaniacal hitch-hikers that came straight from the readers' letters pages of the porn magazines they read. The wall of the Goldfish Bowl was plastered with page-three cut-outs, and centrefolds from magazines so basic that they could have been used as a gynaecologist's wallchart. One picture was taped to a dartboard, and every morning the Lads would play at trying to hit the spreadeagled woman's nipples while they waited for the day's addresses to come spewing out of the IBM.

'Real charmers,' Eddie said, when Marion asked what they were like.

They, like Miles, called women 'it'. Even their wives were called 'it'. Their children were 'sprogs'. Monday morning had its own special routine. The Lads would swagger in, stretching, yawning, wincing, arching their backs. This was because of the strain of 'homework', their euphemism for making love to their wives. 'Had to farking give it one,' they'd say, 'otherwise there'd be 'kinell to pay. It'd suspect I was playing away from farking home or something.' And they said it week in week out, for every weary Monday morning that Eddie lasted.

The newspapers they read seemed to be composed entirely of ten words – martian, melons, loony, poofta, bonk, panties,

Kraut, raving, moist and Thatcher, or, more usually, Thatcha.

All of this disgusted Eddie, but he needed the job, and as it turned out, he got good at it too. He developed the knack. If bullshit was an art, Eddie would have been an old master. That's what Miles said, and he should have known.

'You're the best farking liar I ever met, Eddie,' he said, 'and hey, you know what, that's a compliment.'

The secret was to get in fast that the estimate was free. Eddie discovered that this was all he had to do. He called himself Eddie Smith, because Virago was just too much of a mouthful, and too many valuable seconds got wasted in repeating it to the bewildered victims on the end of the line. Miles helped him out with his technique. He gave him all the theories and acronyms and mnemonics he'd picked up on his course, whispering them in the pub at lunchtime with the furtive air of a KGB agent.

Miles seemed to like him. He said he'd invite Eddie and Eddie's little woman round to his tepee some night, but Eddie said he didn't have a little woman, and anyway he was too busy most nights with his music. Miles didn't seem to mind.

'Some other time,' he told Eddie. He said, 'See, you and me, Ed, we're different.' Eddie admitted that this was certainly true. 'But in some ways we're the same, Ed,' said Miles, 'and you know what? I like that.'

There was a problem, though. As time went on, the Lads got harder to take. He couldn't even discuss it with Marion, because he knew that if he told her about half the things they said, she'd blast him for not having the guts to leave.

Christmas was coming anyway, that's what Eddie figured. He'd hold out till the New Year, see if anything better turned up. It was bound to. He phoned up his father and asked for a plane ticket home on Christmas Eve. His father objected. He wanted to know why Eddie couldn't pay for it himself. Eddie told him he was a bit pushed actually.

'Bit of a liquidity problem, Dad,' he said. 'Just temporary, you know.' After a tornado of sighs, his father conceded, and said he'd send it. But it would have to be Eddie's Christmas present. There'd be nothing else, and no complaining. That was the deal. He wasn't made of money. Eddie said OK.

Then, only three weeks into the job, something happened.

They'd all gone down to the Mucky Duck to have a drink with Fitzy, the office junior, who'd decided, much to the Lads' amazement, to leave the world of the now officially rechristened

'Natty Sax'n'Bagz' after Christmas and go to college. Miles was happy. He'd just managed to sell 57,000 black supa-whoppa size refuse sacks to the Chilean Ministry of Security, and things were looking up. Drinks were on him. The night had started off well, lots of free snakebite, which Miles kept saying was 'worth it to keep the tribe happy'.

But then Johnny K came back from yet another of his doomed forays to proposition the barmaid, flapping his arms in excitement and muttering incoherently. He grabbed Keith and Eddie, and dragged them over to the bar.

'Look at that,' he said, in awe, 'isn't that just something else?'

It took some moments to ascertain that Johnny K was pointing at a large circular clock on the mirrored wall behind the bar, with the names of just about every cocktail Eddie'd heard of – and quite a few that he hadn't – emblazoned around the numbered circumference.

'Fark me,' sighed Keith, 'I see what you're on about.' Johnny K had had an idea, and the Lads were not to be put off. They were going to drink all the way around to midnight. Death or Glory. Pukesville or bust.

When the chorus of 'Here we go, here we go, here we go' finally died down, the weary-looking landlord advised caution. He said these cocktails were lethal stuff and he wouldn't be responsible for anything. But Miles insisted. He pulled two fifty-pound notes from his wallet and stuffed them ostentatiously into the manager's breast pocket. He said this was the best god-damn sales team in Christendom and he wasn't going to let them down now. The Lads whooped and hammered the tables as the barmaid tottered nervously over to them, bent under the weight of her full tray. Hands grabbed glasses, full of exotic foliage and psychedelic colours. Eddie laughed. He knew he'd end up heaving it all back down the toilet at the Brightside, but still, just then, that wasn't the point. He was happy. He was OK for cash. And as the first few elegantly named and syrupy concoctions slipped down his throat, he was so drunk he didn't care any more.

'Right,' chirped Miles, red-faced, waving his watch. 'Last one around the clock's a Liberal Democrat. Alright, Ed?'

'Miles,' he slurred. 'I'm pissed drunk, I'm tired, I'm hungry, but I just don't care any more.'

Johnny K told him that was the spirit. And it was good to be hungry sometimes. He said the Irish ate too many potatoes anyway, so that it affected their brains. Eddie said the English would eat anything, once it was in a tin.

'If General Galtieri had really wanted to fuck the English up,' he said, briskly stirring his Long Slow Screw Against the Wall, 'he should have just left the little keys off all the tins of Argentinian spam.'

Sipping delicately at his third Harvey Wallbanger, Keith chuckled.

'That's not very nice, Eddie, that's not very Christian.'

'Well, I'm not a fucking Christian.'

'You're not bloody Jewish, are you?' said Keith, horrified.

'I'm an agnostic, actually,' drawled Eddie, demolishing his Knee Trembler in three swallows.

'Oooooo,' whopped Keith, 'ooo, are you now? Well, I'm a fucking Taurus.'

'How come they have a cigarette machine in the women's toilets?' mammered Johnny K, to nobody in particular.

'That's a tampon machine, you idiot,' sighed Maria.

'Religion is the opium of the people, Keith,' gabbled Eddie politely, blowing the froth off his Multiple Orgasm. 'As Marx said.'

'Groucho, was it?' chuckled Miles, to hysterical laughter.

'But I mean seriously, Ed, mate,' intoned Keith, picking his nose 'what about, you know, seriously, nature and all that, no, stop laughing Johnny, you cunt . . . How do you like, explain all that?'

'What are you saying?' lisped Eddie.

Keith's bleary eyes stared into the middle distance, as he thoughtfully scratched his crotch. He swigged a mouthful of Thigh Opener, snorting as he dribbled a little of it down his tie.

'Well, think of a little flower, right, I mean, a farking flower, OK, I mean, why the fark, shaddap Maria, why the *fark* should it exist even? Little poxy scabby cunt of a flower, no use to anyone? Makes no sense, does it?'

'S'very simple,' gulped Eddie. 'Evolution.'

'Evofuckinglution?' scoffed Keith, 'stuff it up your junta, Eddie, willya? It's 'cos God put it there, innit? I mean, stands to farking reason.'

'Lads, lads, lads, lads, lads, lads,' said Miles, 'lads, please.'

'Fuck off, you,' snapped Keith, 'and give me another one of those things with the little paper farking umbrellas in it.'

Eddie's brain felt like it was beginning to implode in slow motion.

'No, look, Keith,' he argued, polishing off his Rambo Rupturer in one slug, 'you have to understand this, man, OK' – he wiped his lips with the back of his hand, feeling warm and glowing and contented, noticing suddenly how oddly kind and pleasant and generally wholesome Keith's blue eyes were – 'I mean like, I love you man, so I want to make you see the truth.' Bewildered and blushing, Keith noticed a hand clutching at his lapel. 'You have to understand, Keith, you have to fucking liberate yourself, man. I mean, tune in to reality, you know what I'm saying? Like, have you ever read Keats? Or William Blake?'

'He's right,' sighed Johnny K, pursing his lips, nodding, glugging haplessly at his Exocet Missile. 'He's so right.'

Eddie threw his arm around Keith and hugged his shoulder.

'Fark off, you farking poofta,' warned Keith. Eddie laughed and punched his colleague manfully in the chest. Then he emptied a box of safety matches over the damp table, and proceeded to explain the life and work of Darwin, while Keith worked his way with true devotion through a very large Hand Shandy.

Three French Letters, one Roll Me Over and half a For God's Sake Whip Me Now later, Eddie still hadn't made much progress. Keith was getting upset. Quaffing lugubriously at his Bollock Blender, Keith began to thump the table.

'There is a farking God, and I don't give a wank what you say about beagles, you cunt.'

'No,' said Eddie, 'Jesus was a good man, but he was just a prophet.'

'Did somebody say profit?' said Miles.

'Don't start on about Jesus,' warned Keith, vaguely waving a finger. 'I mean it now, Eddie, a joke's a farking joke, but don't start.'

'Peace and goodwill to all men,' hiccupped Johnny K, pink liquid oozing from his nostrils.

'There is not a God,' snarled Eddie, gulping down bitter mouthfuls of his double Prickteaser. 'That is just fucking *fucking* peasant propaganda, Keith, and you fucking know it, you fucker. What's your game, come on, I mean, what's your fucking trip man, tell us, huh? Are you a hit man for the fucking Pope or what?'

Keith glugged his Brewers Droop, folded his arms, belched loudly, closed his eyes, began nodding intensely.

'Oh yes, that's it, it's good enough for everyone else but not our farking so-called educated . . . well, let me tell you, Eddie Virago, or whatever your farking Red Sea pedestrian name is, I am working class and farking proud of it.'

'But Keith,' slurred John K, 'didn't you vote for the Tories last time?'

'Ha,' gulped Eddie, a little too loudly. 'Huh.' Miles looked at him nervously.

'Are you going to be sick or something?' he enquired, covering his glass with his hand.

'I farking did not, you cunt,' barked Keith. 'And anyway, that's not the point. That's different.

'God,' sighed Maria, 'you really are a moron, aren't you, Keith?'

'Well, at least I'm not a farking lesbian,' barked Keith, 'not like some bastards I could mention.'

Eddie was having difficulty moving his jaw. His stomach felt like he had swallowed a washing machine. He noticed that every word Keith said now seemed to begin with the letter 'S'. That annoyed him. That, and the fact that Keith's oddly *nasty* and cunning blue eyes were too close together. Yes. He'd never noticed it before, but they definitely were, there was no mistake. He could see it now, the objectionable bastard. And his nose was too big too. Jesus, the contemptible ugly *bastard*. People like Keith, Eddie reckoned, should be just put up against the wall and shot. Or, better still, clubbed to death.

Hot angry air seemed to rush past Eddie's ears as he swigged his Jerk Me Silly.

'Yes, well it's goose-steppers like you started the fucking Spanish Civil fucking War. Yes you, personally, you fascist. Yes you. Don't look around like that, I'm talking to you, Adolf.'

'Why can't we all just love each other,' whined Johnny K, 'why can't we just all . . .'

'Plans for Christmas, Ed?' asked Miles, brightly.

'Oh, fuck off, you reactionary,' said Eddie.

Suddenly sobbing into his Sink The Belgrano, Keith muttered, 'But I mean the poor little baby Jesus, all alone in his little

stable, just him and the farking cows and shit and straw. All
alone in the world. Nobody to care for him. Poor little bastard.'
And he blew his nose loudly on his green and puce tie.

'Oh, *very* nice,' bitched Eddie, 'very nice, wonder how *that*
would go down with the vicar on Xmas morning, calling the
putative offspring of the omniscient deity an illegitimate love
child. Very nice indeed.'

'That's the fucking trouble with you lot, over in Ireland, you
don't have any farking religion. You're all bloody sun-
worshippers.'

'Too much fucking religion,' growled Eddie, 'that's the real
trouble. What we actually need, actually, is for the organised
mass of the working class' – he found himself rising to his feet,
clenching one fist at this point – 'to join together, cast off
the chains of bondage and overthrow their common capitalistic
oppressors.' Somewhere in the back of his mind he heard a roar
of heroic proletarian applause.

'Who are you calling common, you cunt?' snarled Keith.

'Did someone say Chains of Bondage?' asked Miles. 'I think I
had one of those earlier.'

'Working class, my bollocks,' announced Johnny K.

'Oh Christ, here we go,' moaned Maria, reaching for her coat.

Silence came down very suddenly over the group. Music
tinkled from the jukebox. Miles drained his J Danforth Quayle
and lit a cigarette. Everybody seemed to be looking at him,
everybody except Keith and Eddie, who were too busy looking
at each other. Then Keith's head fell forward, and his hands
touched his eyes. He began to cry. His shoulders shook, and
Johnny K gave his thigh a reassuring squeeze.

'I'm off then, lads,' said Fitzy, 'thanks very much for the send
off.'

'You're a cunt,' wept Keith, 'you're a heartless cunt, Eddie.'

'And you,' screeched Eddie, 'are a fucking monotheist.'

Behind the bar, the landlord sighed deeply and clicked his
fingers. The black bouncer lumbered over from the door and
placed his massive hands on Eddie's shoulders, pushing him very
gently back into his seat.

'Right on, man,' said Eddie to the bouncer, 'Nelson Mandela
all the way, yeah? One bullet, one fucking settler, alright?'

'Don't talk like that, Paddy,' Keith said, smiling, suddenly
confident, 'you're not in 'king Belfast now.'

Eddie stood up again, feeling oddly sober now, totally sober, blackly sober, more sober in fact, than if he had not been drinking at all, more sober than he had ever been in his whole life actually, if anyone was asking, not that it was anybody's fucking business. Pure distilled hatred dribbled through his veins. Contempt burned through his brain. He opened his mouth, but no words came. Everything blurred in his hot eyes. Heat seeped from his pores. Everyone in the pub seemed to be looking at him. He stared at Keith and he realised quite casually, as he began to sway rhythmically from side to side, that he wanted to murder him, in some preferably bizarre but excruciatingly painful manner.

'Hold on now, Ed,' said Miles, 'don't get crazy now. Here, have another Multiple Orgasm.'

Eddie threw back his head and he began to howl at the reproduction oak rafters.

'Maggie Maggie Maggie, Out Out Out,
Maggie, Out,
Maggie, Out,
Maggie Maggie Maggie . . .'

'Out Out Out.' said Miles absent-mindedly.

''Kinnel,' said both Keiths, shaking their leering and terrible heads, 'it's no wonder, is it?'

'What's no wonder?' spat Eddie.

'It's just no wonder what's going on over there in Leprechaun Land.'

Four Johnny Ks sniggered into their glasses.

'Shut your face,' roared Eddie, at the army of kaleidoscopic Keiths dancing before his eyes, 'I'm warning you.'

'Go ahead, Paddy,' they sneered, 'make my farking day.'

Miles finished his Missionary Position and tried to say something.

But it was too late. The bar seemed to explode. Drinks and ashtrays and olives and lemon quarters and little pink paper umbrellas flew through the air. Somebody screamed. The juke box skipped. Eddie found himself backed up against a wall and Keith's smiling face was up against his own. He could hear his shirt being ripped, as Keith tugged his lapel. Eddie could see blood somewhere. And he could see Johnny K and Russell holding Miles by the arms. He heard the sound of glass breaking. He could see somebody he didn't know smiling at him.

Keith's lips moved. His eyes closed. His cheeks rolled as he snorted hard. He spat into Eddie's eyes.

Keith's wide freckled forehead smashed forwards into Eddie's nose. Then he rolled his shoulders, gritted his teeth and head butted again. Eddie surrendered to the pain. He felt his body being spun around. His cheek ground against the plaster wall. He felt his arm twisted tight against his back. He saw his blood drop in regular splashes onto the tiled floor, where it slithered on the gloss like it was going to disappear. A knee forced into the back of his own knee, bringing him down like he was praying. The seat of his trousers felt warm and wet. The fire roared somewhere.

Eddie lay on his back staring at the ceiling, unable to speak. He tried to move his arms but pain shot across his back, and it spread up and down his body until he couldn't be sure where it was coming from any more. Faces stared down at him. The room began to spin, first slowly, then stopping completely, then increasing to a whirling merry-go-round of sound and fire. Then everything looked black and white and when he swallowed, the sour and metallic taste of blood flooded the back of his throat. He felt something sticky on his face. It felt like honey. He thought about Marion. In the back of his ravaged mind, all he could wish was that she was there. He saw her slender face in the fire, and he saw her screaming with pain, her eyes dark and her hair glowing, her hands reaching out of the flames to touch him.

When Eddie woke up a pneumatic drill was busily burrowing into his brain. He was flat on his back in a white-tiled room, and Miles was standing over him, with his tie off and his collar open and blood streaked down the front of his white shirt. There were two policemen on the far side of the room, one black, the other very white and very weary-looking.

'Thank fuck,' Miles moaned, 'oh Jesus.'

He told Eddie not to speak. He told him he'd bitten his tongue and inhaled his blood.

The nurse was Irish. She stitched his head and put an icepack on his face. She said she thought U2 were doing great things for Ireland.

'If you say anything about Dean Bean,' Eddie warned her, 'I'll just fucking scream, OK?'

'Poor lad,' she sighed, 'a bit delirious.'

Miles was told that Johnny K and Russell would probably be OK, but that his other employee would be spending the night behind bars. Eddie couldn't speak properly.

'Do you want him charged?' sighed the black policeman. Eddie nodded furiously. Miles put his hand on Eddie's shoulder.

'Now look, Ed, mate,' he said, 'this is crazy, now we don't want to do anything foolish.'

'Charge the cunt,' said Eddie, 'and get your hands off me, Miles.'

An hour later, when he was feeling better, Eddie staggered out to the phonebox in the lobby and rang Marion. She'd been worried sick about him. She said his voice sounded like he had a mouth full of marshmallows. At first she didn't believe he was calling from hospital. But when he collapsed in the door of the Brightside with his face all bruised and scraped, she did.

He told Marion he'd gone to the rescue of a little old lady who was being crowbarred by two skinheads on the All Saints Road.

Marion said there were some absolute bastards in this country. Eddie said yeah, and the trouble was, they'd nicked his wallet, with all his month's pay and now he was skint. She said not to worry. She'd give him a few quid.

Mr Patel chipped in too. He came up to the room as Eddie lay spreadeagled on the bed shivering in his Mikhail Gorbachev boxer shorts, with a wet towel on his face. He asked if Eddie could sit up for a second. Beaming with pride, he handed him an envelope. Eddie gave it to Marion to open. Inside were £200 worth of Thames Water shares. He'd been saving them for Christmas, he said, as their present, for helping him out during the Tube strike, but in the circumstances they could have them now. He hoped it would give them a good start, and that they would use them properly, for their future. It was just that he'd felt really bad, he said, about what had happened to Eddie. He didn't want them to have a bad impression of this country.

'People here are not like that,' he said, sadly, 'these animals are the rotten apple, Eddie.'

Back at work on Monday, Miles summoned Eddie and Keith into his office.

'You're both good lads,' he told them, 'the world is your ashtray. There's a good future for you both in this game, but I can't have you behaving like farking apaches, can I?' He asked them to kiss and make up, smoke the pipe of peace. Keith stared at the carpet and said he was sorry. He had nothing against the Irish at all, or the farking Jews, if it came to that. It was just the gargle. Miles told him he couldn't give a Castlemaine XXXX what it was, it'd better not happen again. Keith said the ball and chain had given him a right bollocking when he'd got home after his night in the cells, if it was any consolation. Eddie shook his hand and said no hard feelings. Keith looked genuinely sorry, and he kept saying he was sorry, over and over again, and that he had nothing against anybody, until it got embarrassing. Miles looked proud as a parent on sports day. He said there'd be a Christmas bonus for both of them. 'But don't spend it all on wine, women and song,' he quipped. 'Money spent on song is often wasted.' Then he said they could go back to work and there'd be no more talk about it. 'We're a team here,' he said, 'when the solids hit the air conditioning, we're a team. Remember that.'

A few days later, as Christmas week invaded London, Eddie's plane ticket arrived. And when Marion came home from work that night, he told her there was some good news, at last. The Hothouse Flowers manager had heard his demo tape over in Dublin, and he was paying for Eddie's flight over to do some session work on their new album over Christmas. She couldn't believe it. She threw her arms around him and kissed his still bruised face, again and again. He asked if she'd be OK going home to Donegal on the boat, on her own, and she said of course. She kissed him again, and she said the news had just made her Christmas complete. Eddie said he wouldn't get a credit or anything, but it'd be mega experience. She said that was absolutely marvellous and she bought a bottle of champagne. Even Mr Patel had a sip. And Mrs Patel too.

Mr Patel said they had good reason to celebrate. Tears filled his beautiful brown eyes. Mrs Patel was expecting again. He beckoned towards his wife, like a magician applauding a sequined lady that had been sawn in two and put back together again.

'I am so very proud of her,' he cried, holding her tiny hand. 'I just wish you two the happiness we have found.'

Eddie wanted to go out clubbing that night, but Marion couldn't. She had to pack up her stuff for the boat. She had an early start the next morning.

'We're not all big rock stars like you, Eddie Virago,' she teased, 'we're not all set up like you.' And then she said she was proud of him again.

'Yeah,' Eddie shrugged. 'I know you are.'

'Happy Christmas, Eddie,' she said softly, 'I'll be thinking of you.'

And they made love in the dark, while the white grids of the passing headlights danced up and down the lettered walls.

O'Connell Street was thick with a grey precarious snow that had packed hard like marble underneath the slush. Roaring groups of Christmas Eve Dublin drinkers spilled out from the pubs and disco bars. Police cars prowled up and down, fishtailing around icy corners, red lights wet in the shop windows, which gaped with sad-eyed mannequins. The water in the Anna Livia memorial – the floosie in the jacuzzi – was frozen solid, crisp bags, Coke cans, condom packets and burger wrappers all fossilised in the translucent ice. The GPO shimmered with pale yellow light and the windows had all been decorated with green sashes that had 'Welcome Home For Christmas' stamped on in gold. Down Henry Street the star-shaped lights glinted suggestively in the purple smog. Talbot Street was the same. Eddie saw a lurching drunk in a Santa Claus uniform hail down a taxi and jump in, pausing only to pull a packet of twenty cigarettes from his breast pocket. Two soldiers waited at a bus stop, fat kitbags by their feet. Queues stretched out from the doors of the fast-food joints. The pool halls and gambling arcades were full of young guys in jeans, cursing, rattling pool balls into pockets. And the whole street seemed to vibrate with the exultant buzz of the jackpot bells and the insistent thud of piped heavy metal. Couples skidded up and down the pavement, Christmas lights in their eyes, laughing, kissing, fighting. Under the statue of Daniel O'Connell, a group of stocky traveller women all wrapped in tartan blankets shared a flask of something steamy, counting out the day's money into a battered mushroom punnet. And all along the Liffey the black water danced with light, all the way down past the silver Halfpenny Bridge and into the Phoenix Park, where the neon rainbow glowed up and down the huge papal cross.

Eddie picked his way down past the black bulk of Trinity College, towards Westland Row, feeling apprehensive and excited in equal measure. Dublin at Christmas was a dangerous town. Too many familiar people, all waiting to jump out of the shadows and wave their latest attitude in your face.

Kennedy's was roaring with people. Hot wet air and the smell of sweat and Guinness blasted Eddie's freezing cheeks as he pushed in the door. Loud traditional music pumped out of the speakers and a couple of duffel-coated students sang along, punching the air when the rebel chorus came around. His ear-lobes and his nose felt raw with the cold, and the sides of his shorn and stubbly head ached too. A huge cloud of cigarette smoke hung under the chandelier, rolling from side to side of the bar, but always holding its purple shape. Frothy pints with heads of yellow cream were passed from hand to hand, high in the air, slopping over the floor and down the backs of people's necks. Eddie pushed sideways through the bodies, seeing faces that he recognised, taking in all the gossiping flirtatious cacophony of Christmas Eve.

'Hey, sucker,' came a voice from behind, 'what's shaking?'

Eddie turned, just in time to see a pair of pink lips descend on his cheek.

'Dean Bean,' he laughed, 'what's going on?'

'Nothing going on, 'cept the rent,' laughed Beano, clasping his hand hard. 'What's shaking with you?'

'I'm great,' said Eddie, 'just great.'

'Jesus, man,' said Beano, 'what the fuck happened to your face?'

Eddie said it was a long story.

Dean Bean was chewing gum, and looking his usual studied, laidback self. His bony knees poked through his Levis, and his puce houndstooth jumper looked like it needed a serious spell in the launderette. He grabbed Eddie's elbow and propelled him into the gents, where he pulled a little tobacco tin from his hip pocket. He glared conspiratorially over his shoulder, innocent eyes flashing, then he pulled Eddie into one of the cubicles. The unscrewed tin was full of fine white powder.

'I'm dreaming,' he croaked, 'of a white Christmas,' and he rolled up a blue twenty pound note. 'Great to see you again, pal,' he said, clapping Eddie hard on the back, pushing the tin into his trembling hands. Eddie could see the broody face of W. B. Yeats staring at him from the bank note as he snuffled hard at the sour white powder. 'Home is the hero,' said Beano, closing his eyes, sniffing hard, tapping his nostrils. Eddie snorted, until his eyes began to water.

Beano said the gang had commandeered a couple of tables in the back room. But Eddie wanted to know just who was there. There were a couple of people in Dublin he really didn't want to run into. And he didn't feel like a heavy good old days' vibe either.

'Vibe?' said Beano. '*Vibe?* Where the fuck have you been, man? Planet Woodstock?'

Eddie, to his surprise, felt his face flush.

Beano told him to chill out and put his eyes back in his head. He dragged him from the gents and into the back room, towards a table around which Eddie recognised various bored faces, including, way down the other end, the faces of Jimmy and Ruth. He slapped Eddie's shoulders again and roared, 'Hey, everybody, there's a new kid in town.' Upturned faces. Glum smiles. Ruth beckoned for Eddie to come and sit down their end. She looked nervous again. And Jimmy looked drunk and sweaty and slightly too old.

'Later,' Eddie mouthed, silently. She looked disappointed.

Eddie sat beside Dean Bean and Ronnie Kavanagh, and somebody got him a drink.

'You like it over there, do you?' said Ronnie, suddenly.

'S'alright,' said Eddie.

'I hate it myself. Been over a few times. Beer tastes like pisswater.' Beano laughed loud.

'You'd know, man,' he said.

'I like it,' said Eddie.

'Welcome to it,' said Ronnie, kissing the beerfroth from his upper lip. 'Beer tasted like *pisswater.*'

Beano said he was drinking too much anyway. He had to watch it.

'I've got an addictive personality,' he said. Ronnie said he'd never noticed that.

'I can take it or leave it, myself,' he said. 'Your personality, I mean.' Beano showed him a finger.

'So how's the rock and roll business?' said Beano, pummelling Eddie's arm. 'Awopbopaloobob.'

'Oh, things are going OK,' said Eddie, modestly. 'I've got a couple of labels sniffing around, you know. Did a bit of session work a while back there, good money.'

'You freakin' mother,' cawed Beano. 'Far out.'

'Oh yeah?' said Ronnie. 'For who?'

'The Jesus and Mary Chain,' said Eddie, lighting a cigarette.

'You absolute bastard,' said Beano. 'How much?'

'Two fifty for the day,' said Eddie, shrugging casually. Ronnie sipped at his pint.

'They wouldn't make it the even three quid, no?' he said.

Dean Bean laughed again and he told Ronnie he was a bollox. The word sounded odd in his Arkansas accent.

'Good one, Ron,' said Eddie, smiling, 'so what are you up to?'

Ronnie was working as a print boy in his father's office and waiting for the civil service job embargo to end. He was still writing a bit, but not much. Just weekend stuff. The odd poem.

'Very odd,' Beano said, but Ronnie ignored him. He was seeing some girl from Germany who was over to study folklore.

'You know the type,' he said. 'Magic leprechauns and Aran knickers.' Into the Greens, apparently, as everyone seemed to be over there.

Beano asked if Eddie was doing anything lovewise over in London. He pronounced it long and languid, *luuurrrrve*, like a soul singer.

'C'mon, Ed,' he said, 'who's whipping your cream, huh?' Ronnie snuffed a laugh.

'Nah,' said Eddie, 'no way, José. Don't want all that again. Not after last time.'

'Once bitten, huh?' said Beano.

Down the far end of the table, somebody knocked over a pint of Guinness, and a tall girl Eddie didn't recognise stood up quickly, cursing, black wet stains down the front of her white dress.

'Twice bite,' said Eddie, and Ronnie giggled into his drink. But Beano was suddenly not listening.

'Well, Jesus Christ,' he sighed, deeply, 'would you look who it is? I mean, talk of the goddam devil.' Eddie sat back very still. He knew what was going to happen.

Someone squeezed between two bodies and put her arms over Eddie's eyes from behind. He knew immediately who it was. It was her perfume. Sweet and expensive and pretentious. He'd always hated it. He touched her fingers and felt them squeeze around his own.

'Can it be you, she said?' said Jennifer. She had this habit of talking about herself from time to time in the third person. She thought it was cool, and sometimes it was. But most of the time it wasn't.

Jennifer was looking well. She'd lost a little weight, but her fabulous eyes were clear and bright, and her skin was the colour of milky coffee. They talked for a while, but Ronnie and Beano were beginning to shout at each other about Descartes, and the place was way too loud. She leaned closed to Eddie so that he could hear her, and her minty breath caressed his face. And then somebody else came flailing into the philosophical discussion on the side of the anti-Cartesians, so that Eddie couldn't hear her any more, no matter how hard he tried, and he suggested they step outside for a few minutes.

Outside in the alley, they got carried away, kissing and shivering in the cold. Eddie put his hand under Jennifer's skirt and fingered her while her hips bucked against the door. It felt like speaking a language they'd half forgotten. Their breath was like smoke and Eddie's heels kept skidding on the ice. Finally, halfway through a particularly enthusiastic lunge, he fell over backwards into a puddle and grazed his hand on a bin lid. She didn't laugh. So he stood again, and they groped each other off while the rhythmic screech of The Pogues' 'Fairytale of New York' boomed out through the fire escape.

When Eddie came she said something in Spanish. And when she came, Eddie said nothing at all.

'She said this probably wasn't such a great idea,' said Jennifer. Eddie said it was a bit late now. 'You probably think I'm a tart,' she said. Eddie said that was ridiculous, of course he didn't.

'Anyway,' he shrugged, 'it's Christmas.' Jennifer, closing her blouse, wanted to know what that had to do with anything.

'Auld Lang Syne,' he said. 'You know. Peace and goodwill.'

'Afterwards they walked around the block and talked about Nicaragua.' That's what Jennifer said, languorously, as she smoothed down her dress. She said it was a beautiful country and all the politicians were poets. And Eddie told her about how brilliantly things were going for him over in London, and how it was the best fucking thing he had ever done, getting out of this forlorn kip of a country. She asked if he didn't miss his friends.

'Friends?' Eddie laughed. 'Oh yeah, great friends, really, a collection of fucking losers and layabouts all jerking each other off and sticking the knife in behind each other's backs.' Jennifer said she thought that was a bit hard. Eddie said it was Christmas. It always brought out the bastard in him.

'You'll never change, Eddie,' she said, 'you're such an actor.' He didn't know what she meant. But he didn't want to know either, so that didn't matter.

When they went back inside a handsome guy in a black blazer was sitting at the table, leaning his head on one hand, sipping at an orange juice, and regarding Dean Bean with a kind of affected quizzical bemusement. He had a haircut like a trendy Jesuit and a slightly turned-up nose. Beano was in his element. The drink and the coke were having their usual effect of rendering him almost totally incoherent. He was waving his arms around and talking about the lost generation again. His eyes were excited as he spoke, and he kept lighting cigarettes, dropping them on the floor and trying to pick them up again.

'*Socialism*,' he yelled. 'The Irish Labour Party wouldn't know socialism if it bit them right in the ass, you mother. They've stood by and watched a lost generation.'

'Jeez,' sighed Jennifer, 'isn't it just so great to be part of a lost generation? I really don't know what Beano would talk about otherwise.'

She introduced him to Leppo. Leppo was a rugby player who played centre for the Irish international team. His handshake was firm and warm, but his breath smelt sour. Eddie recognised his face from the papers, but he didn't want to admit that. They weren't going out or anything, he was just Jennifer's current flingette. He looked like the kind of guy who trails his arms in the dust. Jennifer said something about getting an autograph for Eddie's dad, but Eddie said no way, he wasn't into rugby any more, cycling was his game since Stephen Roche had won the Tour de France.

'Pezzo's game,' said Leppo, throwing back his head and laughing.

'What about South fucking Africa?' slurred Beano. 'What about Nelson Mandela, eh?' Leppo said hey, did he play scrum half or second row, and then he laughed. Then he said no seriously, rugby wasn't a black man's game anyway. Beano said maybe so, but Irish players shouldn't be going over there to support apartheid. But Leppo said if he ever got the chance to go out to the republic and have a decko for himself – he'd jump at it. You couldn't really talk about a situation, he felt, unless you had direct experience.

'I mean,' he cackled, 'I'm not going to ask the bleeding Pope about screwing now, am I?'

Eddie felt bad. Leppo started talking about the bank where he worked in London, loans or something, interest rates, but the coke was beginning to make everything more intense. When Eddie tried to speak, a terrible fear shot through him. He watched Jennifer laugh, and the way she touched Leppo's arm when she wanted to interrupt him and say something, the way his fingers squeezed her hand. The colours shimmered. The music felt electric and weird. Whenever he looked at Jennifer her face rippled, as though it was a reflection in water. And every so often somebody would come over with a soggy beermat or a serviette, and ask Leppo for his autograph. He made the same joke every time.

'Just don't put it on a cheque, OK?'

Eddie excused himself and tumbled into the toilet, where he stuck two fingers down his throat and made himself puke into the urinal. It wasn't Leppo's fault. This was just bad coke, he knew it, and he didn't want to get paranoid, not on Christmas Eve, it was crazy and paranoid enough as it was. The calendar's answer to cold turkey. Typical Dean fucking Bean. He just couldn't be trusted where drugs were concerned. He just wasn't fussy. If you got him in the right mood he'd trip out on a bottle of Domestos. In fact, he'd seen him once after a party in Foxrock, when it was late and cold, rolling up the leaves of an aspidistra and trying to smoke it while he raved about the dawn.

When he came out of the gents Jennifer and Leppo were standing. He was holding her coat like some fucking duke and she was struggling her arms into the sleeves. That made her breasts protrude against her blouse. Beano was rocking back and forth on the stool, eyes closed, humming 'Walk Away Renee' to himself, face contorted. Leppo was smoking a cigarette, holding it like he was Noël Coward, pretending he didn't know half the pub was looking at him.

And something strange happened. All of a sudden, Eddie felt tired. Everything in the mad frantic pub seemed still now, in his stinging eyes. Everything stopped. He heard the sound of waves breaking on stones. All these people seemed like automatons, a faded brown pose in an old photograph, a frozen tableau, with no light, no movement, no possibility anywhere. Eddie had a sensation of being on the brink of something dangerous, and he swallowed hard to drag himself back to reality. He wanted to shiver and lie down, but he found he could not even move.

In the end, Jennifer's laughing voice intruded.

She invited him to the party they were going to, out in RTE, but Leppo said there might be a problemette. It was pretty strictly RSVP, actually.

Eddie said he didn't mind. He said he had two parties anyway.

And he'd been to the RTE party last year. Crap, he said. Posers and dilettantes and overfed talentless bimbos. She laughed again.

'She said goodbye,' she said, and she kissed him on the cheek. Leppo told him to give him a buzz in London some time.

'We'll get together,' he said, 'and do a few bottles to death.'

After she left Eddie sat for a few minutes, remembering all the good times they'd had. Now he hardly knew her any more. She was so confident too, that was what really annoyed him. She was so confident and together and looking so sexy and brilliant and generally surviving without him. Christ. It was maddening.

Dean Bean leaned across Eddie's lap, his grey tongue lolling.

'Once driven,' he said, 'forever smitten.'

'Yeah,' Eddie said, 'something like that.'

When he looked down at the table, he noticed an envelope with his name on it, and a wet brown glass-ring on the top. Nobody knew where it had come from. He opened it, curiously. Folded into four was a ripped out page from *The Face*. 'The Discreet Charm of Salome Wilde,' said the headline, over the white, modest face. Eddie opened the card. 'Arencha just sick of her?' it said. 'Happy Xmas from Jimmy and Roof.' He looked around, but they were gone. He screwed the page and the card into a ball and started drinking Dean Bean's beer.

He walked all the way home, because no cab would take him. Up past the National Gallery, all solid in the snow, down Merrion Row, along the black railings of the Green, up Earlsfort Terrace and Harcourt Street, past the broken windowless shell of the TV Club, over the bridge and through the now deserted flatland of Ranelagh where he'd been to so many parties and used to have so many friends. Some were in Australia. Some were in the States. One or two were in jail. He remembered the night Ritchie Mulcahy and him had talked their way into some lousy twenty-first in the Harcourt Hotel and talked about poetry. And the time Beano had cried on his shoulder outside the Onion Field and told him he was his best friend in the world. And other nights too, a bleary haze of mad parties and other people's girlfriends.

In the twenty-four hour shop an off-duty branchman was trying to chat up the coy girl behind the counter. His pistol was jammed into the back of his belt and his bomber jacket had ridden up so you could see it. He had sad eyes. The moon was cold and red in the sky. It hung over the great green dome of Rathmines Church like some stupid Christmas bauble.

And his stomach felt better by the time he crossed the old railway and ended up in Beckett Road. His head felt clearer now, and even though his spit was thick when he spat, he knew he probably wouldn't throw up again.

When he thought about Marion, he fought back the realisation that he was a lot happier when she wasn't around. She seemed so far away from him and it was almost like he'd never met her. His foreskin ached from the alleyway earlier on and he wanted to piss. Eddie was feeling low.

An expensive car sat outside the house, with the windows all steamed up and the light on. As he got closer, Eddie saw Patricia and her boyfriend, sitting in the back seat, eating hamburgers and talking. Eddie left them to it. She rolled down the window as he passed by, and Cliff Richard tinkled out of the car. She asked if Eddie wanted to meet the new love of her life, but Eddie said no thanks, and walked into the driveway.

'Charming,' she said. 'My big brother, folks.'

The light was still on in the front room. From the street Eddie could see his father engaged in combat with the Christmas tree. He had a screwdriver in his hand, and he kept prodding gingerly at something, as though he expected the tree to bite back, advancing and retreating like a fencer in a swashbuckling movie. He stood in the garden, staring in through the window. Snow-flakes fizzled on his lips.

When Eddie came into the hall his father was standing there, a vision of overweight anger in his scarlet Christmas cardigan. It was the tree. The lights were acting up, the same as every year.

'If I told her once, I told her a thousand times,' he sighed, 'buy a new set. Jesus. Anyone'd swear we were itinerants.' Eddie sat on the arm of the sofa and watched his father prodding the lights. 'One of these fecking years,' he snapped, 'we'll all be burnt to a crisp in our beds.' Eddie started to snigger, dutifully. His father turned and said it was no bloody joke.

A sudden and deafening *bang* shredded the silence. A turquoise flash illuminated the room. Eddie's father howled and stepped back from the tree. He dropped the screwdriver, clamped his hand into his armpit and roared with pain. The lights blazed brighter, then, one by one, they flickered out, from the bottom of the tree spiralling up to the narrow top, followed by the wall lights and the lights out in the hall, until the whole ground floor of the house was in darkness.

The tree toppled sideways and against the wall, sending a painting crashing to the floor. Tiny plastic bells and balls tumbled onto the carpet. Flames licked up the branches. Eddie ran to the kitchen and filled a saucepan with water. He could hear his father, still yowling in the murk.

Eddie sloshed the water over the tree.

'Jesus, you idiot,' his father snapped, 'do you know what that wallpaper cost me? Jesus.'

After they'd lit the candles and sponged the wall dry they sat in the flickering orange light, drinking from the bottle of duty-free Scotch that Eddie had picked up at the last minute in Heathrow. His father was OK now. He'd just got a little kick.

At first he was a little moody, and they didn't have much to say. He kept standing up and trying the light switch, to see if the light had come back by magic. It hadn't. Eddie offered to have a look at the fusebox but his father insisted no, they'd wait until morning and get someone qualified.

'Probably cost forty quid,' he said, 'on Christmas Day, forty or fifty at least, another fucking fifty out of your life.' Eddie kept pouring drinks, and gradually his father seemed to cheer up. He sighed deeply and said he was sorry for calling Eddie an idiot. 'Second Christmas without Mam,' he said, 'it's just got me down a little.' Eddie said forget it. He told his father to look on the bright side.

He asked if Eddie ever saw his mother over in London.

'No,' Eddie said, 'not much.' His father nodded into his glass and his fingers drummed on the coffee table.

'You know I was fond of her,' he said, suddenly, trying to be disarming, 'don't you?' Eddie laughed and said sure, he knew that. His father said, 'I don't know why, but that's important to me now, it's becoming a big bloody thing with me these days.' Eddie said not to worry. He knew that.

'Things just don't work out, sometimes,' he said. His father said you just never knew where things were going to end up. You just couldn't see what turn your life was going to take. They had another drink. He could see his father loosen up. 'Tell me what's on your mind, Dad,' he said. 'I know there's something.'

And Eddie's father laughed softly, and he told him a story, about a man named Pascal who'd once worked in the bank, when he'd been in the Baggot Street branch. Pascal was a loner. He'd lived in digs, with a Jewish family in Rathmines, had no friends, never went with girls. Well, one year his colleagues had said, 'Look, Pascal, don't stay by yourself this Christmas, go on holiday somewhere.' He'd been reluctant at first, but eventually he said he would. He'd booked two weeks in Spain, gone out every night, got drunk, had a fling with a German woman. He'd phoned Eddie's father and mother up on New Year's Eve to say Happy New Year, and he was having the time of his life and thanks very much for persuading him to take this trip. He'd even put the German woman on the line, Greta her name was, to say hello.

'But she didn't speak much English,' his father said, 'and you know what Mam and me are like for languages.'

'Yes,' said Eddie, 'I do.'

'When he came back from Spain, you know what he did?' Eddie said no, he didn't. His father took a mouthful of whisky. Eddie prepared himself for the corny punchline. 'He killed himself, Eddie. He took an overdose of sleeping pills one night. When they found him he was already dead, no note, nothing.'

There was silence in the room for a few moments. Out on the street they could hear the catcalls of a few drunken kids coming home from Midnight Mass. The clock ticked solidly. It seemed like a long time before either of them spoke.

'Jesus,' said Eddie, 'that's terrible, Dad.'

'Yes,' his father said, 'I think he just realised what he had wasted, in his life, do you know? I think he just saw all that, the way people do sometimes, you hear about it.' There was silence again. 'It happens,' his father said. The sweet and mournful smell of the pine needles hung heavy in the room. 'And it's just that I always think of him at this time of the year.'

'Yes, Dad,' Eddie said, 'I'm sure you must, Jesus.'

'Yes,' he said, 'I really do,' and again, there was silence in the room, a silence that seemed to go on and include the ghost of this sad and dead bank clerk, who had died in a bedsit, dreaming of sangria and on his own.

The silence lasted so long that it became almost unbearable, and Eddie was on the point of yawning and saying he had to go to bed, because he felt that his father wanted to be alone. And he was *just* about to say it, when his father spoke again, as though he had suddenly remembered something.

'One thing, Eddie,' he said. 'What age are you now?'

Eddie said he was twenty-four.

'It's a thing I meant to say to you when you were twenty-one.'
He smiled, embarrassed. 'It's just a small thing, but the fact is,
I don't like being called "Dad". I really don't. I never have, as
a matter of fact. And at your age, I think you should be able to
call me by name. I mean, if you introduce me to a friend of
yours, I don't want you to have to say, and this is Dad, y'know?
It's just a small thing.'

'What,' said Eddie, 'me call you Francis?'

'Frank,' his father said. 'That's my name, that's what everyone
calls me.'

'OK,' Eddie said, uncertainly, 'it'll feel weird, but if that's
what you want.'

'Yes,' he said, decisively, 'that's what I want. I'll be Frank
from now on.'

'And I'll be frank too,' said Eddie. His father laughed and
poured them both another inch of whisky.

'Yes,' he said, 'that'll be the day, Eddie, that *will* be the day.'
The clock struck two, out in the hall. They drank the whisky
and talked about perestroika.

At four in the morning, his father asked Eddie to go check
outside and tell Patricia it was really time to come in. But when
Eddie went out to the road, everything was quiet and black, and
her boyfriend's car was gone. Snow was falling into the road,
banking up on the roofs of the cars and against the sides of the
footpath. White dust.

'They stay out all night sometimes,' his father sighed, shaking
his head dolefully. 'All night long.'

Eddie poured himself one more drink, and he found himself
wondering silently what his mother was doing right then, and
whether she'd remember this pathetic little ghost that his father
had spoken about.

On the stairs, Frank said he thought Patricia should have a
little more respect for herself.

'All night long,' he said, 'it's really not on. She'll get a name
for herself, and then she'll be sorry.' He stood on the stairs for
a moment, fingering the bannister and running his hands through
his hair. Then he turned, and began to slowly climb.

Half-way up, he stopped. He touched the bannister rail again,
gripping it hard, and then releasing. Eddie stared at him from
the hall.

'I love you, son,' he said, without turning, 'you do know that,
don't you?'

'Yeah, Frank,' Eddie said, softly, 'I know that.'

'We don't say that too much in this country,' said Frank. 'Specially man to man.'

'No,' said Eddie, 'we don't.'

And when Frank was gone, Eddie stumbled back inside to finish off the whisky. He sat still in the soft light, trying to drive away the memories of long-gone Christmases. He drank remorselessly, until the bottle was empty. He drank until his stomach ached, and the room was spinning and his head was full of the sound of rushing wind. When he lit his last cigarette his fingers were trembling.

In the silence Eddie tried to imagine the loneliness of fathers, the terrible depth of their loves, their power, their unspeakable vulnerability. Smoke drifted into his eyes. Hot stinging tears began to spill down his face. Eddie hung his head, and he cried like the child that he knew he would always be.

The rest of Christmas passed off, the way Christmas does, in a haze of flatulence and sentiment. The subject of Eddie's mother was not mentioned again. On Christmas morning Patricia fixed the fusebox in five minutes. Then she microwaved the bedraggled turkey, Eddie did the washing up, and afterwards they sat in the TV room with Frank watching 'Twenty-One Years of The Two Ronnies', and drinking flat gin and tonics.

The only rough moment came after the dessert, when Frank raised his glass for a toast.

'To absent friends,' he said, and he started to blink hard, before coughing loudly and disappearing rapidly off to the bathroom. Patricia told Eddie he'd be OK, it was just the wine. Eddie said he knew that.

Patricia must have phoned Rod about fifteen times in the course of Christmas Day. She called him 'funny bunny' and spoke to him in a gurgling baby voice. Eddie said it must have been great to be young and in love and Patricia told him not to be such a cynical old wanker.

'Lovely language,' said Frank, wiping the dust off the Monopoly board with weary resignation, 'oh yes, that's beautiful.'

Over the next few nights Eddie went to a couple of parties with Patricia and Rod, who had a Ford Sierra and a taste for thrash heavy metal. Rod was a trainee auctioneer, but he was

OK. His biggest ambition was to emigrate to Australia. He seemed to like Eddie, even though Eddie didn't like him much, and made it pretty obvious. But Rod was one of these people you can take the piss out of and they think you're kidding around. They think you're being ironic. That type.

Soon as they arrived at these parties, Rod and Patricia would disappear for the night, leaving Eddie to fend for himself. He did his best to consume as much free drink as was humanly possible, chatting up women, laying down the bullshit about what he was up to in London. Sometimes he was a roadie for Terence Trent D'Arby, other times a trainee designer for Katherine Hamnett, other times an investigative journalist for *New Statesman and Society*. But whatever line he laid down, Eddie always ended up staggering home on his own. He could have hung around to get a lift from the funny bunnies, but it was a matter of pride. He'd walk six miles home in the rain, just so's he could tell Patricia the next morning that he'd scored, and left early, while she was upstairs in the coats' room chewing the gob off Rod.

As if it mattered to her, one way or the other.

'Eddie Virago,' she teased him, 'the man who slept his way to the bottom.'

Marion phoned once. They didn't get on well. They had very little to say. She sounded far away, and very down. It was snowing in Donegal, and it had been for days. Eddie thought that sounded picturesque but she said no, it was just cold, and the reservoir had frozen over, and there was nothing picturesque about not bathing for four days. There was a slight echo on the line, so Eddie could hear his words repeating, like he was talking into an iron bucket. There was no crack up in Ballybracken, she said. It was dull. And the hairnet factory had just announced that it was closing down and moving to Portugal, so everybody in the town was depressed.

She said she missed him, and she thought that he didn't miss her as much. She accused him of trying to make small talk. For some reason, Eddie didn't contradict her. When there was a silence on the line she'd say, 'Hello, hello?' as though she thought the line had been cut off, and Eddie found that infuriating. He told her she was getting too dependent. She hung up the phone, and when Eddie rang back there was no answer. He imagined her footprints in the snow, trudging back into the town, cursing him.

That was a bad day. Eddie felt gloomy, sitting around the house with his feet on the furniture, waiting for the phone to ring back, which it never did, not for him anyway.

Yes, that was a bad day. And the next few days too, when she never rang back, they were bad days too. But things were about to get worse. And the day before New Year's Eve, well, that was the day it all went wrong.

At eleven in the morning the doorbell rang. Patricia prised herself wearily up from the kitchen table and sloped out while Eddie sat munching his toasted turkey sandwich, nursing his hangover and trying to make sense of the interminable Reviews of the Year in the papers. Frank had gone to Uncle Joe's house to watch American horse racing on his satellite TV. The kitchen smelt of tangerines, bought by Frank on Christmas Eve, and left untouched in the big white bowl on the table.

Out in the hall Eddie heard a voice, asking if he was in. At first he didn't pay much attention. He was half-way through an article about Bono's ambitions for the nineties. It didn't quite register. Then it came again, and Eddie thought he was hearing things.

He folded the paper, swallowed hard, stood up quickly, stared at the window, wishing somehow that he could disappear. For some reason, he picked up the remains of his turkey sandwich and chucked it in the bin. Then he sat down again, folded his arms and tried to look cool and casual.

He heard Patricia call his name, then the thump of her stockinged feet running up the stairs. A chill licked down his backbone. He heard the front door close against the whistle of wind. He heard his name being called in a voice that was little more than a whisper. He looked through the full-length kitchen window again, and way out over the back wall, out to where the clouds were fleshy and shocking. He heard his name again, a little more boldly this time. Eddie licked his fingers and ran them along his eyelashes, checking his bloated reflection in the kettle. Then he walked into the hall.

'Jesus,' he said, 'great to see you. Unreal.'

Standing just inside the door, rucksack half-capsized on the floor in front of her, was Marion.

She stood very still at first, pulling at her hair and staring around the hall like she was in a church or a museum. She was smiling. She looked healthy and well. Her skin was pink from the cold. She seemed to be wearing layers and layers of clothes, a yellow oilskin, a woollen Dexy's hat and black mittens. She rustled when she moved. When she smiled again, her teeth were whiter than Eddie remembered. Her breath smelt of smoke.

'Surprised?' she said, unbuttoning her coat.

'Yeah,' said Eddie, 'gobsmacked.'

Upstairs the bathroom door slammed, and the muffled sound of the radio burbled against the hiss of water.

'That's such an English expression,' she said.

They kissed, under the sprig of mistletoe that Frank had optimistically sellotaped to the hall lampshade the week before. Eddie kept saying this was amazing, and she apologised for not letting him know in advance.

'No sweat,' he said, 'no big deal. Really.' Marion said the kitchen was bigger than the entire downstairs of her house. 'Oh yeah?' Eddie laughed. 'Is that right?' He looked around, as though he expected the walls to shrink. Then he laughed again, and he said he supposed it was quite big, now that she mentioned it. But Marion wasn't laughing. She scrutinised the sheaf of bills, jammed to the front of the fridge with little banana-shaped magnets. She stared out into the garden, as though she had seen something odd in the grass. Then she took off her coat, and hung it over the back of a chair. 'That's it,' said Eddie, 'just chuck it anywhere.' They sat in the kitchen having coffee and cigarettes. Eddie's head swam with vague panic. His fingers drummed on the table. She kept saying the house was unbelievable. 'So,' he asked, 'what's been going down? Fuck. It's great to see you.'

'Nothing,' she said.

'Really?' he said. 'Quiet, yeah?'

They talked for a while about the wallpaper in the living room. She asked him how much the stereo was worth.

'I knew you wouldn't want to see me,' she said, half-way through her second cup of coffee.

'Don't be crazy,' Eddie laughed, 'I'm just a little surprised, that's all.' He found he was beginning to get a headache. She said she'd just got sick of the bullshit at home, family arguments, the boys rolling in drunk, the sisters all force-feeding their yowling babies around the table.

'Oh yeah?' Eddie giggled. 'Not a baby fan?'

'No,' she scowled, 'I'm really not. Whatever that is.' So she'd hung out till this morning and caught the first bus out. Eddie said his own Christmas had been OK, pretty busy of course, with all the parties he'd been invited to, but OK all the same.

She gave him a parcel. She yanked it from the rucksack, wrapped in blue paper, a yellow sports shirt with a little crocodile over the breast pocket. It was his present. She'd got it in the New Year sale. He told her it was beautiful, although it wasn't the kind of thing he would have picked himself. He hadn't got round to getting anything for her, but he would. She said he didn't have to, it was just a last-minute thought. 'Don't worry,' she told him, 'it was very cheap.'

She came and sat on Eddie's knee, kissing him pretty seriously, and their hands explored each other through clothes.

'Is there anywhere we can go?' she said, after a few minutes.

'Well, we have to be careful,' he told her. 'Gloria will be in later.' Marion asked who Gloria was. 'Nobody. Just a woman,' Eddie said, 'just a woman who comes to do the ironing for Dad, y'know.' Marion laughed out loud. She thought Eddie was joking.

'This is like "Upstairs Downstairs",' she said.

'C'mon Marion,' he said, biting his fingernails, 'Dad just needs a bit of a help.' Marion pinched his arm.

'Now that your ma's gone?' she said, accusingly. Eddie said well yes, actually.

They went up to the spare room and locked the door. When they started making love Eddie could hear the radio in the bathroom being turned up, louder and louder. 'Drugstore Woman'. John Lee Hooker. The bed was too creaky, so they lay on the carpet and continued. Eddie got carpet burns on his knees. John Lee's howling guitar rattled through the walls.

Afterwards she sat on the windowsill in her underwear, smoking the inevitable joint. Eddie said that wasn't exactly a great idea, that they better get dressed, Gloria really would be tumbling in any minute now.

'Oh well,' she sighed, pulling her skirt on, 'we don't want to disappoint Gloria. It's so difficult to get good staff these days.'

She asked him how it had gone with The Hothouse Flowers. Eddie said it had gone brilliantly, much better than he'd expected. He winced as he pulled his denims on over his grazed kneecaps.

'The thing of it is, though,' he said, 'it's all a bit hush hush, contractual, you know, they're not really supposed to be using session musicians, tax reasons, something like that, so if you'd keep it quiet I'd be more than grateful.'

Patricia was down in the kitchen, drying her hair. Eddie introduced her to Marion.

'Yes,' she beamed, in the mirror, 'we've met actually, haven't we, Marion?' Marion said yes, they'd met. Patricia said she had to split.

'Oh yeah?' said Eddie. 'Funny bunny's calling round, is he?' She didn't answer. 'Private joke,' he said to Marion. She shook her head, as if she didn't care. They had another coffee. Eddie pulled out a pen and told Marion to stick her Dublin number down on a piece of paper and they'd get together later on. 'It's so great to have you in town,' he told her. 'We'll have a good time. There's so many people I'd really love you to meet.'

'The thing is,' she said, 'I don't really have anywhere to stay in Dublin.' Eddie said that was a real drag. He scratched his head. 'Yes,' she continued, 'so I was hoping I could maybe stay with you for a couple of days.'

'What?' laughed Eddie. 'You mean here? In the house?'

'No,' she said, 'I'll sleep in the garden shed.'

Eddie began ripping tiny pieces from the newspaper and absent-mindedly chewing them. He suggested another coffee.

Eventually she said that as Eddie obviously didn't want her to stay she'd go to her brother's girlfriend in Cabra. Eddie's laugh became a shrieking falsetto, so amused was he at the prospect that he wouldn't want her to stay. Of course he wanted her to stay. Hell, that was the obvious thing. It just hadn't occurred to him, honest. He just never would have thought of that.

'I'm a bit slow today,' he stammered, 'but that's really a swell idea.'

Eddie took one of Marion's cigarettes and phoned his father at Uncle Joe's. When his father answered the phone he said, 'What's wrong, Eddie, why are you phoning?' Eddie said just to say hello. His father sighed, 'OK, OK, what do you want, Eddie?'

'Something's kind of come up, Frank,' he said.

'Not Mam, is it?' Frank asked, worried. Eddie told him no, it wasn't Mam. She was just a friend from London. Frank asked what did Eddie mean, a friend, and Eddie said really, just a friend, a girl who lived in the same place. Frank asked if they were linked, romantically, and Eddie said no way, absolutely not. Then he said yeah, he supposed they were, that was one way to put it, in a way. He paused.

'Ish,' he admitted. 'Vaguely.'

Frank was very reluctant at first. He really didn't think it was a great idea. But Eddie said he really couldn't throw her out on the street, and her only other option was someone she knew in

Cabra. That seemed to swing it. Frank conceded, provided that they slept in separate rooms and she went around the house in a decent state. He didn't want the place turning into the Folies Bergères – 'even if your mother *isn't* here'. It wouldn't be good for Patricia. Eddie said Frank worried way too much about Patricia.

'She *is* twenty-one,' he said. Frank said twenty-one might seem old to Eddie, but it didn't to him. He said, 'Look, Frank, when you were twenty-one, you were married with a kid.'

'Exactly,' Frank sighed. 'Need I say more?'

At mealtimes Frank seemed shy of Marion. She called him 'Mr Virago' and he said, 'Please, Marion, call me Frank. Feel free.' But when she called him Frank he didn't seem to like it. Neither did she. And in a weird way, neither did Eddie.

Frank didn't say much. He'd eat his dinner with the paper propped up against the milk jug most of the time, clicking his tongue or shaking his head in resigned disbelief at the breath-taking stupidity of politicians. When he did talk, he seemed to say the wrong things somehow, and Eddie was embarrassed. He asked her one day whether living in London she felt like 'the nigger in the woodpile'. Another night they talked about literature and Eddie's father asked who her favourite writers were. She said she never read. She just didn't like books. Eddie said yes she did and she snapped at him, closing her eyes, gritting her teeth, that she didn't. Patricia said she was sure Marion was well able to speak for herself and Marion's face went purple. Then his father said, 'Oh well, coming from up there you must know lots of folk tales, I suppose, fairy stories and the like.' A look of bewilderment settled over Marion's face. 'In the country-side, I mean,' said Frank. That seemed to make things even worse.

When she said her father worked in a sausage factory, Frank said, oh well, that his own grandfather had been a tramp, apparently. Or so he'd heard once, from his brother Joe, who'd once done the family history.

'There's a few skeletons rattling in *our* cupboard Marion,' he beamed, and he laughed, for a very long time.

Eddie knew Marion had taken a dislike to Frank. When he wasn't there, she didn't say much about him. Eddie would tell his collection of funny father anecdotes, but Marion didn't seem to find them funny at all. She didn't seem to like Patricia too much either. She said Patricia dyed her hair too blonde and said 'actually' all the time, something which Eddie said he had never noticed. Actually.

Patricia didn't like Marion either. She didn't say anything much, but Eddie knew. Patricia told Rod that Marion was 'a real character' and a 'totally unique human being' and 'surprisingly different from the other girls Eddie's gone out with'. A pretty damning indictment, coming from Patricia.

It was a strain having her there, and in a way Eddie knew it couldn't last. Something had to give and that much was obvious, even to him. But what happened in the end was a fight, not between Eddie and Marion, not even between Patricia and Marion. The final jawbuster, when it came, was between Marion and Frank. And when it happened, it was the OK Corral all over again.

New Year's Eve had passed off alright, better than Eddie'd imagined, in fact.

Dean Bean and Marion had got on like a house on fire. Beano thought she was one wild chick, for sure. Every time she said something he roared with laughter, grabbed her shoulders and shook her from side to side like a puppy playing with a doll.

'You're so weird,' he roared, 'the way you talk, man, Jesus, it's awesome.' She laughed at Beano too. He told her why he had changed his name and she said he was a fucking idiot, with little to worry about. 'Yeah,' he nodded, 'you're right, Marion, you're so right, man.'

But Eddie'd felt uneasy because Jennifer had showed up at the party too. The rugby player was gone, she said. Tonight her date was some blow-dried and besuited publishing company researcher who looked like he probably still had his communion money. When Jennifer met Marion she said, 'I hear you have the misfortune to be doing a lap of the track with Eddie just now.' Eddie wondered who had told her. When Jennifer turned her back, Eddie saw Marion and Beano taking the piss out of her walk.

Ruth and Jimmy turned up too, but thankfully they didn't stay. Eddie managed to keep them in the hallway, talking about how they should come over for dinner some time in the New Year. He was desperate for them not to meet Marion. He knew there'd be a total blowout if they did. Fuck. It'd be Chernobyl city. When Ruth came back from the toilet, she said there was some really tedious and awful girl on the dancefloor, getting on everybody's nerves.

'You know how it is at these parties,' Eddie shrugged, 'there's always one, isn't there?'

When Jennifer left, Eddie saw her into the hall.

She said, 'She seems very nice, Eddie, pity you didn't tell me.' She pulled a small mirror from her bag and combed her hair.

'I thought you'd be jealous,' he said. Jennifer laughed. She rolled her lips, firming her lipstick.

'Jealous?' she laughed. 'Of her?' Then she kissed Eddie on the cheek and said she'd see him next Christmas. Eddie said maybe he'd come out to Nicaragua to see her some time. 'Yeah,' she sighed, 'sure, Eddie, you do that.' Eddie said he really would, he'd been wanting to see what was going down over there for years.

'*Hasta luego*,' he called, and she waved her mother's car keys at him, disappearing down the drive, bewildered and besuited publisher in hot pursuit.

When he went back into the room Marion was dancing to Elvis Costello's 'Pump It Up', with a long-haired girl in a thigh-length jumper, jumping around arm in arm with Dean Bean and Freda and some other girl that Eddie didn't recognise. Beano was out of his mind as usual, strumming an invisible guitar and stamping his feet, wrenching his head from side to side in time with the drums.

Eddie stood in the kitchen doorway, just looking, swigging from a can of Red Stripe. The music was so loud that the floorboards throbbed. Every time she whirled past him, she either pretended not to see him, or laughed even louder, until he was convinced that she was doing it on purpose. She knew it was bugging the shit out of him.

At midnight she threw her arms around everyone in the room except Eddie.

A couple of hours later Beano spiked their tequilas with angel dust, which was his idea of a good New Year's joke. Marion quite liked it, breathing hard and waving her arms like a windmill, but that's what annoyed Eddie particularly. She seemed so at home and happy, much more so than she ever was with him. When he criticised Beano she said, 'Oh man, don't guilt trip me, don't get righteous on me now.' And she told him not to be such a fucking dry shite, that it was only a bit of fun.

On the way home they were both sick in the taxi. Marion said her New Year's resolution was to be happy with Eddie, forever and ever, and the taxi driver murmured a laconic 'Amen'. When they sneaked into her bedroom and collapsed, she kept saying it, murmuring it in her sleep, along with all kinds of other weird shit about her family that Eddie hadn't heard before and didn't particularly want to hear now.

At the kitchen table next morning she bit her nails and lit a cigarette. Smoke drifted through the room and it made Eddie want to crap. He felt absolutely dreadful. He had terrible diarrhoea and his ass ached whenever he moved. When he closed his raw eyes he still felt out of it. When he opened them he felt worse. No matter how much water he poured down his throat, his tongue was completely parched.

Frank had gone out for his morning jog and Patricia had gone out to Mass. Weird thing to do, Eddie said. But she told him the folk group was quite good actually, and anyway, there was nothing much else to do and they'd probably all go for a few drinks afterwards, all the gang. They were welcome to come along, she said, but Eddie said the very thought of drink made him want to barf his spleen up. Patricia thought that was a shame, and she tried her best not to look relieved. So Eddie and Marion sat in the chilly kitchen alone, listening to Gay Byrne on the radio, pretending that everything was alright.

Frank bustled in, pink with sweat in his shabby black tracksuit, panting softly. He stood legs apart in the middle of the kitchen floor, hands on his thighs, bent over, sucking at the air.

'Health,' he said, and he made a thumbs-up sign. Just that, when he stood up. 'Health.' He started running on the spot, jabbing at the air like a boxer. He looked like he was about to have a heart attack any minute. Eddie told him to take it easy, but he laughed, swallowed a long glass of water, and spat into the sink. 'And how are the lovebirds this morning?' he chuckled, clapping his hands, and slapping himself on the chest.

'Great, Frank,' said Eddie.

'Great,' said Marion, 'Frank.'

Frank turned off the lights. He said there was enough light in the room to light up Broadway. Eddie knew it was going to be one of those days.

Frank made a great show of cooking the fry, chiselling lumps of solid lard off the cold block, scraping the spatula against the greasy edge of the sizzling pan. He peeled rashers off the pack and threw them in, like a pantomime witch throwing frog's legs into a cauldron. When he threw something in, he would stand back, left hand in the air, like he expected it to burst into flames. He cracked eggs and dipped the broken shell up and down, getting every last bit of white. He whistled. He was in a good mood. He was play-acting.

The argument was about abortion. There was some crummy article in the paper about the huge number of Irish women who'd had abortions in England that year, and Gay Byrne said something about it on the radio. He said, 'And of course, we have absolutely no abortion in Ireland, that's what we like to think, oh yes, holy Catholic Ireland, my friends,' just before going to the commerical break.

Marion said it was all disgusting.

'Yes. What can they do?' said Frank. 'They don't have the money, poor things. It ought to be made legal here.'

'That's not what I meant. Money isn't everything,' Marion said. 'It's just wrong. It's taking life.'

'These *priests*,' Frank scoffed, mouth full of sausage. 'Money helps a lot,' he said, 'there's nothing money can't sort. People who tell you otherwise, well, it's all very well, you know. Take it from me, love,' he said, laughing, and he touched her arm.

Marion stared at Frank's fingers, on the sleeve of her sweater. he looked her in the eye and his laugh died away. Her face was dark with anger. His eyes looked watery. She shook her arm slightly, and he withdrew his hand. He held his fingers to his mouth, and coughed. Marion looked even more angry now. She pursed her lips and flicked open a page of the paper. Eddie looked at Frank, and Frank shrugged.

'Hey, chill out, Marion,' Eddie said, 'I think people should be allowed to have abortions, if they want to. I mean, nobody's talking about making it compulsory.'

'Well,' she said, 'I don't care what anyone says, I think it's wrong.'

'Well, I think *you're* wrong,' said Eddie. 'Woman's right to choose, right-on,' and he did a little fist clench in the air.

'Typical man,' she said, spitting the words. 'Leave it all up to the woman.'

'But look, love,' said Frank.

'Don't "love" me,' she said. 'I'm against it and that's that. Sometimes you have to take a stand.'

'But I mean, say if you were in that position yourself?'

'Are you saying something about me?' she snapped, putting her hands on her hips.

'No,' said Frank, 'of course not, I'm just saying, for argument's sake, say if you ended up you know, whatever, in trouble.'

'I'm not that kind of person,' she said, 'don't say that about me.'

'Now, hold on,' he said, 'I'm not saying anything. It's just that I would have thought most educated people could see a case for it, that's all.'

'And I'm not educated enough, is that it?'

'Jesus, love, no, I'm just saying, maybe you look at things differently, I suppose.'

'Well, I wouldn't expect anything else from *you*,' she said, standing up suddenly. The milk jug jolted to its side and spilled its contents into Eddie's lap. 'It's no wonder your marriage broke up,' she hissed.

She stalked from the room, slamming the kitchen door as hard as she could, so hard that the crows in the back garden leaped into the air. Eddie put his throbbing head into his hands.

Frank stared into the garden. He laughed. Then he looked like he was going to break something. The swing was moving in the breeze, and the black chain clanked against the mainframe. He folded his knife and fork, delicately across his plate.

'I want her out,' he said, quietly, without looking at Eddie. Then he stood up with exaggerated calm, walked to the sink, washed his cup. When he had finished he let the water run hard, swishing around the sink with the little red plastic brush while his other hand touched the back of his neck. His fingers worked. He seemed to be actually tugging at the hair on the back of his neck. And then he turned to go into the back garden. He pointed at Eddie and raised his eyebrows. His face was red. He had bags under his eyes. 'I want her out,' he said. 'Now.' His voice trembled.

She cried out on the road, and there was nothing Eddie could do. Every single fucking neighbour seemed to be out walking dogs or children, and every one smiled knowingly but said nothing as they squeezed by on the path.

Eddie said he was disgusted with her.

'Jesus H Christ,' he said, 'how could you speak to him like that? Jesus Christ. He's my father, for Christ's sake.'

She cried even more then. She said Eddie was the one who was always going on about standing up for your principles.

Eddie said yeah, but he knew very well she wasn't opposed to abortion.

'How do you know that?' she said. 'We've never even talked about it.'

'Stop jerking me around, Marion,' he said, 'I know you well enough.'

'You know nothing about me, Eddie Virago,' she said, 'you're so full of bullshit it's coming out your ears.'

Eddie started doing his calm voice.

'You said it on purpose,' he said, 'I don't know what's got into you these days, are you fucking jealous or what? What's with you?'

'Jealous of what?' she said.

'Of my relationship with Frank,' he said, 'you're jealous.'

'*Frank*,' she laughed, 'that's another thing.'

'Yes,' he said, 'Frank.'

'Oh yes, there's a few things I could tell "Frank" about his darling boy alright. Some relationship alright. The man doesn't know the first thing about you. You're terrified of him.'

Eddie said he knew she didn't mean that. He knew it was hard for her. He said he knew coming to stay with him, well, it probably made her aware that he was different, that he came from a different background.

'But money isn't everything,' he said, 'you should realise that, and hey, Dad's as working class as they come, really.'

She slapped Eddie's face, hard.

'You bastard,' she said, 'you're a fucking jumped-up snob, Eddie Virago, you make me sick. Fuck you, and your whole family.'

Eddie turned on his heels and walked away, his face throbbing in the cold. That was fine. That was absolutely fine. She was crazy anyway, there was no doubt about that. Fucking space cadet. He didn't ask to be born middle class. He'd show her, the fucking cow. Jesus. She had a screw loose and no mistake. Toys in the fucking attic or what. Well, she could fuck off. He'd phone Mr Patel right now, tell him he wouldn't be back, tell him to send his stuff on somewhere, to his mother's place maybe, yeah, that would show the fucking bitch. Jesus. It was all over between them, and not a minute too soon. He'd fucking show her.

Half an hour later, Eddie caught up with her down in Rathmines. She tried to get away from him, but he held her arms and wouldn't let her go. She said she'd scream but she didn't. Not at first. Only when he said that she wouldn't dare. Then she hollered like a madwoman. An old woman with a zimmer frame stared at them, as they roared at each other in the middle of the street.

'You're a fucking fool, Eddie, all your friends say it about you, behind your back, they're wise to your act.'

Eddie told her she could make things up and scream as much as she liked, that this would have to be sorted out.

'What's the matter with you?' he kept saying, 'are you sick or something? Is something on your mind?' Marion began to cry again, and she wept like a baby, and her face twisted in choking tears. 'I love you,' he said, 'you know that, come on, I love you.'

Marion said she thought she was cracking up.

'I feel so awful,' she wept, tugging wildly at her hair, 'something's going on in my head.' She wanted to go see a doctor. She said she really didn't feel well and she wasn't putting it on.

So Eddie sat in the lobby of Saint Vincent's hospital for a couple of hours, wondering how the fuck he had ever got into this and how he was ever going to get out. When she came out she felt better. She'd had a good chat with one of the nurses. 'It was just a women's thing,' she said. 'Hormones. I don't want to talk about it. Just a small thing. You wouldn't want to know about it.'

Eddie told her that if she needed a prescription he'd go get it, but she said no, she didn't, she just wanted some fresh air.

They bussed into town and sat on the crisp grass in Stephen's Green, watching an overweight brass band up on the bandstand. Later a troop of little girls in ornate green dresses spangled with harps and Celtic swirls came on and did some Irish dancing. Husbands and wives strolled down the damp paths, with children being dragged reluctantly along, and forced into feeding the ducks.

Eddie said he wasn't sure exactly where they were going any more. He sometimes wondered whether she really knew exactly who she was, and if they still wanted the same things from a relationship.

She said, 'Does that mean you want to break up?' He told her no, he wasn't saying that at all, he was just running a few ideas around the block, and how come any time he said anything, that was the first response? 'You just haven't the guts to walk out,' she said, 'that's your problem.' He looked her in the eye.

'This relationship means heaps to me,' he said, meaningfully, 'I don't want to give up on it now.'

But he knew he was a liar. They sat in the snug of Kehoe's, where Marion laced into the gin and tonic like it was about to go out of fashion, and Eddie felt dog-tired. He was terrified somebody he knew would come into the pub. Even though he had shaved, his face felt bristly and uncomfortable, and his eyes and the top of his stubbled head itched savagely.

She looked so beautiful, so vulnerable, the way she laughed when the colour came back to her face, the way she held his hand between hers, the way she spoke to herself.

'Happy New Year,' she said, bitterly.

Eddie sipped deeply at his pint of Guinness. It tasted sour and poisonous. It made him shiver.

The day she went was bright and cold, a sharp winter day when the frost lay sugared across the spine of the Dublin mountains. The trees on Beckett Road looked like black lace against the sky. Shrieking children disembowelled snowmen on the lawns. And Eddie felt so good he could almost believe everything was going to work out alright.

In the morning he went to collect Marion from Dean Bean's pad in Donnybrook, and she was standing on the doorstep hugging her rucksack when he arrived. Beano had gone out, she said. Into town. Had to see somebody, she said, but he'd catch Eddie later in the Crombie Inn for a drink.

'He's a sweetie,' she said, 'isn't he?' Eddie said yeah, he was, one in a fucking million. 'No, really,' she said. 'He's an absolute dote.'

They went out to Dun Laoghaire early, and they walked around the shopping centre, stopping for coffee and ice cream in one of those horrendous open-plan restaurants, idling up and down the malls with the tracksuited housewives, browsing through the bookshops. When Eddie's back was turned she bought him a slim volume of Samuel Beckett's poetry. She said she had a grandfather who looked just like Samuel Beckett. Eddie said everyone had a grandfather who looked just like Samuel Beckett, that was the thing about grandfathers.

Marion didn't much like Beckett's stuff usually. But there was one poem she'd read once, where he wished his lover was dead, and he'd be walking the streets thinking about her, in the rain, all by himself, in a long coat.

'It was beautiful,' she said, 'so sad.' They couldn't find it in the book, but Eddie said they'd look through properly, later.

Then they walked through the People's Park, watching the pensioners bowling on the dog-turd strewn lawn. Some of the pensioners looked like Samuel Beckett too, but not all of them. Marion pointed to an old couple, the woman in a print dress with bandages round her ankles, the man in a bright shirt and yellow flares and a sun hat. She wondered would that ever be her and Eddie. Eddie said no way. He said he wouldn't wear yellow flares to save his life.

They walked all the way down the East Pier and sat at the end looking over to Dalkey Island. Way out near the mudflats was a little green boat, and a young boy was rowing, all on his own, straining back and forth with the oars. In nearer the beach, brave-hearted rubber-clad yuppies skimmed in close on windsurfers, howling and whooping with joy. On Sandycove a gaggle of nuns tiptoed along the beach, wind buffeting their wide white wimples, roaring around the stern shadow of the Joyce tower and the architect's house. Eddie told Marion all about Stephen Dedalus, how he left university to become the uncreated conscience of his race.

'Jesus,' she said, 'that must have got a few laughs in the student bar.' Marion was happy. She sang bits of Bros songs in her awful voice, with her eyes wide open, conducting herself with her fingers. Up the top of the tower she walked around the edge, running her hand along the stone. She said it would be a good place to make love, and Eddie said that was a very Joycean thing to say. 'Typical Irish. Everything has to be Joycean with you,' she sighed, 'it can't just be dirty.'

'Typical Irish,' said Eddie, 'is actually the most typical Irish thing anyone could say. Specially when you say it like that.'

Standing outside Embarkation, she made him promise not to go immediately. She made him say he'd stay there waving on the pier until the ship had slipped through the harbour walls and couldn't be seen any more. And Eddie told her he didn't go for this sentimental trip, but in her case he'd make an exception.

She said she was sorry for what had happened, but she just hadn't been feeling well lately. Eddie told her it was OK.

'Things will get better,' he said. She asked him would his father ever speak to her again. Eddie said he didn't think they were destined for a beautiful relationship, no. She pursed her lips and nodded.

'My nerves,' she said. 'My mother used to complain about her nerves, and I never used to know what she meant. Now I do.' Eddie said his mother used to complain about her nerves, too. He said he guessed that was just part of being a mother. Marion said yes, that was probably true, not that she'd know. 'There were no photographs,' she said, 'in your father's house, no photographs of your mother anywhere.' Eddie said he was sure he had one somewhere. He'd dig one out and show her some time.

'People say she looked like Audrey Hepburn,' he said. She told him he really should go see his mother when he came home to London. 'Yeah, yeah,' he said, 'tell me about it.'

'You will come back to me,' she said, 'won't you, Eddie Virago?'

''Course I will,' said Eddie, planting a kiss on her cold cheek, 'I'll see you tomorrow. The plane's at seven in the morning. I'll be home before you're even out of bed.'

'Don't forget to wave,' she said, 'you promised. I'll be watching. And if the boat sinks and I'm drowned think how awful you'll feel.'

Eddie said he would, but he didn't. As soon as she slipped through the barrier he raised his collar, furtively, and shuffled off to the bus stop. He knew she would never be able to see, not from way down the other end of the pier like that. No way.

He sat in the Nora Barnacle Lounge of the Crombie Inn, right up at the top of the shopping centre, looking out over Dublin Bay and writing her a letter. He just felt he might be able to express himself more clearly in words. But every page, every line almost, seemed so clichéd and inarticulate that he either crossed it out or shredded up the paper. He watched the mailboat slide across the water, way past Howth, out into the mist, until it was just a tiny black snail, with a silver trail of water behind it. He wondered would he ever be able to leave her.

Dean Bean showed up, late of course. But he bought the first round so Eddie didn't complain.

He said no hard feelings about the other night, the angel dust, all of that.

'I'm a royal asshole,' he admitted, 'I know that, I'm just a complete dork, man, you were right to mouth off at me.'

They drank a pint, in silence. But they were good friends, so silences didn't bother them. Eddie got another round.

'Marion,' said Beano, sipping the black liquid up through the froth, 'Jeez, man, she's one great girl, you know, I think she's just ace, I gotta tell you that.' Eddie said yeah, she was. 'Have to hand it to you, Eddie boy,' he said, 'you've really struck gold with that girl.' Eddie said he was sorry for landing Marion in on top of him, but she just had nowhere else to go. Beano told him to forget it. He said they'd really clicked, and hell, it was only for a few days, anyway. And it was great to meet someone like her. 'You come over here like me,' he said, 'and you just meet college types, makes you think all Irish girls are into deconstruction and debs balls, y'know. But it's like another country up there.' Eddie laughed.

'Yeah,' he said, 'that's what all the hassle is about.'

They drank a few more pints and a whisky each, and they went into town to McGonagle's. Eddie wanted to go home. He told Beano his flight was at seven, but Beano said come on, his last night in Dublin, they'd have to sink a few.

'For old times' sake.' Eddie laughed.

'Beano, you're twenty-five, you're not old enough to say "for old times' sake".' Beano said he knew that, but fuck sake, he was young and single and fixing to mingle. Eddie said OK, he'd go, but he'd no Irish money left. Beano said no problem. He paid.

In the cavernous darkness of McGonagle's Beano met some girl he knew, some blonde swatchdog with a fake Dublin accent. They stumbled into each other on the floor, while the DJ played some awful glam number from the mid-seventies and Eddie tried to slam dance. The girl seemed to be either very drunk or very stoned and Eddie had to watch while she and Beano went on at each other, roaring into each other's ears, laughing in each other's faces.

Afterwards they sat, all three, in one of the freezing alcoves, drinking a bottle of Polish beaujolais out of plastic cups. Couples clung to each other under the revolving mirrorball. Some asshole was walking round the floor with a smoke machine in his hand, and the dry ice made everybody's eyes water. Beano got up to talk to the guy, started arguing, ended up shaking hands and going outside. Eddie winced as he polished off his cup of wine. He recognised the signs. Beano was onto a score.

The girl started talking to Eddie about her boyfriend, who she'd just got rid of.

She said to Eddie, 'I think my growth just threatened the balance of the relationship, y'know?' Eddie said he was sorry to hear she had a growth, and he hoped it wasn't too painful.

She ordered another bottle of wine, and Eddie sat there helping her with it. She had more and more to drink, and she started crying and saying she just didn't know who the hell she was any more, and she wanted to get in touch with the deeper parts of herself. Just then Beano swaggered back over.

'Yeah, well,' he said. 'Who doesn't?'

They danced for half an hour, Eddie, the girl, Dean Bean and some guy with long dirty hair and a tie-dye army surplus jacket, who seemed to want to hold hands in a ring.

Afterwards the girl left with the hippy and Beano and Eddie stood in McDonald's doorway on Grafton Street for a while. Beano seemed reluctant to go home. He was in a weird mood. He kept clapping his hands and saying he was just waking up now.

'How about coffee?' he laughed.

'Let's give our arteries something to think about, eh? What you say, Eddie? It's still early. Hows about it? Huh?'

Everywhere was closed, so Beano paid for a cab back to Eddie's place. For half an hour, Eddie said, not a minute longer.

Frank had gone to bed, and Patricia was out, as usual. Eddie showed Beano into the living room and told him to keep real quiet.

Beano kept giggling. When he raised the rizla to his lips to lick the skins closed, he forgot to stick out his tongue. He rubbed the papers against his lips, cursing and laughing as the tobacco and dope scattered all over the front of his shirt.

When Beano rolled up his sleeves, Eddie could see the marks on his forearms, little blueblack pinpricks, some of them still bloody. Beano was at it again, but Eddie said nothing. He didn't want to spoil things. This time tomorrow he'd be back in London, and Beano would just have to look after himself. He'd said it all before anyway. Beano knew the chances he was taking. And if he didn't, he should have.

Beano was in one of his sentimental moods. He always got sentimental when he'd been taking drugs. He wanted to talk about mistakes. All the mistakes he'd made with girls. And the time in first year when he and Eddie had gone swimming in the lake the night the exam results came out, Jeez Louise, that was the biggest mistake of all. The things that what's her name had said about him. What he tried to do and what he didn't try to do. He'd tried to open her shirt. She'd told everybody he was a rapist.

'Can you believe it, Ed,' he scoffed, 'me, a rapist? Can you dig it? I mean, sickorama.'

They talked about their friends. Fergus wanted to be a film director. Now he was unemployed. Casey wanted to be a novelist. He was illegal in New York, working as a hospital clerk. Jimmy Sterne, the great future criminal lawyer and defender of the poor, was now working in a television repair shop in Auckland. Paul O'Brien, Ireland's first anarchist Taoiseach, was managing a disco bar in Carrickmacross. Tim Stoker, the man who put the Boomtown Rats on at Belfield when he was Ents Officer, now ran his uncle's pornographic video store. The women had done better. Michelle Gratton was working for a big ball-bearing company down in Cork, raking in the dosh. Sinéad and Maureen were both on travelling scholarships, a year in Geneva, a year in Rome, a year in Budapest. Susan Lever was reading the news on Century Radio. Eimear was working for Aertel. Jennifer was over in Nicaragua. Katie Ross was editing some women's magazine over in London. And that Salome sodding Wilde of course, the cow, she'd hit the jackpot, presenting that pseudy arts show on Channel Four. Yeah. The girls were all doing fine. But the guys, Jesus, the guys. A collection of primadonnas and has-beens and never-weres and casualities and out and out chancers.

'If bullshit was energy,' Beano sighed, 'we could have put Sellafield out of business.' He laughed as he sipped his beer. 'We believed it, Eddie, that's the funny thing. We were the worst. All that future leaders crap.'

Eddie said he'd never believed it. Anyway, he was doing OK and no way was he a failure. Things were shaping up well for him, and the new year would be fine. He was writing more now than ever before, had a whole album of stuff together, really good stuff too. And his guitar playing was improving every day, everybody said it. He said Beano'd be OK too, soon as he decided what he wanted to do with himself. That took time these days. You had to understand that. But Dean Bean was a talented guy. He'd rise to the top of the pot, no problem.

'Like scum,' Beano said.

'Come on, man,' Eddie laughed, 'you get back to the writing, Beano, you're a real wordsmith.' Beano said he didn't write much any more.

'Anyone can write,' he scoffed. 'Oh yeah, the Great Irish Novel, Jesus man, a computer could write that. A bit of mother-love, a touch of suppressed lust, a soupçon of masochistic Catholic guilt, a bit of token Britbashing, whole shitloads of limpid eyes and flared nostrils and sweaty Celtic thighs, all wrapped up in a sauce of snotgreen Joycean wank.' Eddie laughed again. 'Like I say,' said Beano, 'anyone can do it.' Then Eddie said there was nothing worse than having ambition without the talent to match.

'Sad people,' he said, shaking his head dolefully.

They prised open the door of Frank's drinks cabinet and poured two large glasses of port. Eddie filled the bottle up with Ribena and replaced it, carefully.

'One thing, Ed,' said Beano, 'I've known you for a long time, yeah?'

'Yeah,' Eddie said, with trepidation. He didn't like conversations that started like this.

'There's just one thing I want to say to you, man. It's just – I don't want you to get uptight now, OK, but I think when you're in a tight corner, Eddie, it's always best to be straight about it, you know. That's what I find, myself.' Eddie asked what he meant. He said he meant nothing. Just to be straight, with your friends. He said it was just a thing people said about Eddie sometimes. Maybe he could be a little straighter with people, nothing heavy, just maybe a little straighter, that was all. 'And with Marion, too,' he said, 'it's none of my business Ed, but you wouldn't ever bullshit her, would you?' Eddie said of course not, and he wanted to know what Marion had said to him.

'We have a very honest relationship,' he said.

Beano said she hadn't said anything at all. She just seemed very kind of fragile to him. Eddie said he did know that actually, he had noticed, and Beano said hey, chill out, he knew that.

'Nobody knows that better than you, Ed,' he smiled, 'I'm just thinking out loud, you know, it's just the Mary Jane.' He offered the joint but Eddie said no. He leaned over and slapped Eddie on the thigh. 'Come on, Eddie, lighten up, willya?' Eddie said he was fine, really. Beano rolled up another joint and said it had been great to see Eddie again, and he was a really good friend.

Eddie said the feeling was mutual. But the atmosphere in the room had changed, and they both knew it.

Beano left at four-thirty, when the birds started to sing and the milkvan was chinking up Beckett Road. Just before he left Eddie said, 'Oh yeah, I forgot, I got you a Christmas present.' He went to his pocket and handed Beano a paper bag, without looking him in the eye. This would show him.

'Aw, Jesus, man,' said Beano, 'you shouldn't have, really.'

'Well,' Eddie said, 'I knew you liked Sam Beckett, so I couldn't resist.'

Beano was knocked out. He thumbed through the book looking shamefaced. He told Eddie he was a great guy, and he was sorry if he'd said anything to upset him.

'Jesus,' he said, 'I feel so small, if I'd known you were gonna get me something, I'd have got you something.' Eddie said forget it. 'You're a generous guy, Eddie,' said Beano, 'you really are.' Then he stumbled down the driveway, turning to wave the book. ''Preciate it, Ed,' he called. 'Stay on top, man, yeah?'

'Wanker,' Eddie said, as he closed the front door.

Eddie turned on all the lights and cleaned the place up a little. He tried to stay awake, because he knew that if he went to bed he'd never wake up for his flight. He walked through the house, tidying, thinking all the time, despite himself, of how his mother used to haunt the place with her presence.

He couldn't get her out of his head. Pictures and images and silly things she used to say drifted through his mind, and he wondered why. Then in an instant, he knew. It was that fucking smell again. The Christmas smell of the dying pine needles, thick on the carpet, all sweet and mysterious. It just reminded him of so many things. It was Proust city, it really was. But the more he thought about her the more distant she seemed. He looked at his watch. It was way too early to ring her. But he missed her so much that he'd almost forgotten what she looked like. He couldn't conjure up her face, no matter how hard he tried. So he stopped trying and left a note for his father.

His head was beginning to pound. His fingers shook as he held the pen. He thought about his father, and hoped he'd be OK. He wanted to say, 'Frank, I love you', he really did. But for whatever reason, he found that he could not.

At five-thirty the taxi came, and at six-fifteen Eddie found himself slumped over a table in the Departures lounge, sur-rounded by businessmen with sharp, still shower-wet haircuts and expensive suits, and women in smart red dresses and lime-green coats.

When he reached out to take the cup of coffee his fingers trembled, and the waiter gave him a look of camp understanding.

Out on the tarmac, the stink of the sea howled in from Donnycarney. Eddie looked at the squat, round, black and yellow hulk of Dublin Airport, his favourite place in the whole of Ireland. He wished there was a bank of photographers there to record his departure. He wanted to punch the air and make V-signs.

'Good Christmas?' the stewardess said.

'Yeah,' said Eddie, 'you?'

'Quiet,' she said, 'but yeah.' She continued down the aisle, offering the basket of sweets. 'Good Christmas?' she said, to everyone. 'Good Christmas?' her voice rising to a whoop of sincerity. 'Good Christmas? Quiet? Oh well, mine was quiet too.'

As the plane climbed upwards the sky was still white, and the clouds were tinged with yellow where the sun was trying to overcome them. Steam flowed from the wings. Eddie tried to read the *Irish Times* but he couldn't hold his eyes open. He fell into a paranoid sleep, from which he woke every few minutes, with a sudden and nauseating jerk, whenever the plane bucked or banked. Once when he woke up the whole seascape seemed to have tilted over on its side, and Eddie stared numbly through the port-hole at the foaming grey water in front of his eyes.

He tried to say a silent prayer that he wouldn't throw up, but he realised that he'd forgotten the words of the Hail Mary. 'Wow,' thought Eddie, 'this is a big day.'

In the absence of sickbags, he vomited into a rolled up copy of the *Daily Telegraph*. Then he fell into a mumbling sleep again. And somebody put a blanket over him.

When the plane hit the tarmac at Luton Eddie woke up gibbering. He hauled himself down the steps and into Arrivals.

A handsome black man in a sky-blue jacket asked him some questions. Just for the sake of security, he said. Eddie couldn't take his eyes off that jacket. It had the letters 'LA' on the breast pocket, in snazzy gold letters. Eddie almost laughed out loud.

'LA' stood for Luton Airport. Not the other LA. Luton Airport was about as far from the other LA as any place could be. No doubt about that.

It was just the kind of funny little thing that gave Eddie a thrill to notice. LA. Coming into land at LA. Christ. Wait till Marion heard about this one.

Eddie finally staggered into the Brightside at three that afternoon. Marion had gone to the bank on the far side of town. She'd left a message with Mr Patel.

'She hoped the traffic will not be too bad for you,' he said. Then he told Eddie it was great to have him back, and that he'd missed their chats. Eddie asked how Mrs Patel was doing. Mr Patel said she was well, a little sick in the mornings, but OK, considering. He crossed his fingers on both hands. Eddie asked was there any chance of a glass of water, and Mr Patel lifted two glasses, smelt them, then filled them at the tap. 'Yes,' he said, 'I'm praying for her every day.'

'That's great,' said Eddie. 'I'm happy for you.'

'Yes,' said Mr Patel, 'it is great.' Eddie clinked his glass. '*She* is great,' said Mr P.

'Yes,' said Eddie, 'she is.'

'No,' said Mr Patel, holding one finger in the air, 'she is great with child.' He mimed a bump over his abdomen, and he laughed. 'Is that true?'

'That's true,' said Eddie, 'now, if you'll 'scuse me, I have to crash.'

Upstairs, the room seemed too full. Papers and bills and other junk seemed to fill every inch of space. Shirts and towels lay folded over the balcony, drying. Eddie's guitar case was on top of the table, with a vase of wilting geraniums on top of that. A pile of dismembered magazines sat on the chair, with the scissors beside them. There were a couple of new alphabet letters on the walls, but the place was getting too small and the letters didn't help. You could hardly see any of the wallpaper now, just a tiny patch here and there. All those stark and frozen letters seemed to suck the air from the room and make the walls close in a little.

And all of a sudden Eddie started feeling really weird. Just in an instant. He was hot and cold at once. He shivered. The day was cold but when he touched under the arm of his shirt, the cotton was soaked through with sweat.

He lay on the bed for a few minutes, hoping he hadn't got flu. He opened his shirt. Then he closed it again. Then he got bored. He stood up and walked up and down the carpet, kicking at things. He looked over his shoulder. Then he went to the door and turned the key in the lock.

He undid his damp shirt and took it off. Then he pulled open his fly buttons and stepped out of his jeans and underpants in one go, yanking them over his shoes. He pulled the shoes off then, and the socks, clattering them into the far corner of the room.

He touched his forehead and tasted alcohol on his fingers.

Then he knelt down on the floor and slowly pulled open the drawers, as though the creaking might give him away. He felt like a burglar. He scattered her sweatshirts and her blouses through the air. He held one of her bras against his chest and he laughed. In among some fancy underwear that she never wore he found some letters. One from her bank manager saying her overdraft was becoming considerable. One from her mother that said she hoped things had improved, and that we all had to put the past behind us, and that life wasn't all full of terrible things, that there was joy too.

Her mother's handwriting was almost identical to Marion's.

He read her letter again, wondering what she was talking about. He sat on the bed for a long time, going over it and over it again, looking for some clue. Then he put all the stuff back, convinced she was going to notice.

Eddie didn't know what he was looking for.

Bored again, he lifted the pillows, looked under the bed, felt on top of the wardrobe, reached in behind the radiators. You never know what people are going to leave behind in hotel rooms, specially in a cheap hotel like the Brightside.

He lifted the mattress. The galaxy of letters glared down from the wall.

Eddie pulled out the folder. It was a blue plastic file folder, with the words 'The Doors' scribbled on in biro. Marion's politics notes. Absent-mindedly he flicked through the photocopied pages of illegible scrawl, then to the back of the pad. He saw his name 'Eddie Virago' written out a few times in the margins, in different scripts, then 'Marion Mangan', then 'Marion Virago', then 'Eddie Mangan'. Eddie smiled.

Slipped into the clear plastic sleeve on the back cover were a couple of photocopied pages, folded over. Eddie pulled them out.

It seemed to be some kind of list, or maybe a directory. It wasn't alphabetical. You could see the rough black lines around each entry, where each one had been cut out of a sheet and pasted down. Names of judges, politicians, policemen, with their addresses underneath. One or two were circled in red biro. Others had tiny words that Eddie couldn't understand, scribbled in the margins. One had a red cross drawn carefully from bottom right to top left of its square.

Eddie lay back on the bed. He read the entire document from start to finish. He had seen stuff like this before. This was serious shit.

Outside, the moon was coming down already through the clouds, a red scar slashed across the flesh of sky, and the clouds behind were like great purple bruises. Those letters were really getting out of hand, marching up and down the walls like that. Like dumb silent soldiers. Or pretty maids, all in a row. Eddie lay on his back and when he closed his eyes he almost thought he saw flames.

The next thing he knew he was howling, his hands clawing at the air. Marion was in the room, sitting by the window, slowly strumming an open chord on his guitar. In an instant she was by his side. He lay back on the pillow and his heart pumped harder than he could ever remember, so hard that he could see his chest move in and out.

'It's alright,' she said, 'just a nightmare.' Eddie craned his neck and looked around the room. There was a bucket on top of the wardrobe, and water dripped into it. He tasted salt when he licked his lips. 'You must have a guilty conscience,' she smiled.

Eddie lay back down and covered his face with his hands.

'I don't have a conscience,' he said, 'I had it surgically removed.'

'It's eight o'clock,' she said.

'You look thin,' he said, 'are you losing weight?'

'My project notes,' she said, grabbing the folder from the bedspread. 'What did you think you'd find? Love notes?'

'Why do you need all those addresses?' he said.

'For my nightcourse project, of course,' she said, stuffing the folder into a drawer. 'I have to write to all these old tossers and send a questionnaire.'

'Are you sure that's all?' he croaked.

'Eddie,' she laughed, 'what's the matter with you?'

She told him he was welcome home, and she said she'd take him out for dinner to celebrate. She'd found a new place down the end of Montgomery Street and it looked cheap. Eddie wasn't in the mood, but she insisted. She made him go and shave.

'Marion,' he said, still shaking when he came out of the bathroom, 'do you mind if I ask you something?'

'No,' she said, suspiciously.

Wind threw dust against the windowpane. The draught threw a paper into the air, where it bounced, like it was on a string.

'I'm sorry to have to ask,' he said, 'but I think you should tell me the truth.' Marion stood up and looked frightened. She walked to the desk and pulled a cigarette from the packet.

'You can ask me anything you like, Eddie, you know that. If you're really prepared for an answer, you can ask me anything you like.' Eddie snapped at the floating paper, and he put it on the bed. He wondered exactly what she meant.

'It's just Beano,' he said, eventually, 'crazy, I know, but there wasn't anything between you guys, was there?' Marion's face melted to a smile.

'You must be absolutely crazy,' she laughed. 'Dean Bean's far too nice for me.' She pointed to her neck, then she nodded at Eddie. 'There's blood here,' she said, 'you've cut yourself.'

Ten minutes later, while he lay on the bed counting his money, Marion picked up a pillow and held it hard over Eddie's face, giggling like crazy. It was her idea of a joke.

In January, Marion got a part-time job on the checkout of the Navarone Supermarket on Cypress Avenue.

And if there was one thing she really liked about working there, it was catching shoplifters. It wasn't a sadistic trip. Sometimes she even felt sorry for them. But it used to amaze Eddie that her day was only complete when she'd caught one of them in the checkout line and made them face up to what they were doing in front of all the other customers.

At first Eddie argued. He pointed out that anyone who was desperate enough to shoplift deserves a break. But she said that was the whole point. If they got caught they'd be nicked, and they'd be the very people who'd be sent to jail. So it was important to stop them from doing it. Eddie had to concede that she had something there.

'That's the trouble with you cappuccino liberals,' she scoffed, 'you're too busy saving the world to think anything through.'

After that, it became a joke between them. She'd come home in the evenings and Eddie would say, 'Catch any today?' He told her she should paint little shoplifters on her till, tiny little bewildered cartoon ladies with tiny little bulging carrier bags, one for every shoplifter she nabbed. Sooner or later it caught on. Even Mr Patel would say it.

'Hello, dear, bag any today?'

Once, even Mrs Patel said it, and Mrs Patel wasn't exactly the loquacious type. Marion said they were all jealous, because her job was more exciting than theirs. And when it came to that, Eddie couldn't argue.

B'n'S continued to be a total drag. In February the office pipes all froze up in the cold snap, and Eddie sat in the Goldfish Bowl miserably shivering and blowing his fingers. Miles was in a bad mood. The cold weather was a godsend, he said, as far as B'n'S was concerned. The council workers were bound to go on strike, and people's rubbish would be piling up in the streets. But half the motorways were closed down or generally fucked up, so he couldn't get the product out to the people. He seemed to spend all day in his office haranguing bureaucrats over the telephone and screeching at the secretary.

'This world is full of assholes,' he said. 'That's my fucking motto.'

Eddie stopped being shocked by the Lads. But now their crude jokes and their Next suits and their horrible pimples were beginning to irritate and bore him so much that he often contemplated just chucking the whole thing in and going home. They sat around the office all day constructing phalluses out of paperclips, waiting for the telephone to ring and having competitions to see which of them could fart the loudest. That was bad enough. But when the Lads flipped into philosophical mood, it was unbearable.

One particularly cold afternoon there was a discussion in the Goldfish Bowl about whether Princess Diana had been a virgin or not, when she'd got married. Johnny K claimed to know for a fact that she hadn't been.

'Look,' Keith said, 'how the fark could you know something like that? Goes down Peckham way much then, does she?' Johnny K tapped the side of his nose and said he just knew, he had it on very good authority. Ketih said that was crap. 'I mean, you can't have someone coming along in a few years time saying "I fucked the Queen", can you, Johnny? It'd be all over the *Sun*, wouldn't it, you farking wally. There'd be questions in Parliament and everything.'

Eddie sat in the corner, with his arms folded, just listening, and wishing silently that he could get away.

Marion got moody sometimes, specially in the evenings, but as time went on Eddie got to handle her better. He realised that when she stormed out of the room shouting to be left alone, she really did mean that she wanted to be left alone. Marion wasn't the tactical type, and Eddie found that hard to get used to. The girls he'd known before, well, he just wasn't accustomed to taking anyone at face value. Half an hour walking up and down President Street and she'd be fine. Eddie'd sit on the bed strumming his guitar and waiting for her to come back. And once he'd learnt not to refer to anything that either of them said during an argument, things were OK. Most of the time.

On the morning of Valentine's Day they had a ferocious row about the best way to boil an egg, and she went out to the supermarket without saying goodbye. In work that afternoon, Eddie wanted to call her up, but he was too proud. That night she was late home and Eddie was worried. He spent a half-hour opening the anonymous Valentine cards he'd sent to himself and propping them up on the windowsill. At nine o'clock he came down and asked Mr Patel if he knew where she was. He could tell by the look on his face that Mr Patel knew they'd been fighting. They sat in the back room watching the news and telling each other they were sure she'd be OK. Mr Patel said women were temperamental.

'You have to give them enough rope,' he said, 'she's probably just gone to see a friend.' At eleven o'clock she still wasn't home. Eddie started pacing the lobby like an expectant father, chainsmoking. At half-one she rang and Mr Patel came up to tell Eddie it was bad news. Marion was in the hospital.

They drove down to the hospital together, thinking the worst. In the car Mr Patel looked more terrified than Eddie. He said if she needed to go private they could arrange it on his insurance.

'I'll handle it, Eddie,' he insisted, 'just don't worry about a thing.' Eddie's jaw felt too numb to speak.

But when they got to the hospital she was OK, standing outside on the steps with her hands bandaged in gauze and a scared look on her face. Her clothes were black and scorched and her hair was plastered to her forehead with sweat. Soon as she saw Eddie and Mr Patel she ran to the car and burst into tears. She hugged Eddie hard, and Mr Patel put his arms round both of them, clapping them on the shoulders. He said everything would be alright.

What'd happened was that at lunchtime Marion had gone out to get a sandwich. One of the other women, Muriel, had dozed off in the staff room and that was when the fire had started. Lunchtime was busy, so nobody had noticed. It must have been a cigarette. That was Mr Patel's theory.

'When I got back, she was on fire,' Marion giggled. 'Her back was burning and I tried to put it out.' She was still a little hysterical. She kept laughing, for no good reason. She told Eddie, 'She said "I'm burning", just like that, and she kept saying it.' Eddie told her to try not to think about it. He was sure Muriel would be alright. 'No,' she said, 'I don't think so. They said she'd be in hospital for weeks.' Eddie told her she shouldn't blame herself and she gave him a weird look. 'I don't,' she said, 'she'd be dead if it wasn't for me.' Mr Patel said that was right, and that she should be proud of herself. She laughed again. Then she went very quiet.

That night Marion didn't sleep at all. She sat by the window reading by torchlight, staring down into the street. When Eddie woke up at seven she was still there, naked, with a cup of coffee and a full ashtray beside her. Her eyes were dark. There was a pile of cut out letters on the desk, and it must have been an inch high. She looked very thin.

Eddie took a few days off to look after her. He could see she was badly shaken. She stayed in bed for two days, with the curtains drawn in the room, smoking endlessly and drinking bottles of cheap wine. Eddie told her maybe she should cut down a bit.

'It really does you no good,' he said, 'it really doesn't.' But she wouldn't listen. She kept telling Eddie not to start, that she just wasn't able for him. She said if he wanted to give lectures he should fuck off back to UCD. When he tried to hold her, she squirmed. He brought her sandwiches, but she wouldn't eat.

Eddie wrote a couple of songs in the weeks after that. One was called 'The Old One Two'. Another was called 'Waxman'. He played them both to Marion to cheer her up, and she said she liked them. He told her to be absolutely honest. She said they were fine, really. He told her not to pull any punches, he could take it.

'OK,' she admitted, 'I like them, but I don't like them that much.' They had a fight.

Eddie said he was sick to death of the way she discouraged him. He wanted to know how come he was supposed to help her all the time, and whenever he looked for the tiniest scrap of reassurance she let him down. She sat very still in the bed, with her bandaged hands resting on the pillow in front of her and her eyes closed.

'Can't you see why I'm not honest with you?' she said, very calmly. 'Can you not see that?'

Later they forgave each other. They made love for the first time in weeks, but something was different, and it wasn't just that Marion had to keep her aching hands by her side. Afterwards she got up and went down to the kitchen. She said she just wanted to check the oven was off. She thought she could smell something burning. She was convinced. Eddie said he'd go, but she wouldn't let him. She pulled on his shirt and went down. That was the fifth time she'd done this, since the fire. She came back to bed with a glass of milk.

'You just never know,' she whispered, in her sleep. 'It's only the wallpaper keeps us apart.'

Clint found a lock-up garage for The Honey Bees to rehearse in, a cold concrete-floored place that smelt of mouldy carpet and battery acid, with racist graffiti daubed over the door. It was in an alley at the back of Gray's Inn Road and it belonged to Clint's deaf uncle. A dump, with the acoustics of a diving bell, but at least it meant they didn't have to pay for rehearsal space and they could have it for as long as they wanted. The drums were always way too loud and the valves were blown in the communal amp, so the sound was ropey and full of screaming feedback. There was no microphone either – they just couldn't afford one – so Eddie had to howl until his throat ached just to be heard above the clatter.

Ginger had been practising like crazy over Christmas. She'd

picked up a couple of bass riffs off Buzzcocks records, but she was still no virtuoso. Her right hand was always wrong. She attacked the strings like she was scratching an itch. And her left hand was graceless and clumsy, wrapped around the neck like she was trying to strangle some animal to death.

The others had all been writing, and they revealed their songs with the pride of Renaissance sculptors unveiling statues. Only Eddie was reluctant to come out with his new stuff.

'I'm just not ready,' he said, 'you can't rush art.'

Brian said he hated Ginger becase she was a crappy musician. In fact he hated her because somebody had told him she was a lesbian. Clint said he had nothing against lesbians.

'If it comes to that,' he said, 'that's just about my favourite fantasy, you know, two women together.' Eddie said he didn't think that was exactly right-on.

When The Honey Bees played, they sounded like a group doing an impression of what they thought music should be. They all did the correct things, but it never sounded quite right. It never really gelled, and as Clint said, mysteriously, 'If it doesn't gel, it isn't aspic.' For a start, the timing was always just *slightly* out. That was Brian's fault. Brian had Van Gogh's ear for music. When Clint told him that he said, 'Hey, that's great, thanks Clint,' like it was a compliment. Sometimes Eddie had to sit a number out just so he could stand beside Brian's high hat, banging out time with a brush, and going 'one two three four' with the long-suffering air of a medieval martyr.

Marion got them a gig in the Pride of Erin. If they wanted it. One of her awful friends was going out with the assistant manager. Séamus Mulligan, the guy who booked the bands. 'Famous Séamus', he called himself. It was usually trad and country, but she said they might give The Bees a break.

'They're always looking for cheap acts,' she said.

Eddie sent a tape. Famous Séamus called one night and said he thought they were a load of shite, to be absolutely honest, it just wasn't his type of sounds, a bit too groovy for him, but if they wanted to open for The Hounds of Ulster in two weeks he'd arrange it. Eddie said OK, he wasn't proud.

'No,' Séamus laughed, 'I wouldn't be, but fair play to yiz for giving it a go.'

When Eddie told the rest of the band they almost broke up on the spot. Brian said no way were they ready to appear in public.

Eddie said it wasn't exactly Madison Square Gardens and they'd have to start somewhere. Clint said he hadn't anything to wear. Only Ginger thought it was worth doing.

'Fuck it,' she said, 'why not?' There were a lot of reasons why not, but Eddie contradicted all the facts with the unyielding certitude of a Stalinist.

'It's time,' he said, 'that we kicked some ass.'

On the day of the gig, Eddie took a day off work. Miles wasn't too happy about that. He said Eddie's close rate was going down faster than Cecil Parkinson's trousers and he'd better watch out. Eddie promised to work on it.

'Give me a break, Miles,' he said, 'I've had a lot of personal hassle lately.' Miles shook his head and looked exasperated. He pointed to the door.

'See that, Eddie?' he said. 'That's where you leave your personal life. When you come in here.' This wasn't some two-bit cowboy operation. Eddie said he knew that, and he swore it wouldn't happen again.

He met Clint in the car park of the Pride at four o'clock to assemble the PA. Clint had liberated a post office van from his flatmate's postman boyfriend to haul the stuff over from the hire company. As they humped the bass bins into the bar, Famous Séamus didn't look happy.

'Do yiz really need all this amplification?' he asked. 'We have the council regulations to think of, you know, the locals and so on.' Eddie promised they'd keep the decibels reasonable. 'Yeah,' said Séamus. 'I mean, if we'd wanted The Rolling Stones we would have phoned them up.' He seemed to think that was very funny.

The stage was a collection of upturned plastic beer crates, under a giant green plastic shamrock that glowed when Famous Séamus switched it on. Eddie and Clint spent an hour plugging leads into sockets, saying 'Give me a level' and frantically trying to give the impression that they knew what they were doing. On the wall, a large notice announced, in Celtic script, 'NO JIVING WILL BE TOLERATED!'

Marion came over straight after work. She sat in a corner studying and sipping an orange juice while Eddie and Clint went through the sound check. She was in a strange mood again. Eddie kept asking her if she thought they needed a little more treble or a little more bass, until finally she told him that she didn't know what the fuck he was talking about. Clint asked if she was Eddie's girlfriend and Eddie said yeah, kind of. Clint looked like he'd been about to say something insulting but had decided against it at the last minute.

'Fair enough,' he shrugged.

Marion's friends arrived, in twos and threes. All girls. All from Donegal. She introduced them to Eddie, who'd met most of them once or twice before, but couldn't remember their names. They stared at his haircut.

'So you're the famous Eddie Virago,' Angela said.

'Yes,' said Eddie, 'that's me.' Angela said she'd once seen a photo of Eddie.

'You looked sneaky as a foreigner in it,' she giggled, 'sneaky as a foreigner.' Then she started talking about her own hair. She was thinking of splashing out on highlights.

Ginger and Brian arrived at seven, both very nervous. Brian hauled his kit out of the taxi and dragged it sweatily into the Pride.

'Why didn't I take up the fucking flute?' he groaned. Ginger wandered around the dancefloor as though she was looking for something. Then Famous Séamus showed them all to the dressing room, a tumbledown prefab cubicle out in the back yard, the walls of which were covered with IRA slogans.

Eddie had a quick drink with Marion and her friends, but they were talking about things 'back home' so he didn't have a clue what to say. He tried to talk to them about their jobs. May Rose was temping. Angela was an insurance clerk. Bridget was an assistant in the only chemist in London that didn't sell condoms. They were all talking about some primary teacher called Maxwell who'd just got another sixth-year girl pregnant back in Ballybracken.

'You shifted him once,' chided Angela to Marion.

'I did not, you dirty liar,' blushed Marion, glancing at Eddie.

'You did,' said Angela, 'the night of Mary O'Connor's wedding. And I have the photographs to prove it.'

In the dressing room Clint struggled into a pair of tight leather trousers. Ginger shivered in the corner, in a flimsy black cocktail dress, holding her fingers to her temples, 'attuning'. Brian was wearing bermuda shorts and a white T-shirt. He folded a pack of Marlboros into the sleeve, like James Dean.

'Brian,' said Eddie, 'you don't smoke.' Brian said it was all to do with image.

They wrote out the playlist and smoked a few joints. Clint

kept asking if they could do his latest song, 'Whose Dog Are You?' He just wouldn't let it drop, no matter how much Eddie objected.

'Can we?' he said. 'Please, come on guys, can we?'

The trouble was that 'Whose Dog' hadn't been unanimously popular at rehearsals. Eddie said it sounded a little corny, and he didn't understand the words. And Brian said it sounded like just about every other garage-band song he had ever heard, but if everyone else wanted to do it, he wouldn't say no.

'Come on, guys,' pleaded Clint, 'I know it's not great, but let's give it a shot. Huh? Just for the hell of it?' Ginger shrugged her assent.

'OK,' said Eddie, 'let's do it,' and he stuck it down last on the list.

'Just don't be too loud,' pleaded Famous Séamus, before they went on. 'Seriously, lads, it's my bollocks that's on the line, you know?' They stood at the side of the stage, and Clint kept panting 'Rock and Roll, Rock and Roll' like it was a prayer. Séamus said The Hounds would be on at eight-thirty, so The Honey Bees had to be off by eight-fifteen, come hell or high water. The Hounds were very fussy about things like that. They were real professionals.

Famous Séamus stood on the stage in a silver lamé jacket, throwing the microphone from hand to hand, sweating very slightly. He tapped the microphone nervously, and when he blew into it, the sound was like a hurricane invading the pub.

'My lords, ladies and gentleman,' he began, 'as you know here at the Pride, we're always on the lookout for the bright young things of the future, and quite a few of them have played here for the first time, a galaxy of stars, Big Bob and his Rambling Baddies included.' Séamus held the microphone under his armpit while he led the applause. 'But anyway, something different tonight, more from the top of the pops field, a new and talented combo, who've promised not to be too loud, hee hee hee, so say hello if you will' – Séamus glanced at a card in his hand – 'to Eddie Virago and The Honey Bees.' He stuck two fingers in his mouth and released a piercing whistle.

Clint looked at Eddie.

'*Eddie Virago* and The Honey Bees?' he said. 'Since when?' Eddie shrugged.

'Mistake,' he whispered. 'Never mind, get up there quick.'

There were fifteen people in the pub when they started. Seven of them Eddie knew personally. Then there was Brian's boss, Clint's brother and Ginger's cousin. And five strangers.

Brian clicked the intro with his sticks. They started with 'Mind Dross', a solid and pseudo-hippy thing written by Ginger, with lots of fretless bass and weird guitar noises and minor-fifth harmonic chords. Ideally, it was supposed to end with a hole being hammered into the wall with a hydraulic drill, but the manager of the Pride said no way would he have that. Ginger had insisted Famous Séamus check with him, just in case there was any chance. But they'd just had the renovations finished, so it was a non-starter. There was a tape that went with it, of headlines from the TV news and snatches of adverts. An ironic exploration of the perils of Western Civilisation, or so Ginger said. As people drifted into the bar, the point seemed lost on the audience.

'Do you know any Pogues?' somebody shouted.

'Christy!!' came another call. 'Spancil Hill, Rifles of the IRA.'

A slow handclap started during Brian's 'Extra Extra', the only semi-country song they had. Ginger sang the words surprisingly well, with her eyes closed, clutching the mike stand like she was going to fall over on her face if she let go.

> Extra extra
> The news is out
> You're leaving town
> And there's no doubt.

During the middle eight, Eddie and Clint tried to sing a harmony, fingers jammed folksily into their ears. But they both just ended up doubling the melody, until Ginger glared at them to cut it out. Clint's solo started way off-key, meandered tortuously through the fretboard, and somehow managed to stagger back into G-minor by the time the chorus came round.

> The gossip column's
> Working overtime.
> We're old news baby.
> We're all sold out.

When she'd finished Brian did a little roll on his snare, and he clapped, behind his kit. Marion's friends went crazy, whooping and cheering. Ginger bowed, a little self-consciously Eddie thought.

'Good evening,' said Eddie, 'we're The Honey Bees.' The sound of his voice in the microphone surprised him. He stepped back and laughed.

After a couple of cover versions the place started to fill up. 'Madison Blues' went OK. But they hashed up Iggy Pop's 'Cry for Love' so badly that they had to stop half-way through and start again and not even Marion's gang applauded. Eddie did a solo spot, Brian's song 'Fear of the Freedom', and that went down a little better. The audience seemed to think it was a rebel song. Three thick-set guys at the back clapped along in the air, mocking Eddie as he spat out the words. Then the rest of the band came back on and, with great gusto, Clint immediately hit the distortion pedal and pounded out the introduction for 'Whose Dog Are You?'

'Come on, Eddie,' he roared, hopping around the fragile stage, 'give it a shot, OK?' And Eddie stepped up to the microphone, nerves jangling as he started to sing.

> Sometimes. Sometimes. Sometimes.
> I wish I was a terrorist
> Far across the sea
> With a neutron bomb
> And a 47 gun
> For everyone to see.
>
> And I'd ride across the riversides
> And tumble through the plains
> In the sweltering sun
> When the morning's come
> And the snowstorms and the rains . . .

Clint looked ecstatic. He mimed the words as he lashed at his strings, wincing in agony as they cut into his knuckles. Ginger bopped efficiently from side to side, looking cool and unimpressed. Brian pounded his kit so hard that the whole stage shook. And half-way through 'Whose Dog', something weird happened. Eddie could see that people were watching him now. The underlying babble of conversation seemed to be dying away. He felt like he'd just woken up. He started really hearing the drums, clattering at the back, and the smash of the cymbals, reverberating through the room. He felt Ginger's bass slapping up through his spine. In the corner of his eye he saw Clint posing and strutting, lashing out manic power chords and concentrating like crazy. Something started to gel. The music lifted him. At the back he could see Marion, shaking her shoulders from side to side. Eddie swallowed hard. His heard thudded as he closed his eyes. 'Fuck the begrudgers,' he thought, 'this is it,' and he started spitting out the words, as though he really did understand what they meant, through clenched and snarling teeth.

Won't be a dog for the solid citizens
A dog for the CIA
Won't be a jumped-up jewel
A trumped-up fool
Making heroes for a heroin age
Won't be a dog for the masters in the penthouse
A dog for the pentagon thing
A dog digging dirt
On the teenage flirt
A dog for the microwave gang . . .

Eddie's guitar sputtered out notes from way up on the neck. And lower down the sound was broody and growling and menacing. His fingers slithered up and down the frets, hammering on, thrashing at the tremolo arm. Way up top again, the treble notes screamed. The veins in his neck throbbed. Brian's drums were holding up, solid and thumping. Coming into the final chorus, Clint and Ginger hollered into the mike.

A dog for the needle in the haystack
A dog for the winning smile
Burying lies in truth's disguise
With your finger on the Judas dial.

And I'm wondering how
It's all I can do
Yeah I'm wondering now
Whose dog are you?

A tidal wave of wailing guitar and rolling drum finished it off with a heavy-metal flourish. And when it was all over the audience went crazy, clapping and cheering and roaring for more. Marion was on her feet, with her fingers in her mouth, whistling. A thunderstorm of footstamping pounded through the room. Behind the bar, Famous Séamus raised a glass. Eddie stood very still, and he felt like crying.

They ran through the whole repertoire one more time, and then Clint pulled the plug and said to quit while they were ahead. Brian tossed his drumsticks into the audience. In the dressing room they threw their arms around each other.

'That was amazing,' whooped Brian, 'we really hit it out there.' Ginger and Clint opened a bottle of tequila. Eddie sat simpering with his head in his hands, and the one conscious thought he could form was that he wished to Christ Dean Bean and Jennifer had been there to see it all.

Afterwards they went to sit with Marion and her friends, out in the bar. Ginger was more relaxed than anyone had ever seen her. Angela told her she was brilliant.

'That was my favourite song,' she said, 'the one you sang.' Ginger said it was Brian's song, so he had to take the credit. Brian said no, really, it was the way she'd sung it. Clint, already drunk, said hell, they'd all been brilliant.

Marion held Eddie's hand and told him he was fantastic.

'I couldn't believe it,' she said, 'you were really good.' Eddie told her not to be so surprised. She handed him a cassette. May Rose had taped the whole thing on her walkman. Eddie passed the machine around the table and each Honey Bee listened in turn, transfixed and glowing. Brian drummed in the air with his fingers. Clint looked like he was about to expire with happiness.

Half an hour later the pub filled with wild whoops and cheers, and all the lights went out.

'My lords, ladies and gentlemen,' said Famous Séamus's voice, 'time for the main event. Will you put your hands together now and give a big downhome Pride of Erin welcome to Cricklewood's own' – Famous Séamus wriggled his hips – 'The Hounds of Ulster!'

The spotlights flickered on. The neon shamrock started to glow, green, white and orange tubelight running around the stage. Applause ripped through the bar. Like an explosion. In a way.

The Hounds of Ulster turned out to be two middle-aged men in matching Aran sweaters and moustaches. The drummer looked like something from an anti-smoking commercial, his face all grey and thin and sad, stretched over his skull like a mask. He was half bald, but he had let the russet hair on one side of his chrome dome grow long, and then swept it across his scalp. It looked terrible. When he shook his head, and it all fell down over his ear, it looked worse. Every time it did that, he stopped drumming just to allow himself to sweep it back into place.

The other guy played a bontempi organ with the walking bassline built in. He was fat and he wore tight white trousers, over which his belly protruded, and white leatherette shoes.

'Good evening, Kilburn,' he roared, after the first number, 'greatta see yiz again.' Pints of Guinness were brought up to the stage. 'That's it,' said the keyboard player, 'put another coin in the jukebox, baby.' Every time he told a joke the drummer did a short snare roll and a crash of cymbals. 'Want to hear a good one?' he said. 'Paddy's walking down the boreen in Donegal, right?' A big cheer went up from Marion and her friends. 'Aye,' he said, 'in Donegal, when this Brit pulls up in a car, you see.' Boos and hisses. 'Brit says, "Hey, Paddy, can you tell me the way to Donaghadee?" Paddy says to the Brit, "Bejayzus and begorrah, how do you know my name, sir?" Brit says, "I guessed, Paddy, I guessed." Paddy says, "Well, you can guess the way to fucking Donaghadee."' Another crash, and the sound of laughter.

They struck up an introduction that the crowd recognised with a roar.

The place was packed now, swelling with the babble of Irish accents. The room smelt sweaty and hot and male. Ginger had to push through the bodies to get to the bar. Cigarette smoke filled the air. Unshaven men in denim coats went from table to table selling *An Phoblacht: Republican News* and *The Irish Struggle*. Intense girls in leather jackets collected money 'for the movement'. The Hounds of Ulster sang:

> England, your sins they will haunt you,
> The seeds of your hatred are sown,
> Ireland's brave sons, with their armalite guns,
> Will show you the way to go home.

The chorus lifted and swelled through the room, bouncing around from corner to corner. Behind the bar Famous Séamus waved his fist in the air, and he sang the words with his eyes closed, one hand clutching his heart through his silver lamé jacket.

When the girls with the collection boxes came to their table, tins were rattled in everyone's face. Eddie was the only one in the group who didn't contribute. Even Clint and Brian put in something. Nobody said anything, but Eddie felt all their eyes.

'Are you not one of us, Eddie?' chided Angela. 'Are you not proud of your country's struggle?' Marion told her to shut up.

'Not tonight,' she said wearily, 'please.'

Another scream of applause deadened the rest of her sentence. Eddie said they'd talk about it later.

'Any requests?' came from the stage.

'Fuck off,' shouted someone from the darkness, and everybody laughed.

'Sit back in your seat there, and I'll plug it in,' said the organist. The drummer did his cymbal thump again.

May Rose asked Eddie if he wanted a drink. He said he'd have a tequila, and she glared at him with a weird look, pantomiming snobbery.

The Hounds of Ulster played 'Blueberry Hill' and it segued into 'Danny Boy' followed by Elvis Presley's 'One Night with You'. Then the rumba switch got switched on by accident, and it jammed all the way through 'Molly Malone'.

Half-way through the chorus Eddie felt a tap on his back. When he turned, a very fat guy with an upturned nose, stupid droopy eyes and a flabby face was standing behind him. He had a military-style haircut, shorn real short, but dyed peroxide white. His eyebrows were black. He wore a heavy black frieze overcoat, and when it fell open Eddie could see a scarlet waistcoat underneath. He wore leopardskin drainpipe trousers. His ears were studded with tiny earrings shaped like parrots.

'You Eddie?' said the man, in a high-pitched effeminate cockney voice.

'Might be,' said Eddie. Clint and Brian rolled their eyes. Angela and May Rose giggled.

'Yeah,' said the fat guy, 'well, I might be able to do you a fave, Eddie.'

'Oh yeah?' said Eddie. 'I'm always in the market for that.'

'The name's Jake,' he said, sitting on a stool that was much too small for his vast bulk, 'but hey, you can call me Jake. Liam?' he shouted, clicking his finger at the barboy. 'Another salvo of refreshments over here, please.' Jake ordered drinks for everyone at the table. He'd caught the band earlier, and he'd totally got off on them. 'Orgasmic,' he said. 'Fucking ace. Jesus and Mary Chain meets Dylan meets fucking I dunnno, fucking Stravinsky or something, one of those class cats.' When Marion came back from the ladies, Jake introduced himself. 'Jake Mullan,' he beamed, 'Motorvatin' Management Productions. I think you're gonna be huge.'

'That's right,' said Eddie, 'we are.'

Jake had a lot of experience with Irish acts, going all the way back to poor old Phil Lynott and Thin Lizzy, and the showbands before that. He'd been over to the States on the first Lizzy tour.

'Jesus, man,' he sighed, 'I could tell you stories about the guy, his motel rooms, Christ, wall-to-wall bed, you know?' After that he'd handled The Radiators, The Boomtown Rats, Van the Man, The Petrols, Chris De Burgh, all those Irish cats. He knew the scene well over there, been over loads of times checking out new bands. 'Mr Sham Rock,' he said, 'that's me. Do you know The Hedge?' he said. 'From U2, do you know him?' Eddie said not very well. Jake nodded. 'Love that guy,' he grinned. 'Beautiful guy, seriously, lovely kids he's got. And as for his lady.' Jake shook his head from side to side, eyes closed, as though he couldn't find sufficient words to extol her charms. 'She's a livin' doll,' he said, 'a real three-times-a-lady, you know what I'm saying?' He made an O with his index finger and his thumb. 'A class act,' he said.

Jake was so fat that he got breathless when he spoke, and he had to keep pausing, swallowing hard, before going on. His hands moved when he spoke, clenching, pointing, counting out points on his fingers, thumping the table. He had to shout to be heard above The Hounds of Ulster. He said he wanted to level with Eddie and the guys.

'And you too,' he said, nodding at Ginger, 'pardon the pun, yeah? Like, I think you got a real happening thing, you know, a real serious potential, and I'm talking all the way. But you need a bit of help.' Ginger and Brian started speaking, very intensely, in the corner. 'Like I could really hear a bit of brass on that last one,' said Jake, 'y'know, a touch of hornography, that's what you need, really bring it out of itself.' Eddie told him to get to the point. Brian put his hand on Ginger's hand and whispered something in her ear. She laughed.

Basically, Jake wanted money. He said for a hundred quid he could set them up an appointment with a major label by the end of next week. Hundred quid down, money back if no return. Ask no questions, tell no lies.

'I got expenses,' he said, 'money honey, y'know, like the song says. "If you wanna mess around with me."' Eddie looked at the others. 'Take it or leave it, guys,' he said, 'it's no epidermis off my proboscis.' Ginger looked sceptical.

'How do we know you're not jerking us around?' she said. Jake said Ginger could jerk him around any time she liked, then he laughed and said he was just kidding.

'Seriously, honey,' said Jake, 'I take your point.' He gave them his card, and said they could call his office any time they were unhappy and he'd return the money right away. He couldn't say fairer than that, could he? 'Stick your lettuce on that,' he said, 'go on,' offering a piece of paper. He glanced guiltily at Ginger again. 'I'm sorry,' he said, 'just ignore me, OK, I didn't mean that, what I said . . .'

'Lettuce?' said Clint

'Lettuce and cucumber,' said Jake. 'Phone number.'

'What do people think?' asked Eddie.

'I don't know, Ed,' said Brian, suspiciously, 'I really don't.'

'I'm straight up, guys,' said Jake, 'ask anyone in this business. Jake Mullan is a man of his word, and that's the truth.'

'Fuck it,' said Clint, 'let's take a chance.'

'No chance, man,' said Jake, 'you're signing up for the big time.'

Clint had twenty. Eddie borrowed twenty from Marion. That was all they could come up with. Angela said she'd slip out with her bank-link card. Marion said not to be ridiculous, but Eddie said that'd be great, if she wouldn't mind.

'I don't,' she said, 'even if you are a West Brit.'

Ginger said she didn't think it was a good idea, but she'd abide by the band's democratic decision.

May Rose hissed 'Shhhh'. The Hounds were about to play 'Amhrán na bhfiann'. That, Eddie explained to Jake, was the Irish National Anthem. Jake stood with all the others, head bowed and arms behind his back. The words were in Irish, so Eddie didn't know them. May Rose sang at the top of her squeaky voice. Angela came back with the money.

Outside in the car park, Eddie helped Ginger and Brian pack up the van. Jake bent down to tie the lace of his purple brothelcreepers. Then he slid the hundred quid into his shoe. He told Ginger he was sorry again, for being so crass.

'I can't help it,' he said, 'I'm cheap. That's the way the big bopper made me.' Ginger said she'd let it go, this time. 'OK,' he said, backing across the car park, 'see you guys soon.'

'Hang loose, Jake,' said Brian. It sounded all wrong.

'Yeah,' said Jake, making a telephone shape with his hand. 'Be in touch. Ramma Lamma Ding Dong, OK? Keep hangin' on the telephone.'

Just before he got into his car he plucked at the back of his trousers, pinching the material out from between his enormous buttocks.

'Weird guy,' said Ginger.

Famous Séamus, stripped of his lamé jacket now, came running out of the Pride, as the Cortina chugged out of the car park. It was about a round of drinks. Thirteen altogether, ordered by their friend with the funny haircut. He held the order between his finger and his thumb. Still had to be paid for. If it was up to him he'd have let it go, but the boss was strict about that kind of thing. The breeze made the paper flap in his hand. He looked like Neville Chamberlain in an Aran jumper.

Eddie watched, with a heavy heart, as the tail lights disappeared past the wire grille.

Marion said that'd be the last time they'd ever see Jake or their money, but Eddie ignored her.

'We'll have to owe it,' he said.

Ginger and Brian started to laugh, and they put their arms around each other, in the back of the van. Famous Séamus began rolling up his sleeves. He said it was no laughing matter.

A week dragged by and Jake never called. Eddie double-checked with Mr Patel every night when he came home and every morning before he went out. Marion got downright smug about it, saying that Eddie should listen to her a bit more often.

'That guy was a chancer,' she laughed, 'anyone could have seen it. Anyone except you.' Eddie told her she had no faith in human nature, and she said no, she didn't, not where other people's money was concerned. Her friends' money, especially.

But just as Eddie was about to give up hope and swallow his pride and blame the whole thing on Clint and Brian, Jake did ring back. He came round to the Brightside a couple of nights later to chew a few things over.

The hundred quid wasn't mentioned at first, and when Eddie plucked up the courage to ask, Jake said he was right to bring it up, but have no fear, things were already going well. Nothing definite, he said, but certain wheels were starting to turn. It was a process, he said. You didn't want to push things too hard. But he could see a very bright future for Eddie, seriously bright, we were talking dazzling city.

'Listen, man,' he said, 'like the song says, the future's so bright I gotta wear shades, yeah?' He told him he'd played the tape to a few important people, close personal buddies of his, and basically, they'd dug it, that was the up side. But it was a yin and yang situation. There was a down side too. The down side was that Eddie would have to face some tough decisions. 'Rock and roll,' Jake said, smiling philosophically, 'it's not just chicks and cadillacs, you know, it's not just dreams, Ed, it's a business.'

Eddie said he knew that.

Jake said it was a jungle out there, crawling with alcoholics, child molesters, nervous wrecks and primadonnas, and Eddie needed a shark like him to keep the barracudas at bay. He said he wanted to ask Eddie something. Straight up.

'Are you loyal, Eddie? Are you, like, loyal to people?' Eddie said yeah, and Jake nodded in approval. *'Moi aussi,'* he said 'Disloyalty's not my thing Eddie, but let's face it . . .'

Eddie asked him what he meant. In fact Eddie spent half an hour asking him what exactly he was talking about, with very little effect. Jake had a politician's way with words. 'Hey,' he said, in the end, 'like I told you, loyalty's my middle name, Ed.' Jake made a V-sign with his fingers. 'He ain't heavy man, he's my brother, that's what I say. Jake Loyalty Mullan, that's me. Ask anyone in this business.' Eddie said he knew that. The smile froze on Jake's flabby face. 'It's just Ginger and the others,' he said, 'I mean, they're great kids, don't get me wrong.' Eddie said he wouldn't. Jake said he wanted to be absolutely up front. 'Let's have a bit of fucking glasnost here, Ed, OK? Let's just tell it like it is.'

'Please do,' said Eddie.

'OK,' said Jake, 'I'll be Franklin D. Roosevelt with you, OK, Ed?'

Just then Mr Patel came over and said there was a phonecall for Marion. He looked at Jake as if he didn't fully approve of him, a useful weapon for an hotelier to have in his facial armoury. Eddie said Marion was up in the room. Jake resumed his conspiratorial tone.

'Anyway, Ed, what I'm saying, that Brian for instance, well, I mean, we're not exactly talking Mr Percussion here, are we? I mean, my freakin' grandmother's got a better sense of rhythm than Brian, and she's had a colostomy bag for the last four years, Ed, you know what I'm saying?' Eddie said he had a vague idea, yes.

Jake said he wasn't talking anything definite, just running a few ideas around the block. But you needed a shit-hot sticksman. That was just essential. He said a good rock and roll band was like a ship, and the drums were the engine room. It was all very well having the captain prancing around on lead guitar and everybody else frigging in the rigging, but if things weren't hunky dory down in the rhythm department it'd be Titanic city, over and out before you could say bebopaloola, she's my baby.

'Which brings me to Ginger,' he said. 'Again, great chick, good looking too, but I mean to say.' Marion walked through the lobby and into the callbox. 'She wouldn't be prepared to kind of tart things up a little, would she? Image-wise?' Jake shook his ample front from side to side and pouted. 'Ginger, I mean,' he said. He shimmied again. 'Crank up the sex appeal factor. Get the old threepenny bits out?' Eddie said he didn't think so. And anyway, he didn't want to be in that kind of band. Jake said he was right, and that's what he'd thought. 'You're a man of principle, Eddie,' he said, 'just like me. Woman is the nigger of the world, yeah? Clint is OK. Clint I can handle. Clint I can just about get my head around. Shame he's called Clint, but what can you do about that? Well, change it maybe. Anyway, he can handle his guitar and that still counts for something in this business, Ed, ha ha ha, I mean it's not all Lucy in the Sky with Diamonds . . . LSD,' he explained, 'pounds, shillings, pence.'

What Jake was saying was that sometimes in this business you had to make tough old decisions, and he just thought that this was one of those times. He said if Eddie was prepared to be flexible on the personnel front, maybe they could talk some serious turkey. He had a couple of musicians in mind for Eddie, frighteningly good guys, he'd been using them on and off for ages now, for different bits and pieces, and they were just starting to really cook.

Eddie said, 'So the bottom line is, when you say you want me to be flexible, you want me to get rid of them?'

Jake said it wasn't exactly a question of what *he* wanted. It was a question of a professional attitude. It was utterly immaterial to him. What he wanted, he said, was for Eddie to have a little think about it and then, like the movie said, do the right thing.

'They're gone,' Eddie said, immediately, 'that's fine by me, honest.'

Jake started to speak, lowering his voice suddenly when he saw Marion emerge from the phonebox and walk through the lobby.

'If that's what you want, Ed. Now personally, I have to say I think you're right, but I'm happy to leave it up to you.'

'Yeah, yeah,' said Eddie, 'they're out.'

Rather dramatically, Jake drew two red lines through the names in his notebook. The tip of his tongue protruded between his lips as he nodded, slowly, thoughtfully. This was a whole different ballgame. Jake could see things a bit more clearly now. Things were gelling.

'Love the lady, by the way,' he said, nodding vaguely in the direction of the stairs. 'Mary Anne, is it?'

'Marion,' said Eddie, 'as in Faithful.'

'Yeah,' Jake laughed, 'I hope so, Eddie, I hope so.' Eddie asked if there was anything else, he was kind of busy. 'Just one last thing, Ed, just a small thing, the name.'

Jake said that frankly, The Honey Bees was an awful name. He said it reminded him of some crummy Motown girl group. It was pure corn. Eddie agreed. The Honey Bees had been Ginger's idea, he said. 'Yeah, thought so,' giggled Jake. He said they needed something more aggressive, more happening, more scruff of the neck, something, frankly, with 'a bit of bollocks'. Jake closed his notepad.

'The Diehards,' he said, 'think of it, man. The Diehards. A real kick-ass name.' Jake's fat, excited face peered up at the ceiling, and his hand picked out invisible letters in the air. 'Eddie Virago,' he said, slowly, 'and The Diehards. It has a certain *cherchez la femme*, yeah? Think you could get your head round that, Ed? Do you? Yeah. Thought you would.'

Eddie said yeah, it had possibilities. So Jake arranged to set up a meet with his people, and said he'd start the ball rolling straightaway on a new demo tape.

Then he had to split. He was expecting a couple of long-distance calls, then he was going to John Peel's fiftieth birthday party. The Undertones were reforming specially to play at it. Not one to be missed. Eddie said he'd love to come along, but Jake said, 'Sorry Ed, no can do, it's strictly RSVP. Catch you later. Hang loose, babe.'

Mr Patel's eyes scrutinised Eddie as he crossed the lobby. He was speaking into the telephone in his back room. He held the phone between his chin and his shoulder. He was doing his superior look.

Eddie knocked on the bathroom door, and he told Marion the good news.

She turned off the shower, but she didn't open the door. She was happy to hear Jake was so confident. Eddie walked to the window, his head swimming with happiness.

'I told you you were wrong about Jake,' he said.

'Yes,' she said, 'you were right.'

'We're on the way, babe,' he yelled. 'I'm kicking ass. I'm up and running.' He punched the air.

'By the way, Eddie,' she said, her voice trembling an echo in the bathroom, 'that call I got.'

'What about it?' he laughed, beginning to roll an enormous joint.

'My mother's dead,' she answered.

Eddie wasn't so keen on going to Belfast, but what else could he do? They weren't so hot on the idea at work either. Miles said it was a question of commitment. He said B'n'S required a lot of commitment, it wasn't just a job. He said he was sick to the back teeth telling Eddie this.

Eddie said please. Miles sighed. He bent his head and put his fingers against his temples. Eddie noticed he was getting thin on top, but he reckoned this wasn't the time to point that out. Miles said Eddie was pushing him. Eddie said it was an important personal thing.

Miles said, 'Look Eddie, stop sucking my cock, alright?' Eddie said he certainly didn't want to give the impression that he was sucking Miles's cock, or any other part of his anatomy. He said, 'Jesus, Eddie, you really can talk, can't you?'

Eddie said, 'Come on, Miles. Give me a break.'

'OK, Eddie,' Miles snapped, 'you may as well go, but do us both a favour and don't come back.' Eddie said was Miles sacking him and Miles said he was letting him go, yes. He could collect what was owed him, plus a month's pay, and just get the fuck out. 'You've got the wrong attitude, Eddie,' he snapped. 'People like you just fuck other people up. You're just not dependable.' Eddie said Miles was being unreasonable. Miles thought that was a good one, coming from Eddie. Eddie said OK, he wouldn't go, if Miles wanted him that much he'd stay. Miles said he didn't. Not any more. 'You blew it, Eddie,' he growled. 'You had your chance and you made an Arab's armpit of it. Now fuck off out of here.'

Eddie told Marion that Miles wouldn't give him permission to go to the funeral, so he'd told him to stick his job where the sun didn't shine. Marion wasn't impressed. As it was, she didn't want him to come with her, or so she said. But Eddie knew she was just saying it. So he had to insist.

The flight was OK. And apart from a few bored-looking soldiers squatting in the shrubbery outside the airport and a couple of armoured cars parked in the centre of Belfast, there was no sign of trouble. Here and there the kerbstones were painted green, white and orange, or red, white and blue, but that didn't bother Eddie. He'd seen it on television so many times. What bothered him more was the air of struggling normality. Tired women doing their shopping, big sisters pushing prams, corner boys slouching against the walls of the RUC stations, fags stuck to their lower lips.

When the coach stopped to let everybody use the toilet, Eddie combed out his mohican, gelling it down over his ears. Then he took out a can of black spray dye and zapped his hair. Then he pulled on a black tea-cosy hat. He looked ridiculous, but it was an improvement, and although Marion said nothing, he knew that she was grateful. He couldn't go to her mother's funeral dressed like a cross between Joey Ramone and Hiawatha. Even Eddie knew that.

On the Irish side of the border a couple of Gardai got onto the bus and swaggered up and down for a few minutes, checking passports and trying to look tough. The hills of Antrim were slate grey and yellow and by the time the bus got to Ballybracken Eddie had got thoroughly bored with the landscape.

Marion was quiet. After the initial tears, she'd been philosophical. She said she was happy her mother had gone early.

'She would never have been able to cope without Daddy,' she said, 'if he'd gone first.'

Her brother Mario picked them up at the little station. He kissed Marion awkwardly and shook Eddie's hand without saying anything at all. He looked Eddie up and down and Eddie got the feeling he didn't like him too much. He was very quiet, and his eyes were a little too close together. He wore a tartan shirt and a pair of green cord flares. He wanted to stop at the hotel for a drink on the way into town, but Marion said no.

'*Mario?*' whispered Eddie, in the back of the car.

'Lanza,' she explained, 'my father used to like him.'

The first time she really let rip with the tears was when she walked into the house on Factory Street. The place was stuffed full of cigarette smoke. There were neighbours everywhere, filing up the stairs to the bedroom to see Mrs Mangan laid out in the coffin. Somebody nudged Eddie, nodding towards his hat. But he didn't take it off.

A framed picture of the Sacred Heart smiled smugly from the bedroom wall, and the room smelt of incense. Little cards with black borders and crosses covered the yellowing lace mats on both the bedside tables. A glass of water stood on the windowsill. A pale blue shirt, on a hanger, adorned the front of the wardrobe.

Mrs Mangan's hands lay clasped across her stomach, with a set of rosary beads tangled between her nicotine-stained fingers. Her face looked well, considering. Her skin looked waxy. She looked like she might open her eyes any minute, and that was a little freaky. Eddie looked at this dead woman, and he could see a real resemblance to Marion, in the high pronounced cheekbones especially, and in the curve of her pale lips. It felt weird meeting her like this for the first time.

It occurred to Eddie that this was probably the bed in which Marion had been conceived. A strange thought maybe, but that's what popped into his head, and he couldn't make it go away.

In the room downstairs her father was sitting on a low armchair by the aga stove in the corner, with his head in his hands.

'Daddy,' she said softly, 'this is Eddie, the one I told you about.' But Mr Mangan didn't look up. The backs of his hands were red and wrinkled. He sobbed silently, and his whole body shook, as people on both sides tried to comfort him.

Eddie said maybe he shouldn't have come. He felt like he was intruding. Marion told him not to be silly. She told Eddie to go outside for a while, have a walk around the village. She wanted to have a chat with her father.

Eddie walked up and down the main street, past the chip shops and pubs. People stared at him on the footpath. They all looked like victims of botched forceps delivery. Eddie felt like a stranger in a Wild West town. That feeling was enhanced by the way everything in the main street seemed to have an American name.

There was a Stars and Stripes Pizza Joint, a Yankee Doodle Bar and Fried Chicken, a Boston Tea House, a Hollywood Hairstyles, a Route 66 Grill Bar, a Prairie Moon Burger Bar, a Miami Vice Fashions, complete with an enormous confederate flag in the window and a lifesize Uncle Sam on the pavement.

Old men doffed their hats and said, 'Soft day.' When he went to buy cigarettes the guy behind the counter talked to him for fifteen minutes about the government's road licence scheme, and how it was banjaxing the tourist industry.

'Are you a tourist yourself?' he said.

'No,' said Eddie, 'I'm from Dublin.' The guy said that's what he meant.

Eddie walked out the far side of the town, out past the concrete housing estates to where the electric fences stopped and the stone walls began. Beside a tiny old ruined church was a Protestant graveyard, full of the graves of women who had died 'in childbirth' or 'during confinement'. The stones were green and mossy. There wasn't one woman buried there who'd lived past forty.

Eddie gaped out over the fields, trying to imagine what it was that poets and killers had seen in this barren and perverse landscape. In the misty distance the spindly black army observation towers seemed to have sprouted like weird plants from out of the landscape, and Eddie thought of giants and beanstalks. Nothing seemed to move, not even the mangy cows. It occurred to Eddie that this was one of the few places he'd ever been where what was fascinating about the scenery was not what could be seen, but what couldn't be.

At half-past four Eddie came back up Factory Street, and he stood in the hall of Marion's house for a while, drinking tea and chatting to one of her older sisters, Katherine. Katherine was a nurse. She had a plump, pleasant face and orange lipstick. He said he was very sorry about her mother, and she said not to worry, her mother had had a hard life and was better off out of it. She had never been the same since Daddy was let go at work, she said. She was bad with her nerves.

'Are you the one who lives in London?' Eddie said. Katherine looked confused.

'No,' she said, 'the only one of us in London is Marion.' Eddie said he thought Marion had told him there was another sister over there. Katherine said no, not as far as she knew, not unless Daddy had been misbehaving himself, and she laughed, 'God forgive me,' she chuckled, crossing herself, 'for laughing. And poor Mammy lying up the stairs.'

Eddie was standing in the hall on his own, smoking a cigarette, thinking about something, listening to the distant growl of the thunder, when the door opened and Marion called him into the front room. She looked strong and capable. She looked like she was ready for anything.

Her father was bent over the stove now, squatting on his hunkers with his back to the doorway, stoking the flames with a poker, the end of which was glowing red hot.

'Daddy,' she said, 'this is Eddie now.' He grunted, put down the poker, wiped his hands on the front of his tweed trousers and turned to face Eddie. He held out his hand. Eddie almost laughed. His own hand slipped, and tea slopped into the saucer.

Because Marion's father had no nose. Under the hooded dark eyes, where his nose should have been, was a scar of purple scaly tissue, and two black holes for nostrils. Eddie's eyes scanned the face. He couldn't believe anybody could have no nose. He looked for a nose, any kind of nose, but there was none. He looked in the dead eyes of Marion's father. He wanted to say, 'You've got no nose,' but he didn't. He wanted to turn to Marion and ask for help.

Eddie's head reeled. Dumbly he shook the hot damp hand that was held out to him. He tried not to stare, but he couldn't help it, and the man kept looking away, embarrassed at Eddie's embarrassment.

'You're a good lad to come over,' he said, gruffly, glancing over into the kitchen that adjoined the tiny room. He smelt of turf.

'Least I could do, Mr Mangan,' croaked Eddie, red-faced.

'James,' he said, turning away again, towards the window this time, 'you don't have to call me Mr.'

Marion's father beckoned to them to sit down, and he looked into the stove again. Eddie said he was very sorry about Mrs Mangan, and Mr Mangan nodded rapidly and said thanks.

'It's a tragedy, Eddie,' he sighed, 'but it's God's holy will.' He asked about Eddie's trip, about the British Airways flight, about Eddie's college career and his music. He was a music lover himself, he said. He seemed to know everything about Eddie. It was obvious that Marion had been talking about him and that made him flush with pride, which surprised him.

At eight o'clock Mr Mangan sent his youngest son Pascal down to the shops for a message. Marion and her sisters busied around, setting the table while the boys smoked and watched television in silence. Fifteen minutes later Pascal came back, clutching a bottle of cheap wine in a plastic bag. Mr Mangan uncorked the wine, and handed the first glass across the table to Eddie.

'What do you think of that, Eddie?' he asked. Eddie laughed, uncertainly. Everyone in the room looked at him. He told Mr Mangan he wasn't exactly an expert on wine. 'Just give it a sniff,' Mr Mangan said, 'tell us is it only rubbish or what.' Marion kicked his ankle under the table. Eddie took the glass, sniffed, tasted a mouthful and said that it was very nice. 'That's fine so,' said Mr Mangan, spreading butter over his potatoes.

'Aren't you having a glass yourself?' Eddie said, when he had poured his own.

'I'm not, Eddie,' he said, 'I only ever drink milk. That's for you.' Eddie's face felt like it was on fire. 'And whoever else, of course,' Mr Mangan said, gesturing vaguely. 'If they want any.' Apart from Marion, nobody else did.

Later they went out for a drive in Katherine's Fiat. They parked the car behind the District Court and made love in the passenger seat, a tangle of elastic and passion. Afterwards they sat in each other's arms listening to Dave Fanning playing Van Morrison on the radio, with the gearstick nudging into the back of Eddie's thigh. The rain waved across the windscreen, washing out the world. Eddie touched the side of her face. Marion knew what was on his mind.

'Jesus,' he said to Marion, 'you could have told me.'

'I *did* tell you,' she said, 'don't you remember?'

'I thought you were joking,' he said.

'No,' she said, 'I wasn't. He has no nose.' She laughed, and shrugged. Then she pulled away from Eddie and began closing the buttons of her shirt. 'Some people don't,' she said. 'It's not his fault.' Eddie flicked off the radio. 'He caught his face in the machine in the factory,' she said. 'It's the machine they use to strip up the pig's stomachs, to get them into sausage skins. He was wearing a tie. It got caught in the machine and pulled his head in.'

'Jesus,' said Eddie.

'Yes,' she said, 'the worst part is that he can't get over the idea that his nose ended up in somebody's sausages. They said they cleaned out the machine, but he didn't believe them. He can't eat them now.' Eddie felt sick.

'No,' said Eddie, 'I can see how he wouldn't.'

'Mammy used to say it was a shame,' she said, 'because you get them free, sausages you know, if you work in the factory, free for life. But Daddy won't allow them in the house now. He won't wear a tie either. He's never worn a tie since then. Never. Mammy used to say he looked like a tramp, going to council meetings in an open neck shirt.'

'Please,' Eddie said, and she smiled suddenly, looking very young.

'I wish you could have met her,' she said. 'You'd have got on.'

She said she knew she'd said it before, but all this went to show, you never knew what was coming with people.

'So?' said Eddie. She kissed his face, gently.

'So please give your mother a ring, for God's sake, Eddie. You never know really. You just can't tell what's coming around the corner.' Eddie said he knew she was right. He promised.

The windows had steamed over now. She said they'd better be getting back to the house. Eddie wiped the squeaking glass with the back of his hand. Then he switched on the wipers.

'Jesus Christ almighty,' he gasped. 'Fuck.'

A man was standing in a doorway, maybe ten yards in front of the car, in the rain, staring in the windscreen. When Eddie flicked on the white headlights he recognised him, with a shudder.

Mario stood still in the pouring rain, staring into the car. He looked angry, but he said nothing. Then he smiled, and his crooked teeth were yellow. He turned, dug his hands into his trouser pockets, and walked slowly away.

Rain rattled on the roof of the car. Marion said to pay no attention to him. He was a bit simple. He couldn't really help it. Eddie's heart pounded. He was a bit of a loner, she said.

Eddie felt suddenly sick. He watched Mario disappear around the corner, his broad shoulders hunched in the rainy streetlight. He opened the window to get some air. The darkness seemed closer than usual.

The night before the burial Marion went to stay with her father and her sisters, in a bungalow a little way out in the country, where her eldest sister lived with her husband.

Eddie had to sleep back at her parents' house, in with five of her brothers, on the floor of the tiny bedroom at the top of the stairs. He couldn't sleep. The airless room smelt sweaty and foul, and he was lonely for Marion. And he was acutely conscious that there was a dead body in the next room, just on the other side of the wallpaper.

At three in the morning one of the younger brothers, Leo, woke him and whispered, 'Eddie, is it?' Eddie said yeah. He said, 'Listen, Eddie, do you take a drink at all?' Eddie told him it had been known occasionally, yes. 'Well, d'you fancy one now?' he hissed.

'Jesus,' said Eddie, 'it's three-thirty.' The boy looked at Eddie like he was stark staring mad.

'Well, you won't mind if I do?' he said, nervously.

'I couldn't care less,' said Eddie.

When he lay down again, he was sorry he'd spoken to him like that. As the sun came up, Eddie could see the boy's fist beating up and down under the sheets.

Next morning the family waited in silence for the hearse to arrive. When the men carried the coffin down the stairs Mr Mangan looked at his watch, and then he turned away. 'Daddy,' said Marion, 'won't you put on a tie?' He said no, sharply, and then he broke into sobs again. His sons looked at each other, vaguely. 'Don't just stand there,' Marion said, 'get him a tie, for Christ's sake.' Pascal took off his own tie, and he handed it to Marion. Mr Mangan wept, head bowed low, as his daughter fingered his hard collar and slowly knotted the tie around his neck. Tears trickled down his wrinkled yellow skin. He leaned his head on her shoulder and bawled, like a child, while she stroked the back of his bald head.

'There, there, love,' she said, 'there, there.'

Eddie noticed that the hem of her slip was showing under her black dress.

It rained all through the funeral. In the church the men sat on one side and the woman and children on the other. Rain spattered coldly on the windows. Coughs echoed up and down the aisle.

They walked from the church to the little graveyard by the new power station. It was only half a mile away, over a humpback bridge at the far end of the town, past the itinerants' settling site. A policeman on duty outside the prefab Garda station saluted as the coffin passed. In the graveyard a man tried to put a tricolour banner over her coffin, but Marion's father said no. She wouldn't have liked that.

'She wasn't a political woman,' he said.

That man was another Sinn Féiner, Marion whispered to Eddie. He looked like a nice man, awkward, fiddling with the crumpled flag as he fingered his rosary beads. He closed his eyes when he prayed.

The priest said the graveside prayers in Irish, and the babble of mourners replied in Irish too. All except Eddie, who couldn't remember any Irish, not even a prayer, and didn't feel much like praying in any language. The priest held his hand like a magician over the grave as he invoked Saint Peter and Blessed Matt Talbot to come down and guide the soul of this sinner past the gates of hell and into paradise. The rain came down harder, beating on the leaves like applause, battering the black felt hats the young men wore, until most of them took their hats off, and stood bare-headed, like all the older men. Most of them, except for Eddie.

The trees were still dormant, snaking cruelly against the wild white sky. Misty translucent light hung over the fields. The country smell of cowshit and bottled gas and slurry and frying rashers drifted in over the graveyard. Plaintive sheep bawled at the clouds.

Eddie's cold damp sleeves clung to his wrists. When Marion's father threw the clod into the grave, her face twitched, and she turned sharply away.

Afterwards they went to the hotel in the town and everybody got slowly but determinedly drunk. There were so many people at the funeral that the hotel said they could move out of the bar and into the ballroom. Weeping people kept coming over to Marion, saying they were 'sorry for her trouble'. Most of them she didn't even know. Distant friends of her mother's. A couple of cousins over from Manchester.

After a while, a sing song started at the far end of the room, led by the priest, and the local Fianna Fáil TD. The sound grew louder as more people drifted down to the circle of plastic seats, joining in the choruses, swaying from side to side, arms tight around each other.

And Marion's father sang a song, a slow Irish lament, drawing out each syllable in a faltering and slurred tenor voice. Silence came down over the ballroom. People looked at each other guiltily as their glasses clinked. Complaining children were slapped into silence.

I wish, I wish, I wish in vain,
I wish in vain I was a youth again.
But a youth again I ne'er shall be
Till the apple grows on the ivy tree.

But the sweetest apple is the soonest rotten.
And the hottest love grows the sooner cold
And what can't be cured love must be endured love,
So now I'm bound for the coast of gold.

For love is teasing, and love is pleasing
And love is a pleasure, when first it's new.
But as it grows older, the love goes colder,
Till it fades away, like the morning dew.

At the end of the song Marion cried. Eddie held her hand
and told her not to be upset, but he felt the prickle of tears in
his own eyes. She said she wasn't upset. It was just that it had
been such a beautiful day, with all the songs and the crack. An
old-fashioned day. The kind of day her mother would have loved.

Just before closing time, Eddie went to the gents. He'd had
way too much to drink, and he splashed water over his face to
sober himself up. He had to be strong, for Marion's sake. It was
the least he could do.

Outside in the lobby, people were coming in for a dance that
was just starting up in the marquee. Billy Joe Boland and the
Bronco Kings. The thump of country and western bass throbbed
outside in the night, meshing with the doleful faraway wail of
pedal steel guitar.

As people pushed past him, all dressed up in suits and fancy
new dresses, Eddie saw a strange, handsome young man taking to
Marion by the cigarette machine. He seemed to be whispering. He
leaned close to her and spoke, smilingly, but with a certain care.
She nodded back, expressionless. He talked very intently, rocking
back and forth on his heels. He wore a black leather jacket and he
carried an umbrella, which he shook gently from side to side,
sending raindrops spinning. She looked up at his face, asking a
question. He shook his head violently and looked around the lobby
before bending down close to her face, clenching his fist by his side
as he whispered. Eddie felt jealous. The drink had stripped him
down. Lust dribbled into envy. The young man slipped out the
door and into the rain, and Eddie watched Marion for a minute,
the way she moved through the crowd.

He asked who the strange man was and she said he was Tom Clancy, an old friend of the family, who was in studying for the priesthood now.

'His family own the Prairie Moon Burger Bar,' she said, 'in the town.'

'If that guy's a trainee priest,' said Eddie, swaying, 'I'm the fucking Dalai Lama.'

'The who?' she said.

'No,' he said, 'the Dalai Lama.'

'No, really,' she laughed, 'he is. Why wouldn't he be?'

Eddie felt the anger possess him like a drug. He looked at her upturned and confused white face for what seemed like a long time. And he knew that what he felt was not love, but hate, and that he was too drunk to care.

'Look, Marion,' he snarled, 'just stop sucking my cock, OK?'

Tears welled in her green eyes. Her lips quivered. Marion put her hands over her ears, like she had just heard a loud noise.

'Eddie, please, don't start, not today.'

'That's it,' he told her, 'that's it, guilt trip me. Go on.'

'Leave me alone,' she said.

They argued on the way back from the hotel. Eddie said she was lying. It was the drink. It made both of them brave. She told him he was possessive and he told her she was a lousy little cockteasing flirt, without even the guts to admit it.

'One of your farmers, is it?' he whined, mimicking her accent. 'One of the local clodhopper studs?'

'You've got it all wrong, Eddie,' she wept. 'Tom's just a friend, that's the way it is up here.'

'Oh, it's different up here, is it? What's different, Marion, come on, tell me, I'm just a southside boy, the noble peasant, is it? What? Brighten up a few of your charming harvest barn-dances, did he?'

'Please, Eddie,' she said, 'stop.'

'Please, Eddie, stop,' he whinged. 'I bet you didn't say that to him, did you, Marion?'

Marion stopped walking. She turned to Eddie with flaming eyes.

'And even if I didn't,' she shouted, 'is that any of your business?'

Eddie said it *was* actually, and that two could play at that game. Oh yes. He felt the cold violence of rationality descend over him, a murderous calm in which he knew he would say anything, *anything*, to hurt her.

He told her if it was just a fling he didn't mind.

'I mean,' he panted, 'we've all had our flings. Don't think you're alone.' The road was quiet and black and things crawled in the wet hedgerows. 'Just be honest,' he said, 'I don't care. It's not as if I give a shit, but I think I'm owed honesty, at least.' He heard his own angry breath, and the beat of his heart. 'Just tell me the truth,' he said, 'that's all I ask.' He allowed himself a sardonic bitter laugh. 'I mean,' he sniggered. 'I know we've all done it.'

Marion began to walk quickly, ahead of him. He caught up with her and grabbed her shoulders, spinning her around. Tears had made her mascara run black down her cheeks. 'You fucker,' she sobbed, into her cupped hands. 'They're welcome to you.'

She pulled away from him again, her feet clicking on the hard stone road. He could hear her sobs as she walked away from him, shadow lengthening in the yellow streetlight as they rounded the corner. She bent low, and took off her shoes, and then she walked in her bare feet, weeping all the time, weeping loudly, carrying her shoes in her hands, limping over stones. She turned to face him.

'Eddie Virago,' she screamed. 'I rue the day I met you.' Her voice seemed to come from every hedge and corner of the black little turfsmelling secretive town.

Afterwards they sat in the front room of the tiny council house on Factory Street. Marion refused to speak to him all night. The television was on in the corner, and everyone watched 'The Rockford Files'. Mario seemed to be taking a plug to pieces with a screwdriver and putting it back together again, for no particular reason.

And something strange occurred to Eddie as he sat there breathing in the smell of cabbage and coaldust, swallowing back his fury.

There was such a strong family resemblance, it was uncanny. The babies, their mothers, their grandfather. It was unmissable. He couldn't quite place why that bothered him. Not at first. But he looked at Marion's father in the tiny kitchen, the way he touched her, the way he put his arm across her shoulder when she went to move away from the sink, the way she slowly dried her hands on her apron before delicately removing his tie. Thoughts floated. Suddenly she caught Eddie's eye and scowled. She looked away from him then, and she slammed the kitchen door closed with her foot. And when she did that, every single person in the room looked at Eddie, every single one except Mario, who kept fiddling with his plug, his face a map of concentration, taking it apart, putting it back together again, as though nothing in the house was wrong. But even that didn't bother Eddie any more. Eddie was too busy thinking.

They were a close family. There was absolutely no doubt about that. A real Irish traditional family. The kind you read about in books. He looked around at the babies, at their baleful dead eyes, and their wide open howling mouths. He tried to think where he had seen eyes like these before, shallow eyes, weird eyes, Sandymount green eyes that seemed to mock him fiercely. And suddenly, with a sickening shudder, he knew.

'What's the matter, Eddie?' said Mario, with a sneer, 'something on your mind?'

'Leave him alone, you,' snapped Katherine.

'It's a secret,' croaked Eddie, blushing. Mario laughed, a little too loud.

'Oh we all have those,' he said, and he began to unscrew the plug again.

Eddie closed his eyes. He felt cold now. All he could hear was the sound of Mario sniggering, and the babies crying, and the rush of whispers. He thought of the way she had touched her father's face that morning. The way her father had pulled her soft body close to his chest. The way his gnarled purple hands had stroked her hair and her lips.

When he opened his eyes again, the light stung. Katherine was staring at him. Her eyes were nervous. After a moment, she turned away. She put her hand to her cheek, so that he could not see her face. Eddie gaped at the closed kitchen door. He swallowed hard at his whisky. He told himself he must have been even more drunk than he thought.

They didn't speak all the way home. Marion sat with her headphones on, doing her defiant look, and when Eddie went to pour some milk into her coffee she called the hostess, smiled with a sweet hostility and asked for a fresh cup. She sat still, arms folded, mouth closed very tight. Later, when he touched her wrist, she pulled it away and turned a page of her magazine so hard that she ripped it.

Then she pulled her nail scissors from her handbag and started snipping black letters out of the headlines, with unnecessary vigour. Eddie looked at the tiny yellow man on the aircraft safety leaflet, strapping on his tiny red lifejacket, smiling his tiny yellow smile, putting his arm around his tiny yellow smiling wife. Then he looked at the scissors. It occurred to Eddie that maybe dying in a plane crash wouldn't be the worst thing that could happen.

As soon as they came in to the Brightside she changed her clothes and went back out again, still without saying a word. The door slammed so hard that Eddie's interview suit, suspended on its hanger by the window, fell to the floor like a corpse. He didn't bother to pick it up.

Eddie sat alone in the room strumming his guitar and waiting for something to happen. He noticed that there was hardly any space at all left on the wallpaper now. The alphabets had spread all over the place, completely covering the wall by the bed, the opposite wall, the surround of the window, the skirting boards, and most of the back of the door, an impenetrable forest of fading newsprint. After the customary half hour, she still wasn't back. 'Fuck her,' Eddie said, out loud. He opened the bottle of whisky that Katherine had given them and poured himself a large one. But the glass tasted of toothpaste, so he slopped the whisky down the sink, like a reformed alcoholic in a soap opera, and after another hour he went downstairs to talk to Mr Patel about the funeral.

Mr Patel said it was very sad, but he had to go to the whole-salers. He looked harassed, and in a very bad mood. He asked Eddie to look after the desk while he was gone. Eddie said he'd really rather not, so Mr Patel said fair enough, if anyone wanted to ransack the place, let them, why should he care? And he took his van keys and stalked out.

Behind the desk, Eddie called up a few people, but everybody seemed to be busy. Ruth and Jimmy were decorating their spare room. Clint was out, and Ginger and Brian weren't speaking to him any more. He dialled Jake's number and Jake was out too. His answering machine said he was gone to a rave and wouldn't be back until the morning. It was four in the afternoon. Eddie wasn't sure whether the message referred to the night before, or the night to come. 'Rave on,' Jake said, in his best Buddy Holly hiccup, 'it's a crazy feeling.'

He looked through the desk drawers, but he couldn't find anything interesting.

He signed a couple of Australian backpackers in, but otherwise things were quiet.

'You can check out any time you like,' he beamed, 'but you can never leave.' The Ozzie girls looked at each other. '"Hotel California",' he explained. 'The Eagles.' They didn't seem to get the joke, but they laughed anyway. Then they told him about all the countries they'd been to, like they were ticking them off on an invisible list. When he asked which one they'd enjoyed most, they said that El Salvador had been the cheapest. They hadn't made it down as far as Nicaragua. 'Pity,' Eddie said. 'It's a great country, I believe. All the politicians are artists.' They said it sounded a bit like Australia.

'Piss artists,' they said, and they laughed.

'Hey, girls,' called Eddie, as they went for the stairs, 'hear the one about the Australian student? Took a few years off Europe to bum around college.'

When Mr Patel came back he was still in a bad mood. He'd been wheelclamped outside the cash and carry and got a flat tyre on the way home.

'Fucking typical,' he said, 'fucking sonofabitch.' It was the first time in a while that Eddie'd heard him swear. Mr Patel looked at the hotel register as though he expected the place to have filled up solid in his absence. 'Sometimes,' he sighed, 'I don't know why I bother.' He said Marion was spending far too much time at her other job. That wasn't the arrangement at all. He hoped she wasn't taking advantage. He said Eddie should take it up with her.

'Get outta here, Mr P,' chuckled Eddie. 'Take it up with her yourself.'

Mr Patel's washing machine was bust, so Eddie unpacked his dirty stuff and hauled it down to Bubbles launderette on the Markham Street junction. He sat with his head in his hands watching his clothes revolve, eating a hamburger. Young guys shuffled in and out from time to time, glared round shiftily, and left. Old women came in to use the public phone. Hardly anybody wanted actually to wash their clothes. Eddie wondered how the place kept going.

The woman behind the counter had a gold tooth cover with a star-shaped hole in it. Her fingers were almost black with nicotine. She asked Eddie if he wanted a cup of tea but he said no. She slogged up and down the launderette in slippers, talking to herself. The radio played a record that sounded off centre. The whole place smelt of stale sweat and cigarette smoke. On top, it smelt of soap. But under the soap it smelt just like anywhere else in London. Old.

'You wouldn't believe the state some people leave their clothes in here,' she mumbled. 'People have no shame.' Eddie said that was true.

When he came back to the Brightside he sat in the lobby for a while, hoping somebody would ring. Mr Patel asked where was the lady friend and Eddie told him he didn't know. Mr Patel said that wasn't so good, and Eddie shrugged.

'Communications breakdown,' Mr Patel tutted, 'that is bad for a man and a woman.' Mr Patel had an infuriating way with words sometimes. Eddie got up and went out. He left his sack of clothes perched on a seat in the lobby. He didn't even put on his jacket.

Eddie walked around the city for a while, trying to get things together.

On Piccadilly Circus he realised he was in way over the top. He knew that. That kind of weird behaviour, all it could mean was that she was really into him. Eddie knew that too. God, she must have really loved him. She was too much in love to handle, and so was he, though he didn't know why any more. Maybe he'd never known why. Or never would. She was so sensitive about everything. She was like someone who'd had a layer of skin peeled off. Hell, she was like someone with no skin at all, just pure flesh and blood and bone. Everything from pain to pleasure, the whole damn spectrum, she felt it all more deeply than anyone he'd ever known. That was the trouble with Marion. She was all feeling.

He drank three glasses of beer in the French House and he bought a pack of Gauloises. But then a bedraggled madwoman sat down beside him and started talking about General de Gaulle, so he left. He walked up and down Chinatown looking at the dismembered ducks in the windows of the little restaurants, their bodies flattened out like they'd been run over by steamrollers. The air was full of the smell of garlic and ginger, and upstairs, from over the shops, Eddie could hear the chatter of angry conversation and the rattle of dice in cups. He scored a couple of acid tabs from a dealer he knew whose patch was near Covent Garden. Then he came back down into Chinatown and tried to get into Krugers, a German pub frequented by Irish yuppies. New Irish Professional People in London. Nipples.

The doorman wouldn't let him in. It was his hair.

'You look too rough, man,' he said. It wasn't up to him. It was policy. He said Eddie'd better believe him. There was honestly no point in arguing. Eddie argued anyway. He said he was a personal friend of the manager. The bouncer told him he didn't care whether he was J. Edgar Hoover, he still wasn't getting in. Eddie asked for his name, and he wrote it down in his notebook.

'Right,' he said, 'I'll see you next time the licence comes up.' The bouncer sighed wearily.

'Look forward to it,' he smiled. 'It's a date.'

Just as he was turning away, the door of Krugers opened. A couple of suited Nipples pushed out past him, talking about some girl, and from inside the smoke-filled bar, above the exuberant wail and clank of Motown, Eddie heard laughter that he recognised. He looked through the window. He rubbed at the dirt with his sleeve.

Sitting up at the bar, talking to two guys in double-breasted suits, he saw Jimmy and Ruth. Their backs were turned, but it was them all right, the lying curs. He rapped on the window, but they couldn't hear him. Jimmy had a pink paper crown on his head, and he was talking excitedly, hands on his hips, his torso rocking from side to side, wiggling his ass, as he impersonated someone. Ruth put her hand on the thigh of the guy standing beside her, and she laughed until she was red in the face.

Eddie decided to walk home. He wasn't in the mood for the Tube.

'You can't trust anybody,' he thought. 'This city is full of liars and dickheads.'

When he came back down President Street, Marion was home. Eddie could see the light from the street as he sat on the pavement, with his head in his hands.

He slipped into the back kitchen and made a cup of coffee. He was feeling bad. Everything was murky, with an upside-down and underwater feeling. He couldn't concentrate on any one thing. Worry unfolded inside him, like a perverse tapeworm, uncoiling through his gut.

When he got into bed, she rolled away. She wasn't asleep. He knew from the way she was breathing.

The room was hot and stuffy. The breeze made the paper letters rustle on the walls. Sirens kept him awake half the night.

Next morning she was already gone when he woke up. He looked around for a note, but there wasn't one. Something caught his eye. Peering up, Eddie saw it, 'ABC' in stark black lettering that seemed to defy him, up on the ceiling. He lay back on the bed again, staring, right in front of his eyes. For a long time he didn't even blink. And then he did. It was at that moment Eddie knew things just couldn't go on like this for very much longer.

Eddie had to look for a new job. He checked out the Job Centre but it turned out to be the most ironically named place in King's Cross. Then he looked through the papers. Selling ad-space or computer programming, that was it. He knew he couldn't handle that. There was just no point in trying. He tried restaurants, asking if they needed waiters, but it was the same old story. His hair. He asked Mr Patel if he needed any help with the carpentry business, but Mr Patel doubted whether Eddie knew one end of a chisel from the other. And anyway, business was too slow to take anybody on. As it was, they were pushing it just to break even. It was all Nigel Lawson's fault. Since the mortgage rate went up nobody wanted to shell out on home improvement.

Finally he called into the burger bar on Euston station, where he'd seen a sign saying help was wanted on the nightshift. The manager was called Jason, and he said OK, but the pay was basic and the hours were long. Eddie told him he wasn't fussy. Jason said that was the best news he'd heard all decade. He was a sarcastic fucker.

They put him on long grills to start. That meant standing over the hotplate for five hours at a time with a silly cardboard hat on, turning slabs of burger meat with a spatula. He burnt his fingers and got hot spitting grease all up his forearms. Sweat dribbled from his forehead, in rivulets down his face, and it dripped onto the hissing metal. Every worker got a fifteen-minute break every five hours, when he or she could eat £1.37-worth of food. The amount of food you could eat depended on the length of time you'd been working there. Eddie never ate anything. On his first day he'd seen a fat guy with red hair and freckles blow his nose over the grill, and the snot had gone all over the chicken balls.

But even that wasn't the worst thing. The worst thing was just the amount of food. The vast cardboard boxes of burgers, splitting at the seams, the plastic ten-stone sacks of chips, the barrels of sweet-stenching quadruple thick shake, the enormous jars of bitter gherkins in green brine, the vats of tomato ketchup, the obese bins bulging with rotten leftovers and soggy bits. The thought of all that food. The first night he got home, Eddie thought he was going to be sick. The second night, he was. He heaved up in the bathroom until there was nothing left in his stomach.

He asked to be put on the counter but Jason said no way.

'You get rid of that hair,' he said, 'and we'll talk about it. Until then you're out of sight.' That night Eddie puked again.

Marion must have felt sorry for him. The sick was gone from the bath when he got up next day. He thought it was a sign of relenting. He called her at the supermarket, and some stupid penpusher said there was nobody of that name working there, and even if there was, she wouldn't be free to come to the phone. Eddie said he knew for a fact that Marion did work there.

'Well,' the guy insisted, 'she's not on my list.' He said Eddie didn't understand. If she was there, she'd be on his list. Eddie told him to stick his list, but when he rang back later the same thing happened.

When she got home that night, Eddie had already gone to work. When he came in, she was fast asleep. And when he got up, she was gone again.

In this manner, they didn't see each other properly for a few days. Then, after a week, they hardly saw each other at all. Time seemed to speed up. Apart from her body, dozing in the bed, the only evidence of Marion's presence in Eddie's life was the smell of her perfume late at night. And the inexorable spread of little bastard cut-out letters all along the ceiling towards the window.

Eddie tried to get onto days, but Jason said no way. Days were full. Days were when the OAPs and students came in. If he wanted days, he'd have to look elsewhere. Eddie started feeling desperate.

Jake told Eddie about the Lump. This was a car park in Cricklewood where you could turn up at eight in the morning and maybe get picked out of three hundred men for a day on the buildings. Thirty-five quid a day, no questions asked, no insurance, you could stay signing on the old rock and roll if you wanted. It all sounded a little corny for Eddie, but his money was running low, and there was nowhere left for him to turn.

He went down one morning, but none of the gangers picked him. The car park looked like a Chicago backstreet during the Depression: lines of silent men with red Irish faces and stained overalls and World Cup T-shirts, coughing up phlegm and pulling on cheap cigarettes. The bosses arrived in Mercs and Jags, fat greasy bastards with dandruff all over their Savile Row suits. They looked like the kind of guys who would have been urban district councillors back home in Ireland. The type who've got handmade Italian shoes but never change their socks. That type. They said Eddie looked like a Pretty Boy, who'd never done a day's hard work in his life. Pretty astute. They asked if he knew the difference between a joist and a girder. Eddie said yeah, Joyce wrote *Finnegans Wake* and Goethe wrote *Faust*. They didn't see the joke.

Eddie used to wonder where everything had gone wrong. He was obsessed with a sense of failure, not of love. Sometimes he thought of leaving. Other times he reckoned all they needed to do was talk things over and sort out their problems. But any time he tried to talk, in the middle of the night, Marion was cold. He told Jake about it. Jake was philosophical. 'If you want to keep your beer cold,' Jake pronounced, 'keep it next to my ex-wife's heart.' That was the title of Jake's favourite country and western song. He didn't seem to realise that the Marion situation was getting Eddie down, and making it hard for him to concentrate on his music. He said Eddie was too selfish. Eddie said he wasn't being selfish, he was just being a sensitive human being. Jake said that in his experience, there was a thin line.

'Love hurts, Eddie,' he smiled, sadly, 'sometimes you have to understand that. It's not all moonlight and Cadbury's Roses.'

'Jesus, Jake,' said Eddie, 'you're a real fucking help.'

On his spare days, Eddie played with The Diehards. The way things were going, he had a lot of spare days. Jake would sit in the corner rolling endless joints which he rarely seemed to actually smoke, slapping his thigh in time to the beat.

Spider Simms was the new drummer, a coolsville dude who liked wearing all the latest clothes. Spider dressed like a feature from *The Face*, with a permanent pout all over his mouth. He had a weird walk. He walked like he had a clothes hanger still inside his shirt, but he could thump the hell out of those drums. Spider had been in the army band for a couple of years. He had a soldier's rhythm, and he was always the first to turn up. At first, he and Eddie found it hard to talk. They'd stand outside the rehearsal room waiting for Clint and Andy and Jake, and things would sometimes be a little strained.

Spider was an acid house fanatic. He spent all his weekends driving up and down the motorways looking for draughty barns and abandoned warehouses in which to get stoned. He told Eddie he didn't know what he was missing. Eddie said he'd take his word for it.

Andy was the bass guitarist, a handsome soulboy from Edinburgh, with a flat-top hairdo, and a flat-top Chevvy, secondhand. He was the most accomplished musician of the lot. He'd been in the business for years. Jake referred to him as Andy 'LA' McCrory, because Andy had once been in California on a job, and he'd been bragging about the time he saw Prince in a nightclub ever since.

Andy and Spider were both ex-session players, competent, efficient, but a little on the soulless side. Eddie would jam through a chord sequence and they'd repeat it exactly, but sometimes a little too exactly.

'More soul,' Eddie said, 'give it a bit of guts, you know.' Andy said he was used to playing on Kylie Minogue records.

'Guts didn't exactly come into it,' he'd say, scratching his head. And Spider's solution to the guts problem was to play louder, which wasn't necessarily what Eddie wanted at all.

'Try to feel it,' urged Eddie, 'in here, you know, in your bones.'

Some nights Jake brought along a couple of the guys from The Sax Machine, his other band, just to thicken out the sound here and there. Eddie wasn't a brass fan, but he had to admit these guys were good. Still, it just bugged the shit out of him the way they insisted on doing their stupid choreographed finger-clicking whenever they weren't actually playing.

In between numbers Andy and Spider jammed hard-rock riffs, usually 'Stairway to Heaven' and 'Layla', which they never got exactly right, and The Sax Machine played John Coltrane, until Eddie nearly went crazy.

He'd come home with his throat hoarse, more from screaming at everybody than singing. Jake said you had to expect that. He said music was a great big melting pot, and Eddie had to be open to other influences. Eddie said the trouble with melting pots was that when the heat got turned up the scum came to the top. Jake said he was too cynical.

'You don't understand people, Eddie,' he'd sigh, 'sometimes I just don't know about you.'

It all came to a head one night in May.

Eddie came in late that night from a lousy frustrating practice, and he went straight to the kitchen. He'd got stoned again after the session and made up his mind to break up The Diehards and start things all over again. He'd had it with Jake. Always watching his watch for when the rehearsal time was up, never going a minute over. Clint was getting pissed off too. He reckoned they'd been better off back in the lock-up garage, hacking it out with The Bees.

Things weren't helped by the fact that The Bees, with new guitarist and singer, had just landed the support slot on The Stone Roses European Tour. When Eddie read this in the *NME* he almost collapsed on the spot with envy. Jake was dismissive about it. Support slots were a graveyard, he said.

'When I'm finished with you cats,' he promised, 'The Roses'll be down on their bell-bottomed knees, begging to support *you*.' Eddie said maybe, but in the meantime The Honey Bees were gigging all over Europe and The fucking Diehards were still stuck in Nowhere Land. Jake said it was all a matter of time. 'Patience is a virtue, Eddie,' he chided, 'as Billy Bragg said.' Eddie said maybe, but it wasn't a virtue he had much of left.

Eddie sat in the Brightside lobby with his coffee and everything started to spin. He sat very still, because he couldn't do anything else. The only conscious thought he could form was that this was why they called it stoned. Because it turned you to stone. Hey. So this was mind expansion. Eddie was pissed off. His band was crap. His girlfriend wasn't speaking to him. He had no money. The ceiling somersaulted and whirled around. When he looked out at the lights, all he could see were wispy streaks of neon. And just to make things worse, the smell of burnt curry powder and rotting rubbish bins drifted out to the lobby from the kitchens.

On his way up the stairs Eddie noticed that the carpet was wet. At first he thought it was just him. He thought he was imagining it. He stood on the stairs for a few seconds, stamping his feet, giggling softly to himself, thinking maybe that was good

Lebanese shit after all. But the carpet was squelching. There was no mistaking it. He walked up further and it got worse. The 'EXIT' signs glowed green in the dark. Every flight of stairs was wetter than the last. By the time he got to the fourth his ankles and the hems of his chinos were soaked. This was getting seriously unfunny. A horrible stink came from somewhere. Eddie stopped again. Somewhere in the back of his frantic and ravaged imagination he could hear a noise. A slow, turgid, mechanical sound that just didn't sound right. One of those sounds you know is wrong, it doesn't matter what else you're thinking. A sound that didn't fit.

He turned the corner, hand gripping the bannister.

Up ahead, on the landing outside their door, Eddie could see Mr Patel's washing machine, rocking gently from side to side, as soapy water came leaking out through the little door at the front.

Eddie stood still, watching the water surge from the machine, in regular waves. He blinked, hard. Then he walked over to it, nervously wishing that he was a million miles away.

Eddie tried to close the door properly but it burnt his hand, and when he touched it, it seemed to give a little growl, as though it was alive, and it didn't want to be touched at all. 'Fuck,' he winced, sucking his finger. Smoke drifted from the motor hatch at the bottom. An acrid chemical stench assaulted his nostrils.

Eddie went to the bathroom and got a towel, which he wrapped tight around his hand. Kneeling, he tried to force the door closed. The catch seemed to be broken. He jammed a chair hard against the door and water started spurting out through the top of the machine. Suds slapped against his face. The washing machine began to make loud farting noises.

Eddie stood up and ran his fingers through his mohican. Water was trickling down the stairs now, dripping over the edges of each step. All of a sudden, Eddie started feeling pretty unstoned.

He wondered what to do. He didn't have his watch, but he knew it was pretty late. He walked into his room and tried to wake Marion, but she was out cold, lying on her back, breathing deeply. Her pressed uniform hung blithely on the back of the door. He shook her and said her name, but she didn't wake. He shook her again, and she mumbled a soporific complaint. Eddie stood in the room looking at her.

He looked at the ABCs, all up and down the walls, and now in a straight black line that cut the ceiling in two. Then he gazed back at her. She looked innocent, and even though he knew she wasn't, he let the iilusion come. He looked at her hand, clasped tight around the sheet. Just for a second he seriously contemplated getting into bed beside her and pleading the fifth the next morning. He looked out on the landing. He couldn't see the carpet now. It was thick with grey fizzing foam.

The washing machine started to vibrate now, and a dull death rattle came from the motor. He went back to the bathroom. He splashed water on his face. Somebody had scribbled a phone number on the bathroom wall. Eddie looked in the mirror. This was just so fucking typical.

He tiptoed down the damp corridor and knocked on Mr Patel's door. There was no answer at first. He knocked again.

'Go away,' growled the voice, 'I sleep.' Eddie cleared his throat and steadied his mind. He leaned his forehead against the door. 'Mr P,' he hissed, 'it's me, Eddie Virago, can you, like, ease on out here for a minute?' There was no answer so he knocked harder, and said it again.

He heard the click of a switch, and some curses he didn't understand. Next thing Mr Patel was standing in the doorway, blinking in the light, tying the belt of his scarlet dressing-gown. He looked angry, but he said nothing at first. He just looked over Eddie's shoulder, down the corridor, straight at the ailing machine.

And then he started cursing.

'Motherfucker,' he said, 'Jesus, Mary and Joseph.' Eddie didn't even get a chance to tell him what was wrong. He could see for himself. 'Oh Jesus,' he kept saying.

'Yeah,' said Eddie, 'that's what I thought.'

They went to the machine and pressed a few buttons. Eddie said he was a bit of a Luddite when it came to machines, but Mr Patel didn't know what he meant. The stoned feeling kept creeping back over him. Whenever he thought about being stoned, the feeling came back. He felt like a character in a cartoon, running over the edge of a cliff, not falling until he looked downwards. He couldn't take his eyes off Mr Patel's hands. They looked so beautiful, long and elegant, like a sculptor's hands, the fingernails so beautifully manicured, the knuckles sharp. It occurred to him that Mr Patel would have made a great blues guitarist and he giggled at the thought. Mr Patel started to lose his temper. He kicked the machine, hard. He kicked again, and then he howled with pain, and began to hop, clutching the side of his slippered foot. He brought his fist down hard on the machine top. Hot water welled out and spilled down the crotch of his dressing-gown. He clamped his eyes closed and whimpered with pain.

In a sudden fit of inspiration Eddie said, 'Hey, Mr P, why don't we unplug it?'

'Well, don't just stand there,' he snapped, 'don't just talk, do it.' White foam had given him a Santa Claus moustache. Eddie ran his fingers through his hair again, then he bent to touch the plug. Mr Patel really started to freak out then. 'What the fuck are you doing?' he roared, slapping Eddie's hand. 'What are you doing, idiot, do you want to electrocute us all?' Eddie stared blankly at Mr Patel. 'Water and electricity,' scoffed Mr Patel, snorting in mock astonishment, 'they don't mix, you fool. Didn't they teach you anything in college?'

They stared at each other for a moment. Eddie said he'd majored in English Lit., actually. He said, 'If you want me to talk to it about semiotics, I'm your man.' Mr Patel put his hands on his hips.

'Do I have to spell it out?' he shrieked, making a pulling gesture. 'Yank on the flex. Like this.' And he did his pulling motion again. 'Pull the sonofabitch.'

'Do you really think I should?' said Eddie.

The machine groaned, and a tidal wave of evil-smelling gunge slobbered out of the top. It dribbled down the white enamel, leaving bits of filthy silt in its wake.

Mr Patel started hitting himself in the face.

'Get out of my fucking way,' he whinnied, 'I'll do it myself.'

Mrs Patel appeared in the doorway, wrapped in a pink blanket that revealed her thighs when she moved. Her hair shone, glossy and loose. It flowed down her back and when she shook her head she looked beautiful. Mr Patel said something to her, but she refused to leave. She looked at Eddie, and pulled the blanket tighter around herself. She pushed her hair behind her ears. Her purple eyes were dark with sleep.

Mr Patel started pulling on the flex, foot up against the wall. He heaved and panted and sweat poured down his face. The veins in his arms throbbed. Mrs Patel motioned Eddie to help him, but her husband said he didn't need any help. Eddie shrugged. She winced.

Sparks began to fly from the wall.

'Fuck me,' said Eddie, stepping back.

A bright blue electric flash illuminated the landing. The flex came away from the plug in Mr Patel's hand. He tumbled over backwards, banging his head on the bannister. Half the plug remained in the socket, and a waterfall of sparks began to shoot out, sparks everywhere, spraying through the air, crackling over the edge of the bannister, battering against the walls. The washing machine kept going for a few moments, churning round and grinding. Then it gave a sickening creak, juddered and went dead. Its timer ticked, ominously.

That was when Marion came out of the room. She wore a T-shirt and a pair of blue knickers. Her eyes were bleary, her face pale. Eddie looked at her, but she looked away from him. Water flowed across her bare feet and into their bedroom, but she didn't seem to notice or care. She asked Mrs Patel what was wrong. Her voice was hoarse. There was no time to answer.

'Get back,' roared Mr Patel. The washing machine gave one final whine and with a deafening crash, it exploded.

The top blew into the air and over the bannister, shattering the chandelier on its way down to the lobby. Great waves of water washed down the stairs. Mangled sopping clothes burst out through the door. Mr Patel clung to the leg of the bannister, as though he was going to be swept away. He gurgled furiously, in the foam.

Mrs Patel began to laugh. Mr Patel picked himself up and looked at her. He looked like he was going to slap her. She pointed at his face and imitated his angry expression. Then she laughed again. And she slowly closed the door.

Then Mr Patel began to laugh too. He threw back his head and laughed out loud, cackling and wiping his eyes, and Eddie laughed too, uncertainly. Some of the other guests came out and they laughed as well. Everybody laughed, except Marion. She stood very still, wrapping her arms around herself to keep warm. Her face was white. She looked down at her feet, and a horrified expression darkened her eyes. It was as though the dirty water was blood. She said nothing. She held her hands to her head and looked disgusted. She backed into the bedroom and closed the door, like a silent wooden weatherlady on an old-fashioned clock.

An hour later, when he had helped clean up the mess, Eddie came to bed. She was still awake. The carpet in the bedroom was sopping and ruined. The sweet smell of washing powder seemed to seep out of the walls.

Eddie took his shirt off and draped it over the chairback. He said he was sorry he was so late home. For a moment, she didn't speak, but Eddie wasn't surprised.

'It's three o'clock,' she said then, 'I was worried.' It was the first time they had spoken in a month. 'Where were you?' she asked.

'Look,' he said, 'I'm tired, let's douse the Edisons and get some kip.'

He flicked the switch and everything went dark, except for the inkblot clouded sky, purple and red outside the window, and the electric rainbow of the neons on the street. She rolled on her side, and moved against the wall, as far away as possible from Eddie.

The closeness of her body made everything seem worse. Eddie's feet were cold and wet. He lay on his back, with his hands behind his head.

'Marion,' he said, carefully, 'this is crazy. We can't go on like this.' She said nothing. 'I care about you,' he said, 'this is cracking my head up.' He moved his thigh across hers and pushed his hand up the front of her T-shirt. His fingers touched her breasts. 'Come on,' he pleaded. 'Can't we make up?'

In the dark, she screamed. She sat up straight and punched his face.

'You don't care for me,' she yelled, 'you don't take care of me, all you want is fucking, you think *nothing* of me.' Eddie held her arms but she spat at him, and Eddie could hear tears cracking her words. 'All you do,' she screamed, 'is confuse me. You're so fucking controlled, aren't you, Eddie? Everything is just a little thing to be made up.' Yellow light swept in under the door, from the landing, and Eddie could see her face now, twisting in rage. They wrestled in the bed and she tried to escape from him. Eddie was terrified. She fell onto the floor. He fell on top of her, and he felt his knee connect with the soft flesh of her abdomen. She yelped with pain, like an animal in a snare. They rolled around the wet floor, grunting, panting, struggling against each other, and she tried to scratch his skin with her blunt fingernails. Thighs on each side of his chest, she pummelled his face.

And the dreadful noise they made as they struggled, the hollow and parodic cacophony of two lovers fighting, the absurd symphony of two lovers whose love was dying – Eddie knew where he had heard it before.

He pulled away from her and flicked the lights on.

Marion stood in the centre of the room clutching a pair of

scissors in her hand. Blood stained the side of her cheek. Her eyes were furious. She was shaking. A rip ran down the side of her T-shirt. Eddie wondered whether it had always been there, or whether he had done it. He found himself laughing as he took a step towards her. She stepped back.

'I'll do it,' she warned, 'one of these days, I'll do it. That's what you want, isn't it, Eddie Virago? Isn't it?' Her hand brushed her hair behind her ears. She held the scissors like a child holding a pencil, her face purple with hate. 'Isn't it?' she screamed. 'Answer me, you fucking bastard.'

'Please,' he croaked. 'Jesus, Marion, please calm down.' His torso was wet, with sweat and water. His boxer shorts were soaked through, and they clung to his buttocks and testicles and thighs. 'Take it easy,' he said.

She screamed again.

'Don't *speak* to me like that,' she warned. She lunged at the bed. The scissors cut into the pillow, and white feathers spilled up through the air. She hacked the scissors from side to side, speaking in a terrible and calm rhythm. 'Don't. Speak. To Me. Like That.'

She slashed the pillow again and again, until she was almost hysterical. Every stab felt to Eddie like it was aimed at him. He found himself clutching at his chest. He backed against the door.

'You're fucking crazy,' he laughed. She picked up the ruined pillow and tossed it out into the street. Then she threw the scissors to the ground and without saying anything, ran to the bathroom. Feathers clung to her wet T-shirt and her naked legs. The door slammed. Feathers drifted back in from outside the window, and they settled on the floor like snow.

Eddie started to cry. He held his fingers over his eyes and he sobbed. Outside he could hear Mr Patel hammering on the door, and he could hear his own voice telling him to go away. In his mind's eye he saw her cutting herself, lying back in a bath full of red water. But he didn't care. He saw her graceful arm draped over the edge of the bath, as though she was reclining in a boat on a summer's day, trailing her hand in the mossy water. Tears came from somewhere they had never come from before, some bitter and truthful part of him that he had always submerged. Tears emptied him out and left him folded across the bed like a crumpled suit.

She sat in the bathroom all night, and Eddie lay on the bed. Once or twice he knocked on the door, but she didn't answer.

Then he was afraid to knock. As the sun stained the windowpane, Eddie fell into a flickering sleep. When he woke up he had a headache, Smokey Robinson was on the radio somewhere and she was beside him, naked, wanting to make love.

In the end, he never even told her he was leaving. He just started, day by day, to take his clothes and his books and his tapes with him to work, and he stashed them all into a couple of hired lockers at the back of Euston station. Sometimes he worried that she would notice his stuff disappearing from the room. But if she did, she never said anything. In any case, they hardly even spoke any more. Whenever Eddie came into the room she picked up her stuff, pushed past him without a word and went down to the lobby, or into the breakfast room, where she'd sit for hours, writing letters, smoking endless cigarettes.

He began sneaking out of the Brightside in the mornings, wearing as many shirts and jumpers as possible. He squeezed his suit trousers on under his leathers and smuggled those out too. He stuffed his shoes and his books into the soundbox of his guitar. And on the very last morning he got dressed, took his guitar case and strolled out the front door, telling Mr Patel he'd probably be late home that night. Mr Patel hardly even looked up at him.

'OK, Eddie,' he murmured, scribbling something, 'OK, see you then.' That morning Eddie handed in his cards at the burger bar. He told Jason that if anybody came asking for him, he was going away to South America.

At the rehearsal, he asked Jake if he could stay with him for a few days, at his garden flat in Blackheath. He said he was having a few domestic difficulties and he needed a place to lie low and get his act together for a while. Jake shook his head. It was just the wrong time. He couldn't help. He had a troop of twelve French reggae musicians crashing at his place just now, so there wasn't room to swing a pussy. He'd brought them all over from Paris to do a couple of demo tracks with The Sax Machine.

'It's only a garden flat,' he whined, 'it's not Madison Square Gardens, Ed. Any other time, man, but not now.'

'Jesus, Jake, I'm really stuck here,' said Eddie, 'I'll sleep in the bath or something.'

'Christ, Ed, I've got two of them in the bath already, pal, and one in the fucking bidet, you know? I mean, the joint is jumping, Ed.'

'Jake, look, I wouldn't ask you except I'm stuck.'

'Eddie, you know me, I'd give you the shirt off my back, kid, but I really can't help.'

'Don't you have any friends, Eddie?' asked Andy.

''Course I've got friends,' he pouted, 'I mean, Jesus, of course I do, but I just need to be away from everyone right now.'

Spider stopped battering his bass drum and peered up at Eddie.'

'You can stay with me for a while,' he said, 'I mean, if you're really stuck. You can crash at the squat.'

'Spider,' said Eddie, 'you are a wonderful human being.'

'Yeah,' said Jake, 'that guy's blood should be bottled.'

So Eddie moved in with Spider, into the squat on Electric Avenue in Brixton. They sat up late the first night and Eddie drank himself stupid. He told Spider that he'd caught Marion screwing his best friend in the world, and he just had to get away from her for a while. Spider nodded, understandingly. He agreed that disloyalty was a terrible thing. But he said he didn't want Marion arriving around here and causing a humungous scene. Eddie promised she wouldn't.

'I don't want you guys washing your dirty linen all over my place,' he warned, 'I mean it, Eddie.'

'Spider,' slurred Eddie, 'cross my heart, pal. Swear to God.'

'I mean, you can tell her you're here,' said Spider, 'but just do your peacemaking on neutral ground, OK?'

'Listen,' said Eddie, 'I'm not even going to tell her I'm here. She'd be around here to get me straightaway.' Spider said he didn't think that was very fair. 'You don't know her, Spider,' said Eddie. 'Believe me, that girl is capable of anything.'

For two days and nights Eddie stayed in Spider's spare room, pretending he had some kind of obscure summer flu. Sometimes he heard a creak on the stair, or the sound of a footfall out on the landing, and that freaked him out completely. He slept for hours, in the middle of the day, and when he woke up he felt numb and stupid from the sleep. At night he lay awake thinking about Marion, and the way he had left her. Sometimes he fell into flickering dreams, seeing himself sneaking down the stairs of the Brightside, seeing her on every landing, standing very still in the shadowy alcoves, with her arms folded across her chest, and her eyes wide open, and her fragile face covered in alphabet letters. He took far too many drugs.

One night after the first week Spider asked Eddie if it hadn't bothered him, just walking out like that, without even saying goodbye. Eddie told him he thought that was a really sexist assumption actually, that Marion would fall apart without a man to keep her together. And anyway, Eddie was doing the right thing. His conscience was completely clear. It took real guts to leave somebody and take all the guilt on yourself. Spider laughed.

'I thought there wasn't any guilt,' he said.

Eddie couldn't seem to make him understand, but Spider told him to relax. He said he didn't really give a shit one way or the other. It was Eddie's problem and he didn't want to get involved in it. Spider had adjusted his attitude a while back. He was going through what he coyly referred to as 'a period of celibacy'. In Spider's book monogamous relationships only led to trouble. You met someone you really liked, then you ended up slowly tearing each other to shreds. Hell. It wasn't his idea of a fun time.

'Happy loving couples,' he said, 'spare me.'

The squat didn't look like any squat Eddie had ever seen, not that he'd seen too many, except in late-night documentaries on Channel Four. The furniture was all tubular steel and black leather – Spider worked part-time as a security guard in an office supplies warehouse – and there were weird plants in earthenware pots all over the place. Spider had a big thing about plants. They swung from the ceiling, they sprouted in the airing cupboard, under sheets of flapping black plastic in the allotment at the back, everywhere. Spider was a closet hippy, in fact. He really was. He denied it frantically, but he had a mobile of white paper swans hanging in the windowframe and the complete works of Joni Mitchell stashed under the sink. When he got drunk he'd start talking lugubriously about Woodstock, as though he'd been there, slopping through the mud himself. Also, he was writing a novella 'about birth'. What further proof could anyone want?

Eddie had the spare room to himself, but the mattress was thin and lumpy, so when Spider was out during the day, he lay on his futon and tried to get some sleep. In Spider's room there was a word-processor on a black table by the wall. In the corner sat a bookcase full of all kinds of impressive stuff – lives of Renaissance painters, novels in French, slim volumes of poetry – that had obviously never been read. The books were arranged very neatly, from top to bottom, by colour, starting with red spines and moving, shelf by shelf, through the spectrum to violet.

The squat was fine. The only problem was the damp. Spider's clothes got mouldy and stiff during winter, so he covered the walls of the wardrobes with thick layers of tinfoil. This took Eddie a while to get used to. Sometimes he'd open a wardrobe door and jump at his reflection. But Spider seemed to spend all of his money on clothes. Every weekend he'd come trailing home from Soho or the King's Road, great bags of garish garments wedged under his armpits. So Eddie had to put up with the homemade insulation system.

Brixton was a good place, specially in the summer, full of fruit stalls and chancers and great secondhand record shops and people trying to sell you things you didn't really want. Eddie liked just walking up and down the main street, looking in the windows, glaring at the soulboys and rockers, and the beautiful girls, listening to the hip-hop that came booming out of the minicab offices and the cafés. He saw people more black than he'd ever seen in his life, men and women so black that in the strong sun their skin looked not black but dark blue, like in the Irish for a black man, *fear gorm*, a blue man. For the first time ever, Eddie got to understand that phrase.

In Brixton there was always music. Wailing soul and reggae beating out of the flats, ska and bluebeat in the street market, bebop jazz in the barber's shops, and on Sunday mornings the sound of hymns from the Pentecostal church.

Spider took him to a speakeasy club over a launderette that played blues all night. Muddy Waters and Howlin' Wolf. Robert Johnson and Elmore James. Johnny Winter, Sonny Terry and Brownie McGee. Strictly speaking the club was blacks only. But Spider was OK because he had once done the manager some favour that he didn't like to talk about. And Eddie was OK – just about – because he was Irish. The place was dark and small, and it smelt of dope. There was sawdust on the floor, cans of beer, bottles of rum. The tables were planks of wood laid across beer crates. The records were played loud, with the bass turned up as far as it would go. Sometimes they had live acts too, young guys with out of tune guitars, blues shouters and torch singers, an angry dreadlocked girl who hammered the battered piano and screamed about the police. Spider said this was the real blues. He said the feel was the deal with this music. It wasn't to do with middle-class kids from Surrey singing about the Delta on electric guitars their mothers bought them as graduation gifts.

Sometimes they sat there together all night long, saying nothing at all because the music was too loud, the only white faces in the room, oblivious to the hostile looks around them, laughing, completely drunk, almost even happy.

Then one Friday night they went down to the Academy to see The Pogues. But the queues were too long and they couldn't get in. Spider was pissed off, but Eddie was relieved. The place was crawling with Irish people, all young, all drunk. He was still paranoid about meeting Marion, or one of her friends. He just couldn't have handled it, but he didn't want to admit that to Spider. On the way back to the squat he had to pretend that he too was pissed off. He knew it was irrational, but being told how irrational it was only made him feel worse.

Sometimes in those early weeks he wanted to telephone her, just to say he was OK, and to see how she was doing. Several times he found himself in the phonebox late at night, with the receiver in his hand, dialling the number of the Brightside. Once he actually rang it, and Mr Patel answered, sounding friendly and warm. For a moment he considered speaking, just saying hello, asking for Marion, explaining the whole thing and saying he was sorry and how he still wanted to be friends. But then Eddie hung up. And the next time he rang the phone was answered by somebody he didn't recognise, a young Asian man with a soft lisping voice.

He tried to write letters too, long paragraphs of self-justification, subtle mixtures of great frankness and total evasion. And then one night he drank a bottle of Southern Comfort, sat down and wrote it all out, as honestly as he could, holding nothing at all back, not trying to spare her feelings, or his own either. But next morning he screwed it up and threw it away. He didn't even bother to read it over. In his heart he knew that the time for honesty had already gone. It was now nearly a month since he'd left. How could he just write now, as though anything between them was still capable of explanation?

'Let's face it, Eddie,' said Spider, 'you've been a bastard. It's no crime. Everyone does it sometimes, but you shouldn't pretend you can sort it out now.'

Summer smooched its way down over Brixton. Everyone donned cycling shorts and mirror shades. Stand pipes were delivered to the street corners when the water was rationed. Heat made the food rot in the shops. The streets hummed with the stink of rotten pears, pineapples, bananas. A couple of kids got busted for selling buckets of water to old-age pensioners. Young men sat on the steps of the town hall, swigging cold bottles of Guinness. A woman went heat-crazy in Brockwell Park and told one of the gardeners that she was Jesus. July melted into August. And still Eddie didn't get in touch with Marion.

Spider was good about things. But he said he couldn't keep paying for everything. He didn't want to get into a big material- istic situation, but Eddie would have to get work, or go on the dole, or sell his body, or some damn thing. So Eddie got another burger-bar job, this time in Victoria, where he thought he'd be safe enough from Marion.

There was a black guy working there who could make a snare drum sound with his teeth. That was the height of the excitement. Otherwise it was pretty much the same deal as Euston. Except that now Eddie was used to the work. It didn't bother him any more. He didn't throw up when he came home at night, and he didn't expect any favours from the management. He even got to like it. Almost. People laughed at his mohican, peaking up through a specially cut slit in the top of his embarrassing paper hat. The customers seemed to get a kick out of him. He had a quick fling with a beautiful Dublin girl, a first year at Trinity, who was over in London for the summer. The next week she left. Eddie was just as happy. He made up his mind to take Spider's advice. No more relationships, for the moment anyway. He tried to put Marion out of his mind. Most of the time, to his surprise, he succeeded.

And then one day in work, a strange thing happened. Eddie thought he saw her, in the middle of the afternoon, standing in the middle of the station concourse, as though she was waiting for somebody. He squatted behind the till and watched as she looked around. She'd lost a little weight, but she looked well, in a white sweatshirt and tight black shorts. She stood very still by the ticket machines, flicking through a magazine, gazing from time to time at her watch. Looking at her, Eddie felt the blood drain from his face. Just for a moment he contemplated walking straight over to her, just to say hi, and how he was sorry for everything, the way he had treated her, and the way things had turned out between them. He stood up straight, cleared his throat, stared across the concourse at her back. But then he changed his mind. He ducked out the back of the burger bar, telling the boss that he felt ill. He hid in the gents for an hour, pacing up and down, smoking cigarettes. A middle-aged guy in a suit offered him thirty pounds to come to a hotel with him. Eddie told him to fuck off. When he came back up to the stand she was gone. He asked his boss whether anyone had come looking for him while he'd been away. Nobody had. Eddie really didn't feel well now. He sat on the floor behind the counter with his head in his hands, sweating, shaking. After half an hour, his boss sent him home.

For a few days Eddie sat in the flat, wrapped in a blanket, looking like an H-block hungerstriker and not feeling much better. Whenever the telephone rang he jumped. He began taking it off the hook, and that drove Spider crazy. He worried. When he stopped worrying, he felt guilty. When he stopped feeling guilty, he began worrying again, about why he didn't feel guilty any more.

He tried to give up cigarettes and dope, but he couldn't do it. When Spider came in at night they'd sit up for ages, smoking themselves stupid and listening to strange sitar music. Other times they went back down to the speakeasy, but even there Eddie didn't feel calm. People down there didn't like him. He could tell by the look in their eyes. 'Boss,' they called him, with a half sneer.

He tried to throw all his energies into the band. By the middle of August they'd settled down into some kind of steady routine, and once or twice, rehearsals even went well. Spider and Clint made a good writing team. The new demo got made and Jake started sending it out to the record companies, kissing each envelope personally before he dropped it into the letter box.

Spider tried to introduce Eddie to some new friends. Girls mainly, who hung around with him and Clint after gigs. Some of them were OK, but Eddie never showed much interest. Spider and Clint began to wonder if he was gay, and if this was why he and Marion had parted. Spider sat him down one night and told Eddie that he had friends he could trust, that we all felt confused about things sometimes, and that human sexuality was a drama, not a monologue.

'Spider,' groaned Eddie, 'what the fuck are you talking about?'

And then Eddie started worrying that Marion would start checking the listings in *City Limits* and show up at one of The Diehards' gigs. She never did, but still he got cagey and secretive. He started wearing a black balaclava when he walked down the street. When Clint and Spider and Jake went out clubbing to the

West End, he'd invent ridiculous excuses to stay at home. He went out less and less, only to the shops, or to sit on his own for hours in Brockwell Park. And then it got to the stage where the only time Eddie ever went into town was to play a gig. Even then, he'd turn up last, and afterwards leave straightaway in a cab, like he was Elvis fucking Presley, as Jake said, speeding back to a teenage schoolgirl and a double cheeseburger in Graceland. Eddie told everybody that singing put him up on such a high that he just had to be alone afterwards. For a while, they had the good grace not to laugh.

But then one night Spider finally tackled him. Another gig had come up at the Pride of Erin, and Eddie'd refused point blank to do it. It was the acoustics, he said, they just weren't up to scratch. Spider said that was bollocks, and that The Diehards had played in places with the acoustics of a metal bucket. Eventually Eddie backed down, and admitted it was Marion. He just couldn't bear to meet her. Spider lost his temper and said Eddie was being totally paranoid.

'What's the worst thing that can happen,' he asked, 'even if you do bump into her somewhere? I mean, she's not going to castrate you, is she?' Eddie said he wouldn't be so sure about that. 'You know sometimes, Eddie,' Spider said, 'I suspect there's more to this relationship than you like to tell people.'

'*Et tu*, Spider?' said Eddie. 'Just get off my case, OK?'

On a Saturday night near the end of August, Spider finally gave him an ultimatum. He said he couldn't take it any more. He said it was at the stage where *he* felt guilty, and he'd done fuck all. He said he felt like he was living with Charles Manson. Eddie had to shape up or shift his ass.

'I'm going out to a rave tonight,' he said. 'You're either coming with me, Eddie, or you're getting out of here. I'm sorry, man, but somebody has to kick your ass out of this.' They argued. Eddie asked who the fuck did Spider think he was.

'When I want your advice,' he said, 'I'll ask for it.' Spider said Eddie was driving him bats.

'I don't want to lay this pressure on you, man,' he implored, 'but if this goes on, Eddie, you're gonna end up where the doors have no handles, and so the fuck am I.' There was an acid house party. It was somewhere in a circus tent off the Magic Roundabout – Spider's name for the M25 – and they had to call a number at eleven to get the details. 'You're coming with me, Eddie. Be there,' said Spider, 'or be sleeping rough.'

'No way,' pouted Eddie, 'you can't push me around like that, you fucker.'

In the car Spider apologised for being such a fascist. He said Eddie'd enjoy it.

'Come on, man,' he beamed, 'you can't live like a hermit just 'cos you're scared of your old chick. Plenty more snakes in the pit, y'know.'

Eddie tried to pretend he couldn't read the map properly, but it didn't work. Spider knew the way.

The first sign they'd got to the rave was the massive row of cars. Clapped-out Minis, Morris Minors, and one or two Jags. Guys with thick necks groped them outside the tent. They wore shirts that said InterCity Firm. They didn't look like the kind of guys you'd fuck with, in any sense of the word. Doc Martens, belts, braces, buckles, tattoos all up and down their forearms, and in the case of one or two, all over their faces. They carried baseball bats and bicycle chains, and one or two hauled at snapping rottweilers on leashes. Spider said wistfully that it was just like The Stones at Altamont.

Inside the tent was thick with the scent of poppers and fresh sweat. The floor was damp and slippery, tacky with spilled Lucozade. Almost everybody seemed to be drinking Lucozade. Either that or currant juice. Music pumped out of huge speakers hung from the mainframe of the tent and rainbow lights swept across the sea of heaving bodies. A huge flashing green strobe announced the words 'DON'T BELIEVE THE HYPE'. A gang of DJs filled the circus-band balcony.

These guys were amazing. They spat words into their microphones, hopping from foot to foot, faster than anything, faster than Eddie could even hear the words. While one of them rapped, his posse stood behind him, cheering him, urging him on, clapping him on the back, swigging from bottles of something that looked like it might be tequila. One tiny black guy in a red tartan hunting cap coaxed a roar of applause from the audience. He screamed rhythms into the mike, swaying from side to side, legs apart, knees bent, holding his cap on with one hand, bellowing into the thing like he was hysterical, but never missing a beat. Bass pounded up through the floor, rattling the tent supports, vibrating Eddie's spine and his gut. Snatches of James Brown and Aretha Franklin came screaming over the PA, double mixed and looped back.

Spider looked like he'd died and gone to acid heaven. He closed his eyes and mouthed the words of the chorus, dipping his shoulders and skanking gently from side to side. In the ultra-violet light his white shirt looked purple and glowing. Half-way through 'Paid In Full', he pulled a tiny brown bottle from inside his underpants.

'Amyl nitrate,' he crooned, 'we love you.'

Eddie had never tried poppers before. But he closed his eyes and sniffed, and almost immediately he felt his heart jump. He sniffed again and his chest felt like something alive was flapping inside it. His eyes streamed and Spider slapped him on the back. A sensation of nausea followed by the most intense well-being came down over Eddie. He could almost feel it starting in his tingling toes and licking its way up his thighs. It was like he'd got pins and needles before, and now he could feel blood flowing back through his body. Spider made a thumbs up sign.

'Put hair on your chest,' he said. 'Blow your blues away.'

Spider seemed to know lots of people. People seemed happy to see him. Pretty girls wandered up behind him and kissed him, one or two pretty guys too. He greeted them with his usual sardonic grin. He held one hand in the air and his friends would reach back like they were going to punch him, then slap his hand, high above their heads. He introduced Eddie to a couple of people.

'This is Eddie Virago, folks,' he said, 'he's been hibernating over the summer, but now we've coaxed him out.' For the first time all summer, Eddie could feel himself relax.

The clothes helped make everything weirdly asexual. Almost everyone wore the same kind of stuff. Loose psychedelic T-shirts that came down to the knees, baggy jeans, expensive looking trainers. One or two girls wore tight-fitting cocktail dresses, black or red, and one or two guys wore sharp-looking suits, but mostly they didn't, and the ones who did looked hot and uncomfortable and out of place. They danced with their eyes closed, and they moved their arms in the air like they were underwater and trying frantically to get to the surface.

Spider didn't want to dance. He left Eddie talking to some girl called Rowena who was bonking the guy in the Levi 501 commercials, or said she was. She was a stylist, apparently. She said it wasn't exactly a job you could define. Eddie said he could believe that. He sucked on his beer can and nodded every few seconds, in time with the beat, watching Spider weave through the crowds. He was prowling around the tent looking for somebody, with a hungry look in his eye. Way across the middle ring Eddie could see him shaking hands and exchanging banknotes with a seedy guy in sideburns and a leather jacket. Rowena said she used to go out with Roland Gift from The Fine Young Cannibals, but now he was in LA. Eddie expressed his sympathy.

A camp black guy on roller skates came by selling raffle tickets. He had a Japanese headband round his forehead, white, with a red disc in the middle. Eddie said no, but the girl explained. Acid house parties couldn't get licences, so you had to buy a raffle ticket. The prize for every raffle ticket was a can of Red Stripe.

'There's no losers here,' the guy said, 'that's the theory anyway.' Eddie bought two, and he gave one to the girl. 'Big spender,' the black guy said, bitchily, and he sped off into the crowd.

She didn't want to take it at first. She said she didn't drink, but she was obviously on something. Her eyes were moist and she looked like she'd been crying. Her breath smelt sweet as brandy. Eddie said to be absolutely honest, he'd be into making a score. She pointed out the dealers, strung around the hall like Christian Brothers at an Irish school dance. Eddie said he thought there were no drugs at these things, and that's why everybody'd got searched outside the tent. She told him some dealers paid to be allowed in. It was like a franchise, she said. They paid to cut down the competition.

Eddie and Rowena danced for a while, not looking at each other, but the floor was way too packed and stoned people kept crashing into them and standing on their ankles. So they went and sat on the rim of the circus ring, and they talked for a while about Spider.

'Did you know he was in the army,' she said, 'over in Northern Ireland?'

'Jesus, no,' said Eddie, 'I never heard that.'

'Oh yeah,' she said, 'got into deep water over there. His best friend got killed by a car bomb. Spider had to pull him out of the car.'

'Are you sure, Rowena?' he said. 'I mean, he's never told me.'

'Oh yeah. He doesn't like to talk about it much. He's never

been the same, you see,' she said, sadly, 'he's just so weird now, I can't figure him out any more, you know?'

'Christ almighty,' exclaimed Eddie, 'I'm not surprised.'

'Spider's a real space cadet,' she slurred, 'I think he's crazy, but he never listens to me.'

But Eddie wasn't listening either. In the middle of the circus ring, something had caught his eye.

A thin girl with long auburn hair came walking through the crowd of heaving bodies with a microphone in her hand, talking furiously to a camera. On all sides of her, guys in jeans scuttled along holding lights that shone down on her hair. An intense-looking woman in red glasses marched in front of her, hooshing dancers out of the way.

'Hey,' said Rowena, 'that's Salome thing, isn't it, from "Art Attack"?'

Eddie squinted into the middle of the ring.

'Jesus, yeah it is,' he said, 'Salome Wilde.'

'Yeah, big deal,' she said. Eddie was on his feet.

'Want me to introduce you?' he asked, as he closed the top button of his shirt. 'She's an old friend of mine.'

Rowena said no. She said it was seriously untrendy to pester these celeb types. Anyway, she had to go meet somebody. She said maybe she'd see Eddie later for another dance, and he said, 'Yeah, sure, catch you later.'

Eddie stood over by the circle of people, watching Salome Wilde doing her piece to the camera. She was prettier than he remembered, that was for sure, and more confident too. She was talking quickly at the lens, gesturing around her and running her fingers through her long hair. But the music was so loud that Eddie couldn't hear what she was saying. Every time the director lowered his hand, some guy came over and dabbed makeup on her face.

Eddie went to talk to the woman in the red glasses.

'Look, Toots,' she said, 'we're making a television programme here, OK?' Eddie said he didn't think they were doing open-heart surgery.

'She's a friend of mine,' he said, 'go ahead, ask her.'

Salome Wilde did remember him, too.

'I know you,' she said, shaking his hand, 'I remember your hair.' She stared into space and tried to think of Eddie's name. 'And you were a friend of Dean Bean, weren't you? All those socialist types.' She said the word 'socialist' like she was talking about a native of the Seychelles. Eddie said yeah, that was his big claim to fame. She said, 'No, seriously, it's the haircut I recognise,' and he told her he recognised her from the TV. 'You're very kind,' she said. He told her his name was Eddie Virago. 'That's right,' she said, as if it was in doubt.

'You busy?' he said.

'You know, Eddie,' she said, touching his wrist, 'I don't think they've invented a word for how busy I am.'

She asked what he'd been doing since he left UCD and he said nothing much, hanging around, getting a band together. She thought that was great. She loved to see people from the old days doing something with their lives. She said the problem with Ireland was the way everyone sat around moaning all the time.

'I know it's such a cliché,' she said, and she made a yawning gesture with her hand, 'but I mean, we really are a nation of knockers, don't you think, Eddie?' Every time she said his name, it gave him a real thrill. She looked fantastic, in a blue one-piece thing that showed off her figure. Her hair was glossy and well-cut and her fingernails were painted black. Her skin was amazing, tanned and smooth, like Jennifer's. She looked rich. Eddie told her that and she laughed. 'If only,' she said. She asked about Dean Bean again.

Just then Spider staggered over, looking like he'd anticipated something. Eddie said this was one of the guys in his band, the drummer, Spider Simms. Spider told her he wasn't just a drummer. He was doing a bit of creative writing as well.

'What,' she asked, 'in an advertising agency?'

'No,' he said, 'in a squat. I'm writing a novella about birth.' Salome pulled a face.

'Deep,' she smirked. She picked up a hand radio and said, 'Cat. Send Tex in here, will you, if he's around?' Tex was a friend of hers. She thought he might be able to give them a bit of advice. He was bisexual, she told them, for some reason. Then she laughed and said, 'Oh, don't worry, he's into girls, at the moment. It goes in waves, apparently. Something to do with the moon.'

Tex was an A and R man from Red Tape Records, and he told Eddie to send him a tape some time. Eddie said he'd get his manager to do it, and the guy looked impressed.

'Hey,' he said, 'you've got a manager, who is it?' Eddie told him. Tex nearly laughed his fillings out. 'Jesus, Jake Mullan. That guy's not a manager, sweetie, he's a hoodlum.' Then he said he was only kidding around, but Jake had been in and out of the music business for years and he'd left more than a few broken hearts behind him. Eddie said, oh yeah, he knew that, but it was a tough old business and he needed a shark like Jake to keep the barracudas at bay. Tex said, yeah, that was one way of looking at it. But the road to rock and roll heaven was strewn with the bleached bones of people Jake had made promises to. Salome said he was a real poet. She nudged Spider and said, 'You two should get together.' Spider grinned, stupidly.

Tex told some good stories about Jake, and Spider listened with growing unease to every word. The more stuff came out, the more worried Spider looked. It turned out that Jake had turned down the Boomtown Rats. In 1978 he'd told them punk was finished. Six weeks later they'd signed to Ensign for a million up front and Jake had gone around telling everyone he'd negotiated the deal. 'Instrumental' was Jake's word, Tex said.

'If Jake ever tells you he's been "instrumental", you better run.' Another time, he told them, one of Jake's bands was offered third support on The Clash tour, and Jake'd turned it down. 'Can you believe it? He turned the fucking thing down.' Eddie said no way, he couldn't believe that. Jesus. 'The way I heard it,' giggled Tex, 'he told his boys, who are now, incidentally, currently residing in the where-are-they-now file, he said, get this, by the time he was finished with them, right, The Clash would be down on their knees pleading to support *them*.' Tex spluttered with laughter, hand over his mouth. '*What* a bull-shitter,' he sniggered.

Eddie felt embarrassed listening to all this. Salome Wilde kept giggling, and telling Tex he was a terrible old bitch, but Eddie felt like a naïve idiot. Spider went quiet and broody. He said he wanted to be alone, and he wandered off into the crowd again.

'What's eating him?' asked Salome. 'He's not a very happy bunny, is he?' Eddie said no, he wasn't, not just now.

'But he's like that,' explained Eddie, 'creative, you know.' Tex apologised.

'No offence to your friend,' he said to Eddie, 'I just don't know the mischief my ole tongue can do.'

Salome told Eddie to stick around, they were nearly done shooting, and maybe she and Eddie could have a beer afterwards. So he hung out in the middle of the ring, watching her do her piece again, and trying to sidle into one of the shots.

When she was finished, the crew got busy packing their stuff away, and she asked Eddie if he felt like a bop. He didn't really. But he said yes anyway.

Salome danced like a robot. She never moved her feet, just swayed her hips from side to side, and moved her arms with awkward grace, as though she was shadowboxing, and not dancing. She kept leaning over and shouting names from college into Eddie's ear, and he roared back either that he didn't know who she was talking about, or else told her whatever gossip he knew, which wasn't much.

Everyone else was doing the Lambada, a pretty sexy Latin dance that was the latest thing that summer. It was the closest thing to vertical fucking Eddie had seen since one hot night out on the balcony with Marion in April. He watched the lithe thrusting bodies of the dancers around him, and he felt a feeling that was a little too close to embarrassment for his liking.

But Eddie and Salome Wilde clicked. She laughed at his jokes and he laughed at hers. When he held her hand coming off the dance floor she didn't seem to mind. Tex and the red-spectacled woman were waiting for her, looking impatient. She had to dash.

She told Eddie she'd love to do something some time. Like dinner. Catch up on old times. Eddie said that'd be great and she gave him her card. On the back she scribbled her home address and her number, in St John's Wood.

'Hey,' said Eddie, 'I'm impressed.'

'Oh, you shouldn't be,' she laughed, 'it's only rented.' He meant he was impressed that she had a card at all, but he didn't say that. He said he'd get in touch soon. 'No really, do,' she said. She stepped forward and kissed him on the cheek. 'Yes,' she smiled, 'do. We can have that chat about Dean Bean. You never did tell me what he was up to these days.'

They shook hands, until the woman with the red glasses looked like she was going to explode with impatience.

'Come on, Salome,' she urged.

'OK, OK,' Salome sighed, and she turned quickly to Eddie again. 'Just by the way,' she said, 'don't worry about what Tex told you about your manager. He's just a bitch. He exaggerates everything.'

'Oh yeah,' laughed Eddie, 'that's exactly what I thought.'

After they'd gone Eddie wandered around the tent silently cursing Dean Bean and trying to find Spider and Rowena. He felt good, but the music had got way too heavy for his liking, serious hard-core reggae, all pumped-up drum machine and manic bass. The acid freaks were still on their sneakers, bopping wearily from side to side like they were on strings. But everywhere else people had collapsed on the floor, asleep or snogging, or staring up into the roof of the tent like it was a planetarium, which, at that stage, it probably was. For some people anyway.

He drank another beer, sticky, warm, and he looked around for Rowena, again, but she was gone. He sat on the edge of the ring, watching the dancers, and Marion came into his mind. Hell, it hadn't all been that bad. He tried to think happy thoughts. The day they went sightseeing. The night they went to the Hippodrome and found a twenty pound note on Charing Cross Road. And even that day she ripped into Frank, hell, Eddie had to admit, it had its funny side. But now it was over. These things happened every day of the week. It was nobody's fault, that was the thing to remember. He told himself that. He could see that now. Every day people met and they parted. And it was just life. That's all it was. Not Heathcliff and Catherine. Just men and women, an everyday thing. Nothing, Eddie told himself, possibly lasts forever.

And anyway, she was much better off without him. He had to be honest about that. Dean Bean was right. It was good to be straight with yourself. She really was much better off now. Eddie was sure of it. He could see everything clearly now. Hell, he'd done her a favour. In a few years' time she'd probably look him up and say thanks very much, pal, you did me a real favour that time. Sometimes in life you had to make tough decisions, just act like a man, take your responsibilities seriously. She'd see that one day. If she hadn't already. She really would. He knew it.

Eddie leaned his hot face into his hands, wishing the music would stop.

'What a fucking *sap*,' he thought. 'Why the fuck did you ever let her go?'

Eddie found Spider in a heap outside the back of the tent. Crusty dried vomit decorated his face, but he was lying on his side, and he was still breathing, which was something. The dew had fallen and his clothes were soaked through. Eddie nudged him with his foot, but Spider didn't seem to want to wake up.

Way across the damp hedges the light was coming up over London. Eddie could see tower blocks in the gloom. Cowpats lay like landmines across the grass. Everything was cold. Birds had started to sing somewhere, but Eddie couldn't see them.

When Spider woke up he didn't know where he was. Eddie told him he had vomit on his face.

'I wonder whose it is?' groaned Spider, and he laughed. Then he clutched his ribs and winced, in real pain. He was in a bad way. He told Eddie that he'd had this pretty freaky hallucination where he thought he was a banana. Eddie started to laugh. Spider said it wasn't that funny. He thought people were trying to peel his skin off. 'Just think about it, Eddie,' he said. 'Seriously bad.'

Someone had snapped the mirror off the car, but Spider was past caring. Eddie drove. All the way back to London Spider talked to himself. He was worried about Jake. He thought that guy Tex had really seemed to know what he was talking about. Eddie said he was sure people had said stuff like that about Brian Epstein. Spider said maybe, but at least he had The Beatles. He leaned his head against the side window.

'We ain't no Fab Four, Eddie,' he sighed.

'Yeah, well,' said Eddie, 'let's look on the bright side. Things can only get better, OK?'

Outside the squat, Spider sat crying with his face in his hands.

'Oh Jesus, no,' he whined, 'I don't believe this has happened, man. The first night in Christ knows how long the place is empty.' His face went red, white and blue, in quick succession, as he punched his dashboard. Eddie chewed his fingernails, looking at the smashed windows, smoking his last cigarette. He knew it was going to be one of *those* days.

Soon as Eddie touched the squat door it kind of slipped forwards, off its hinges, and it crashed into the hall like a drunkard hitting a bar-room floor.

Inside, quick-drying cement had been poured down the toilet and all the pipes had been smashed up. Mortar and tiling lay scattered across the carpet. Eddie's guitar lay shattered in two pieces, held together only by the strings. The word-processor was gone.

'Oh man,' wept Spider, 'my novella was on that thing.'

'Fuck your novella,' said Eddie, 'what about my fucking guitar? Jesus, how did she find the place?'

'What are you talking about, you dickhead?' barked Spider.

'It was the fucking landlord. He's been trying to get in here for months.'

Clothes, books and records had all been taken. The wardrobe doors lay unhinged on the floor. When Spider hit the light switch nothing happened. In the back garden he wept again, as he surveyed his ravaged plants, uprooted and strewn in an earthy heap.

After they'd sifted through the ruined stuff, they decided they'd have a coffee and talk things over. The kettle was gone. So were all the cups. And so was the coffee. Spider ranted, totally appalled.

'Fuck,' he gasped, 'imagine nicking somebody's fucking *coffee*. Jesus.' He would have broken something, but there was nothing left to break.

They sat out on the step, drinking water out of a stainless-steel soup bowl that, for some reason, was in the boot of Spider's car. Spider kept putting his head in his hands and saying this couldn't be happening. He said he'd have to liberate a new place and it'd probably take time. Eddie'd have to find somewhere else.

'Gee, thanks pal,' said Eddie, 'thanks a lot, OK?' Spider said it wasn't his fault.

Magnificent golden sun slid out from behind a cloud. There was only one thing to do, and Eddie knew he had to act fast. He walked briskly to the end of Electric Avenue, to the graffiti-covered phonebox, and he almost laughed with relief when he picked up the receiver and heard the dial tone. He patted his pockets for change. With shaking hands, he dialled the number. The line clicked and buzzed, and then, at the other end, the tone started to sing importantly. Eddie raked his fingers through his stubborn gunge-filled hair. The soft voice sounded like it was still asleep. Eddie swallowed hard. He stroked his unshaven chin.

'Hello?' he said, huskily.

'Yes?' yawned the woman's voice.

'Salome?' he said. 'It's Eddie here. Eddie Virago. You know? We met last night?'

'Oh yeah, hi. Jesus, Eddie. What time is it? Christ.'

'I know, I know. Look, Salome, I'm really sorry about this, but could I meet you, do you think?'

'What? Is anything wrong? You sound a little uptight, Eddie.'

'Well, it's my flat actually. When I got home this morning my flat had been taken over.'

'Eddie, is this a joke?'

'I wish it was, Salome. I know you're not going to believe this, but this gang of squatters right, skinheads I think, they broke into my place last night when I was out at the rave, and they won't let me in. All my stuff's in there, my clothes and everything, my wallet. They've barricaded the doors. I don't know a soul in London. Everyone I know's away, Bank Holiday weekend, you know, I've no money or anything.' Silence buzzed down the line. 'They've got knives, Salome, and fucking I don't know, rottweilers or something, it's pretty freaky, I can tell you.'

'Jesus, Eddie. What a downer. Have you called the cops?'

'Nothing they can do. Apparently it's all fucking legal, pardon my French. I mean, it's a council thing or something, I don't know.'

'I don't know what to say. God. That's terrible.'

'Jesus, Salome, I'm really sorry about this. You don't know how embarrassing this is. I'm scarlet here. I'm cringing. I mean I really am. I hate myself for doing this, but please, can I see you today?'

'Well, I don't really know, Eddie.' Eddie began to snuffle down the receiver.

'Jesus, Salome. I'm at my wits' end here, I swear. I'm gonna have to sleep on the Embankment or something. I'm really sorry for calling you like this, but I had your number on me and well, these guys, they've got my address book in there you know, and Sunday morning, it's so hard to find people.' A trickle of tiny sobs oozed down the line, followed by a tornado of energetic nose blowing.

'Cut it out, Eddie,' she said, 'don't panic. OK? Please, stop crying. OK, look, come on over and meet me. Do you know the Wild West café? Yes, well, that's just across the road from me. By the old church. Meet me there, and I'll buy you a brunch. And calm down, for God's sake. It's not the end of the world.'

'Salome,' he said, genuine relief in his voice. 'I won't forget this, you're an absolute angel.'

The church bell was striking twelve as Eddie arrived at the coffee house. By two-ten he was staying the night. By three they were back at Salome's place, talking about relationships over a bottle of wine. By five-o-seven he'd finished the story of his life. By six-thirty he was staying for a week. By seven-fifteen she'd left for the studio, Eddie was on his second long-distance phonecall, and the evensong bell was tolling over the avenues and verdant gardens of St John's Wood.

Spider drove over with Eddie's cases. When he arrived Salome was on the TV narrating the piece on the acid party. He said it looked a hell of a lot more enjoyable on the screen than it'd been in real life.

'I don't know how you'd know,' said Eddie. Spider looked round the enormous luxurious apartment, whistling in amazement.

'Jesus,' he sighed, 'you always land on your feet, don't you, Eddie?'

'Yeah, well,' said Eddie, 'it's just for a month or so, I mean six weeks at the absolute most, until I get myself sorted, you know.'

Eddie gave Spider a bottle of Salome's wine to take away. To say thanks for all the help, and for putting him up for so long. He said he was sure Spider would be OK. He said he'd been feeling bad for a while anyway, about abusing his hospitality. He'd been meaning to make other arrangements for absolute yonks. He didn't like being a burden.

'Gee, thanks, Ed,' said Spider. 'You're all heart, man.'

'Hey, don't worry about it,' said Eddie. 'I mean, that's what friends are for, yeah?' Just as Spider turned to leave, Eddie thought of something. 'Listen, Spider,' he said, and Spider turned, expectantly.

'Yeah?' he said.

'It's just, you know, speaking of friends, something I wanted to ask you. About Ireland?' Spider scratched his head, looking confused.

'What about it?'

'Well, I mean, you've been over there, haven't you?' Spider was silent for a minute. He seemed to be looking around the room.

'I don't think so, Eddie,' he said.

'Oh, right. It's just I heard something, you know, about the army and stuff. I mean, if you ever want to talk about it, I'm here, you know?'

Spider shrugged. He looked Eddie straight in the eye.

'Some mistake somewhere,' he smiled. 'I've never been there, Eddie.'

'Oh well,' said Eddie, after a moment, 'some mix-up somewhere.'

'Yeah, Eddie,' said Spider, turning to go. 'There's some terrible fucking liars in this city, and that's the truth.'

Moving in with Salome Wilde wasn't just a career move.

Salome laid down the rules from day one. Eddie was welcome to stay for a couple of months, no more, while her flatmate was away on a singles' safari in Swaziland. It'd be a separate rooms situation. It was strictly a favour, seeing as how he'd nowhere else to go, and, of course, how he was a friend of Dean Bean's.

During the day Eddie had the place to himself, whenever he wasn't working. He'd be expected to do his share of the cleaning and other stuff. Salome didn't have a home help. That kept her feet on the ground. At nights, if she wanted the place to herself, Eddie had to stay in his room, or better still, go out. He could have the guys from the band over, when she wasn't there. But there was to be no drug taking on the premises. That was a total no no. Salome had her reputation to think of. Eddie said it all sounded fine.

'Hey,' he assured her, 'no sweat. I'm very easy to live with, really. You wouldn't believe it.'

After a couple of weeks it felt like they had known each other all their lives. Or at least for longer than they had. They sat up late when she got in from the studio, saying how it was so amazing actually, that they had so much in common. They did the same crossword, listened to the same bands, hated the same people. They even pretended to have read the same books. And one was almost as ambitious as the other, something which tended to come out whenever Salome thrashed him at Scrabble, which was pretty often. Salome was vicious on the Scrabble board. She knew all those amazingly irritating little words that nobody ever uses – pathetic words like yogh, li, zax, tigon – and she whipped them out with a smug mercilessness. The night she got 'aardvark' down on the triple, with the fifty-point, seven-letter bonus, Eddie realised he was living with an intellectual.

Salome's parents had split up too, but it had been a long time ago. Her father had run away with a large-breasted metermaid who'd slapped a ticket on his BMW one morning. It was a long story. She didn't like to talk about it much. She said if Eddie really wanted to know about it she'd give him a photocopy of a profile of herself that had appeared in *Cosmopolitan* earlier in the year. She'd lived with a guy for eighteen months, but she'd called a halt when she discovered he'd spent all her money helping out his friend's floundering soft-porn publishing company.

'Messy,' she said. He was in some religious cult now, on an island off Cornwall. They had to sleep in coffins, she said, on this island. Weird.

She said most of the guys she'd met since then had been too stupid to brush the dandruff off their Ray-Bans.

Sometimes Eddie talked to her about Marion. He talked about her as being part of the Old Days, like some drink-sodden chartered accountant bitching about his ex-wife in a singles' bar. Salome said it all sounded seriously intense, but when Eddie told her about their sex life together, about how Marion seemed to want to do it all the time, she laughed. She couldn't see exactly what he was complaining about.

He knew he would never make her understand, and for some reason, that was important to him. That bugged the shit out of him, but there was no denying it.

'It's just that sex means something to me,' he said, *sensitively*, 'I mean it's not just an animal experience.' Salome laughed again.

'Sure,' she said. 'That much is obvious.'

The really frustrating thing was that the more he talked about Marion, the more Salome said she sounded OK by her. She said it was about time women started being sexually up front. She said Irish women were brought up to be a cross between the Virgin Mary and Florence Nightingale. She said Eddie had it all wrong about women, and that underneath all the egalitarian bullshit he was just as big a chauvinist as anyone else. He told her he really resented that actually, and she said they'd have to agree to differ.

'Sexism is right out,' he said, 'I'm all for women's liberation.'

Salome said male chauvinism was like flared trousers. It'd never really go away for good. She couldn't trust men who said they were feminists. It was just another form of seduction. Cleverer, admittedly, but transparent, nevertheless.

'They all have the same voice,' she said, 'these men, all soft and syrupy and ideologically correct and non-predatory. They've all done the same bloody course somewhere.'

He said that he and Marion hadn't broken up because he was sexist, if she really wanted to know. She said she didn't really want to know, but he told her anyway. They'd broken up because he'd slept with other girls.

'But she got the wrong idea,' he sighed, 'I mean, I *slept* with them, that's all I said, I didn't do anything with them. I mean, I often sleep with my friends. Don't you? I just find it very comforting, sleeping with somebody. There doesn't have to be anything physical.'

Salome said that was a nice try. Then she said it was pretty feeble. Eddie couldn't have it both ways. Either he wanted to be the tough-guy macho stud fucking everything in sight, or else he was Mister Right-On-New-Man-I-Don't-Want-A-Car-Shaped-Like-A-Penis. He couldn't just give out one set of vibes when the set-up suited him, and another when it didn't. She said Eddie was a sexual chameleon, and that he'd have to make up his mind. And she said either way, Eddie had a lot to learn about women.

'The thing is, Kiddo, the best ones are hardly ever as good as you think they are, and the bad ones are probably never as bad.'

When she didn't call him Kiddo, she called him Hun. At first it drove him crazy.

'Don't call me that,' he'd pout, 'I'm not a bloody German.'

But very slowly, as the weeks went by, Eddie got used to it. Then things got worse. When she called him stupid names, he found that he began to like it. He sat in the kitchen one day thinking, 'Jesus, I'm a grown man, and I don't mind that she's just called me Cup Cakes.'

He began to think about her during the day when she wasn't there. He began to think of Salome's face, the curve of her body, the breathy sound of her laugh. Sometimes when he looked at her, curled up on the sofa, jabbering into the phone, caressing the heel of her naked foot, he wanted to weep with desire. The way she ran her fingers through her hair, the way she wrote her name, the way she flashed that dangerous smile of hers, all of these things began to devour him.

'Christ, Beano,' he wrote, 'I've got it bad. I don't know what's happening to me.'

One windy Sunday afternoon they sat on Hampstead Heath together, eating bagels, saying which of the passers-by they'd like to see on a jury, if they had murdered somebody and had to face a trial. This was a favourite game of Salome's. Eddie said his own version was to point out which passer-by you'd like to fuck, if the world was going to end in ten minutes and you had your choice. It was particularly good in Tube delays, he said, it made the time pass very quickly. Salome snorted, choking on her bagel. Then she put her hand to her mouth and laughed out loud. In that instant her moist blue eyes fell on him, with the air of a startled animal. She touched his knee to steady herself. Eddie stopped laughing. He stared at her and he felt like he was falling through space. She stopped laughing too. She pushed her hair out of her eyes. When she leaned over and kissed him on the corner of the mouth, Eddie was gone.

'There is a God,' he thought, as her tongue began to force its way down his windpipe. 'Thank you, thank you, thank you, Jesus.'

That night when they went back to the flat they made love. It started in the living room, horsing around on the sofa while Melvyn Bragg tried to keep up with Gore Vidal on 'The South Bank Show'. She curled up in his arms, caressed his face and his chest. When he held her tight he felt her shiver. Their hands groped each other through their clothes. They panted and drooled while the cat looked on, rubbing its ass against the coffee table, with smugness in its yellow eye. When half the buttons on her shirt were open, and her skirt was up around her waist, and Eddie felt like he was about to explode with lust at any minute, Salome pulled away and said, 'Listen, Eddie, I know this is a revolutionary suggestion, but maybe we should take our clothes off.'

'Sure,' he said, 'hey, I'm a liberal.'

With the casual air of an accountant disrobing in a Bangkok sauna, Salome opened the remaining buttons of her shirt and took it off. She folded it very carefully across the back of the chair. She reached into her handbag, and took out a packet of condoms. Then she unzipped Eddie's tight jeans, and tugged them off, with some difficulty, over his Doc Martens.

'You can take the boots off yourself,' she said, 'this isn't Texas.' Eddie tittered frantically as his fingers clawed at the laces. 'This is just a fling, Eddie, now, OK?' she said, cautiously, stepping out of her shoes.

'Fine, fine,' Eddie panted, 'listen, I've forgotten about it already, I swear.'

Then Salome pulled her skirt down over her hips and they lay on the carpet, shivering in their underwear, legs intertwined, grinding their crotches together like they were trying to start a fire with the friction. At the touch of her body Eddie felt like he was melting. She lay on top of him, with her thighs around his, and her long hair down on his face. When she pulled off her pants, she laughed. Her breath smelt of wine. Then she kissed him so hard that he couldn't breathe. She tugged his T-shirt off over his head. He managed to open her bra. He touched her breasts and her face and her flat stomach. He bit her shoulder. She peeled off his boxer shorts and licked his navel. He kissed her abdomen and moved his tongue between her legs. She sat back with her thighs over his shoulders. With her hands, she squeezed the sides of his bald head.

And then, for some minutes, all Eddie could hear was Salome gasping, and Gore Vidal being sarcastic about Ronald Reagan on the TV screen, and Melvyn Bragg going 'Yes, I see, yes,' every few moments.

After she came, Eddie stared up at her face, doing his best to look adoring. But Salome was sniggering guiltily, with her hand across her lips.

'I've never done it with a mohican before,' she said, 'your head looks just like a stick of candy floss down there.'

'Ha ha ha,' said Eddie, wondering whether this was a compliment or not. He knelt on the floor and rolled on a condom.

Salome pulled away and said she had an idea. She wanted to do it in the bathroom. So they slithered around the shower for a while, until the hot water ran out and Eddie's limp mohican was flopping down in his eyes. Then, soaking with soap and sweat, they did it on the hall carpet. Then they did it on the stairs, and leaning over the huge table in the study, flailing around in between Salome's fax machine and a tottering stack of copies of the Governmental Report on the Future of the Deregulated Broadcasting Industry.

They ended up two hours and three condoms later, stark naked in the kitchen, wedged up against the fridge, with the kiwifruit-shaped magnets wearing into Salome's back, and her legs clasped around Eddie's buttocks, howling while the national anthem boomed out on the television inside.

Afterwards they lay on the floor in the dark listening to the rain, while jazz played on the radio and Eddie tried to get some sensation back into his jaw.

'How was it for you?' he said, after some minutes.

'Oh,' she answered, yawning, 'I suppose it was OK.' She shot him a glance of what looked disturbingly like sympathy. 'I'm kidding,' she said, 'it was fine.'

'Fine?' he said. 'Oh, great.'

'I mean, the earth moved, Eddie, what do you want, an announcement in *The Times*?'

'Salome,' he croaked, 'I think I've fallen in love with you.' Then she smiled, sadly, and she touched the side of his face.

'Don't be so silly, Eddie,' she said. 'Don't spoil everything.'

'Jesus, what does it spoil?' he said. 'Does it always spoil it when it's with someone who loves you?'

'Not always, Hun,' she said, 'but usually.' And she stood up, poured a glass of water and plugged in the kettle.

'Jesus,' Eddie said, 'I can't figure women out.'

'Oh really?' said Salome. 'Well, maybe you shouldn't try so hard.'

They did it three or four times more after that night, in his bed, and never in hers. After that first night the sex was competent, efficient, acrobatic even, but never as much fun. And when Eddie woke up, Salome would almost always have gone back to her own room. At first that didn't bother him too much. Secretly he was relieved. Eddie found it weird waking up beside somebody he saw on television every night. Somehow it felt vaguely sacrilegious.

But then Salome started seeing other guys. Eddie sometimes met them over breakfast, where he tried to freak them out by talking knowledgeably about Nietzsche when her back was turned. Salome tended to go for what she called 'the strong silent type'. What this seemed to mean was guys with pointed heads, minuscule intellects, and enormous nipples that stuck through their denim shirts.

'I don't see what you see in them,' he'd whine, 'I really don't.'

'They have hidden talents, Eddie,' she'd answer, meaningfully.

He began to think about her *all* the time. He wrote long passionate letters to her, which he couldn't bear to send. He invented reasons to call her at work. In the middle of the night he would lie awake, mouth dry, face hot, every sinew shaking with thoughts of her thin white body. One morning he woke up and heard John Lee Hooker on the radio moaning, 'Woah, I'm a crawling king snake for you, baby.' Eddie closed his eyes, swallowed hard, stared glumly at his erection and thought, 'Jesus, John Lee, you think *you've* got problems?'

One afternoon in September Eddie decided he'd taken enough. He'd spent all the night before with his ear pressed to her wall, and all that morning ironing some other guy's Y-fronts. He walked into the study, took off his apron, and told her he loved her.

'And I mean it, Salome,' he announced, 'I've never said that to anyone in my life.' Salome looked up from her word-processor, sighed deeply and took off her glasses.

'Eddie,' she said, 'you've known me for six weeks. Give me a break.'

'What about us,' he said, 'what about that Sunday night?'

'What about it?' she asked. 'If you think just because we played a bit of tonsil hockey I'm all yours, well, you're all wrong.'

'Tonsil hockey?' screeched Eddie, 'I did things with you that would have made Caligula barf.'

'Well, that's not my fault,' she said. 'If you're too immature to handle it, Kiddo, that's fine.'

'You're too bloody independent,' he snapped. 'You don't seem to need anybody.' Salome folded her arms and attempted to whistle the theme music of 'The Lone Ranger'. Then she looked up at him and said, 'Finished?'

'That's it,' said Eddie, 'go on, that's really mature, that is.'

She said she liked him, but she just didn't want anything heavy, and at the first sign of heavyosity she'd have to kick for touch. What this would mean in practice would be that Eddie would find himself packing up his kitbag and dossing down on the Embankment.

'Oh well, if I'm any trouble,' he huffed.

'I'm warning you now,' she snapped, 'don't come the sizzling martyr with me, Eddie.' Then she put her head in her hands. Salome began to speak very slowly. She said she didn't mind him being there, for the moment, until he got somewhere else, but as far as she was concerned they weren't living together, *per se*, they were just living together. Sharing the same space. 'That's the deal,' she shrugged, 'take it or leave it.' Eddie insisted. He wanted to know where they stood. Salome sighed. 'You're doing it again,' she said. 'Why does everything have to be so defined?'

'Who's defining?' Eddie bawled. 'Jesus, I ask you a simple question, all of a sudden I'm Pol Pot.' Salome started tapping her biro rather threateningly on the rim of her cup. She said Eddie was getting hostile. Eddie pointed his index finger at her face. 'I,' he growled slowly, 'am not getting fucking hostile.' She looked him in the eye, and unleashed her smile.

'Can't we just see what happens?' she asked, patiently. Eddie said no, he wanted an answer. He performed his best pout. Salome said that as far as she was concerned they were good friends, who had sex with each other once in a while. That was it. 'C'est tout,' she smiled, 'Hun.' It wasn't a chastity-belt situation. They were both free to see whoever they liked. He told her she was afraid of commitment. She couldn't go around acting the social butterfly for the rest of her life. She said she didn't actually see why not. 'Anyway,' she beamed, 'I'm not going to argue with you, Eddie. I make it a principle never to argue with people I've slept with.'

He went back to scrubbing the kitchen floor.

One night shortly afterwards, Clint seemed a little bothered at the rehearsal. He kept playing the wrong chords and staring meaningfully out the window. When it was time to go, he asked Eddie to stay behind. In the pub he said he had something to say. He didn't want to butt in, but he'd been to a gig at the George Robey a couple of nights before, and he had some news that he just wanted to run by Eddie.

He'd seen Marion. She'd been sitting way at the back of the Robey with all her friends, and she seemed to be in bad shape, very drunk, kind of hysterical and out of things. When he'd gone to talk to her she hadn't seemed to know who he was.

'She didn't look so good, Eddie,' he said. 'I gotta tell you that, pal, she really didn't.' She'd been with a couple of creepy looking guys who were all over her. Eddie sipped his pint.

'Was she depressed?' he asked. Clint said not exactly, not depressed, just drunk. Eddie asked why Clint was telling him this. It wasn't his problem any more, and it certainly wasn't Clint's business either way. 'A lot of water's been passed since then,' he said. Clint told him no offence, but he just thought Eddie would want to know. Eddie said he'd enough hassle as it was, love-wise. So Clint said forget it.

They spent the rest of the evening bitching about Jake, and taking the piss out of Andy's shirts. But Eddie was preoccupied, and the more he drank the worse it got. He wished Clint hadn't told him about Marion. 'File under bad memory,' he thought, lurching home in the rain.

No matter how hard Eddie tried, Salome continued veering clear. The way she fended him off, it depressed the hell out of him. One night when he'd made a serious attempt at the world sulking record she flicked off the Peter Greenaway video and sighed, 'OK, Eddie, I'll ask you what's the matter. That's what you want, isn't it?'

'I don't know what's wrong,' he whimpered, 'but I just want it to stop.' He put his head in his hands and tried to screw tears out of his eyes.

Salome wasn't having any of it. The lovesick swain routine just didn't cut it with her.

'The problem is, Eddie, you're not looking for friendship. You're looking for somebody to hose your pubic hair out of the bathplug, and it's not going to be me.'

He told her that crudity didn't suit her. She said she was going to bed.

Eddie knew that none of this would last long. Salome's flatmate was due back any week, and then he'd have to move out. In the nights he felt a painful sensation of things fleeting and dying away. He tried to write a song about unrequited love, but nothing would come. He strummed the sad, mysterious minor chords, hoping their echo would drag something out of the back alleys of his mind, but it wouldn't work. He told himself that this was just so typical, soon as he met somebody he really liked, he couldn't have her. But no matter how he tried, he couldn't get that into a song. And nothing rhymed with Salome anyway. Except boloney. Even her name conspired against him. It was a hopeless situation.

In early October, Salome came home with a decision. When she announced this, Eddie thought he was about to be thrown out. But not yet, she said, this was a different decision.

'Art Attack' was doing a Battle of the Bands special, where eight new bands would come on and play live, and the audience could call in afterwards and vote. She'd got The Diehards a spot on the show. At first Eddie wasn't keen. He felt they just weren't ready. But Salome insisted. She'd had to bend over backwards and, as she said, that was a pretty difficult position. When he said he'd have to ring the rest of the guys and consult them she told him she'd already done it.

'They all seem to think it's an excellent opportunity,' she informed him. She'd phoned Jake too, and he'd nearly flipped out completely, because it was such a great chance. 'Come on, Eddie,' she smiled, 'it'll be the biggest fun.'

As it turned out, it was a lot of fun. The Diehards arrived at four in the afternoon, got wrecked on tequila in the Hospitality Suite, sobered up in time for the sound check and gave an absolutely brilliant performance, the best ever, of 'Whose Dog Are You?'. Spider put his stick through his tom tom at the end, then he tried to convince everybody he'd done it deliberately, because Keith Moon was his hero. Jake spent the whole night eating as much smoked salmon as was physically possible, and trying to get off with the production assistant, an irritating pallid woman who wore black and spoke like she had marbles in her mouth. The Diehards got two hundred votes, second-last place. An all-woman anti-sexist heavy-metal band came top of the poll. An intense guy with atrocious acne and a drum machine came last.

The producer called Eddie next morning to tell him the final tally.

'Punk's just dead,' he said, in his lispy voice, 'why don't you get into New Country or something?'

'Because we don't do songs about fucking sheep,' Eddie said.

The producer asked did he mean songs about fucking sheep, as in the expletive, or fucking sheep, as in the verb. Eddie told him to go swivel on it. The producer said fine, if he wanted to be like that, and the phone went dead. Just for a second Eddie could understand why frustrated rock stars chuck television sets through windows. He called the producer back to apologise, but his secretary said he was in a meeting. So he tried to call Jake. Jake was out at a rave. It was the same fucking message for the last six months, 'R-R-R-Rave on,' it said, 'it's a crazy feeling.'

Salome rang and gave him a bollocking for being so aggressive. He told her to swivel on it too.

'I told you we weren't ready,' he snapped, 'I never should have listened to you.' She said they'd have to speak about this later. 'Well, I won't be here,' he said, 'I'll be gone when you get back.' The line was dead by the time he'd finished his sentence.

When she'd gone Eddie went into her room. He looked through her stuff, not knowing exactly what he was looking for. He walked into her walk-in wardrobe, and it smelt like a perfume shop. He wanted to tear her dresses off the hangers and shred them into bits and leave them strewn around the flat like confetti. He wanted to find a horse, decapitate it, and put its head under the sheets. He wanted to ring the Iranian Embassy and say he'd found Salman Rushdie's address. But he didn't.

He sat around the flat for a couple of hours, watching TV. Then he went into the kitchen, took all the glasses out of the cupboards and washed them, first in hot water, then in cold, and he dried each one until it squeaked. It didn't make him feel any better. The anger kept clawing its way back into his brain. When the glasses were almost all lined up on the draining board, his wet fingers let the last one drop and it smashed into a million fragments on the floor. Eddie opened his mouth and shrieked. He head butted the fridge. He kicked the kitchen door. He karate-chopped the dishwasher. He opened the kitchen window and flung the clean and brilliant glasses one by one out at the dog below, a pathetic little poodle called 'Noodle' by its pathetic little owner, a blue-rinsed aristocratic lady who'd had her face lifted more often than a toilet seat.

Later in the day, while Eddie was addressing envelopes for the demo tape, Frank rang to congratulate him on the show. He said it didn't matter what anybody else said, he was proud of him, and that was that. That was the good news.

'You were tremendous,' he said. That cheered Eddie up a bit.

But there was bad news too. Dean Bean had just been signed into Jervis Street suffering from hepatitis B. Someone had told Patricia in a pub.

'You know what it's like over here,' Frank said, 'small town.'

Eddie listened to Frank, and he felt nothing. Not even surprise. Not even coldness. He continued addressing his envelopes, while Frank spoke. He clamped the receiver between his chin and his shoulder and kept on writing.

Frank said he'd never known that Beano was into drugs. He kept trying to sound sympathetic, but Eddie could hear real disappointment in his voice. A dirty needle, apparently.

'You better come over,' Frank urged, 'he's really not too good.' Eddie said he couldn't come. He just hadn't got the time.

'He's fucked himself up before,' Eddie said, 'he'll be OK, believe me, the guy's a born survivor.' His father said he hoped that was right. Eddie said he was sick to death of this. The least he'd expect of his friends was that they'd look after themselves. It wasn't his baby. If Beano thought that people could just drop everything and come running to supply the required attention, he had another thing coming. 'The guy's so full of shit,' he said, 'it's coming out his ears.'

'Eddie,' Frank interrupted, firmly, 'I hope you're not into all that scene. That druggie business.' Eddie said no, he wasn't. Frank said he didn't mind the couple of odd blasts on a joint. He knew that went on, but anything more than that was bad news. Eddie reassured him that he had absolutely nothing to worry about. 'Yes, well,' said Frank, apprehensively.

'I don't need drugs, Frank,' Eddie insisted, 'I'm just not that type. I'm disappointed, actually, that you think that.'

'Come on, Eddie,' sighed Frank, 'get off the fucking stage, son.'

When Salome got back she didn't refer to their argument, until Eddie brought it up, metaphorically, over the lasagne. She lifted her eyes from the book on her side plate.

'Calmed down, have we?' she asked sarcastically, her eyebrows almost disappearing into her hairline. Eddie said he was sorry. He told her it was just the pressure. She said everybody had pressure, and she went back to her book. She told him if he couldn't stand the heat he should get in off the patio. She said that thanks to Eddie she was in the dog house with her producer. It was a serious loss of brownie points. It was the last time she ever did him a favour.

'Some favour,' roared Eddie, 'some sodding favour.' She kept saying she wasn't going to argue.

'I know you want me to,' she sighed with infuriating calm, 'but I just won't, so there.' Eddie started bending the cutlery.

'That's just so typical of you,' he yelped, 'you're just so controlled, aren't you, Salome?' She said Eddie was the only person she'd ever met who could use the word 'controlled' as an insult.

'That says a lot about you, Eddie,' she smiled.

The telephone rang while they were arguing about whether to have an argument or not. Neither of them went to pick it up. Salome sat at the table, very still, with her fingers massaging her temples. Out in the hall, Eddie heard Jake's voice crackle on the answering machine.

'Eddie, man,' panted Jake's voice, 'sidle your ass over to my place soon as you get in. I mean as SOON as you get in, know what I mean? I got some big news for you and the guys. It's happening, kiddo. Jesus. But one thing. I need six hundred quid, Eddie. I don't care how you get it, borrow it, anything, sell your ass, I'll get it back to you next week, but don't forget it. Jesus. I hate these frigging machines.'

Eddie said nothing to Salome. He stalked out of the kitchen, closing the door behind him. When he phoned Jake back, his answering machine was still stuck on. He hung up and dialled again. 'Rave on,' it said. Eddie screeched.

'Jake,' he roared, 'pick up your fucking phone!!' Nothing happened. 'Rave on,' hiccupped the message, 'you got me reeling.' Eddie slammed the phone down and it made a little 'ding' noise. 'Jesus,' Eddie muttered, 'one of these days I'll murder that bastard.' When he came back to the kitchen Salome was grinding up coffee in one of those machines that make your teeth feel itchy.

She pointed to her cashcard, on the table. And when she turned the machine off, she said he could borrow her car.

Eddie said no thanks, he didn't want any more favours, and as of now, he was officially moving out. She told him not to worry, it wasn't a favour, it was a loan. And if he wanted to move out, that was fine, but at least he should wait until he'd calmed down a little. She thrust the card into his hand.

'It's just to show I've nothing against you, Eddie,' she said. 'We may be a walking disaster in the amorous department, but I would still like to be your friend.' She held his hand and he felt his rage subside. 'Lighten up, Eddie,' she smiled, caressing his hot face, 'your future's in your own control, you've got to stop blaming everybody else.' He told her the cashcard wasn't much good without her PIN number.

'Greater love hath no man,' she smirked, 'or woman,' and she scribbled the number on a piece of sticky yellow paper, which she attached, very carefully, to the side of Eddie's bald and goosepimpling head.

Jake's garden flat in Blackheath turned out to be a basement in a clapped-out Victorian Square near Peckham. The kids stared at Salome's yellow 2CV when Eddie stepped out. They looked like tough little fuckers. Down the steps, a folded brown envelope taped under the cracked doorbell announced, 'Motorvatin' Productions; The International Home of Rock and Roll'. When he came to the door Jake was draped in a scarlet Japanese-style dressing-gown which was covered in dubious-looking stains. He waved the glass of milk in his hand.

'Bit of a rough quarter this,' said Eddie.

'Yeah,' said Jake, 'it's OK when you get used to it.'

'Where's your motor?'

'Fucking repo men bastards,' spat Jake, 'they came and took my baby away. They don't understand, Eddie, I've got the dough, it's just an accounting problem, you know? I've so much overhead I sometimes get lost.'

Eddie laughed. He asked Jake if Salome's car would be OK. Jake said yeah, the kids all knew him. He staggered up the steps to the street.

'Hey, guys, mitts off that motor, OK? I'm like the fucking pied piper around here,' he chuckled, 'I really am. The pied piper of fucking Peckham.'

Eddie asked for the good news. Jake asked if he'd brought the money.

They walked into the tiny front room, which smelt warmly of sour milk and vinegar. Jake snatched a pair of underpants from the battered coffee table and threw them over an old-fashioned dressing screen in the corner. His eyes were wide and excited. He looked like a fat little boy who'd just been picked for a basketball team for the first time.

'Eddie,' he croaked, 'I'm so happy for you.' He grabbed Eddie's hand, shaking frantically. 'It's *Melody Maker*,' he said, 'they want to put "Whose Dog" on a flexi-disc they're giving out free with the Christmas edition. Isn't that just the most fucking wild thing? Ain't that the mostest?'

Underneath the vinegar stench, the room smelt of cheap aftershave, sweet, like dying flowers. A faded poster of Little Richard, screaming, his foot hammering a piano, covered a damp crack that ran down the length of one wall. Over by the window squatted a shabby television with a coat hanger stuck into the back as an aerial. Up at the top, near the ceiling, the floral wallpaper was peeling away from the brown wall. Mysterious black plastic sacks bulged. A heap of dirty clothes lay on the floor. Every corner seemed to have huge piles of yellowing newspaper, all tied up with twine. Every corner except one.

In the corner furthest from the door stood a massive stereo system, sleek, black and glossy, with more buttons than the control panel of Concorde. Tiny lights flickered on the front. The speakers, suspended from the walls, were enormous, *obscene*-looking things. It all looked alive. It seemed to throb quietly in the corner, and to gaze at Eddie, exuding a dangerous calm. It looked more expensive than everything else in the room put together. It probably was, Jake said, but he'd got it wholesale.

'That's my desert island thing, Eddie,' he laughed, 'if I'm ever washed up somewhere, that's the one thing that's coming with me. Jake stood with his hand on top of the smoked-glass deck cover, beaming proudly, as though somebody was about to take his photograph. Then he breathed on his sleeve, and he wiped the place where his hand had been. 'Anyway,' he said, 'great news, huh?'

Eddie said yeah, but his face gave him away. Under the onslaught of Jake's enthusiasm, eventually he caved in. He confessed that he'd thought it was going to be a record deal. Jake looked miffed. He said it was another step on the ladder.

'Who else is on it?' asked Eddie. 'On the record, I mean . . .'

'Couple of other unknowns, I mean, sorry, Ed, but that's, you know, new up-and-coming bands, all that bullshit.'

'Who?' insisted Eddie.

'Some thrash-metal outfit, Agonising Death or something.' Jake looked at the ceiling, counting off on his fat fingers. 'Then there's you guys, there's Jimmy Lightning and The Hip Replacements, there's The Sex Things, who else, oh yeah, The Four Whores Men of the Apocalypse, they're doing "Fuck Thatcher", and a couple of others. You know, small fry. You're definitely the most happening of the lot.' A kettle whistled mournfully from the kitchen.

'They want to call it "Young Pretenders",' he said. 'It's like, the bands most likely to make it in the nineties.' He looked excited again. 'That's you, Eddie,' he said, punching him gently on the shoulder, 'that's you, pal.'

Eddie asked was there anything in writing. Jake said not yet, but they were biking over the contract first thing tomorrow morning. He needed the six hundred smackers because the song would have to be rerecorded properly. He'd booked the Roundhouse already. He'd produce it himself, to keep the costs down. He'd called up The Sax Machine and they were coming down too, for no fee. The deal was that after the record came out *Melody Maker* was going to reimburse everybody. Eddie slapped the wad of notes against his open palm.

'This better not be a wind-up, Jake.' Jake looked hurt. He put down the kettle and picked up the phone.

'Ring 'em,' he said, 'call 'em now.'

Eddie said, 'Fuck off, Jake,' and he laughed.

Jake said, 'No. Fuck you, Eddie Virago, come on, I work my fucking ass to the bone here for you guys, this is my thanks, come on, call them up now, come on.' Eddie apologised.

'Yeah, well,' Jake said, getting breathless, 'let me tell you something. You're full of shit, Eddie.' Eddie said it wasn't that he was ungrateful. Jake started smoking, violently.

'Gratitude,' he sneered, 'you wouldn't know the meaning of the fucking word.' He sucked hard on the cigarette and he started coughing smoke across the room. Eddie put the money on Jake's table. 'Put it away,' Jake spluttered, 'go on, take it back, you little fuck, you explain to the rest of the band that one of the most happening and ABC-penetrative music magazines in the entire fucking country isn't good enough for Mr Eddie fucking Hendrix big dick Virago.' Eddie said he was sorry again.

Jake stalked back into the kitchen, slamming the door. Five seconds later he came back in again. He bowed his head and apologised. He put his fingers against his fat face.

'Sorry seems to be the hardest word,' he said. It was just the excitement. It had gone to his head.

'Chill out, Jake,' said Eddie, 'I'm thrilled, really.'

They sat in Jake's kitchen, talking and sharing a joint.

Autographed pictures of rock stars covered every inch of the kitchen wall. Bob Geldof. Sid Vicious. Morrissey. And right in the middle was a photo of Jake with his arm round a fun-furred and bewildered-looking John Lennon. It said, 'To Jake the Fake, with love from John the Con. NYC 1975'. Jake said he'd been stoned out of his mind at the time.

'Lennon,' he said, sadly, 'what a loss, man, what a loss.'

They talked about the future. This was it, Jake said. It'd be all-systems-go after this. There'd be deals, tours, interviews, offers of TV. Jake said the only way was up. Eddie and the guys were knocking on the door of the big time. He said building a career in this business was like building a wall. You needed a solid foundation, and oh baby, this was it.

As the light came down outside, Jake broke out the last few tabs of ecstasy he'd been saving for Christmas. He said he didn't usually do this stuff, but hey, this was a big day for the race.

'What race?' Eddie said.

'The human race,' Jake said, and he started to cackle. When Jake went out to get some beers, he told Eddie to show himself around the flat. 'Give yourself a tour,' he said, 'the place isn't at its best, but fuck it.'

The bathroom looked like a medieval hovel. The ring of dirt around the enamel looked like it'd been spray-painted on. In the bedroom, Jake's sheets looked like they'd probably shatter if anyone tried to pick them up.

In the bedside drawer Eddie found a thick copybook lined in blue. His fingers idled through the pages.

'To Jake from Elvis,' it said, on the first page, and Eddie was impressed. He turned over. 'To Jake from your good friend Buddy.' The next page. 'To Jake from Al Green. To Jake from Philip Lynott.' And the next. 'To Jake from Janis Joplin, with lots of love and French kisses.' And the next, 'To Jake, number one homeboy, from Prince.' Every single page, covered in florid and exaggerated scribbles, and all in the same hieroglyphic handwriting that Eddie had seen too often not to recognise.

Eddie stood on his own in the foul bedroom for a few minutes, listening to the rattle of trains going past. He caught his reflection in the dirty cracked window. His eyes burnt and he felt suddenly that he wanted to cry. Then very slowly, he replaced the book in Jake's bedside drawer.

Jake was so long at the off-licence that Eddie got worried. When he finally did get back, clutching the beers to his enormous chest, there were flakes of snow on the shoulders of his coat. Jake said it was snowing like a bastard outside.

'Jake,' Eddie asked, 'there's something I've always wanted to ask you.' Jake bustled around the kitchen trying to find glasses.

'Yeah, Eddie,' he said, 'go ahead, ask and you shall receive.'

'Why the *fuck*,' snapped Eddie, 'don't you ever change the message on your answering machine?'

Later they got drunk and Jake started talking about the old days. When he talked, he mentioned a woman called Marge, and Eddie asked who she was.

'Used to be my lady,' he sighed, and he brushed something off his knees, embarrassed. Eddie said he never had Jake down as a ladies' man.

Jake said yeah, they'd got married one day in Vegas, in the early seventies some time, he couldn't remember exactly when, in one of those drive-in places you read about. They'd both worn purple crushed velvet bell-bottoms and it'd lasted only six months. 'She gave me the bell-bottom blues alright,' he chuckled. Jake pulled out his wallet and showed Eddie a picture. The woman had a thin face, long straggly blonde hair and a mountain of mascara. She wore platform shoes with silver stars, and a shaggy yellow waistcoat, and she was laughing as she held a baby up in the air. 'That's her,' Jake beamed. 'Lips as pink as a teddyboy's socks. And that's my kid, Elvis.' Elvis and Marge were still over there now, living in a camper van in Great Falls, Montana. Eddie looked at the picture for a few moments, trying to find something to say. He asked whether Jake ever saw Elvis now, and he said not too often. 'We'll catch up on it,' he said, 'when he's older.' Eddie asked what happened. Jake looked away and he squeezed his nostrils. 'I guess we just lost that lovin' feeling, Eddie, you know how it is.'

'Yeah,' said Eddie, 'I'm sorry, Jake.' Jake shrugged.

'Don't be sorry, man,' he said. 'It was a good experience, but things were just too heavy back then.' He sipped his beer. 'It was a very heavy time, Eddie,' he said, 'everything was just too intense, you know? People did crazy things.' Jake wanted to talk about Marion. He said she'd seemed reet petite to him. Eddie said they weren't exactly the first words that sprung to mind. Jake laughed. 'OK,' he admitted, 'bit free and easy in the mouth department, but still, nice enough.' He didn't like Salome much. Eddie knew that behind his back Jake referred to her as 'Salami'. 'All tits and attitude,' he sneered, 'you know what I mean? Nothing personal, man, but chicks like that just give me the pip. I gotta say it.' Eddie said he shouldn't call them chicks. Jake said sure, he knew that, but still. 'Women like that,' he sighed, 'they think every guy's got it in for them, you know? They're like, obsessed.' Eddie asked if Jake ever got lonely. Jake said no way. 'Are you kidding, man?' He laughed. 'Yeah, I got loads of chicks, y'know, groupies and stuff. They're knocking on the door here, it's like Fellini's fucking "Satyricon" sometimes, know what I mean? It's like the fall of the fucking Weimar Republic, y'know. It's crazy, I mean, *look* at the place. The funny thing is, I know you don't believe me, Eddie, and I don't blame you. But it's true.'

'I believe you,' said Eddie.

Jake sighed, 'Oh yeah, oh yeah,' and he nodded into his drink, 'loads of chicks, oh man, the stories I could lay on you.'

'I believe you,' said Eddie again, more gently.

Jake appeared to drift into thought, and silence came down over the room, a silence broken only by the irritating hum of the electric fire and the drum-like rattle of the trains outside. A long time passed before either of them spoke. In the end, it was Jake who broke the silence.

'But one thing, Ed, that chick, Mary Anne, she was nice, man. She was cool. What happened between you two?' Eddie said he didn't know.

'It's *Marion*,' he said.

Jake said it sure was a shame that Mary Anne wasn't around now, to share in Eddie's new success. He said it was such a pity, and a thing you often saw in the business, bad vibes between people for no good reason at all.

'Oh, the games people play,' he muttered, sadly, into his drink. Eddie said things were getting a little morbid. 'Yeah,' sighed Jake, 'guess life goes on, huh?' He stood up, smiling, wobbling a little, and he stuck a cassette into the stereo. 'My favourite band of all time,' he beamed, and he hit the switch. Words came screaming out of the speakers, and Jake nodded in time, mouthing the chorus.

> I'll make you feel my promises
> You'll recite them when you fall
> With your finger on the trigger
> And your ego getting bigger
> You'll recite them one and all.

Jake's face distorted as he closed his eyes and snarled out the words. He shook his ample hips and strummed hard at his invisible guitar.

> Dogs in the moon
> Dogs howling at the light
> And I'm wondering who
> Whose dog are you?

Eddie drained the last beer can, and he was happy. He listened to the words. He saw things very clearly now, and he knew what had to be done.

'Jake,' he shouted, and his words slurred above the wail of his guitar solo, 'you're a great human being, you know that?'

'Hey,' Jake said, 'that's what I'm paid for.'

Eddie stood up and said he wanted to go home. He started looking for his keys. Jake turned the sound down and grabbed his arm.

'Eddie, man, you can't drive. You're not in a fit state. Let me call a cab.' Eddie said no, but he knew Jake was right. He was drunk. 'Here, lemme call you a cab,' he urged. 'Here, I'll pay for it, Eddie.' Jake hammered the receiver against the arm of a chair, and dialled a number. Eddie sat staring at the pile of money, still on the coffee table. 'Fucking telephone,' Jake sighed, bashing it again. When the cab came Jake peeled a twenty off the wad and stuck in it Eddie's shirt pocket. 'There's your advance off the first album,' he said solemnly, and he punched Eddie on the arm, and laughed, and said he was just plucking Eddie's strings. 'See ya soon, Eddie,' giggled Jake, 'I'll look after the wheels for you. Send someone over in the morning.'

'Yeah,' slurred Eddie, 'listen, thanks a lot, man.'

'Forget it,' said Jake. 'You're my investment for my old age. I gotta look after you.' He helped Eddie up the steps into the street.

Snow was falling heavily now, and it fizzled on Eddie's bare head. The children ran up and down the paths, screaming, holding their mouths open to the snow, like fish gulping in a tank.

Just before the cab pulled away, Jake came puffing back up the steps from his place. He rapped on the back window, and Eddie rolled it down. Snow was sheeting into the street now, long slivers of snow in the yellow street light. The cab driver said he wanted to get a move on. Word had come over the radio. The Blackwall Tunnel was closing down and the streets were like an ice-rink.

Jake told Eddie to leave the keys to Salome's motor. He said he might take it for a little run round the block later. Nobody would mind. In fact nobody would ever know.

'Go on, Ed,' he said, 'go on, how about it? Do this old raver a favour, huh?' Eddie looked up at Jake's innocent babyish eyes, all wide with drink and hope. He sighed as he fished in his pockets, and handed them through the window. He told Jake to look after it, for God's sake. 'Baby, you can drive my car,' Jake sang, clenching the keyring in his fat hand, 'beepbeep, beepbeep, yeah.' Eddie lay down flat on the back seat.

'I'm trusting you with my balls, Jake,' he said.

'Goodbye, Eddie,' Jake laughed, as the car pulled off. 'Don't worry, I'm trustable. Stick with me, baby.' He closed the front door behind him. 'Goodbye, Eddie Virago,' he said, again.

Salome was home from the studio when Eddie got back. She understood about the car. She said she was happy, in fact. You didn't want to take chances when you'd been drinking, specially not in this foul weather. She'd get somebody to pop around in the morning and collect it. If she could persuade anybody to go to Peckham. 'Joke,' she said.

When Eddie told her the news she opened a bottle of M and S Chablis and said she was really proud of him. They sat up talking, although it was already very late. She said all this must have been a terrific vindication, and a great motivating force too.

'You're going places, Eddie,' she said, 'see what happens when you've got a positive attitude?' He told her then what Jake had said to him about Marion. How it was such a pity what had happened between them, how they couldn't even speak to each other any more. He laughed sardonically when he told her, as if to put a distance between himself and what Jake had said. But Salome thought Jake was right, as Eddie knew she would. 'Whatever else about her, Eddie, she stood by you when you were on your own. She had faith in you. I can't believe you're going to turn your back on her completely.'

'What do you think happens to love?' he asked. 'I think that's what I really want to know. I mean, where does it go?'

'If I knew that, Kiddo,' she said, 'I'd be a rich woman. And I'd probably never love anyone ever again.'

At three in the morning Eddie phoned out for a takeaway.

'How do you want your pizza,' he asked her, 'deep or shallow?'

'I like my pizzas like I like my men,' she pouted, in what she thought was a Mae West voice. Eddie ordered shallow, but she didn't laugh. Then they went into his bedroom and looked out at the snow, holding hands.

Salome told Eddie he really should phone his mother. She'd be absolutely thrilled to hear the good news, and it'd been such a long time.

'Yes,' admitted Eddie, 'too long.' And she said he should call to see Marion too.

'Why not?' she urged, softly. 'Where's the harm?' Snowdrops spattered against the black window. She squeezed his fingers hard. 'You know you're still in love with her, don't you, Eddie? I mean, even you can see that.'

Eddie gazed out at the snow, falling through the air like ticker tape. For a couple of minutes he was silent. He looked up at the silver stars, and he remembered scraps of some faraway conversation. He felt Salome's hand on his own.

'I feel like I'm in *The Dead*,' he said, eventually.

'What?' she laughed softly. 'As in Grateful?' He rested his forehead against the cold grey glass.

'No,' he sighed, 'the Joyce short story, with all that fucking snow at the end.' She nudged him in the back.

'I *do* know what you mean,' she said. He turned to her, expecting her face to look beautiful in the moonlight. But Salome had the kind of face that looks best under electricity. He touched her cold lips, and she pulled away.

'Have you read it?' he asked. She said no, but she'd seen the movie.

Eddie was afraid Marion would hate him. But Salome said not at all.

'I'd say you're impossible to hate,' she told him. Eddie looked at her sweetly and said thanks. Salome didn't necessarily mean it as a compliment. 'You're too arrogant to believe any woman could hate you, you'd think it was all suppressed desire.'

Then he laughed and told Salome that she was the best friend he'd ever had, and she said yes, that was probably right.

'You're really never jealous,' he said.

'No,' she told him, 'I am sometimes, but I haven't got to that stage with you yet, Eddie. I'm not saying it'll never happen, but it hasn't yet.' Eddie put his head in his hands.

'It's just that things are looking up now,' he said, 'I just have to stop fucking everything up.'

Salome sipped at her glass. Sinatra burbled out of the stereo.

'You have to try to be straight with people, Hun,' she told him, 'I like you, you're a nice guy, but you're just not straight, and that gets people into deep water.'

'Jesus,' said Eddie, 'this is always what it comes down to. Everyone tells me this crap, and I don't know why.'

She looked him straight in the eye.

'Honest Indian?' she asked.

'Really and truly,' chortled Eddie, 'I mean, when have I been unstraight with you?'

Salome laughed, and swallowed a mouthful of wine.

'Well, for instance, when you moved in here, Eddie, I knew all the time you were lying, about your little army of grubby proletarian squatters. You made it all up, and you used me.'

Her fingers ran around the rim of her glass, and her sad eyes twinkled.

'I really resent that, Salome,' he pouted.

'Eddie, please,' she laughed, 'Spider told me all about it, months ago.' Eddie gaped at the floor, feeling his face redden.

'So why did you let it go on?' he asked quietly.

'At first because it was fun. Then later because I felt sorry for you, and I thought I could help.' Eddie lit a cigarette.

'Any other reason?' he asked. Salome laughed again.

'Yes, Eddie. Because I liked you, I suppose. But let's not go on about it. I mean, I'm not really miffed any more. Let's just say, lessons are there to be learnt, and not just for you.'

The pizza never arrived. They called to say the snow was just too bad and all deliveries were off.

When it was time to go to bed, Salome kissed Eddie, hugged him close, and told him she'd see him in the morning, after he'd got back from seeing Marion.

'And I want to be told what happens,' she warned, 'all the gory details. I want you to make up with her, Eddie, because I think you do too.' He asked, as politely as possible, if he could come to bed with her. 'Not until then,' she whispered, and she kissed her index finger, touching Eddie's cheek. 'We'll take it from then, if you still really want to.'

That night Eddie dreamed of being alone on a great white stage, an outdoor stage in a grassy amphitheatre, with the rain drizzling softly down over an audience that had come just to see him. He saw dark faces, great lines of them, stretched far back from the stage and up over the surrounding hills. He saw a forest of outstretched pleading hands. When he strummed his guitar it sounded lush and mournful, with depths he'd never heard before. He stood alone for a minute, holding his hands high in the air, listening to the rumbling of applause. And then one by one The Diehards came on behind him. The sky sang with weird colours. He heard a slow prowling blues figure pounding out from Spider's drums, and a great slapping bass that seemed to throb through his guts. He heard Clint Saigon's guitar screeching and echoing against the night. He heard a great roar of applause that reminded him of the sea. And up on the hills he saw fires licking at the edges of the deep blue sky, and fields full of camper vans with gay flowers painted on the sides . . .

When he woke up, Salome had already gone to the gym.

In the bathroom Eddie stared in the mirror, at his huge comb of wild scarlet tufts. He took one long and lingering look. He thought about all the weird things that had happened in his life, and the strange turns it had taken lately. And he thought about the things that Salome had said, when it was too late last night to lie any more.

He plucked a few razorblades from a pack in the cabinet, noticing the shake in his hands. This was a big deal. He didn't want to botch it. He looked at his face again, pale and bristly and slightly too thin. Then he sighed very deeply and walked down the passage to the kitchen.

He took a pair of scissors from the worktop drawer, and walked very slowly back down the passage to the bathroom, very slowly indeed, feeling the coldness of the metal in his fingers, half-hoping that a nuclear bomb would drop, or that some other catastrophe would strike him, before he would push open that bathroom door and turn on the tap, to fill the sink with hot soapy water, and do what had to be done.

It occurred to Mr Patel that morning that President Street had changed a little lately. On his way back from the newsagents, it really struck him. Things were undoubtedly looking up. Maybe it was the sharp frost, but the street seemed to glisten in the hard sun that day, and it made everything seem extraordinary. There was a spanking new kebab shop where the old tobacconist used to be, a gleaming modern place, all stainless steel and plastic plants. Bubbles Launderette had closed down, with a steel barrier over the front, plastered over with posters for rock concerts and left-wing meetings. But that was only temporary. Soon, he knew, it would become a high-class vegetarian restaurant with lots of parking and an extensive wine list. He'd read about it in the local free-sheet. New double yellow lines ran up and down the street, bright sunflower yellow, not the mangy brown things you saw everywhere else in the city. A proud block of red-brick apartments was already sprouting from the rubble of the old car park. The air sang with the hum of diggers and the rumble of pneumatic drills. Urban regeneration all around. And the Brightside too had played its part.

He stood on the pavement, admiring the front door of the Brightside, with its bright and glossy blue coat, and the window frames white and gleaming and the morning sun glinting on the new rooftiles. He stroked his chin thoughtfully as he studied the calligraphy on the new sign over the front door, 'The Brightside Hotel, est. 1840, props N. and H. Patel', it announced, in gold letters that were *perhaps* a little brash, as his wife had argued, but still, no point in hiding one's light.

He pushed in through the new revolving doors, and there, in the pine-smelling darkness of the back room, master of all he surveyed, Mr Patel sat down, bent himself over a copy of *The Independent*, with a pen in his mouth, and his pipe by his side, deep in his soul, genuinely happy.

But an hour later, just as he was just settling into his second cup of tea, something very disturbing happened. He had noticed the man earlier, pacing up and down outside in his black clothes and his black balaclava and had presumed he was just a bewildered courier looking for a contact. Mr Patel had even contemplated strolling out to offer help, but then the telephone had rung for another booking and his attention had been distracted. Now a sudden shadow caught Mr Patel's eye. The man was standing on the other side of the street, smoking a cigarette. He seemed to be staring up at the top floor, then in the window at Mr Patel. Slowly, he crossed the street, looking right and left. Mr Patel began to sweat a little. In through the swing doors stepped the man in black leather, with the tight black and orange balaclava over his face, black leather gloves. The man moved furtively, like he had no business to be there. He glanced quickly around the lobby, then right over towards the desk, before clearing his throat and taking a few rapid steps.

'Hold it right there now,' Mr Patel warned, 'we have no cash here, what do you want?'

The man stood very still, and he began to laugh. He rocked back and forth and his shoulders shook. He opened his mouth wide and roared with exuberant mischievous laughter. Mr Patel laughed too, as he reached down slowly under the counter, groping for his cosh. Then, moving very slowly, the man reached up one hand and pulled at the hem of the balaclava, laughing all the time, peeling it delicately backwards over his egg-bald head.

'It's me,' he said, 'it's me, Mr P.'

'My God almighty,' gasped Mr Patel, 'Eddie Virago's come home.'

Mr Patel rushed out from behind the counter and threw his arms around Eddie and hugged him hard, slapping him on the back. He said he was so glad Eddie had returned. He said they knew he would. One day. They knew he wouldn't leave them without saying goodbye. He held Eddie at arm's length, looking into his face with moist eyes. He said, 'Oh Eddie, we'd almost forgotten what you looked like. And I barely recognised you with your new hairstyle. I mean you're bald as a bloody coot.' And he said he was so thrilled, because now he could see the new baby, a little girl, Yasmin. Eddie started to apologise for disappearing so quickly, but Mr Patel put up his hand. He understood that these things happened, and anyway, he thought they both knew who really deserved the apology.

Eddie said of course, and that was the other reason he'd just come around, to bury the hatchet with Marion.

The happy expression froze on Mr Patel's face.

'To see Marion?' he said, and he laughed, softly, as though he expected Eddie to say that he was only joking.

'Yes,' giggled Eddie. 'Does she still stay here?'

Mr Patel said, 'Not really.' He looked uncertain. Eddie laughed again. 'Don't you know what has happened, Eddie?' Eddie said no, he didn't know what had happened. Mr Patel started looking pretty serious. He put both hands to his nose, and stared at the ground, thinking. 'My God,' he sighed, 'I thought that was why you'd come.' The telephone rang in the back room, but Mr Patel let it ring. He raised his voice, so that he could be heard above the noise. 'Let me ask you something, Eddie.'

'Shoot,' he said.

'Didn't you know anything about her?'

'What do you mean, Mr P?'

'About her past?'

'Not much,' he said. 'What do you mean?'

'About her history?' Mr Patel looked away, as though his irritated look could silence the telephone. 'About her family history? Did she ever talk to you, about that?' Eddie said no. He didn't know anything at all about her family history. 'Or the reason she came over here?' Eddie said no. He didn't know much about that either.

They stood in the lobby of the Brightside for what seemed like a long time, although in fact, it was not. They stood very still, as though it was some child's game and they weren't supposed to move. The telephone stopped ringing and then it started to ring again. When it stopped, Mr Patel clicked on the answerphone.

'She saw some very sad things, Eddie, in her life.'

'What's happened? She's not sick, is she? Is she alright?' Mr Patel turned to look at him.

'Oh yes,' he smiled, 'Oh yes, don't get the wrong idea. I mean, she's fine. Of course she is.' The smile illuminated his handsome face. He grabbed Eddie by the wrists. 'Of course she is,' he giggled again. 'Don't you really know?!!' Eddie said no, he really didn't know. 'She's married, Eddie. She's married. Our little Marion.'

Eddie felt like he'd been punched in the stomach. He couldn't breathe.

'She's back in Ireland now. I felt sure you'd know. She told me she was trying to get in touch with you. Tom Clancy. Some boy from her home town. He was studying to be a priest and then he left. She met him again not long after you left us. She was upset when you went away, naturally, so we sent her home for a few weeks. Next thing we knew we got the phonecall. She's living back there now. Terribly happy. Mrs P and me went over for the wedding. Her husband owns a little catering business in the town. A hamburger restaurant. Met her father. What a character.'

'Yes,' croaked Eddie, 'he has no nose.'

'That's right,' nodded Mr Patel, 'that's him. He spoke very highly of you, Eddie, and everybody said it was a shame you couldn't come over for the ceremony.'

'You really met her father?' said Eddie.

'Yes,' cawed Mr Patel. 'Of course, he and Marion, well, they had their problems over the years, there's no denying it, a sad business, but basically he's a good man, and they're all sorting themselves out now. They're facing up to everything. And she's living on the same street, with a little baby already on the way.' Eddie felt his legs turn to water. 'Such a beautiful country, Eddie,' he said, 'I've never seen sunsets like it in my life. Never. And tremendous whopping mountains.'

Eddie felt sick. He leaned on the counter, splaying out his fingers to support himself.

Mr Patel stopped talking about the little stone walls and the thatched cottages and the deep blue lakes and the great friendliness of the ordinary people. He said Eddie didn't look well. He thought Eddie'd better come in for a drink. Eddie tried to speak, but he couldn't say a word. He knocked back a whisky and it burnt his gums, unleashing tears. Mr Patel offered to sing him an Irish song, to cheer him up. His fingers wagged, conducting himself, as he lilted . . .

> Love and porter make a young man older
> And love and whisky make him old and grey.
> What can't be cured love must be endured love
> And now I am bound for Americay.

Mr Patel stopped singing, and a dreamy look came down over his beautiful eyes.

'Such a beautiful country,' he sighed, shaking his mournful head, 'it's such a shame about everything. The history. So sad.' The screech of the telephone shattered the silence. 'Don't you think so, Eddie? Don't you think it's sad? The things that happen over there?'

'What do you mean?' croaked Eddie.

'I mean the things that you still do to each other,' said Mr Patel.

'Oh that.' Eddie said yes, he thought it was very sad, but Mr Patel had picked up the phone now, and he wasn't paying attention. He handed Eddie the receiver, with a surprised look in his eye.

'Eddie Virago!' the voice crackled. 'Been trying to connect with you for months, you sly old dog. Kieran Casey here . . . It's about that student loan. I'll have to put out a contract on you, Eddie, heh, heh, heh. If you're not careful, Eddie, I'll have to go on the warpath. I'll have to scalp that toilet brush off the top of your bloody head!'

When Eddie's mother opened the door she didn't look like his mother.

She wore a pair of smart blue Levis and a thick white shirt with a black and white appliqué cowboy design. Her hair was in a stylish cut and a different colour, a golden red that made her look almost young, and prettier than Eddie remembered, if that was a word an Irishman could ever use about his mother. She looked like some Tennessee country and western singer, not like an assistant deputy bank manager's wife from Dublin 6. She looked like she was surprised to see him too, but she was chewing something when the door opened, so she couldn't speak at once. But her eyes bulged and she gestured joyfully with her hands. And almost as soon as he stepped into the hall she started to cry.

'Let me look at you,' she wept, touching his face.

The hall of the small house was clean and white, and little rectangular watercolour paintings went up the grey wall by the stairs. The smell of warm bread and garlic drifted out from the kitchen. When she pulled Eddie close to her, he started to cry himself, and he hugged his mother hard, stopping only when he saw a big man saunter into the hall from the back room. The big man wore a worried, curious look on his face. Tiny black and white tiles covered the hall floor. Eddie's mother was barefoot. Her toenails were painted light pink.

'Raymond,' she said, without looking at the man, 'this is my son, Eddie.'

Raymond was a squat, stocky man, maybe sixty, maybe even a little older, with a sunburnt face and big hard muscles and a happy smile. He spoke with a cockney accent. He had a thick mop of Brylcreemed grey hair combed backwards across the top of his head. He wore a collarless green tartan shirt and his belly flopped out over his belt. He looked like a builder's labourer, or maybe a plumber, but he was neither of these. He was in jacuzzis. That was what he said when Eddie's mother prompted him to say something about himself. He rubbed his hands on the thighs of his trousers before shaking Eddie's hand with a firm grip, for a long time. He'd come in from the shed where he'd been splitting logs. He smelt sweet, like woodchips. His trousers were corduroy. He gave Eddie a piece of chewing gum. He had hair on the back of his soapy hands. Eddie smiled.

'You're in jacuzzis?' he said.

'That's right,' said Raymond, and he laughed. 'I've heard all the jokes,' he said, 'I don't mind if you laugh at me, Eddie. I've heard them all before.' Eddie smiled again. 'You're the image of your mother,' said Raymond. His red face crinkled when he smiled. He spoke gently. 'We're so glad you've come,' he said, 'aren't we, May?'

'No,' she said, 'he's the image of his father. When I opened the door just now, I thought it was him. I really did.' Raymond looked at Eddie, as though he knew what Frank looked like.

'Did you?' smiled Raymond. 'Did you really? Isn't that queer?'

The house shook as a plane roared overhead. The windows rattled in their frames and a throb licked across the floor. Out on the street the children whooped in terrified joy.

'Make us a cup of something, Raymond,' she said, and she led Eddie by the arm into the front room. 'God, I wish I'd known.'

'Oh yes, Boss,' said Raymond, pretending to sigh, rolling his eyes at Eddie, as he straightened a picture on the wall.

The little room had a piano in the corner, but it was covered with a white lace tablecloth, on which stood tiny useless china things and a crystal glass vase. The room was cold, and the furniture was all a shade of cold sea blue, and that made it worse. The coffee table had a map of the world design. Magazines lay in tidy heaps on the rack.

'So that's Raymond,' said Eddie, not sure of what else to say.

'Yes,' she said, 'that's him.' His mother looked into the fire-place, which was empty. She looked at it for a long time, as though the fire was full and burning. 'We're making a life together,' she said, suddenly, and she lit a cigarette. Eddie's fingers drummed on the armrest.

'Yes,' he said, and then there was silence.

'I smoke now,' she said, brightly.

'Yeah,' said Eddie, 'so do I.'

'And I paint a little,' she said.

'That's good,' said Eddie, surprised, 'that's very good.'

'In moderation,' she said, handing him one, 'I don't worry about it too much.' Eddie chewed his gum. 'The cigarettes, I mean,' she said. 'Not the painting,' and she chuckled, nervously. Eddie said nothing. His mother nodded, blowing smoke across the room. 'I telephoned your father last night,' she said seriously. 'Raymond gets the *Irish Press* for me on Fridays. We were so worried when we saw the terrible news, in the papers. We just felt for you.'

'Yeah,' he nodded, 'I wanted to get over, but I didn't have the time.'

'I suppose you will go,' she said. 'For the funeral.' Eddie said no, it was back in the States. It was all arranged now. Dean Bean's parents were coming over to collect him any day.

'Well,' he said, 'you know what I mean. Collect his stupid body. Or whatever.' Smoke drifted into his eyes. 'His remains,' he said. 'I think that's the word.'

'Of course,' his mother said, and she almost laughed. 'It's odd,

I got so used to poor Dean, I almost thought of him as one of our own tribe. Irish, I mean.' Eddie said nothing.

She said it was a terrible thing, really awful. Eddie agreed that yes, it was, wishing she would talk about something else.

'He often asked about you,' Eddie said, 'I think he was very fond of you.'

His mother looked as though she might cry again. She said that was nice, and that Dean had always been such a gentle, handsome boy, and that it was such a waste, and how it made you think.

'Frank and I,' she said, and then she nodded quickly and said, 'your father and I,' as though Eddie didn't know exactly who she was talking about. 'Your *father* and I,' again, in a trembling voice, and then she said nothing.

Raymond came in with a tray, which he placed on the map of the world table. The tip of his tongue protruded in concentration as he lowered the tray down, cups clattering upside down on the saucers. Then he clapped his hands together and said something about putting on the heat. It was still cold in the room, getting even colder as the light grew copper outside and the afternoon came down. Eddie said he was fine but Raymond insisted, turning the thermostat on the wall with a theatrical flourish.

'We don't use it much,' he said, 'only for special occasions.' Then he glanced at Eddie's mother, eyebrows raised. She nodded. Raymond clapped his hands again, a little too hard, so the noise sounded vaguely ridiculous in the small room and the discordant aftersound of the piano strings hummed softly in the corner. 'Well then,' he said, 'I just have a bit of work to do, so I'll be upstairs if anyone wants me.'

After he'd left, Eddie's mother smiled, as though she was a little embarrassed.

'He's a good man,' she said, 'he takes care of me.'

'Good,' said Eddie, 'I'm glad to hear it.'

'Your father and I got to talking,' she said, suddenly, 'as you know, it's been a little while.' Eddie said yes, he knew that. 'He said we should have a pow-wow, you and I,' and she looked at Eddie, sidelong, 'about things.'

Eddie said there was no need, really. There was nothing that she needed to say. But he could see his mother needed to talk, so he sat back in the chair and he sipped his tea as he prepared to listen. His mother coughed. She looked into the empty fireplace again, gathering her words.

'It's nobody's fault. It's just that your father and I grew apart,' she said, as though she had learnt the phrase off, as though she had been rehearsing it.

'Yes,' said Eddie, embarrassed. 'Anyone could see it.'

'Yes,' she said. 'I don't blame him, of course, but our lives just didn't turn out the way we planned. It's no crime. But one day I turned around and your father wasn't the man I married. He was different. Not any better or worse, but just a lot different. Tireder, Eddie. He used to get depressed, in the evenings. I used to find him down in the kitchen, in the middle of the night, drinking milk. I don't know what I can tell you. He never was happy, and I couldn't seem to give him what he was missing in his life. I can't explain it. All the work he did, but he never really seemed to be happy. He was dedicated. But he was almost too dedicated, do you know?'

'Yes,' said Eddie. 'I do know.'

'He would wake up, and worry. In the night. And nothing I could do for him would make him stop. He took his responsibilities very seriously. He wanted the best for us. He had such plans. Well, we both did, of course.' His mother stopped speaking and her soft eyes moistened. 'We never thought that things would turn out so badly,' she said, in a cracking, fluted voice. 'We couldn't see that. When you're that age, you don't. You think that if you love each other, things will sort themselves out.' A wet black streak of mascara began to spill down her cheek. Eddie's mother began to blink hard. She held the heel of her hands to her face for a second, and then looked her son full in the face. Her lips quivered. 'You'll see what I mean,' she said, 'when you're older.'

'Yes,' he said, 'I'm sure.' And he reached out to take her hand, squeezing her fingers very hard. His mother began to sob, hunching up her shoulders, trying to stop herself.

'It wasn't that we didn't try,' she said, 'your father especially, Frank especially.' Tears spilled from her eyes again. Sobs broke the pattern of her breath. 'It's just that love can go wrong, Eddie, that's all. But it doesn't mean that it was never love. You mustn't think that. I'll never love anyone like Frank again. He was everything to me, and I want you to know that. Don't think there was never any love. I loved your father and we both loved you. That was the set-up. When you're married yourself, Eddie, you'll see for yourself how these things work, and how people can get sometimes lost in them.'

Eddie swallowed hard. He cradled his mother's sobbing face in his shoulder, and he stroked the back of her head.

And he told her that he knew very well what she meant, and he was sure Patricia did as well. Then his mother sat up straight again, wiping her eyes with her fingers.

'Do you think so?' she asked. Eddie said yes, and his mother nodded carefully, and said well that was something. 'It's funny, but I think when Granny died, I just thought, well, I don't want to be a wife and mother all my life. That was all, in the end. I thought the world was full of opportunity and I wanted to go get some of it for myself.' While his mother spoke, she bit at the ends of matchsticks, and played with them, twisting them between her fingertips. And Eddie kept telling her that everything would be alright, while he held her hand and sipped his tea. 'I mean, I was nearly fifty-seven,' she said, and she laughed.

'Yes,' smiled Eddie, 'you were. I know.' He handed her a tissue and stroked her limp hand, awkwardly, while she dabbed her eyes. And then his mother started to explain about Raymond, how she'd met him at the counselling group after his wife died, all of that, but Eddie said really, no offence, he'd rather she didn't explain it at all. That was a private thing. Why should she explain it to him? 'You're my mother,' he said, 'I don't want to know about that. I don't want to be in analysis for the rest of my life.' He said it was her own affair, and he laughed. 'If you know what I mean.' The clock struck.

'Yes,' she said, and she laughed too. 'I do know what you mean.' So she poured some more tea, and she asked about him. 'I haven't seen you in so long, Eddie. Daddy told me,' she said, 'that there was someone special, some young Donegal lady. Is that right?' Eddie gazed around the room, listening for a moment to the bubbling of the water pipes.

'Not really,' he smiled. 'She was just a friend, you know. We were never close.'

'Yes,' she said, 'well, I must admit Daddy said she wasn't really for you. He just had that impression somehow. He can be very perceptive with people. He said she just wasn't your type.'

'Yeah, well,' said Eddie, 'she was just a friend, like I say. She was involved with this pretty screwed-up guy, and he just left her one day. Just went out one morning, said he was going to work, never came back. Then she discovered he'd been moving out all his clothes and stuff, for weeks before. He just never came home. She went a little crazy, and he didn't find out about it until it was too late. She started a fire in the supermarket where she worked and she told everyone it was an accident. And then she lost her job, but she pretended she was going to work every day, and nobody ever knew where she was.'

'The poor mite,' his mother said.

'Then when he left her, he found out that she tried to burn the hotel down, where they lived, and she took an overdose. She's in a hospital now.'

'The poor thing,' his mother said.

'Yes,' said Eddie, 'he wanted to go back to her then, but he didn't realise. I mean, he realised in the end what he really felt for her, but she was gone, you know. Things had gone too far.' Eddie shrugged. 'It happens. Nothing anyone could do.' His mother said there was a lot of sadness in life, and Eddie had seen his fair share. He shrugged again. 'It was her family,' he said, 'there were things in her family, you know, bad things, in her past. You wouldn't want to know about them.'

'Like our family,' she said, and she laughed, uncertainly.

'Well,' Eddie said, 'kind of. Worse, really. I don't like to discuss it.'

'And why did she come over first, Eddie. For a job, was it?'

'Well, when she came over first, it was for the other reason. You know? It wasn't really for a job. That's what she told people, but that wasn't it. She never told *me* that exactly, but I knew it. You could tell. It was the other reason girls have to come over from Ireland. It was her situation. She had to deal with it.' His mother nodded and stared into her cup. 'She was from a small town, you see.' Eddie laughed. 'She *is* from a small town,' he said, 'I shouldn't say *was*. She is.'

'Yes,' said his mother, 'it would have been difficult for her.'

'Oh, impossible,' said Eddie, 'with a baby, on her own, but I don't like to talk about it much. She had to get rid of it.' He looked his mother in the eye. 'It's a tough situation,' he said. 'But it happens.'

'Life is like a game of dominoes, Eddie,' she sighed, 'events and changes all laid out, standing up like that,' and, with her index finger, she pointed out an invisible line along the map of the world coffee table. 'You start out at a certain point and you end up at a certain point, and what happens in between God only knows. People think they can choose their lives, but really, everything is about what's possible at the time.'

'Well,' Eddie said, 'I suppose there must be some kind of rules.'

'There are rules,' she nodded, 'but you can't figure them out until it's all over. It's crazy. It's like statistics or something, you just can't see them until you stand back from them. Or one of those paintings, you know, the ones with the little dots.' She paused. 'Do you ever see her, your friend?'

'Not much,' said Eddie, 'the hospital's a long way out, y'know. Surrey or somewhere. I wouldn't like to see her like that anyway.' He sipped his coffee again. 'She really isn't very well, she doesn't take to visitors much. She can't.'

And then his mother started talking about a friend of hers from the old days, who'd found her little daughter kissing another girl one day, and had her locked away for a few months. Eddie was grateful for the change of conversation. He listened for a while, then he asked for the bathroom.

On his way up the stairs, Eddie stared at one of the little paintings on the grey wall. A silhouette of a man and a woman, holding hands, staring out over a bright pink sea. They looked young and slender, these black shapes. They looked happy, if shadows can. In the bottom right-hand corner, his mother had signed her name. May Virago. Eddie turned the frame around and looked at the back, but there was no title anywhere.

In the bathroom he filled the sink with water, and splashed it over his hot face. Through the window, the back garden was green and fresh, with ivy climbing up a ragged trellis fence and a solid stone birdbath full of squabbling seagulls.

On the landing, just outside the bathroom, there was a small room in which Eddie saw two single beds, side by side, with a wooden dresser beside each. Raymond was sitting at the desk by the window, tapping on a calculator and pulling on a cigarette. He mumbled to himself as he added up his figures.

'Alright, Eddie mate?' he said.

'Sure, Raymond,' he answered. 'That's one hell of a jacuzzi you have in there.'

'King size,' he said, and he laughed. 'Do you a good deal some time.' Eddie stared at the two single beds, all made up in matching quilts. 'Your mother's a good woman,' Raymond said suddenly, without looking at him. 'I wouldn't want you to think I'm not fond of her.'

'I know,' he said. 'I know that.'

'Well, yes,' said Raymond, blushing.

'I know that, Raymond,' said Eddie, 'you don't have to worry about that.'

'These situations,' shrugged Raymond, looking out the window.

'Yeah, life's a bitch,' said Eddie. 'But there you go. What's new?'

Downstairs again Eddie and his mother talked about the future. Eddie told her all about Salome, and the plans they'd made together.

'Who?' said his mother. 'What class of a name is that?' Eddie explained that she was Protestant and his mother nodded, in embarrassed understanding. Then she recited 'Salome, Salome' a few times, as though it was poetry, and then she told Eddie to be sure and not lose his head, and she laughed.

He told her they were very happy together and she'd got him a job as an assistant researcher on a religious music television programme that would be going out on Sunday afternoons in the new year. They had plans to get married, maybe, after they'd saved up a little money. And he'd decided to give up the music. Their manager had let them down, told them a whole pack of lies. And it just wasn't worth the bother of starting it all up again. He was just going to take this new job and try to settle down a little.

''Course, as you see, I had to get rid of the mohican,' he said, patting the top of his head, still unused to the velvet feel of an all-over inch of new spiky hair. 'For the new job, I mean.'

'Well,' his mother said, 'you're a bit too old for all that now.' She sounded a little sad when she said it.

'Yes,' he laughed, 'I am.'

'But you meet a better class of person in the media,' she said, 'and you look well with hair, Eddie. You look handsome.'

'Do I?' he laughed. 'Do you think so?'

'Yes,' she smiled, 'but you know that, of course.'

They talked a little more, about Patricia mainly, and her boyfriend Rod, and all of the neighbours back on Beckett Road. And just before his mother called Raymond down to join them for a beer, Eddie asked her something.

'Are you happy, Mother?' he said. 'Do you think you're happy now?'

She looked into the fire again, plucking at the shoulder of her shirt. She laughed. She held a tissue to her mouth and gnawed at the corner. 'What a funny question,' she said, and she looked at him, thinking for a moment. 'The truth is, I don't really know about happiness,' she told him, 'but I'm content, I suppose, Eddie. That's not the same, I know. But it's something, isn't it, son?'

'Yes,' he smiled, 'that's certainly something.'

Then Raymond came down and he opened a beer bottle with his teeth, much to Eddie's mother's horror. And they sat in the parlour together until the light greyed down outside the window and the street lamps flickered on, Raymond holding Eddie's mother's fingers all the time, roaring with tears of laughter when Eddie told some embarrassing story from her past.

In the wet porch, just before he went, his mother pressed something into his hand.

'Just something small,' she urged, 'go see your friend. In the hospital. Go bring her something.' She waved off his protestations, and closed his fingers with her own. 'You're like me, Eddie. Me and your father. People like us need good friends. We hang onto the past too long. We just never know when it's time to let things go. We need people to tell us that.'

In Eddie's hot hand was a crumpled fifty pound note. He kissed his mother's face and got lipstick on his cheek. Raymond said to be sure and call again.

'Don't leave it so long next time,' he said.

And they stood outside the gate, waving, until Eddie was gone from sight.

When Eddie got back into town it was already dark. The streets around the South Bank were full of people, all laughing, out for a good time. Neon stained the puddles. The sinful stink of hot dogs and kebabs and fried onions drifted on the air. There was music everywhere, hip-hop throbbing from the windows of cars, snare drums and saxophones punching through the night, raucous heavy metal hammering out from every pub door. Saturday night in London and the streets were heavy with illicit promise. Another kiss-and-tell night. Everybody was dressed up and looking sharp, lithe girls in beautiful dresses, rich men in gorgeous suits. All along the river, everyone looked like a movie star.

Eddie wondered about all the people who were about to meet a new lover tonight, or break up a marriage, or get drunk, all the people who would wake up on Sunday morning with a headache in a strange bed, with a vague memory of having done things they never would have done sober and a terrible realisation that they had fallen into something that could never be a one-night stand. Or those who would wake up in a cell with blood on their hands and a carpet of broken glass on the floor. Or those who wouldn't wake up at all. It was all chance. His mother was right.

Walking across Waterloo Bridge, Eddie dropped a tab of acid, and he saw the whole city dance over the flyover, made of glass, so that he could see into every room. Neon lights snaked up and down the cranes over the Isle of Dogs. The dome of St Paul's shimmered and spun, shooting laser beams into the sky.

He called his father from a phonebox on Charing Cross Road, just to say hello. His father rang him back and they talked for ages, about the strange things that happen when you're least expecting them, about poor Dean Bean, and about all kinds of other stuff, love and work and life. His father said not to worry about Salome's car. The police would find it, and she'd get to see reason in the end. And even if she didn't, he'd meet someone else.

'It's the call of the wild, Ed,' he said. 'Everyone feels it one day. It's nature, that's all. She won't let a Citroën 2CV stand in the way of that.' Eddie said he hoped not. 'I mean,' Frank laughed, 'it's not as if it was a Merc.'

When he hung up Eddie was really beginning to trip out. He wanted to ring somebody else. So he pulled his address book from his jeans' pocket and he flicked through the pages. He knew people all over the world. Australia. America. New Zealand. Even Nicaragua.

Inevitably, his fingers found the page where Mr Patel had written Marion's new number. The blue lines shimmered on the paper. And the longer Eddie stared, the weirder it got, until the lines began to roll slowly like a broken-down TV set.

Eddie looked over his shoulder, as though somebody was watching him. He laughed out loud. Then he stuck the phonecard into the box again, the dial tone purred and he rang the number in Donegal. The line crackled and bleeped.

'Hello,' said a man's voice, 'Prairie Moon Burger Bar?' The voice sounded efficient. Eddie said nothing. 'Hello,' said the voice again. 'Tom Clancy speaking, hello?' Eddie listened to Tom Clancy's undulating voice. He could hear him talking to someone in the background, over the doleful lament of the country and western music. 'Hello?' he said again. 'Is there anybody out there?' Eddie pulled the card out. That was when the tears came. At last.

And when he turned hot-eyed into the Strand the lights were on, all priestly purple and mohican red and beer can yellow and acid house blue, glowing in the rain, running together. The whole street was a river of light. It looked like a time-lapse photograph, streaks of fluorescent colour all flowing up and down, as though they had a life of their own.

A troop of ten white horses clopped past the Virgin Megastore. Men in medieval uniforms led them along the wet street and fathers held their children high so they could see, high in their straining arms. The horses whinnied and snorted and stomped and the men had to reign them in hard, laughing and shouting jokes to each other as they tugged at the leather. The children squawked with joy. Camera flashes flickered everywhere. The birds screamed in the air, and feathers rained down into the street.

Eddie walked up to Covent Garden, where he got drunk and told some girl in the Rock Garden the story of his life.

Only October, and already the lights were going up for Christmas. It seemed to get earlier every single damn year. One of these years it would end up being Christmas all the time. That's what Eddie thought, when the girl had gone to the bathroom. The definitions that keep things apart would just disappear. It had to happen.

They'd put the lights up a little early one year, leave them up a little late. And sooner or later it'd just end up all one. What a thought.

Christmas, all the whole year round. Jesus. What a thought.

He waited for the girl to come back, so that he could tell her what had occurred to him.